What People Are Saying About, Finding Home by Jesse Birkey

Finding Home is an incredible story of love, hope, and healing that will have you laughing one minute and crying the next. The final chapter left me speechless. You're going to love this book!

> — **Praying Medic, Best-Selling Author**
> of, *Divine Healing Made Simple* and
> *Seeing in the Spirit Made Simple*

There is nothing more exciting than indulging in the restorative love of God. *Finding Home* masterfully depicts God's heart and invites you into his story, then drenches you in hope and expectancy for your story.

> — **Jeremy Mangerchine, Founder of Bastion Ministries and Author**
> of, *The Longest Bridge Across Water*

I picked up this book with some hesitation because it is not the genre I typically enjoy reading. But, the first chapter hooked me and I had a hard time putting it down. The story line is intriguing and keeps you wanting to know how things are going to turn out. If you need a fresh perspective of the awesome and unconditional love of God for each and every person, this book is for you!

> — **Marlin, Professional Family Therapist**

Finding Home is an absolute treat to read. Jesse's writing reminds me of Frank Peretti's, but the voice is all his own. The characters are alive and the storytelling is brilliant. And the story; Oh the story! He had me deeply involved from the first page, and in tears several times before it was over. I surely hope he plans a sequel.

> — **Nor'west Prophetic, Writer/Blogger**

I really enjoyed reading *Finding Home*. I believe you captured the character of Jesus: always faithful, always forgiving, and full of grace and love.

All of us have experienced tragedy and pain in our lives, and one person's pain isn't greater than another's. It's just different. This is portrayed in the lives of the characters.

Finding Home reminded me of the redemptive love of our heavenly father who never ever gives up on us, and is always moving his children towards healing and reconciliation.

I am learning this first hand in our family. Even though things appear far from finished the story reminds me that he will bring our family to full reconciliation in his time. Thanks for writing this beautiful example.

— **Cherie, Nursing Case Manager**

When I first encountered this book, I thought it would be a great read. But I found it to be so much more than that. I don't read much fiction these days, but this story intrigued me. I really want to know how tragedies are handled in our lives, where Jesus is in all of it. These questions, and the circumstances that provoke them, come up everyday.

What I found in these pages, even if it is a fiction story, showed me a glimpse of a Jesus who is standing right there with us, as one who has suffered everything we've gone through himself. I'd never looked at his suffering that way. It's opened my eyes to consciously look for him no matter what I'm going through. He's there, of that I have no doubt.

Seriously, this book has profoundly changed my heart.

— **Ginny, Writer/Blogger/Baker**

As we each live our lives we quickly learn that we're not immune to adversity, loss, and heartbreak. But in every situation and circumstance, we have a loving Father whose heart is all about restoration. *Finding Home* is a beautiful story that reflects his heart toward us no matter what we walk through.

— **Laurie, Writer/Blogger**

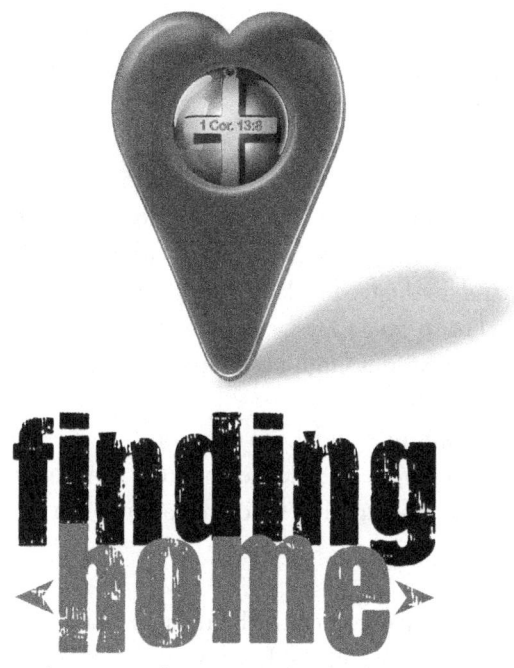

finding home

Book One in The Lost and Found Series

JESSE BIRKEY

Dedication

Finding Home is dedicated to the author of the vision that inspired me to write it, Jesus. The only way the content I write can be life changing is if your heart's infused into it. My deepest desire is to help people know you more, and I pray that happens through this story.

Finding Home is also dedicated to my amazing wife, Kara, who has encouraged and uplifted me every step of the way. Thank you for all of your honest and loving feedback. *Finding Home* couldn't have been written without you. I'm so excited to be on this journey with you, and can't wait to share the many stories God has in store for us. I love you.

Rylie, you are awesome and I am so proud of the young man you are, and are becoming. You are a leader because you know how to love like Jesus. I can't wait to see all that God has for you. I'm so glad I'm your dad. I love you.

Kailyn, the freedom you have in being you makes me smile. You draw people in because the joy of the Lord is in you. You have so much to give, and I can't wait to see all the lives you touch. I'm so glad I'm your dad. I love you.

I'd also like to thank some of my friends who's feedback helped me take Finding Home to another level. Thank you Praying Medic, Nor'west Prophetic, Laurie Hilgers, Ginny Wilcox, Jeremy Mangerchine, and Ann Jennerjahn. I'm so grateful for each of you.

A special shout-out goes to my editor, Lydia Blain. I learned so much from you through this process. Thanks for all of your tireless work and willingness to make that one last pass through the manuscript. You rock!

Copyright © 2015 by Jesse Birkey

All rights reserved. This book or any portion thereof may not be reproduced or used in any manner whatsoever without the express written permission of the publisher except for the use of brief quotations in a book review.
Printed in the United States of America

First Printing, 2015

ISBN
978-0-578-16738-1 (Paperback)
978-1-4951-6569-6 (Ebook)

Jesse Birkey
PO Box 816
Riverview, FL 33568
www.jessebirkey.com

‹finding home›

‹chapter one›

Four graves rested against a gray backdrop spitting in the face of justice, decency, and fairness.

"While life hands us no shortage of questions during tragedies, I also pray that Jesus hands us no shortage of hope… the hope of a life beyond this one. The hope that we will someday see those we've lost here on earth."

John Rister hung in the front row, trying to listen to Pastor Mark. A thick cloud of breath escaped from behind the podium as his voice caught noticeably in his throat.

"That hope…without it what do we have left? It's *that* hope that helps us celebrate the lives they lived…"

For John, there were no tears. Novocain had replaced his blood. He hadn't worked, hardly eaten, and if more than five words had escaped his thin lips it was too many.

He lowered his eyes and dug his right foot into the frozen earth with his Kenneth Cole dress shoe. Oak Harbor always seemed to freeze faster than the rest of Ohio. He ignored the few strands of black hair that fell over his forehead and noticed a sad-looking mist crawl across the ground. He wondered how it knew exactly where and when to appear.

Mark droned on, "…grief, it's necessary in the midst of tragedy. To acknowledge the pain, to deal with the hurt. Each one of us has been touched by their lives and each one of us has been touched by their death. We will all grieve in different ways…"

The assembly behind John was an orchestra of sniffs and restless movement. He could feel their eyes boring into his back like a hammer drill. He thumbed the buttons on his suit jacket. The stares were expected.

After all, it was *his* family they were about to bury.

A few had approached before the service with the well-meaning hand on the shoulder as they searched for the right words. "Is there anything we can do" and "I'm sorry for your loss," were the most common and, at this point, void of any meaning. There was nothing that could be done, no amount of *sorries* that could help John make sense of what had happened.

He shoved his hands deeper into his pockets and shivered. The last few weeks had taken the insulation out of his 6'4" frame. Something wet hit his face. He glanced up in time to see a rain drop splash against the podium.

Mark's voice seemed to echo in the distance, "…reunions again one day…"

Reunions? Finality swept over John like a door slowly closing as Mark paused to rub his eyes.

"…so we will remember them for the light and life they brought to each and every one of us gathered here and even those who couldn't be here today. Amy, Kayla, Jill, and Andy…their reach and impact cannot be measured by the standards of this world, but they are surely receiving treasures beyond anything we can imagine as they rejoice with Jesus, our hope of glory."

Another raindrop slapped John's cheek. It blurred his vision as he caught site of a group of men dressed in black coveralls. He watched them move to either side of the graves and made a quick count in his head. Sixteen men, four to each coffin, two on either end.

Mark moved from the podium to the front row, and settled to John's left. Gears squeaked to life and began lowering the four coffins into the earth.

John studied the container holding his wife's body. "What style coffin would you like, Mr. Rister?" the funeral director had wanted to know. He'd left without a word. Someone else had finished making the arrangements.

He watched the love of his life sink and felt a tremor in both knees. Then something cracked like a whip in his head, and he doubled over as if someone punched him in the stomach. He gasped and quickly glanced at torn faces around him now showing concern. The events of the last week begin to unfold as if he'd hit *play from the beginning* on his DVR. He saw the accident, the hospital, the coroner's office, the funeral home, the

≺ finding home ≻

paperwork…each new slide was a sword that threatened to cut him in two.

John drew in a ragged breath as more cold drops hit his face. The top of the coffin was now even with the ground. "Amy," he cried and staggered toward the opening. The meals, the empty house, the calls, the visitors, the empty beds…every thought struck him as if he was a rookie in the ring with a heavy weight champion.

Raindrops rolled down his face. "No," he screamed and lunged towards the edge of the grave. He clawed at the top of the coffin as people shouted for him to stop in the background. But only one thing mattered. He had to get her out.

Despair wrung his soul. She was almost out of reach. He wouldn't leave her alone. She was his wife. They'd made vows. He needed to stay with her. His right leg was over the brim when strong hands clamped underneath both shoulders like vices. He swung his arms wildly, but there were too many. They were forcing him up, taking him away.

John dug his fingers into the ground. "No, stop!" But the distance between him and Amy grew. "Stop, please." He heard voices behind him. They were muffled like his ears were clogged. "I can't leave her!" he cried. "Don't do this!"

The rain was now a steady curtain. He struggled and watched it fall into the ground where Amy was, where he should be. A moment later he heard a terrible sound rising high above the rain. It was a wail, but unlike anything he'd heard before, as if a heart filled only with pain and sorrow abruptly burst, spewing its contents into the atmosphere.

The strain in John's throat helped him understand that the sound had come from him. His heart had finally split in two and it was letting the world know.

John's soaked clothes clung to his body as his captors pulled him through the rain. He kicked and thrashed and missed the weight he'd lost. He couldn't break free. "AMY!"

He heard a car door open. Moments later, John was slumped over on a soft cushion between two figures. The door closed, the car accelerated, and blackness swallowed him.

chapter two

The slideshow tore through pictures of his family and mangled components of a minivan. Shards of aluminum and plastic littered the dark, wet ground while tall flames licked the night sky.

John grabbed his head and groaned. Maybe he could crush the projector. He pressed on either side but it was no use. The scene clutched him with claws of regret, agony, and despair. His knees shook and gave up. He groaned again and buried his face in his hands. "That's enough! Turn it off!"

To his relief the image faded, leaving him alone in the dark. He blinked and noticed pale light bouncing off a white dotted surface above him. He also felt his position had changed as if someone had rotated the entire room 90 degrees.

Something soft pressed against the back of his head and continued all the way down to his feet. He blinked again and saw that the white surface above his face was a ceiling, and the pale light was the moon flowing in through the window. He was lying on a bed inside a room.

A wave of nausea hit him as he rolled on his left side. John sat up slowly but it didn't stop the dizziness. *A dream? Where am I?* The room wasn't big. A door stood closed beyond the bed. It seemed familiar, but his spinning head made it impossible to recover anything from his brain.

"How did I get here?" The room didn't answer him, but his brain finally sparked to life and he remembered. The service, the grave, the car...Amy. He groaned and dropped his head between his knees. He stabbed for a small garbage can sitting to his left and got it just before his stomach emptied its contents.

John dragged his wrinkled oxford shirtsleeve across his mouth and slid

‹finding home›

the can to the side. His suit jacket hung on a chair just beyond his reach. He pulled himself up and wobbled to the door, bumping into the bedpost along the way. The brass knob was cool in his hand as he twisted, pulled, and knew where he was.

The Summers' house. The Pastor who'd performed the funeral. Mark and Claire's tiled hallway lay before him.

"Did you get a chance to talk to his parents?" Claire's hushed voice floated down the hall.

Mark kept his voice low. "They left as soon as it was over. They looked pretty bad." John leaned towards the sound. "Everyone did."

His hand slid on the cool, beige wall as he made his way towards the lighted living area where he'd spent so much time. Years worth of dinners and games and laughter had probably soaked into the walls. He frowned. They should've just taken him home. He didn't want to see or talk to anyone.

The floor was a sponge absorbing the sound of his footsteps as he moved just past the end of the hall. A tan leather sectional wrapped around an open living room that ran into the kitchen. Mark and Claire slumped on the couch like marionettes whose strings had been cut.

He heard Claire lower her voice another degree, "Do you think we should check on him?"

Mark rubbed his red eyes. "No, let him rest."

Claire clucked her tongue. "Are you sure? That was pretty bad at the burial." She leaned in and folded her hands over Mark's. "Maybe we should—"

John cleared his throat and they both jumped up. "John, I'm uh…" Mark fiddled with his watch. "We didn't mean to wake you we just—"

"Can I get you something?" Claire stepped forward. "Are you hungry? I'll make you a sandwich."

John threw a sullen look at her and remembered Mark sharing how Claire's family figured there wasn't a problem that couldn't be fixed with a good meal.

Claire was already in the kitchen before John could wave her off. "No Claire, I'm not hungry."

"Some coffee then," Claire opened a cabinet. "Or Tea." Pots clanged together as she searched for the required items.

John stood on the line between the great room and the hall like crossing it would commit him to staying. "I'm gonna go."

"Go?" Claire held a teapot in her hand and tilted her head like she didn't understand the word.

John fixed his eyes on the floor. "I can't stay here."

"John, please." Mark hurried to him. "We've got plenty of room. There's no need for you to leave."

John sighed. "It's not about that. I just...can't be *here*." He took another glance around the room and heard his family, sounds that would probably haunt him the rest of his life.

"But, where will you go?" Claire had caught Mark's desperation. "You shouldn't be alone and there's nowhere else for you to stay and…" She threw Mark a plea for help. "Tell him Mark!"

Mark pinched his forehead. "John, please just stay here. We'll get you whatever you need and—"

"Look, I appreciate what you've done but I just want to be alone." Irritation had invaded his voice and his eyebrows narrowed. "I just watched my family get buried. If I wanna be alone I think I'm entitled to it without having to explain it to *you*."

They both straightened like they'd been struck. He felt a twinge of guilt, but pushed it down like bile. He was at the bottom of the driveway when he heard Mark's voice.

"John, wait a sec."

John swiveled to see Mark jogging toward him. He almost sprinted away, but the years they'd spent together earned him a few more minutes.

"John," Mark pleaded when he'd caught up, "I can understand if you want to be alone. I just want you to know that we're here. We're devastated, Claire and I. Amy and the kids, they were family." He hesitated. "You're family, John. However we can help each other through this we, we should…"

Mark sighed and gazed up into the sky. "What happened is more than anyone should ever have to deal with. I know you have a hard time talking about stuff like this but please, if you don't talk to me talk to *h*." He let his hand slide back to his side. "We love you and we're here for you."

«finding home»

John kept his eyes on his feet. His family had never been loved by anyone more than Mark and Claire. If there was an appropriate reply he couldn't find it, or rather, couldn't find one he felt like saying. His heart was a block of ice in his chest. Mark was right on one point, this was more than anyone should have to deal with. He managed a nod before turning down the sidewalk.

He ambled through the night as the cold relentlessly tried to tear through his clothes. He could stay at his house, but with what happened at the burial he didn't want to risk it. His insides were volatile, like a volcano just starting to wake up. He didn't know where to go.

The frigid gusts forced his head down low until a bright light caught his attention. He stopped and stared. The glow of a liquor store shown in front of him. He only paused a second before walking in and out with a bottle of Jack Daniels.

John hovered just beyond the door and scrutinized the bottle. His father was an alcoholic and he'd always stayed away from booze for that reason. But then Amy's face materialized in front of him and an eruption of emotion lit his heart.

He squeezed his trembling fingers around the neck, popped off the cap, and took a long pull. The liquid was fire down his throat and became lava in his belly. He blinked the image of Amy away and continued down the sidewalk feeling a little lighter. The fire was less intense with the second drink. His fingers and toes started to tingle. He licked his lips and wondered why he couldn't feel them.

Main curved into Church Street and John stumbled past an open field the kids used to play in. He groaned and immediately doused the memory and their faces with whisky. It was starting to taste pretty good. He held the bottle out underneath a streetlight and tried to read the label. He would've been able to if the manufacturer hadn't run all the letters together.

John let the bottle fall to his side and wobbled forward. He made a left on Mill and stopped. Off to his right the top of a two-story white house rose above the tree line and glowed in the pale moonlight.

His breath caught in his throat and the whisky dropped to the ground. His feet were cement blocks. "The house of our dreams," he spewed into the emptiness. It'd been five years since they first stood in front of the beautiful two-story custom built home. He couldn't see the wrap-around porch Amy had required. He could only see a portion of the five acres *he'd* required.

It was 4,400 square feet of upgrades. Wood floors, crown molding, granite countertops and so on. For the first time the kids had their own rooms. There wasn't a sad face for weeks after they'd moved in.

John stood in front of the house like a lost statue. The discarded shell of his former life spilled around him in pieces crying for someone to put it back together.

Suddenly, the night in front of him lit up like a projector screen. He saw his babies at the table banging their hands on the tray, sputtering words only they knew.

The scene changed and highchairs became regular chairs. They were a couple of years older chatting about cartoons and telling jokes that didn't make sense. They were spilling drinks and arguing over the last bit of food.

John watched them grow older, talking about sports, friends, and school. He saw Amy setting items on the table and running to the oven where the bread was burning. He could see the joy in her eyes as she watched them all. She had what she always wanted. Love was displayed in all its glory.

Then as suddenly as they appeared, they were gone.

Tears pricked the corners of his eyes as despair rose in his stomach. He scrambled for the bottle but couldn't find it in the dark.

John dropped to his knees and rocked like he was on a ship in rough seas.

Blessed are those who mourn for they shall be comforted.

The verse was one he'd learned a long time ago. He'd never really understood it. It rose in his throat like vomit. *Comforted? By whom, the one who did it?*

He scanned the sky through blurred eyes. "It's supposed to comfort me knowing you did this? Part of your master plan?" He cursed and wiped saliva from the corners of his mouth. "How, exactly, is that supposed to comfort me?"

The sky refused to answer. John stabbed the air with his finger. "You, you took them away. They were so innocent. You left me with nothing. I gave you my whole life and you left me with nothing!" He almost laughed

❮finding home❯

at how good it felt to finally hold him accountable.

"I hate you." The words were barely audible but they were the needed catalyst. The fire erupted through John's body as he grabbed handfuls of dirt and flung them into the sky. "I HATE YOU!" He reached back and found the whisky. Some of the amber liquid ran down his chin as he drained it into the raging inferno.

He climbed to his feet and jabbed the air with the empty bottle. "I don't need you. I never have. I'll survive. I will go on without you."

The bottle flew through the air and shattered somewhere in the night. With a swimming head and burning heart he staggered into the darkness.

chapter three

Boom-Boom-Boom.

Dream merged into reality, but the pounding wouldn't stop. In his dream, John had just been knocking down a wall with a sledgehammer, but now he was awake and it sounded like something was trying to demolish *his* wall.

He rubbed his eyes. *Boom-Boom-Boom.* "What in the…"

It took him a moment to realize the pounding was coming from his front door. He rolled over frantically trying to untie himself from the web of blankets.

"What time is it?" he stammered and stabbed for his small clock, *7:00 AM*. The digital display made his blood boil.

John kicked his blankets through the air as the banging continued. "You've got to be kidding me." He staggered to his feet, his boxers bunching around his thighs.

Boom-Boom-Boom.

"Stop it!" He stumbled over some dirty clothes on the floor. "Son of a…"

Boom-Boom-Boom.

"I'm gonna kill someone." He quickly crossed the spattering of square footage separating him from the door.

Boom-Boom… John threw the door open and two young men flinched at the sudden appearance of his large, half-naked frame. He leveled a glare at them both. "You'd better have a good reason."

Nervous smiles shaped their mouths. The younger one clutched a Bible like a shield in front of his Hurley shirt. John's eyes narrowed.

‹finding home›

"Hey man," chirped the taller one. He brought his hand out of his designer jeans pocket.

John crossed his arms. "Get to the point before I make those stupid grins really sad."

The guy lowered his arm and cleared his throat.

"I'm, uh Sid." He pointed to his friend. "And this is Josh. We're out this morning inviting people to our new church over on 8th and central."

He paused and raised his eyebrows like it was John's turn. "You waiting for a congratulations?" John spat. "Some kind of medal?"

Defeat entered the kid's tone. "We've got free coffee and doughnuts." The grins were fading. "So, uh, what do you say? Wanna come check it out?"

John closed his eyes. What was it his friend Mike was always telling him? *Count to 10.* He made it to three before his meaty right fist was back and flying toward the taller ones face in a smooth motion. The kid didn't have any time to react as John's fist connected with the right side of his face, just underneath his eye. John felt the familiar crunch of nose breaking on impact.

Sid was down on the ground before John could pull his arm back. He twisted to the left and reached back again, but Josh was already stumbling off the step.

"Wait!" Josh fell next to his moaning friend. He scrambled to his knees and held up both hands. "I'm sorry. Please don't hurt me."

John pointed a finger at his face. "You're gonna pass this house next time."

Josh nodded and helped his friend to his feet. They limped away turning the sidewalk into a trail of tears.

John smiled and closed his door. He admired his calloused bludgeons. They had served him well in more than a few bar fights. "If I could start every morning like this I might get along better with people throughout the day," he said aloud as if someone was there to listen.

"Start every morning like what?"

A woman half stood and half leaned in the doorway of his room. Red-lined eyes stared at him from underneath a mop of shoulder length hair that had changed color so many times even the roots were lost. One of his old T-shirts fell to her mid thigh. John scrolled through the previous night trying to unearth some sort of memory from the haze.

"Hey you..." Silence stretched like an empty road to nowhere. "Uh..." *Tina.* "Tina!"

Her eyebrows slowly became one entity. "It's Gina you idiot."

"Right Gina..." He had a name, but the only other thing his brain could produce was a fuzzy bottle of Jameson.

She yawned and eyed the kitchen. "You got anything to eat?"

"Hang on." He shook off the awkward encounter and checked the cabinets. Empty. He'd forgotten to make his bi-weekly trip to the store. He was sure alcohol had something to do with it. Maybe gambling. Probably both.

"Well?" Gina crossed her arms over her chest.

"I said hang on." *Please let there be coffee.* He picked up the tin can and cursed.

"Great..." Gina lit a Virginia Slim and aimed a stream of smoke at him.

John ignored her and shuffled a pair of jeans and a T-shirt into the bathroom. The high from earlier had fizzled out like soda open for too long. He brushed his teeth and caught his reflection in the mirror. The last ten years showed in the lines around his hazel eyes. He fingered the skin on his face, constantly dried out by the Arizona sun and sighed. *A lot of things used to be different.*

He opened the door and almost bumped into Gina. A tendril of smoke rose from the cigarette between her fingers and a deep scowl voiced her displeasure. "What am I supposed to do?"

"I don't know," he pushed past her, "and I don't care." He snatched his favorite old hat, wallet, and house keys from the table. "Just don't be here when I get back."

"Where are you going?"

"You writing a book?"

"You're such a—"

"Oh," he threw her a glance over his shoulder. "Leave the shirt."

He flipped off the light and stomped out.

‹ finding home ›

‹ chapter four ›

The diner was only a few blocks away. Well within walking distance. The morning air was crisp and cool. John shivered and wished he'd grabbed a jacket or found a shirt with long sleeves. Fall was rapidly giving way to winter. He shoved his big hands into his pockets and picked up his pace a notch, trying to stay warm.

Another pair of young men in trendy attire ambled toward him. Their pace was easy, and mindless chatter drifted on the breeze until they noticed him. He could see them turn pale even from a distance. Their eyes found the ground as they hustled past him. He couldn't help grinning as he rounded the corner.

Structures that barely qualified as homes lined the street on both sides. John kicked an empty can towards one. It rolled over patches of brown grass and dirt and came to rest against a tire half covered by a gutted car. He glanced at the house behind it. Missing doors, windows, and parts of roof pleaded for someone to care. He hardly noticed them anymore.

A gust of wind blew a leaf under his foot and he felt the satisfying crunch. It probably should've been harder to leave Oak Harbor for this place. But it wasn't. Every square mile of the town was a tapestry of memories that never let him forget what he'd lost. So, he quit his job at the nuclear power plant and pulled out a map.

Arizona. For some reason John had been drawn there. The more he stared at it the more he felt it was the right place. When he found Blackwater he knew the search was over. He trashed or canceled anything someone might use to find him and changed his last name to Caban. On his way out of town he dropped the title to his house off at the bank.

Blackwater turned out to be a small town, but bigger than what he'd grown up in. Family businesses outnumbered the corporate chains. It was big enough that people were able to keep their privacy, but small enough to keep from feeling crowded.

It didn't take John long to discover the divide between the good part of town and the bad. New construction bordered old. He'd pointed his old truck at the patched homes with brown yards, and drove into his new community.

A gas station that appeared abandoned was the first structure across the line. A black trash bag covered one of the two pumps. He parked his truck and stepped through the front door, narrowly missing oil that had spilled onto the ground. A picture of a woman covered by only her hands hung on the wall over a rack of dirty magazines. The wall behind the counter was a collage of torn posters advertising Skoal, Marlboro, and Camel. John avoided another puddle on the floor and walked to the counter. A weather-beaten man in torn overalls stood behind the register flipping through one of the magazines.

"Just reading the articles right?"

He raised his head like it was the most labor-intensive thing he'd done all day. His eyes were solid beads darkened by experiences he would never release for public knowledge. His fingers trembled slightly as he lowered the magazine, exposing the outline of his ribs. He was maybe in his 60's. Air whistled through missing teeth when he talked.

"You're not from 'round here," he spat.

John shook his head. "Nope."

The old man's words were deliberate, like there was something damaged between his brain and mouth. "Where you from?"

"Don't worry about it. Just put forty on the one without the bag." John dropped a couple twenties on the counter.

The old man considered that for a long time. John noticed his fingers toying with something under the counter. A bead of sweat crept across his forehead like a beetle. Finally the man took the cash and switched on the pump.

John put both hands on the counter. "I need a place to stay."

"For how long?"

‹finding home›

"As long as I want."

He crossed his old, boney arms. "We don't like new people movin' in here."

"I need a place," John repeated.

"There ain't no place for you," he growled spat on the ground.

John leaned closer to the man. "I could break your face with that gun you've got under the counter and ask you again." The old man hesitated, his mind working out the options. For a moment he thought the guy was going to choose the hard way but then his shoulders sagged.

"Try 4th street. They might have some places." He hadn't lived through dark times by being stupid.

"How about a job?"

"Construction's probably your best bet."

John pointed at the pump. "You short change me and you'll lose the few teeth you have left."

The man smiled. "You're gonna fit right in 'round here."

John must've still been grinning at the memory when he reached the diner because Helen, the long time owner, cook, and waitress was staring at him with raised eyebrows.

"What are you so happy about?"

He didn't answer.

"No, really." Helen lumbered toward him. "What's the matter with you?"

"You won't like it."

Helen's hands found her wide hips. Her arms were plump sausages attached to a round torso. She was in her 50's and had lived in the neighborhood all of her life. One thing was crystal clear. No matter how many people were afraid of John, she wasn't and would never be. She tapped her foot on the floor. "Try me."

John finally surrendered. "I got to punch someone this morning."

Helen weighed the possibility that he was joking, but came out on the wrong side. "Congratulations on being a terrible person," she called as he proceeded toward his favorite table.

"Lucky for me you don't discriminate," John called back. "I'll be at my booth excited about my usual."

"Yeah-yeah," she muttered, and vanished into the kitchen.

John reached a booth by the window and sat down, sinking into the old, worn seat that had lost its ability to support pretty much anything. He plucked a piece of peeling paint off of the wall and stomped on bubbled linoleum at his feet. He smiled. The place was perfect.

A quick survey of the room revealed all of the patrons. He nodded to each one. *What a sorry looking bunch of—*

The thought arrested in his brain like a bad heart. John had been eating at Helen's Diner a couple of times per week in the same old, worn, unsupportive seat for years and had quickly realized that Helen didn't have customers, she had regulars. But John wasn't looking at a regular.

The stranger kept his head down as he read over something spread out on the table. His tan pants and flannel long sleeved shirt were old and cheap. He was wearing a hat that could've once been white but was now faded and yellowing around the bottom. Thick, black hair stuck out where the hat ended. The skin on his cheeks was tough and dark like he worked outside. John decided he was probably roughly his own age. Truthfully, he fit in like any regular.

Tiny needles of anxiety surprised John. He didn't *feel* threatened. The man seemed harmless but something wasn't quite right.

"Coffee," Helen announced and filled a ceramic cup with black, steaming liquid. "Your food will be out in a minute."

"Mm-hmm," John replied without looking up. He took a careful sip still studying the stranger. A second later he felt a hand connect with the back of his head. He coughed and faced Helen's scowl.

"What was that for?"

"What's wrong with you?"

"What?"

"Why in gods name did you punch someone so early in the morning? What could they have possibly done to you?"

John rubbed the back of his stinging head. "That was assault Helen."

"John Caban you answer me right now."

John sighed and gave in. "They woke me up and invited me to some stupid church."

Helen cursed. "You hit a church person!" She grabbed John's shoulder.

‹ finding home ›

"You've got to get out of here. I don't want you anywhere near me or my diner when God Almighty rains hell fire and brimstone down on your head."

"Oh, stop it, Helen. *God Almighty* is welcome to try." He shot her a look. "You don't *really* believe any of that crap do you?"

"I believe in some of that crap John. I believe enough of it not to go around punching church people." She crossed her arms. "He was probably holding a Bible wasn't he?"

John rolled his eyes and shook his head.

"Yeah, I thought so. You're definitely gonna get it now. Did it fall? Don't you know the Bible isn't ever supposed to touch the ground?"

John made a face. "That's the Quran Helen. The Quran isn't supposed to touch the ground." He took a slow sip of coffee.

"How do you know preacher puncher? Did you take a class about Bibles and Qurans?"

"I own a TV Helen. I'm connected to information. You should try it." John brushed a napkin over a spot of spilled coffee on the table. "Plus, I used to go to church so I know about the Bible."

"*You* used to go to church?"

"Hard to believe I know."

"So what happened?"

John shot her the meanest look he could muster.

"Oh," Helen lifted her hands. "Yes sir. I'm *so sorry* I forgot the rules. Personal questions…off limits…whatever."

"You know what?" John put his cup down. "I'll answer your personal question this time."

Helen straightened, eyes wide.

"I went to church for years. I believed everything about Jesus and God and whatever else. I was even friends with the pastor." He paused just long enough to clear his throat and take another swig of coffee. "Then one day I realized I didn't believe in the God he preached and everyone talked about. Actually it was more than that. I didn't *want* to believe in the God he preached and everyone talked about."

Helen held her eyes on him for a long moment. "Why not?"

John held the still steaming cup to his mouth. "That, Helen, is a personal

23

question I will not answer."

Helen raised both hands in surrender. "I'll go get your food. There is something wrong with you though."

"And you *did* assault me."

"So sue me."

"So I could get all this?" John gestured around the room. "No thanks." He heard her chuckling as she disappeared into the kitchen. He felt a smile threatening his face and quickly forced it back into submission.

He took a long sip of coffee and remembered the stranger. He lifted his head to see the stranger staring in his direction. He felt exposed somehow, like his own weapon was pointed at his head. The last ten years had taught John that offense is the best defense. He lifted his chin and hollered, "You'd better have a good reason for staring into my business."

The stranger didn't answer. Instead he adjusted his eyes back to the table and continued to eat the eggs smeared across his plate.

A wiry teenage waiter with skin as black as midnight appeared next to John. He put a plate of eggs over medium, bacon, and hash browns on the table and refilled his coffee cup.

"Hey," John whispered. "Who's that guy over there?" Helen hired young people from the community to wait tables and work in the kitchen so he figured the kid might know about any new people moving in. "You seen him around?"

"No sir," the kid answered without looking up. "Never seen him before. Fits in though don't he?"

John picked up his fork. "Whatever." The kid dropped the check on the table before attending to the other regulars.

John ate his breakfast faster than normal, draining his coffee in a few gulps. He dropped enough cash on the table to cover the tip before heading to the front door. He glanced back one more time before leaving. The stranger was still looking down. A chill left goose bumps on his arms. *Who is that guy?* John left the diner and hurried home.

… finding home ≻

chapter five

The piercing brown eyes of the stranger haunted John all the way home. They bore into him like an auger. He pushed open his front door and wondered if the guy knew him. A Private Investigator maybe. Someone hired to track him down.

John paced in front of the kitchen and ran his hand through his hair. He noticed the shirt Gina was wearing hanging loosely on the back of a chair. "People don't affect me like this," he hollered at it. "A Private Investigator? After ten years?" The shirt refused to answer.

He let his forehead rest against the wall. "It doesn't make sense." The words worked through his body and his heart relaxed into a normal pace. "It was just some idiot," he assured himself. "Nothing else."

John switched on the TV. He fell into his recliner and flipped through the channels until he found The Price Is Right. He was about to guess the price of a wristwatch when a knock at the door made him fumble the remote.

He froze and didn't move until the knock came again, this time a little louder. John rose and took a few small steps towards the door but suddenly straightened. He clenched his jaw and tapped his head with the heel of his hand. "Get a grip John," he muttered. With that he took a few large steps and pulled the door open.

Relief flooded him like a storm surge. "What do *you* want?"

"I hope I woke you up."

John shook his head. "Been up for hours." He slid over to let Mike in.

"Oh well. Another day another opportunity." Mike was a tall, lean man a couple of years younger than John. He was a proud man from a family of

Law Enforcement and Military blood. They'd met a couple of months after John moved into the neighborhood.

"This place is a hole." Mike kicked an empty cup into a pile of dirty clothes. "You ever think about *not* being a slob?"

John crossed his arms over his chest. "I didn't make you come in. Didn't even invite you."

Mike ignored the jab and picked up a piece of paper from the table. "You're the only person I know who could care less about garbage on the floor, but care enough to hire pest control." He tapped his head. "You got two different people in there, John? Are you *for real* crazy?"

John grabbed the bill from his friend. "You could show a little more respect. You owe me a lot."

"That song is so tired, man. You know we're more than even. Scale's probably even tipped towards me. Besides, I had that guy."

"You had him only because *I* had him."

Mike smirked. "Eh. Maybe you're right."

John pulled out a chair from his small table and sat down. Neither of them would ever forget the altercation involving John and some huge guy at Joe's, their favorite watering hole. The issue had spilled into the parking lot and someone called the cops. Mike arrived to find the big guy drunk enough to go after him with a brick while his back was turned. John noticed at the last second and tackled the guy to the ground. They'd been friends ever since.

"Remind me why you're here," John demanded and kicked out another chair for his friend.

Mike held up his hand. "I'm good, man." He adjusted his duty belt. "If I sit I might not get back up. Just thought I'd stop by and check on you."

"Nothing illegal going on here. You could go stakeout the doughnut shop. You know, put my tax dollars to their usual use."

Mike waved him off. "Stop it. You don't pay taxes. You can't afford them after losing your money to me every week."

John rolled his eyes, but couldn't deny the statement was partially true. He paid his taxes but Mike was a regular player in their weekly poker game and he was very good at taking home more money than he came with.

Just then John remembered the stranger and straightened. "Hey have you noticed anybody new around here lately? Maybe someone who just

‹ finding home ›

moved into the neighborhood?"

"I don't think so. Why?"

"There was someone in the diner this morning I didn't recognize," John told him. "Guy about our age. Kept to himself but I caught him staring at me like he knew me."

Mike grinned. "Scared you a little huh? You need me to protect you?" He lifted his finger. "Now I can hold your hand when you cross the street, but that's it. I have a life, John."

John rolled his eyes. "Yeah, I've seen your life. Walking me across the street would be the highlight."

Mike laughed as he strolled to the door. "I'll ask around and let you know what I find."

John nodded.

"Oh, I almost forgot. I got a call from a very concerned preacher this morning." He mustered up a serious cop face. "Stop assaulting people, John. I can't keep pulling you out of these holes you insist on digging."

John jumped up. "He deserved it!"

Mike waved him off. "No he didn't and you know it. Your luck is running thin and if you don't stop I won't be able to help you. You might find yourself in a very uncomfortable situation."

"How uncomfortable are we talking here Mike?" John rubbed his chin. "Are we talking like when you walked in on me and your sister or something worse?"

Mike sighed and pinched his forehead. "For the last time I don't have a sister."

"That's not what *she* said."

Mike threw his hands up. The equipment on his heavy belt was a symphony of frustration as he stomped to his squad car. "I don't know why I put up with this nonsense, I really don't."

"Hey," John hurried to the door and tried to hide the laughter from his voice. "Just out of curiosity, how *did* you smooth it over with the pastor?"

Mike opened his car door. "I told him you're mentally retarded and his men scared you. I'm pretty sure that's the truth anyway." He slammed his door and drove off.

John laughed and closed the door.

chapter six

"Brrrrrrr." Alice shivered and shoved her nose deeper beneath the collar of her thick coat, away from the wind biting her with its teeth. She lowered her head and forged on.

"Do you need a ride, dear?" one of the ladies at church had asked her. "It's quite cold out there today."

Alice wiggled feeling back through her fingers and toes and wished she'd taken the offer. "*No*," she muttered into her coat. "Can't let someone *help* can you?" She aimed one of her boots at a snowdrift and transformed it into a mushroom cloud of white powder. The sunlight bounced off the tiny particles and turned them into glitter. It was enough to melt her frustration and she giggled as the flakes fell on her face.

"Well," she exclaimed and wiped her cheeks. "It's not so bad I guess." Alice rotated in a circle looking at the town that'd been her home for the past three years. Snow lay on rooftops, mailboxes, and tree branches like pillows. Everything looked so clean, all stains covered by a layer of purity. At dusk she watched lazy smoke float out of brick chimneys as the street lamps lit up. It was a village snow globe come to life. "Redwood, New York," she whispered like she was sharing a secret. "I never thought I'd love you this much."

Another frigid gust clawed at her fair skin and she retreated behind the collar of her thick coat. "Spoke too soon," she blurted and hurried home.

The snow-white wood panels and sky-blue shutters of her two-story American Colonial home greeted her as she bounded up the cracked, concrete stairs. Alice pushed through the door and quickly closed it against the rush of wind. She leaned back and yanked off her boots. She smiled and remembered the first time she'd climbed those steps.

‹finding home›

It was just shy of midnight almost three years ago. The wind chased her like a pack of wolves as snow swirled in a rage. When she reached for the door it was already falling away and she stumbled across the threshold. Melted snow clouded her eyes as the door clicked shut behind her. She blinked at a woman doing nothing to hide her wide grin.

"Welcome home," she exclaimed.

Alice almost didn't understand the words. Her throat was suddenly too thick for breath. *Home?* She turned the word over in her mind. *Was it possible?*

"You must be Alice."

Alice studied the woman. She was older, like a grandma. Her hands were folded neatly at her waist and slender arms ran the length of her torso underneath a light green sweater. Thin legs hid under jeans that fell loosely over dark socks.

"My name is Melissa," she announced. "My husband Jack and I manage this house and the program. Normally I'm the only one who greets the girls." A knowing filled Melissa's eyes, but her warm smile never left. "We've found it to be easier that way." She motioned at Alice's bag. "Would you like me to take your bag and coat?"

Alice fell back a step and hugged her items a little closer to her lean 5'7" frame. She nervously tucked a strand of jet-black hair behind her ear.

"That's okay," Melissa conceded. "But I'll need to look through your bag before I check you into your room. House rules." Melissa gave her an apologetic look. "I'm sorry."

Alice tilted her head a few degrees. Those words sounded just as foreign as, *welcome home*. And she noticed a look in Melissa's eyes. It wasn't judgment or a sense of obligation. It was only kindness and sincere joy that she was standing in her entryway.

"I'll give you a quick tour." Melissa pointed to the left. "Through that door is the master bedroom…"

Alice's head was stuck on spin cycle as Melissa showed her the first floor. A dining room and kitchen. Original floors and upgraded bathrooms. A small nook off the dining room looking out at the street through bay windows. Alice's feet had become lead. Her eyes were drooping and she was very grateful when Melissa took her back to the stairs.

Melissa nodded towards the 2nd floor. "Come on, I'll show you to your room."

She led her up stairs that creaked every other step. "There are three other girls here with us," she informed Alice when they reached the landing. "Your room is down this hallway on the left."

Melissa showed her to a door with a pretty sign that read, *Alice,* and held out her hand. "I'm sorry, but I *must* check your bag."

Alice recoiled and heat flashed through her face.

"Please," Melissa asked. "Just for a second. I just have to make sure."

Alice felt her feet tense. She teetered on the edge of leaving and staying but after a couple of long moments she handed the bag over. Melissa gave her a grateful look, moved the few items it held around until she was satisfied, and gave it back. "The other girls are asleep. We'll get you all acquainted in the morning." She fixed her eyes on Alice and smiled. "Well…"

Alice raised an eyebrow and stared back until she realized Melissa was waiting for her to open the door. The brass knob was cool in her hand and she couldn't hide a gasp as she stepped into the room.

Soft lighting reflected off of sage greens and lavenders. The white bed frame held a floral quilt with an arrangement of pillows on top. Alice stepped to the window and let the silky curtains run through her fingers like water. Her feet sank into a plush rug resting on the hardwood floor.

Alice felt her eyes water for the first time in years. But there was something else. She hid her face from Melissa and reached for a basket on the bed. It was filled with lotions, perfumes, and toiletries. She clicked open the lip of one of the lotions and the fragrance of candied apples filled the air.

Alice dropped the bottle and wrapped her trembling arms around her body. Fear snaked through her heart that she was dreaming and any minute she would wake up in a dark alley. But then she noticed a purple bow lying against the basket. It was tied around a card that had the words, *Welcome Home Alice,* written in pretty colors.

She wheeled around wide-eyed. "Is…" Alice swallowed. Her voice sounded strained. "Is all this really for me?"

Melissa's bottom lip trembled as she smiled. "Just for you."

‹finding home›

Alice eyed the colored walls again and then the floor. "I've...never had my own..." She clenched her jaw, angry a how stupid she sounded.

Melissa nodded quickly and stepped over to Alice. "I'm sorry if the colors seem a little young, but we want you to remember."

Alice raised her hazel eyes. "Remember what?"

Melissa ignored the tears on her cheeks. "That you're a princess." She placed a soft hand on Alice's cheek. "We're so glad you're here, Alice. Really."

Alice smiled at the memory, and wiped her cheeks. She hung her oversized coat on the rack and stepped up the stairs that still creaked with every other step. At 20, she was the oldest of four girls who'd come together with the Baker's to make a family, the first one Alice could ever remember having.

She snuck past the other girl's rooms trying to keep her steps light enough to let them sleep. Most of them had trouble sleeping and slept in when they could. She hesitated at the last door before hers. "Tabby" was elegantly written on a sign in pretty pastels. Tabby was the second oldest at eighteen and shared a story similar to her own. She was average weight and height with short auburn hair and glasses covered her grey eyes.

They'd grown close over walks, coffee, and late night talks. Alice traced the letters on the sign with her finger. Tabby was the closest thing she'd ever had to a sister. She smiled and quietly moved down the hall to her room.

She pulled her door shut and fell back on her bed, black hair spilling around her like oil. She let her thoughts drift to Melissa and Jack Baker. It could only be the love of God that drove them to keep opening their home to girls like her.

"We've been doing it for thirty years," Melissa told her one day. "There are hard days that can be draining. But when we see God heal the broken hearts and lives of precious girls like you, well," she squeezed Alice's hand, "We can't imagine ever stopping."

Alice blinked at the ceiling and wondered where she'd be without them. Probably dead. She spied a light pink streamer gently fluttering as the vent pushed heat past it. It was from a surprise party Jack and Melissa had thrown on her one-month anniversary. She'd come back from her counseling session to find the downstairs decorated with balloons, streamers, banners, and flowers. Bright pinks and purples glittered and gleamed all around her as Jack, Melissa, and the girls shouted surprise. She'd been so stiff when Melissa hugged her.

Alice lifted a silver cross charm from beneath her sweater and turned it over in her fingers. That was the day something cracked deep inside like the seal on a window. It allowed the smallest ray of light into a dark, abandoned room.

She let the charm dangle from it's thin silver chain and brushed her thumb over the worn inscription on the back, *1 Cor. 13:8*. "Love never fails," she whispered. It'd been safe in her pocket for as long as she could remember. She wasn't sure where she got it but it was a part of her somehow. The small cross never left her side and right now it was reminding her of the way Jack and Melissa introduced her to Jesus.

"When does he scream and throw things?" she'd asked Melissa one night while they shared coffee. It'd been six months and she couldn't figure out Jack. "Does he hit you when we aren't around?"

Melissa took her hand and held it tightly. "Honey, Jack does his very best to show every broken girl that walks through our door that evil isn't all there is, that good men exist and that the love of God is greater than any darkness you could ever encounter. He won't hurt me." She smiled. "And he won't hurt you either."

Alice pulled her hand away and left the room. She continued to watch and expected Jack to hit and scream and hurt like every other man she'd ever known. But he never did. He continued to treat Melissa, her, and the others with nothing but respect. He found ways to help them, protect them, and provide for them. One day she finally admitted that she felt like part of his family instead of a guest.

She'd run to her room. A few hours later she finally had to acknowledge that Jack Baker had been showing his true colors all along. What could be powerful enough to change a man into something she might want to be around?

She found Melissa that same night in the study. Alice stood in the doorway chewing on a nail and almost fled before Melissa noticed her.

"Alice…" Her smile brushed Alice's heart. "Do you need something, sweetheart?"

"I, um…" Alice took a small step into the room. "I wanted to ask

⊲finding home⊳

you…" She shook her head. "No, I *need* to know something."

"Okay." Melissa gestured to an empty chair. "Would you like to sit down?"

"No, not really. I just need to know about Jack."

"About Jack?"

Alice nodded. "About why he is the way he is. I've never…" Alice felt her eyes water and hid her face. Tears? She didn't think she had any left. She shut her eyes tightly forcing them back. Tears were pointless.

She exhaled and faced Melissa. "What makes him the way he is? Does it really have something to do with God or Jesus or whatever?"

Melissa studied her for a long moment before answering. "I would love to answer that for you Alice. But if you're willing I would love for Jack to answer it even more."

Alice felt her heart race. She took a step back. "N…NO!" But then she heard a soft voice all around her, or in her, she wasn't quite sure. The sound was peaceful like waves gently breaking against the sand.

Please let him. It's going to be okay. I am with you.

The voice. She didn't know it. Didn't recognize it. But she was suddenly desperate for more of it. Who are you?

I am love. Trust me.

She stood wrapped in…whatever it was for a few minutes. She'd heard plenty of nasty voices in her life. This one was different. The opposite. "Okay," she finally whispered.

Melissa disappeared to fetch Jack, and Alice willed herself to calm down while her thumbs spun invisible thread. She lowered herself into a chair just as Jack appeared in the doorway. He smiled at her and took a seat on the love seat leaving room for Melissa to sit down next to him.

Jack told her about his journey into what he called, *The loving arms of the perfect father.* As he talked the pain in her had never felt so raw. She was bleeding, like the scabs and scars over her heart and been ripped away. But she also knew who could heal her.

When Jack was finished she raised her head with were tears in her eyes. This time she didn't care. "I need…" tears spilled onto her cheeks. "I need Jesus." She covered her face with her hands as her body shook. "I need Him to heal me. To save me."

Melissa was there and Alice sobbed into her shoulder. "Oh sweetie," Melissa whispered into her ear. "Just tell Jesus he can have your heart."

Alice wiped her eyes. "That's it?"

"Yes," Melissa answered. "That's it."

Alice had never wanted to do anything as badly as that. "Jesus…my heart is yours." She gasped as she was swept into what felt like a whirlwind of joy and peace. But there was something else above the rest. Love. She had always wondered what it might be like, feel like. Now she knew. It flowed in her and through her awakening parts of her thought to be lost forever.

Alice. I love you so much. I always have and I always will. I'm so happy to have you in my arms. I'll never leave you and I will never let you go.

She covered her face with her hands. "I'm so sorry I didn't come to you sooner. I'm so sorry…" Tears streamed down her face. "I'm so sorry for the things I've done, the life I've lived." She crumpled to the floor.

Oh Alice, I forgive you and have already cleansed you. You are pure and whole. I have resurrected your heart. What you thought was dead is now alive. You have always been and will forever be my daughter.

And then everything but her and Jesus was gone. He was holding out his hand asking her to dance. And they did. For the rest of the night she danced with Jesus. She was lost and had been found.

Alice pushed herself off of the bed as the memory faded. She giggled and twirled to the window as if the dance had never ended. The glass was cold against her finger as she traced a heart in the condensation. She'd been certain she was beyond saving. But she was wrong. His perfect love was stitching her heart one day at a time. She'd even found the courage to begin forgiving those who'd hurt her, and experienced some of the freedom forgiveness brings.

She grabbed the personalized Bible Jack and Melissa had bought her from the nightstand and pressed it against her chest. "Thank you Daddy," she whispered as tears gently rolled down her cheeks. She was his little girl and always would be. That's all she needed.

‹ finding home ›

‹ chapter seven ›

The sun was gone, allowing the darkness to intrude with an icy chill that pushed against the protection of John's jacket. He grunted and lowered his head as if he could intimidate nature.

John crossed the threshold of Joe's, right on schedule. He stepped over mismatched tiles and peeling walls and found his stool. The murmur of alcohol-laden conversation buzzed in his ears a little louder than normal. It was the same melody night after night.

"Caban!" A burly man named Al worked his way over.

John grimaced. "You coming over to tell me the jukebox is finally fixed?"

Al laughed a little too loud and slapped John on the back. "That thing is toast Caban. Aint' never coming back." He lifted his half empty glass. "That's what a beer in the coin slot will do fer ya."

"You should know," John grunted. "It was your beer."

Al laughed again and John leaned back. "You look a little wobbly, Al. Maybe you should sit down."

"Ahhhh," Al exclaimed and spilled beer into his beard. "How 'bout I whoop you in pool instead?"

He was pointing to John's left but guessed he was still the intended target. "Maybe later." The pool table was the only thing that worked. That and the taps. And after a few drafts the whole place started to look better.

Al gave up and staggered off to find another challenger. John grinned. Joe's was full of rough looking, vulgar regulars, but the atmosphere was usually pretty tame. They tolerated each other fairly well. The problems typically started when a new face showed. It was the type of place where chairs were earned. John sat down in *his* just as an Indian Pale Ale slid in front of him.

"There you go, hun," Nellie cooed. She was 29 and had been the bar tender for the last couple of years. Many of the regulars wouldn't be regulars without her. "Your usual."

"First of about eight I'm thinking." John took her in. A low-cut t-shirt ended at her belly button showing off her curves and the angel wings tattooed on her lower back. She was tan and lean with auburn hair pulled into a simple ponytail, and her big brown eyes were currently locked on him.

"Take it easy," Nellie told him. A grin spread across her face. "I wouldn't want you to put another nail through your finger."

John shot her a sarcastic smile. A couple of months ago John had gone to work with a hangover and shot a framing nail through his thumb. "Thanks for your concern. But I told you the hangover wasn't the problem; it was what we did the night before. My head never left your room."

"Well," she leaned over the counter on her forearms. Her voice was like poisoned honey. "I guess our little get-togethers will have to stop…you know…for your own safety."

"I've got insurance, I'm good," John assured her. "Plus, I've got next week off. Burning vacation time."

Nellie straightened. "*You're* taking a vacation?"

"I've got too many hours saved up. I have to burn em or lose em. Wasn't my idea." John took a drink and wiped his mouth. "I just wonder how I'm gonna spend my extra time."

"Maybe the same way you've been spending a lot of your regular time." She winked and moved down the bar where others waited.

John watched her hips sway and wondered where she hid the devil tattoo. It started happening after John stayed until closing one night and escorted her home. Neither of them wanted a relationship so the situation was perfect. No strings attached. He swallowed the rest of his beer with satisfaction. The other relationships over the years ended when the woman wanted more. They *always* wanted more eventually. He raised an eyebrow. But not Nellie.

"Hey!"

Nellie's finger was in the face of a crusty regular named Chuck. Chuck had decided to try and self serve a draft. "If I catch you reaching on my side

‹finding home›

of the bar again I'll break your hand," she pointed to a bat resting against the wall.

John chuckled and drained the rest of his beer. Nellie was as tough as she was attractive. And he loved the ego boost. He hit the bar for another beer, and a few seconds later it was in his hands.

He scanned the crowd. No surprises. The same ugly faces as always. He gulped from his mug and almost choked on the amber liquid. Someone was sitting in a chair next to the pool table. John stared hard as the cigarette smoke cleared just enough to reveal a face, a face that chased all the air from his lungs.

chapter eight

The intruder wore the same tan pants and long sleeved flannel shirt he wore in the diner. The same black hair protruded from underneath the same white but yellowing hat. Both feet stuck out in front of him and his arms were crossed across his chest. John considered the possibility that he was sleeping.

But suddenly, as if the man knew he'd been spotted, he raised his head, and his deep brown eyes resumed their assault against John. They were two swords not bothered by the boundaries of distance, skin, muscle, tissue and bone.

John shut his eyes and forced stale air into his lungs. *Ok, John. Get a hold of yourself. It's just some guy, just some idiot.*

The peace his pep talk gave him fled like an army without a leader when he opened his eyes. The man was still staring at him but this time his lips were moving. Somehow, even with the poor lighting and hovering smoke, John could read them perfectly.

I know who you are.

John jumped up and crashed into someone walking by. He didn't feel the beer splash on his shirt and barely heard the sound of glass shattering on the floor.

A drunk named Steve was glaring at a wet stain on his shirt. "What's your problem, Caban? You're gonna replace that beer. And my shirt."

John ignored him and searched for the stranger. The chair was empty. His heart began to gallop. A rapid search of the room produced nothing.

"Did you hear me, Caban?"

"Who's that guy?"

"What guy?"

◂ finding home ▸

John pointed to the vacated chair. "The guy who was just sitting in *that* chair."

"Who cares?"

"Did you see where he went?"

"I don't take care of your boyfriends Caban. Do I look like a babysitter?"

On a regular night John might have taken issue with Steve's comments. But not tonight, tonight he would get away with it.

John hurried to the door and stumbled into the parking lot. Ten or so cars were spaced across the lot, but other than that it was empty and silent. John jerked his head back and forth. Nothing. He was alone.

He pressed his fingers into his temples. After another few minutes turned up nothing, he went back inside. Nellie was waiting for him at the bar holding a rag.

"Thanks for the mess." She peered at him. "You don't look so good."

John leaned over the counter. "Do you know the guy who was sitting by the pool table?"

"Huh?"

John pointed toward the table. "The guy in the back corner. Do you know him?"

She made a face and motioned to the room. "Do you see all these people?"

John slapped the bar. "He was wearing tan pants and a long sleeve flannel shirt. He had an old white hat on."

"Alright calm down." She thought for a moment and shook her head. "No, I don't remember seeing anyone like that. If he was here he didn't buy a drink." She scrunched her nose. "Why would someone come here and not drink?"

She shook it off and studied John. "The hell's wrong with you? You look…weird."

John wiped a line of sweat off his forehead. "I'm uh…I don't feel…" He grabbed his coat. "I gotta go."

"Wait." Nellie dropped the rag and followed him to the end of the counter. "Does that mean you're not coming over tonight?"

He ignored her and whirled into Steve who had blocked the door. His eyes were dark and his face a stone. "You leaving, Caban?" He moved close enough for John to smell the alcohol on his breath. "Cause I don't have my beer yet."

John felt a familiar fire ignite inside and suddenly his hand was around Steve's throat. The wall shuddered as John threw him against it. "You gonna *make* me buy you a beer Steve?"

"No I—"

John shoved him higher on the wall. "You say one more word I'll put my fist through your face." He held the trembling man in place for another moment before letting him slide down to the floor. He took a look around the quiet room and opened the door.

The moment he hit the cool night air again his knees shook and threatened to crumble. He stumbled home and collapsed on the couch with a beer in one hand and bourbon in the other. Different angles of the stranger's face surrounded him like a fun house.

Finally, after he'd drastically reduced the alcohol content of his house, the torment stopped and he faded into darkness.

‹ finding home ›

‹ chapter nine ›

Alice repositioned her head on the pillow. Her eyes were closed and she was trying to ignore the lump on the couch that always pressed into her lower back.

"Alice."

She didn't answer.

"Alice?"

She opened one eye enough to blur Dr. Felling's face. "Hmmm?"

"Are you thinking?"

"I'm trying." The rhythmic trickle of water from a fountain in the corner would've put her to sleep if it wasn't for that lump. She opened both eyes and blinked at the ceiling. Maybe that was the point.

"Can you remember anything?"

Alice rubbed her eyes. "No."

"What are you thinking about?"

"How long we've been trying. How pointless this is."

Dr. Felling sighed. "Let's take a break then."

Alice sat up and fought a wave of dizziness. "Sure, how about forever?"

Dr. Felling's mouth remained a straight line. "I'll take that as a 'no.'"

"It's important Alice."

"Why?" Alice crossed her arms over her chest. "Why is it important? Why do I have to remember?" She stood and stepped to a window overlooking a pond. It was supposed to be a tranquil scene protected by a border of thick trees, but someone with a snowmobile had discovered it. Alice stared at the mess. "The last ten years were bad enough."

Alice rotated so she could see Dr. Felling who studied her through brown eyes and thin glasses. The therapist's face was smooth, despite being in her mid-sixties, and her short gray hair completed a classy look. She uncrossed and crossed her long legs while her hands remained neatly folded in her lap.

Seeing a therapist had been required if she wanted to stay with the Bakers. She picked a name off a list of Christian Counselors and she'd been meeting with Dr. Felling on Mondays ever since.

Alice watched her hands. "What if I can't remember for a reason." She glanced up. "What if they're terrible?"

For a long time nobody spoke until Dr. Felling finally leaned forward and asked, "Do you feel like a *whole* person?"

Alice returned to the couch and sat down. "What do you mean?"

"Do you feel like a whole person or do you feel…fragmented?"

"Fragmented?"

"Yes, fragmented. *Scattered* maybe. Like there's pieces of you that are lost." She motioned to the window. "Out there somewhere."

Alice fell back against the couch and picked at a nail. "Not as much as I did three years ago."

"Are you saying you still feel broken?"

"Well, in a way I guess. I *am* missing half of my life. But it's not like I'm *suffering*." She straightened and set her jaw. "I would be fine living the rest of my life not being able to remember the first ten years. It's not like I'm missing anything." But the words sank like a stone in a lake. She avoided Dr. Felling's eyes.

Dr. Felling leaned back and scribbled something in her notes. "I want you to think back to our first meetings together. Do you remember how long it was before you would talk to me?"

Alice tried to remember. "Couple weeks?"

"It was a couple of *months*," she stated. "And do you remember what your first words were?"

Alice shrugged.

"They were, 'I hate you' with a couple of other words I won't repeat."

"Okay…" Alice let her hands fall to her sides.

"Do you remember what you said to me almost exactly one year later?"

Alice shook her head.

"It was snowing that day. A blizzard actually. You had waited for things

◄ finding home ►

to calm down before going home."

"Dr. Felling I have no idea wha—" And then she did know. That day came into focus slowly like an old Polaroid. "I uh…said that I trust you."

Dr. Felling put down her notes. "We've come a long way haven't we?" Alice raised her head and nodded.

"So I want you to remember how much I care about you when I tell you that I don't believe you."

Alice pulled her hands away. "Don't believe what?"

"I don't believe you're being honest when you say you're not missing anything. I think it *does* hurt you and deep inside you know that you need to remember."

Alice tried to dismiss the truth, but it wasn't long before she deflated like a balloon. "Even if that's true there's no point. I *can't* remember. I… my brain," she touched the sides of her head. "It's broken. Something happened."

"But I don't think that's true. All of the tests came back negative. Your brain is fine, albeit with a thick streak of stubbornness," Dr. Felling teased.

Alice stood and raised her hands to the therapist. "What do you want me to do then? Isn't it possible that those years were so bad that I just… just…shut them out? Doesn't that happen?"

Dr. Felling's voice was calm. "Sometimes."

"Or what about some kind of injury that happened a long time ago? Couldn't it have healed? Couldn't *that* happen?"

"It could…"

"Would it show up on the tests?"

"Not necessarily."

"Then why are you telling me to remember?" Tears leaked onto her face as she collapsed onto the couch. "Ouch!" she cried and slapped the cushion. "That *stupid* lump."

"Alice, I'm telling you to remember because I just don't believe any of those things are true in this case, in your case." She passed Alice a box of Kleenex. "Maybe you did have an injury that healed, but even if you *did* I don't believe it's keeping you from remembering."

Alice wiped her eyes. "How can you say that?"

"Because I watch you when you're trying to remember. I watch you get close and then shut down. It's like you can see the light start to break through but then close the drapes as fast as you can."

Alice sniffed loudly and pulled her hand away. "But I can't—"

"But you can." She moved to the couch. "The only thing holding you back is *you*. You can't remember because you've decided you don't want to."

Alice felt her shoulders sag as the fight left her. Dr. Felling was right. There *had* been times when the darkness seemed to shutter and fade as if a dimmer switch was being turned up. She had never seen anything, but knew she'd been close. "I'm scared," she whispered.

"I know. But it's going to be ok. Do you know why?"

Alice shook her head.

"Because Jesus is going to be with you every step of the way. He'll never let go of your hand. He wants to heal you and make you whole, but you must let him."

There was a soft knock on the door and Carol poked her head in. "I'm sorry but your 10 o'clock is here."

Dr. Felling nodded her head. "I guess we'll pick this up next week. "She stood and brushed the wrinkles out of her skirt. "Think and pray about what we discussed this morning. God has so many wonderful things for you."

Alice stood and slid into her coat. She said good-bye to Dr. Felling and waved at Carol before stepping into the crisp air. Her brain buzzed. *Maybe I can remember. Maybe it really is safe.* She felt the icy grip of fear on her heart and shuddered. Maybe, just maybe it would be ok.

‹ finding home ›

‹ chapter ten ›

John licked his cracked lips and grimaced at the taste in his mouth. Every muscle screamed when he sat up. He blinked a few times making sure he was in his own room. The combination of women and alcohol sometimes put him in strange places. He rubbed his face and glanced at the small clock next to his bed. 10 AM. He did a quick calculation. Monday.

John ignored his aching muscles and staggered to the bathroom, tripping over his boots on the way. He cursed. "Tina, pick this crap up!" He splashed water on his face and remembered Tina was yesterday morning. Or was it Gina? He quickly brushed his teeth and grabbed his razor before remembering he was on forced vacation all week. He put the razor down.

He grabbed some jeans from the floor and a long sleeved shirt from a chair. He fell over trying to put his jeans on, cursed, and finished dressing on the floor. He sighed and felt his stomach growl.

The kitchen cabinets were as empty as a whorehouse for seniors. He groaned and put his hands on the counter. He didn't feel like going to the diner. *The diner. The stranger. The bar.* The night before came rushing back.

John let the cabinet door hang open and grabbed his head. There was a UFC fight going on in there. He remembered the beer and bourbon and grabbed a bottle of aspirin. He swallowed a few without water.

His bed was looking like a good option but someone banged on the door. He rolled his eyes and pulled it open. "What?"

Mike was in full uniform and pushed past him into the small house without waiting for an invitation.

"Don't you have to have a warrant or something?"

"If you need one you're way beyond my help."

John closed the door and eyed the brown sack in Mike's hand.

"Bagels," Mike let him know. He lifted the drink carrier. "And I brought coffee."

"Bagels?" John questioned. "Really?"

"You think I'd show up here with doughnuts? You should know me better than that. I'm not gonna make it that easy for you." He moved to the table. "Come eat some of this. The ones I dropped on the ground are yours."

John followed Mike to the table and sat down. Mike handed him a bagel with lots of oats plastered on the outside. "Got any cream cheese or do I have to eat it plain?"

"You complain a lot for someone getting free breakfast." Mike slid a tub across the table.

"Yeah, well it's still early."

"If you could let me know exactly when you get happy I'll make sure to schedule my visits accordingly," Mike assured him through a mouthful.

"It used to be in the morning and then you started showing up."

"You know," Mike scooped up some cream cheese with a plastic knife. "I'm starting to think you're never happy."

John set his coffee on the table. "That's not true. I was plenty happy after I punched that church guy the other day."

"Church *kid*."

"Tomato-tomahto."

"You're sick."

"Probably." John picked an oat out of his teeth. "You got any information on that guy from the diner?"

Mike shook his head. "Naw. I checked around and there aren't any new renters or owners around here. I told a few people to keep me in the loop." He stirred cream and sugar into his coffee. "If there was anyone new I'd know by now."

"I saw him again last night at Joes. He was sitting in the back by the pool table."

"Was he with someone or alone?"

"It was just him and he seemed to be pretty interested in what I was doing. Caught him staring at me a couple of times."

◄ finding home ►

"Sounds like you have a stalker."

John threw a hard glare at his friend. "I've had just about as much as I want to take. It's time for him to leave."

Deep creases ran through Mike's forehead. "You're worried about this guy, aren't you?"

John didn't answer.

"Seriously? You've never asked me to help you like this. I usually have to clean up the mess after you take things into your own hands. What's going on?"

Heat flashed through John's stomach. "Are you going to help me or not?"

Mike raised his hands. "Relax, man. I'll keep my eyes and ears open, let you know if I find anything. What's he look like?" Mike took a big bite of bagel. "I probably should have asked that the other day."

"Yeah well you're not a very good cop."

Mike rolled his eyes. "So what's he look like?"

"He's weird and he's a guy."

"I'm looking at a pretty weird guy right now. Want me to arrest *him*?"

John cleared his throat. "I don't know. About my age, couple inches shorter. He's got dark skin—"

"Black?"

"No, not black. More like tan. Like, I don't know, Middle Eastern or something. He's got short black hair and every time I've seen him he's been wearing tan pants, a long sleeve flannel shirt and an old white hat."

Mike stood and balled up his trash. "OK, I'll let you know if I find your grungy, dark-skinned stalker." He laughed, grabbed his coffee, and walked out the door.

It was noon when John snatched his keys and wallet off the kitchen counter and stepped outside. The sun was shining brightly, chasing away some of the morning chill. He slid into his truck and cranked the engine. It grumbled to life like a bear whose hibernation had been cut short. He checked the gas gauge, slid his sunglasses over his eyes, and started towards the store. An altercation with the manager of the local store meant that he had to get his groceries from the other side of town.

The disappearance of *lawn art* always told John when he crossed the line that divided the town. He didn't resent the separation. He was living where he was by choice, plus, most of his construction work came from the better areas. He was responsible for how nice it looked.

The traffic was light and his mind drifted to the stranger. *I know who you are.*

John drummed on the steering wheel with his thumbs. He'd worked hard to leave his old life behind. He was free, completely disconnected, like he'd never even lived it. It was the way it had to be.

John curved into the parking lot and found a space near the front. The free coffee staged at the entrance helped his mood. Maybe things weren't so bad.

He ticked off a list in his head. *Coffee, cereal, milk, lunchmeat, bread, and maybe chips or something like that.* It didn't take him long to find most of the items and he was soon cruising towards the chip isle.

Sqqquueeaaakkkk. John narrowed his eyes and kicked one of the wheels on his cart. "Piece of junk," he muttered. It grew louder and louder, grinding his brain like a sander on plywood.

♥

The words of a pop song she'd heard at the gym played through Ashley's head. She pushed her cart against the dairy case and blew a strand of blonde hair out of her face. Ashley thumbed through the assorted yogurts looking for her favorite. She found the Black Cherry and started to reach, but then stopped. There was a tub of plain Greek yogurt right next to her hand. She considered whether or not she really wanted to do that to herself. The sour taste made her gag and most times she poured in so much sugar that any health benefits were lost.

She sighed. She was tired. Tired and irritable. She'd worked all night with cranky patients that never seemed to sleep. It probably wasn't the best decision to have gone to the gym. Her sanity was a fist clutching a hanging

◄ finding home ►

icicle. *Home. Bed.* The thought sent a wave of euphoria through her. Ashley was done trying to decide. She reached to grab them both.

♥

John found the faster his pace the less the wheel squeaked. He was looking down at it, which was why he didn't see the cart in front of him or the woman reaching for something on the shelf.

The crash shot the woman's cart into her side. She fell to the ground with a yelp. The tubs of yogurt she'd been holding went airborne and exploded on the ground.

John watched the whole thing happen in slow motion. Heat rushed to his face as every pair of eyes locked on him. The accusing looks hit him like bullets.

"Arghhhh," the woman groaned and then, "Ouch!" and held her side. An older man and woman hurried over to help her up. She waved them off and leveled a look at John. Her eyes went from wide to narrow and her lips curled in a snarl. John didn't know what to say so he said nothing.

"I'm fine, I'm fine," she told the older couple and carefully stood. She winced as she tested her side. She faced the couple and forced a smile. "Thank you."

They meandered back to their cart and she bent and twisted a few more times. Satisfied that she wasn't seriously hurt, she fixed her eyes on John.

"Are you kidding me?" she exclaimed and threw her hands up. "There's like, twenty people in the whole store and you crash into *me*." She stormed toward him. "How does that even happen?"

A few words formed in his brain but short-circuited on the way to his mouth. The fire in his cheeks grew more intense and he fell back a step. Not only was he dealing with the embarrassment of the nasty scene he'd created, but the woman now standing in front of him was stunning, despite the fury twisting her features.

Her head only came up to his chest, but there was fire in her emerald eyes. Blonde hair was pulled back into a ponytail and reached the middle of her back. She wore gym clothes that hugged her lean frame and there were no rings on the fingers crossed over her chest. John figured she was younger than him, but only by a few years. She tapped her sneaker on the floor waiting for a response.

John's eyes darted between her and the others he assumed were waiting for him to get punched. He finally pointed to the wheel on his cart. "My... uh...wheel was... squeaking."

"Your *wheel* was squeaking?" She said it in way that made him unsure if it was a question or a statement of his own stupidity. He guessed the latter and remained quiet.

She looked like she was going to say something but then stopped and raised her hands. "You know, I don't even care why you think that makes sense." She whirled around and grabbed her cart. "Unbelievable." She stormed away muttering something about him being blind or stupid or both.

A few people around John shook their heads and pushed their carts away, being careful to avoid the small lake of yogurt on the floor.

John put both hands on his cart, but couldn't seem to move anything else. Something was happening to him as he watched her. Butterflies fluttered through his stomach like he'd become a schoolboy with a crush. Despite her anger and his embarrassment, he knew he had to stop her.

"H...hey, hold on a second." He left his cart and hurried after her. "Wait."

She stopped and snapped her head around. "No, really, it's okay. I don't wanna hear about how your squeaky wheel made me invisible."

She started to move away again but John caught up. "Would you just wait a second?"

Her ponytail swung as she twirled. Frustration rang through her voice. "What do you want?"

John wiped a bead of sweat from his forehead. "I'm trying to... apologize." He made it sound like a question.

She crossed her arms over her chest. "I'm not really sure what's happening here. Was that an apology or not?"

John cleared his throat and heard someone snicker from the isle over. His face got even hotter. "I'm sorry, okay?"

"Wow." She dropped her arms except for one hand on her chest. "Thank

‹finding home›

goodness you got that out. You didn't hurt yourself did you? It looked painful." She rolled her eyes and turned down the chip isle.

"Well, it's been awhile," John responded matching her pace.

She stopped abruptly. "Since you've apologized?"

"Well, yeah."

Ashley shot him a confused look. "Strange…"

"What?"

"It just seems like you would get plenty of practice." She peered down the isle and then back at John. "Why are you following me?"

John shoved his hands into his pockets. "Look, I'm sorry. Really. If you want I'll go roll around in the yogurt or something."

Her eyes poured into him and John shifted his weight to the other foot. "Ok fine," she agreed with a smug look.

John blinked. "What?"

She nodded back toward the dairy case. "Go roll in the yogurt."

He stared at her and waited for the sign that she was kidding. But her mouth was a straight line and her eyes didn't flinch. "I'm *not* going to roll in yogurt. I wasn't being serious."

"Humph," she grunted. "Suit yourself." She started toward the register again.

Panic gripped John's stomach. "Okay fine." He did a quick survey to make sure nobody from his side of town was around.

She spun wide-eyed. "Really?"

He raised his hands. "But you have to at least tell me your name."

A small grin pulled at her mouth. "Ashley Cook," she told him and stepped closer. "Are you really gonna do it?"

John started toward the mess.

"Wait," Ashley called.

He stopped when he noticed her hurrying for him. "You're really gonna do it aren't you?"

He lifted his eyebrows. "I told you I was really sorry. Now, if you'll excuse me."

Ashley grabbed his arm. "It's okay, well…" she covered her mouth and when she dropped her hand she was smiling. "No, it's okay. You don't have to roll in that. Apology accepted."

Relief washed through John. "Oh, thank god."

Ashley laughed. "It's not yogurt anyway. It's more like sour Greek puke."

John made a face. "Never had it."

"Lucky you."

He lifted his chin. "How's your side?"

"It's fine. I think I'll still be able to live a full life."

John smiled. "Even so, you have to let me make it up to you." He paused as his stomach did a flip-flop. "If, uh, not the yogurt thing then how about dinner?"

She titled her head. "Dinner?"

John felt sweat on his head again. He was working way harder for this than his usual, *hey baby, get in the car,* approach. "Yeah. There's a pizza place on Main that's pretty good."

Ashley eyed him for a long time before suddenly saying, "Did you plan this?" She stepped close enough to stick a slender finger right in John's face. "Was all this just some stupid way you meet women?"

John backed up a few steps. "What...NO! I just..." He tugged on his shirt collar desperately trying to think of a way to make her understand. "Really, I didn't plan this."

Ashley pulled her finger back and studied him with her deep green eyes. John's heart pounded in his ears as he watched her trying to decide, silently debating. "You should probably tell me your name."

"Really?" he spouted and chided himself as Ashley gave him an amused look. "I mean, John. My name is John Caban." He stuck out his hand.

"Nice to meet you," she took his hand and winked. "Sort of."

The feel of her soft hand in his fired shocks through his body making him dizzy. "I guess I deserved that."

"Alright John." She let go of his hand. "You can buy me dinner."

John couldn't stop the grin from spreading across his face. "Thursday night work for you?"

"Umm," Her eyes drifted to the ceiling. "Thursday night would work I think."

"Seven?"

"Okay." She scribbled down her number.

John's brain spun the whole way home. Ashley herself was a big reason

◄ finding home ►

but the biggest thing bothering him was how he'd acted. "I was about to roll in yogurt for her," he admitted to the Joe Camel bobble head on his dash. Mike had stuck it on there as a joke and he never took it down. "What's wrong with me." The camel responded by bobbling as he hit a bump. "Pfft, whatever." He opened his window and felt the cold wind bite his cheeks. He hadn't been like that in as long as he could remember. So why now? Why her? More questions he couldn't answer.

chapter eleven

"ALICE, LOOK OUT!"

Alice dropped to the ground just as a snowball zipped over her head. She scrambled to her feet and dove behind a big tree as two more snowballs narrowly missed her.

It was late Tuesday afternoon and a fresh snowfall had buried Redwood the night before. The girls living at the Baker's house didn't do everything together, but they were always up for a game of capture the flag, snowball style.

Alice carefully leaned to her right. Her gunner Anna was pinned down behind some bushes. She was thirteen with brown hair cut above her shoulders. Freckles were painted across the bridge of her nose that faded in the winter. She laughed the most out of all of them. The Bakers and years in Redwood had been good to her.

Alice jerked her head toward the sound of crunching snow and noticed Jessie creeping up on their position. She was a pretty fifteen-year-old, tall and lithe with blue eyes and long thin blonde hair. She was shy and hung back from large groups, but when it was just them she forgot about her shell. Alice took in the scene behind her and wondered where Tabby was hiding.

She narrowed her eyes. They could be friends again when the game was over. Alice glanced at their flag, a flowery sheet attached to a shower rod shoved into the ground. It fluttered with the random gusts between her and Anna.

Alice smiled to herself. Tabby and Jessie had never beaten them. She

◄ finding home ►

straightened as snowballs peppered the tree she was hiding behind. "Anna can you see them?"

"I can see Tabby," Anna let out, her voice muffled by a thick scarf. "She's behind the car but I dunno where Jessie is."

"Okay," Alice called back. She waited a moment and then carefully peered around the tree. The Baker's car was parked in the driveway. She saw the tip of Tabby's hood behind it. She was kneeling, probably making more snowballs. "Where'd Jessie go?"

Suddenly a black garbage can with legs burst from the garage.

"What in the world?" Anna poked her head up from behind the bushes.

Alice stared at the can zigzagging across the yard. But then it changed directions and ran straight for the tree she was standing behind. "What the…whoa!"

Alice jumped back as the can hit the tree. The impact knocked the can backwards and over on its side where it rolled a few times and spit out a disheveled Jessie, who squealed with laughter.

It didn't take long for the shock to where off and Alice couldn't stop laughter from taking control of her own body. She caught a glimpse of Anna rolling on the snow, imitating Jessie. That only made her laugh harder.

"You're absolutely ridiculous," she told Jessie as she rubbed tears out of her eyes.

"You're right," Jessie agreed, a huge grin on her face. "But we finally won."

"Wha…?" At that same moment she heard a cry from Anna. She whipped her head around in time to see residue from a snowball hitting its mark, drifting over her teammate.

"Alice, the flag!"

But it was too late. Tabby had crept in behind the bushes while they were both distracted. She already had one hand on the flag when Anna screamed. "No." But by the time Alice managed to take two steps, she could only watch helplessly as their flag went into enemy territory cementing their defeat.

Jessie jumped up and ran towards Tabby who had both hands in the air. They hopped and hugged and did some kind of victory dance they seemed to make up on the spot.

Alice rubbed her face and hurried over to help Anna up off the ground. "Well, it had to happen sometime."

Anna brushed herself off and giggled. "Yeah. But it was an awesome way to lose."

Alice laughed. "I guess it was."

They joined Jessie and Tabby to hand out congratulations and hugs.

"I'll never forget the garbage can with legs," Anna was telling Jessie as they headed toward the house.

Tabby smiled at Alice. "You coming in?"

Alice tucked her hair behind her ears. "I think I'll walk down to the pond."

"Want me to come with you?"

Alice shook her head. "I'd rather just be alone for a bit."

"You okay?"

"Yeah." She saw the concern in Tabby's eyes. "Really I'm fine. Don't worry."

"Alright." Tabby seemed to relax. "I'll tell Melissa where you went. Just be back by dinner so we don't have to wait for you," Tabby smiled as she retreated to the warmth of the house.

The pond wasn't too far away, and she loved how it looked covered with fresh snow. It was lined by pines, which provided a barrier against the wind and the rest of town. It was peaceful and quiet and she felt close to God there.

The sun was shining, making the cold less intrusive. As she plodded along she let her mind wander back to her appointment with Dr. Felling. Was her own fear really the only reason she couldn't remember? Was it the only thing standing in her way?

Alice drifted with her eyes lost in the treetops slow dancing with the wind. She stopped and sighed. *Do I really want to remember at all?*

"Well, do you?"

The strong voice jolted Alice back to the real world. A black woman about her height stood a few feet away. Her face was mature and eyes full of experience. Gray hair poked out from underneath her hood.

"I...I'm sorry?" Alice sputtered and cast a glance around them to see if

◀finding home▶

the woman was talking to someone else. But they were alone.

There was mystery in the woman's smile. "Do you really want to remember?"

Alice felt the blood leave her face and she stumbled back. "How did you…what did you…*who* are you?"

"I'm Nita," she answered like Alice should've known. The woman took in the pond and trees and snow. "Beautiful isn't it?" She turned her smile back to Alice. "So fresh and pure. You might believe we're the first ones to ever stand here."

"I'm sorry…was I talking to myself out loud?"

Nita chuckled, the sound coming from deep within her. "No, I don't think so." She angled her head to one side. "You sure do apologize a lot."

"I'm sor—" Alice cleared her throat. "Why did you say that?"

"Say what child?"

Alice hugged her coat tighter. "About remembering. Why did you ask me if I really want to remember?"

"Oh, that. Well, I figured that if I'm going to listen when God tells me to get up and leave my nice warm house, drive to Redwood, walk down this particular sidewalk and look for a precious young woman with long black hair, I might as well ask her the questions he wants me to ask." She hesitated. "You *are* Alice aren't you?"

Alice's eyes went wide and her knees wobbled. "How do you know me?" She glanced around wildly looking for anyone that might help. "Are you from the city?"

Nita waved her hands. "Calm down, dear. I told you. I'm here because this is where God told me to be."

The concept was a cyclone in her head. "He…God told you to come find me?"

Nita chuckled and motioned to a trail that weaved around the pond's perimeter. "Come and walk with me a bit." She held out her hand to Alice who hesitated a moment before taking it gently.

Nita's sigh came from somewhere deep in her heart. "It *is* pretty isn't it?"

Alice eyed her, still suspicious. "It's one of my favorite spots." She caught sudden movement to her right as a brown rabbit ventured out of a thicket. She could see its little cream nose wiggle in the air for a moment and felt the sting of envy. There were no repressed or forgotten memories. There wasn't the type of cruelty that people inflict on each other. It didn't have any cares stretching beyond basic survival. *How nice to be you.* The rabbit flinched as if it'd heard her, wiggled its nose, and disappeared back into the thicket.

"It *is* safe you know," Nita disclosed.

The sudden voice startled her. "What's safe?"

"Doing the things God asks us to do. If I didn't believe that, I wouldn't be here now." She paused and surveyed the tranquil picture in front of them. "But fear, now," she clucked her tongue. "Fear tells us it's not safe. It tells us that if we listen to God it'll just bring more pain and suffering." She shook her head. "But does that sound like love to you, cause it sure doesn't sound like love to me. God is love, child. That apostle John, he said that there's no darkness in Him at all."

She faced Alice and put a gloved hand on her cheek. "That love, hmmm, it don't lead us into more pain, now. Love leads us into that abundant life Jesus talked about. He leads us out of darkness and into healing while he mends our broken hearts and hopeless lives. Now, sometimes it hurts when the wound is being cleaned. But while fear tells us that pain is all there is, God tells us that the pain will only last for the night, and joy well," she raised her hand, "it'll rise with the sun."

Alice blinked back tears. "Who *are* you?"

"Just a messenger, honey." She smiled. "Alice, our perfectly good and loving Father told me to come and tell you that it's time to remember."

Tears spilled out of Alice's eyes and streaked down her face. "I...I'm scared."

Nita's voice was a salve on her heart. "I know, child. The big question is, 'what are you going to do?' You must trust that the same God that sent me here to ask you to take a step forward, loves you enough to walk beside you the entire way. He will never leave you or forsake you. He never has and He won't start now." She brushed a tear from Alice's cheek. "He loves you too much for that."

Alice wiped her eyes. "But what if I find things I don't want to know? Things that were just *awful?*"

Nita's eyes sparkled. "But what if you find out that things were wonderful? What if you find out things you wish you had always known?"

❮ finding home ❯

Alice sniffed. "I've never thought about it like that before."

Nita chuckled softly. "It's easy to think about the bad things that can happen. *What if I don't like it? What if I can't do it? What if it hurts? What if the person's not healed?*" Nita paused for a moment. "But what if you do like it and what if the person is healed? What if you can do it and what if it brings incredible restoration?" She took a couple of steps toward the pond. "But results aren't what give us courage to step forward. His love gives us the courage. It's a love that promises to catch and hold us even if the results aren't even close to what we'd hoped for. It's a love that promises to put our hearts back together when they've been broken. It promises that we'll always have a place in his lap no matter what we go through in this life. *That's* where our courage comes from."

Alice shook her head slightly and smiled. "Are you an angel?"

Nita laughed hard at that. "Dear me no. I'm just an ordinary daughter, lost in the extravagant love of my perfect Father, doing my best to love and serve him every day."

Alice brushed her hair back. "This is crazy. I mean, not you, but nobody's ever talked to me like this. What church do you go to?"

"*Church?*" A wide grin took over her face. "What do you think we've been having here, child?"

With that she pivoted and started moving away.

"Wait!" Alice took a couple of steps. "You can't…Will I see you again?"

Nita stopped and turned halfway around, shrugging her shoulders. "Maybe, maybe not. Never can tell. Be blessed child. You're about to do things you didn't even know you believed in."

Alice watched her disappear over a hill before glancing at her watch to see she was going to be late for dinner. She ran all of the way home and burst through the front door to find Jack, Melissa, and the girls waiting. She was quiet through dinner and kept the experience she'd had with Nita to herself. Nobody asked her any questions as the other three girls found plenty of things to talk about.

Later that night, after getting in bed and wrestling with some lingering doubts, she made her decision. "Okay God," she declared with intentional determination. "I'm ready to remember." With that she rolled over and fell asleep full of peace.

chapter twelve

Something sticky clung to John's forehead as it rested on the table. "Helen," John uttered out of the side of his mouth. "Don't you ever clean these tables?"

He didn't get an answer and instead of lifting his head he groaned and pressed both hands into his temples. The Aspirin he took an hour earlier was like putting a band-aide on a broken leg.

"How am I supposed to wipe the table with your big head layin' all over it?"

It wasn't Helen's voice. John raised his head enough to see through one eye. A skinny kid with a bushy fro was clearing plates from a table next to his. "Shut up."

The kid smirked. "Yeah, you enjoy that hangover. Lookin' like a cracker from Walking Dead." He held both arms straight in front of him and made a few stiff movements before picking up his tub and heading to the kitchen.

John rolled his eyes and thought about last night. After the bar closed, he'd found himself going a round with Nellie at her place. He slowly lifted his head and fought a wave of nausea. If he could take a time machine back to Nellie's and slap the last couple of drinks out of his hands he would.

"Oh, thank god," he exclaimed when Helen appeared with coffee. She set his cup down hard enough to throw steaming drops all over the table and turned away without a word. "What's your problem?" he asked and wiped a drop off his arm.

Helen wheeled around and stuck a fat finger at him. "Why don't you mind your own business."

"I will as long as I get my food," John hollered as she vanished into the

◄ finding home ►

kitchen. He rubbed his temples again. The headache wasn't the only thing bothering him. There was something else poking him like a thorn. Guilt? He made a face. What'd he have to feel guilty about? It's not like he'd done anything wrong.

Haven't you? "No, I haven't," he replied aloud and quickly dropped his head away from a few curious faces. *What's wrong with me?* He wasn't just questioning his actions for the first time in years, he was arguing with himself...out loud.

John sighed. Maybe it was because of Ashley. But they hadn't even gone out yet and even if they had, it's not like they were married or anything. He shook the stream of thought from his head, which didn't help the throbbing at all. Being with Nellie was the first time in the last three days he'd felt normal.

John covered his face with his hands. He didn't hear the door open behind him and didn't notice the man slide into the seat across from him until he bumped the table with his leg.

"Hey, what—" John flinched. The man opposite him wore tan pants, a long-sleeved flannel shirt, and an old, yellowing hat. The hair on his face showed maybe a couple days' growth. His brown eyes were certainly intense, but not quite as piercing as the night in the bar. John almost spilled his coffee. "You!"

Helen appeared with coffee for the stranger. She tossed a few packets of sugar on the table before it dawned on her that John Caban was sharing his table. She stared hard for a moment, but then just shook her head and disappeared into the kitchen.

John watched the man calmly lift his mug and sip the steaming liquid. "That's not bad, you know?" He placed the mug back on the table, leaned forward on his elbows, and shot John a full-blown grin.

John's eyes became slits. They stayed in a grin to glare lock for a few moments that felt like hours. *Go on the offensive.* He cleared his throat louder than necessary. "You're gonna tell me who you are."

The stranger drummed thick fingers against his warm mug. His smile became a straight line. For a moment John wasn't sure he was going to answer. And then he did. "John Rister."

The words were a fist into John's stomach. The room pitched and he clutched the seat underneath him with both hands. "Wh…What did you say?"

"You're John Rister, right?" His tone was light as if he did this kind of thing every day.

John's eyes darted around the room but no one seemed to notice them. "You're confused. It's Caban. John *Caban.*"

The stranger slowly lifted the cup to his nose and inhaled the rich aroma. "Mmmm, yes. John Caban. I've known a lot of Cabans." He sipped and put the cup down. "But never you."

"You think you've met all the Cabans in the—"

"Now Risters," the man continued. "I've known a lot of them too. You look a lot like one I used to know."

John felt a blast of heat surge through him and he slapped the table. "Who do you think you are? John lowered his chin. "You think you can show up at a bar, mouth some stupid words, and scare me? You don't know me at all." John leaned toward the man. "You'd be smart to get up and leave town before I really get mad."

"John please," he put his hands together. "I didn't come here to fight. I just wanna talk."

John crossed his thick arms over his chest and tried to stare daggers at the guy. "Then talk."

"I'm an old friend John. *A blast from your past* if you will."

Faces flashed through John's mind but none matched the one in front of him. "You're a liar," he spat. "I have no idea who you are."

"Well, it's felt like a very long time. I'm not surprised you don't remember."

"It doesn't matter," John informed him. "Just go back to wherever it is you came from."

The stranger leaned back in his seat and sipped his coffee. He gazed around the room slowly and brought his eyes back to John. "Are you happy with the life you've built for yourself here?"

John's stomach flip-flopped. "Of course I'm happy. What kinda question is that anyway?"

"I can see why you'd say that," the stranger answered and motioned to the room. "You've got your nice little diner filled with people who

⋘ finding home ⋙

keep to themselves. Construction's a good job and you even have a sort of relationship with the bar tender over at Joe's, am I right?" His eyes flickered. "Though I don't think she's very good for your thumbs. But neither was Sarah, was she? I seem to remember a certain Oak tree, a piece of plywood, and a distraction."

John felt his heart race and glanced at two scars, one on each thumb. One scar was from Nellie and the nail, and the other…He was twelve when he'd done it the first time.

Sarah was a senior in high school and John a freshman. She was a lifeguard and liked to work on her tan in her backyard. A massive Oak stood next to a fence separating his yard from hers. In the summer there was always plenty of leaves to hide him as he perched high above the earth, but not enough to obstruct his view. There was just one problem. It was *really* uncomfortable.

A quick survey had revealed three large branches just below him arranged like a triangle. They were close together at the bottom and spread out as they reached past him. John figured he could nail something to the narrow end and have a seat for the show. He found his tools and a piece of plywood in the garage and lugged them up the tree.

The nails were through the plywood and two of the branches and his hammer was coming down to secure the third when he heard Sarah's backdoor open. He flinched and drove the nail through his thumb. He'd nearly bitten clean through his lower lip to keep from screaming and clutched the branch as the earth swayed. Somehow he made it down without falling and into the house before releasing the overdo wail. He told his parents he was trying to build a tree house. He'd never told anyone the truth.

John stared through wide eyes at the stranger sipping from a mug as if nothing unusual was happening at all. Fear skipped through him like a stone on a lake. His voice came out with a squeak. "How did you…" He cleared his throat. "How do you know Sarah? Did you talk to Nellie?"

"Mmm," the man remarked and put his coffee down. "Could use a bit more sugar."

John slapped the table and drew some looks. He kept his voice low. "How do you *know* me?"

63

"There aren't enough books in all the world to hold everything I know," he replied. "But I digress. Where were we? Ah yes, your life. It's better than what you had right?"

A mixture of tension and anxiety poured into John's muscles and he retreated into the back of his seat. "Uh, that's right."

"Better than ten years ago?"

"Ten years ago?"

"Back in Oak Harbor."

Oak Harbor. John was on his feet. "Are you deaf? I said yes." He hesitated and thought about bolting out the door. "Is that how you know me? Are you from there."

"Keep it down, Caban," Helen yelled from across the room. "It's too early for this nonsense."

The man moved his hands like he was quieting a crowd. "John, please sit down. I didn't mean to make you mad. Let me buy your breakfast. Please."

John shot a glare around at the nosy room. "Mind your own business," he shouted and brushed off his clothes. He could leave, but then the stranger would win. And despite the anxiety stabbing him he wanted to know more. He finally sat down. "In that case I'm getting the biggest breakfast Helen can cook up."

The stranger chuckled and signaled to Helen. She took their order and sauntered away. "I guess I should tell you who I am."

"Whatever's gonna end this conversation the fastest," John growled and sipped his freshly poured coffee.

The stranger held his gaze for a few moments. "You can call me J.C."

John blinked. "J.C.?" He considered the name. "Doesn't seem to fit."

The man smiled. "What would fit, John?"

John suspended his cup halfway between the table and his mouth. "How 'bout weird stalker guy?"

The man's eyes sparkled. "That's quite a mouthful. J.C. will do just fine."

"J.C.," John muttered. "Whatever." He set his cup down. "What's that stand for?"

"It stands for a lot of things."

"The hell does that mean?"

J.C. wiped his mouth. "You don't really care about that. Not yet anyway."

‹ finding home ›

"That's right," John growled. "But you won't answer what I *really* want to know. And what do you mean, *not yet?*"

J.C.'s eye's held amusement. "I'm a bit of a traveler John. I go where I'm invited, but many times I end up in places I'm not. Here, for example. You didn't invite me but here I am."

John sat up higher in the booth. "This is stupid."

"Yeah well," the man leaned back. "It is what it is I suppose. I frequently find myself in situations that aren't very comfortable for others: you in this case."

John shot a nervous look around the room. "You from Oak Harbor?"

J.C. smiled. "Sure John. I've been there lots of times."

John shook his head. "That's not what I—"

Helen arrived with their food and she set it down on the table. She refilled their coffee. "Thank you Helen," J.C. told her.

"Mm-hmmm."

"Helen," he called.

She circled to face him. "What?"

J.C. smiled into her eyes. "I want you to know that you are an amazing woman and an incredible cook. You're doing a great job with the diner and you've done so much for the kids in this community. Don't ever forget how important and special you are."

John choked on his coffee and quickly glanced over at Helen. He was sure she was about to rip the guys face off. But instead of anger and frustration there was a twitch that could've been a smile. She looked like she was going to say something but then pressed her lips together and disappeared into the kitchen.

John wondered if he'd fallen into some kind of alternate reality. Or maybe this was a dream.

J.C. took a bite of eggs. "You should try encouraging someone every now and then. You'd be surprised how much it means."

"Whatever," John muttered and cut his pancakes. *I'm a bit of a traveler.* John watched a small piece of egg fall out of the guy's mouth as he ate. There was a rope inside of him tightening around his stomach. "You're a wackjob."

"I've been called worse."

"I bet," John muttered under his breath. "You better make good on paying this bill."

"I'm good for it," J.C. assured. "I always keep my promises."

They sat in silence, a sort of stand-off. Then he cleared his throat. "I've been watching you for a long time, John. Your whole life even. I've seen the good and the bad. The easy times and the times you'd rather forget altogether."

John fought to keep his tone even. "If that's true I'd know you." He paused and thought about his dad. "You knew my father?"

J.C. bit into a piece of toast an ignored his question. "I'm here because you've started to see the life you've faded into isn't all you hoped it would be."

John could hear his heart in his ears. "What are you talking about?"

J.C. wiped some crumbs off his lips. "You *still* remember what happened in Oak Harbor. The long nights are starting to tear away at your body, let alone your heart." He pointed at John's chest. "And the emptiness has never been filled. You use the people around you to try and make it through the days but life has become dull and meaningless."

Terror gripped John's soul with icy claws at the truth of the words. If he could've shed his skin he would have. "Who do you think you are?" He tried to stare fear into his blood. But something unexpected happened. J.C.'s eyes, they were so…intense, so piercing. He moved his hand over his heart like a shield. It was the bar all over again. But it reminded him of something else too. Someone…*Ashley!* Her face flashed before his eyes. The way she watched him…searched him, seeing deeper than the superficial plaster the last ten years had hardened. John tried to close his eyes but they were glued to his eyebrows.

It doesn't have to be this way.

The words echoed through him. He'd been watching J.C. and his lips hadn't moved. His head spun. He didn't know the voice. Then it came again.

Yes, I know you and I love you!

John felt the sweat on his forehead. "I…I think we're done here." His stomach was a kayak caught in rogue waves and his knees shook under the table. "I don't want to see you again." He squeezed his hands into fists. "If

‹finding home›

I do you won't like what happens."

J.C. seemed to take the threat seriously because he stood, dug in his right pocket, and dropped a couple of twenties on the table. He gazed at John and smiled. "It was so good to talk with you again. See you around."

He took a few strides toward the door, but halted just in front of it. "Hey, John."

"What?"

"Things are gonna be different, but don't worry. It'll be okay."

His words tumbled in John's head like shoes in a dryer. *What does that mean?*

"By the way, how's your headache?"

John was so caught up in the strange meeting that he hadn't noticed when the pain left. He turned toward the door but the man was already gone. "Weird," he said half aloud. Helen slid into the booth and leaned toward him.

"Who was that?" she asked.

John shook his head. "J.C."

She nodded toward the door. "He must know how to tap into phone lines. My sister called me this morning and ripped me up one side and down the other. That's why I was in such a bad mood. Everything that guy said was the exact opposite of what my sister told me."

John raked a hand through his hair. "At least you seem to be in a better mood."

"Shut up."

"Money's on the table." He glanced at the bills. "He's *definitely* nuts to tip like that."

Helen spread the bills with her fingers. "Well, if he's going to tip like this I'll make a special padded room just for him."

"I'm surprised you don't already have one for you."

"Shut up," she repeated.

"Right, time to go."

It was a beautiful morning. The air was clean and crisp and the sun was shining against the blue sky. But John was a storm inside. He was trying very hard to convince himself that the guy was nuts, but the Sarah thing bothered him. A lot about the man bothered him. His eyes. The voice. The way he knew things.

There was something else fighting hard to be heard. Something coming from a long ignored source saying, *you need him. You need to see him again.* It was barely there but it was there.

‹ finding home ›

‹ chapter thirteen ›

The dream. She'd had it again. Flashes of light against a dark canvas. Everything so black and unfamiliar, but when the light flickered she knew there was something important hiding in the shadows. It was like trying to uncover treasure in a hole that keeps caving in.

Alice stared through one of the plain, single hung windows in the waiting room at Redwood Urgent Care. The overcast sky painted the town gray and dreary. There was snow to go along with dropping temperatures in the forecast for later on.

She hugged herself and took a look around the clinic. Cushioned chairs bordered the waiting room against walls colored a very light shade of yellow. Alice had read an article once about the psychology of colors and found that light yellow was very calming. A tank with a variety of colorful fish sat against the far wall where everyone could see them. Sometimes people stared at it the whole time they waited. Alice sometimes found herself lost in the activity of the small creatures.

The receptionist job had been Dr. Felling's idea. *A great opportunity to be with people,* she'd said. It was certainly a challenge, especially in the beginning. She'd kept her head down and face straight. But she was getting better. The phantoms of her past didn't emerge as much as they used too.

The people made it easier. They almost always greeted Alice with a smile chatting about town news and rumors. She knew most of them by name. Maybe she'd make something like this her career. Maybe even become a doctor.

Alice thought about the dream again. Two nights in a row now. It wasn't just the strange flashes of light in the dark. A path glowed softly and called to her as it stretched beyond the edge of her vision. She would turn around to see the quiet town of Redwood illuminated by moonlight and long for its comfort and security, but at the same time want to step into the mystery beyond, away from what she knew. Each time she woke in a sweat and her head hurt.

She dropped her chin into her hand. The path. Where did it lead? What if she—

"Someone please help us!"

Alice jumped up to see Martha Tanner standing in the doorway, her face pale and eyes wide. Alice ran towards the door. "What's wrong?"

She made it halfway to the door when Dr. Tishner joined her. Her curly brown hair swung erratically in a ponytail as she hurried to the frantic woman. "Martha?" Dr. Tishner questioned in a voice calmed by years of experience. "What's going on?"

"It's my husband, Hank," Martha grabbed the doctor's arms. "He was trying to put up some Christmas lights and fell off of the ladder. I think his leg is broken."

"Alright, Martha. Take a deep breath and tell me where he is."

Martha pointed to a car in the lot. "He's in the backseat."

"Okay." Dr. Tishner motioned to Alice. "Please get Sam and a wheelchair and meet us at the car."

Alice nodded and returned pushing a wheelchair behind Sam, the nurse practitioner. Dr. Tishner was bent over a large, groaning body in the backseat of a sedan.

Dr. Tishner waved Sam over. "It's a broken right femur. Let's get him inside so we can get it splinted and treat the pain."

"You wanna give him something before we move him?"

Dr. Tishner pushed against a large box of Christmas lights. "There's no room back here."

"Alright," Sam answered. "How do you want to move him?"

"You're gonna have to help us, Hank," Dr. Tishner told him. "Sam is going to help you stand, turn and sit in the chair while I support your leg. Can you do that?"

"I think so."

◄ finding home ►

Sweat mixed with tears ran down his face as wave after wave of intense pain battered him. Alice remembered hearing Dr. Tishner say that breaking a femur was worse than childbirth. He wasn't making a lot of noise, but his face showed that what she'd heard was true.

"We go on three," Dr. Tishner ordered. "Alice, hold that chair tight. Hank, this is going to hurt...a lot."

"Hang on." He clenched his jaw. "Okay, go for it."

"One...two...THREE."

Hank's scream echoed through the lot, but in one smooth movement he was in the chair.

"It doesn't feel better," he moaned.

"It won't until we get the splint on," Dr. Tishner informed him while holding his leg straight. "Why didn't you call 911?"

"He wouldn't let me," Martha said.

"Don't need no stupid ambulance," Hank declared.

Dr. Tishner rolled her eyes. "Yeah this was a much better idea." She nodded to the doors. "Let's go."

A few minutes later they were inside and Hank was positioned on the floor.

"Sam, get me an IV so I can give him some pain medicine. Alice, get the traction splint."

Sam started working at the IV while Dr. Tishner cut Hank's right pant leg up to the hip. Alice went to get the split specifically designed for femur fractures. She grabbed it from the supply room and hurried back to the others.

"Thanks, Alice," Dr. Tishner told her. "Go ahead and call 911. He needs to go to Redwood Memorial." She glared at the man. "Should've gone there from the get go."

Hank lifted his head off the floor. "No ambulances. I'm staying right here."

"See what I mean," Martha cried.

Dr. Tishner slid next to Hanks head. "Hank, it was a very bad idea to come here. I can't fix this. You need surgery." She glanced back to Alice. "Make the call."

Alice called 911 as she watched the crew put the splint on. She gave the dispatcher what he needed and hung up. "They'll be here in a few minutes," she hollered to the others.

Alice took a step back towards the group, but stopped abruptly as if her leash had run out of slack. Something was happening. Warmth flicked her fingertips and slowly moved over her palms and up her arms. At the same time her pulse quickened and butterflies fluttered in her stomach. She leaned against the wall and felt her body for something out of the ordinary. Nothing. She squeezed her eyes shut and tried to calm down. But then there was a soft voice.

Lay your hands on his leg and pray for healing.

Her eyes snapped open and darted around the room. Everyone was focused on Hank. The voice didn't come from them. She hesitated. Did God just tell her to pray for Hank's broken leg? She shook her head ready to dismiss it when she heard the voice again.

Lay your hands on the leg and pray for healing.

Now she was shaking. It was God. She ran a hand through her hair. But that was crazy.

"ARGHHHH," Hank's scream bounced off the walls.

Alice ran into the bathroom and closed the door. Healing? It wasn't possible…was it? She read the Bible and knew all about the miracles Jesus did. But that didn't still happen, did it? She'd never even heard of someone doing what she'd heard God tell her to do. "Are you sure about this?"

The answer came right away. *Of course I am.*

"But…but…what will they think? What if he doesn't get healed? I can't do this. I'm going to look like an idiot."

I love you.

The words thundered through her like an answer to not just her objections right now, but to any objection she could ever have about anything.

Alice stood in the dark a few more minutes before reluctantly surrendering. She opened the door and trudged back to the room. Sam was still trying to secure the IV. The splint was on, but the beads of sweat on Hank's forehead and the grimace on his face bore witness to the unending torment.

Dr. Tishner stood. "I'm going to draw up the meds. If you can't get that

‹finding home›

IV I'll just give it to him intramuscular."

Alice let Dr. Tishner pass and kneeled on Hank's right side. His thigh doubled the size of the other one. There was also some discoloring that had begun to show. *This is crazy.* Alice started to push herself up in retreat but halted when Nita's voice fluttered through her mind, *but what if he's healed.* Alice gently placed her trembling hands on the leg, below the swelling. She closed her eyes and whispered. "I…in the name of Jesus, I, I pray for healing."

She quickly stood and took a couple of steps back. It took a moment for the silence to register. No moaning. No screaming. She shot a look at Hank. He was staring at his leg.

"Hank…" Martha squeaked, concern moving through her expression.

He fixed his eyes on Alice. "W…what did you do?"

All heads swiveled to Alice. Her fingers twitched by her side. Now what? What was she supposed to say? Fear gripped her heart. She was going to have to leave town.

"What did you do?" Hank asked again.

She slowly met Hanks eyes. He was waiting for an answer. They all were. Might as well be honest. "I, uh, prayed for your leg to be healed. I'm so sorry," she gushed. "I hope you're not mad."

Hank stared at her for a moment longer and then his face began to change. A smile slowly spread over his face until she could see his teeth. Then he started to chuckle and then laugh.

Dr. Tishner rushed back into the room with a vial full of Morphine but stopped when she saw them. "What's going on?"

Hank pointed at Alice. "She prayed for my leg and…and it's better." His smile grew even bigger. "I think I'm okay."

Dr. Tishner raised her eyebrows at a bewildered Sam who pointed a shaky finger at Hank's right thigh. "Uh, take a look. Swelling's gone and the color is normal."

"Impossible," Dr. Tishner muttered and kneeled beside the leg. A moment later she slowly lifted her eyes to Alice.

"Yeah impossible," Hank mocked. "Now get this thing off my leg."

"Huh?" Dr. Tishner uttered. "No Hank, I can't do that."

"Well I sure can," he claimed and started pulling at the straps.

"Hank, stop it!" Dr. Tishner grabbed his hands. "I, I can't explain what happened but you need x-rays and the splint can't come off till then."

"Really it's—"

"Hank Tanner you listen to her," Martha demanded.

Hank grinned at them. "I'm going to stand up right now with or without this thing on my leg." He started to roll over.

"Wait!" Dr. Tishner gave him one last stern look before giving in. "Okay fine. I'll take it off."

She slowly removed the splint fully expecting to hear screams of pain as the traction was released, but Hank was laughing.

"Praise God! Thank you Jesus!" he was singing and shouting with tears flowing down his face.

Hank rolled over, pushed himself onto his knees, and stood up the rest of the way. He grabbed Alice's arm to sturdy himself and found her wide eyes. "When you prayed for me I felt this sort of tingly warm feeling run down my leg almost like goose bumps standing up."

He clapped and she jumped. "Then the pain was gone and I knew I was healed." Fresh tears filled his eyes. "I've been running from God for a long time, but not anymore." He hugged her tightly. "Thank you. Thank you so much."

Alice couldn't make her brain form words. She just nodded her head slightly.

Hank clapped his hands. "Marty, let's go home. I've got lights to finish hanging."

"If you even get near that ladder I'll break the other leg..."

They all watched Hank and Martha leave the clinic without a word. The door closed behind them and all eyes found Alice. She fell back a few steps. Hearing God, the fear, praying, and healing. It was all too much for her.

Alice stumbled into the break room and collapsed into one of the hard chairs. She buried her face in her hands and exhaled fully for what felt like the first time in hours. Excitement fought with confusion and her mind raced, desperately searching for something that made sense.

She heard the door open and felt a body sink into a chair next to her. Dr. Tishner gave her a look that was hard to read.

"I'm sorry," Alice gushed. It was the only thing she could think to say.

‹ finding home ›

Dr. Tishner eyed her for a long moment. "What exactly are you sorry for? We had a sick patient who left better."

Alice studied the doctor. "So…you're not mad?"

"Mad?" Dr. Tishner gave a short laugh. "I have no clue what to think about all this but no, I'm not mad."

Relief poured through Alice. "So I can keep working here?"

Dr. Tishner smiled. "Of course you can. I'd lose most of my business if you left. People who aren't even sick stop in here just to talk to you." Her expression turned serious.

Alice felt the floor drop. "What is it?"

The doctor scratched her head. "Have you ever seen or done anything like that before? Praying I mean."

"Never," Alice answered. "I've never even *heard* of anything like that."

Dr. Tishner was quiet for a moment. "I grew up in church but I never saw anything like what happened to Hank." A sigh rose from somewhere deep in her heart. "I've seen a lot of terrible things," she continued. "I figured a God who allowed such great pain wasn't worthy of my time. I guess the only proof I have is that God's pretty cruel. How could I believe in something, someone, like that?"

A terrifying revelation smacked Alice. *She's waiting for some kind of answer.* Alice blinked at the woman who'd become her friend over the years. "Wendy, I don't know what to—"

Share your heart Alice. The words were warm against her soul.

Share my heart?

Yes.

I don't think I can.

I am with you.

Alice drummed her fingers against the table. *Ok God, I hope you know what you're doing.*

"I'm, uh, not sure about a lot of things," Alice began. "But I *do* know what it's like to believe there's nothing in this world worth living for. That bad is all there is. I've been through some things I'll never forget no matter how much I want to." *And can't remember the things that might actually be good.*

"And God," a sad smile worked through her mouth, "the world I knew didn't have room for him unless he was just as bad or worse than everyone else. I was the hopeless, yucky girl nobody wanted. I didn't even want myself."

Dr. Tishner was tight-lipped, but her eyes hung on every word.

Alice's eyes flickered. "But then I came here, to Redwood." She told Dr. Tishner about the Bakers and how different they were than anyone she'd ever known. She shared how they'd made her feel special and loved and pointed her towards God who loved her more than they ever could. Her words felt clumsy but somehow it didn't matter.

"Their world was so different than mine," she continued. "I couldn't help but think that maybe God was the reason. I wanted what they had." She closed her eyes remembering. "The night I gave my heart to Jesus the depression and hopelessness and everything else totally disappeared. I mean, it was gone so fast and I got this feeling…like I was the most beautiful and perfect girl in the world. I felt, no, for the first time I *knew* that I was loved. I was alive for the first time." She paused. "I got my proof that night."

"Proof of what?" Dr. Tishner asked.

Alice smiled into Dr. Tishner's tearing eyes. "That God is light and there is no darkness in Him at all. That His heart only has room for things that are pure and lovely and lovable. For kindness and grace and honor. For joy and peace and gentleness." She handed Dr. Tishner a napkin. "There's just no room for the bad."

Silence lingered until Dr. Tishner rose and dabbed her eyes. She nodded toward the waiting room. "Maybe I just got some proof of that."

You're going to be doing things you didn't even know you believed in. Alice's eyes went wide as she remembered the words Nita spoke to her the night before.

Dr. Tishner hesitated at the door. "By the way, Sam…er, we want to know what church you go to."

A grin slowly spread across Alice's face. "Church? What do you think we just had?"

◄ finding home ►

◄ chapter fourteen ►

A dense cloud of cigarette smoke crept across the ceiling, swallowing the dim light. John was locked in a staring contest with a beer. It was his first drink of the night and he hadn't touched it. He yanked his eyes from the amber liquid. Alcohol didn't ask him questions or demand his attention. It didn't care about his past or follow him around. All it wanted to do was cool his hand, his throat, and his mind. But he couldn't lift the glass. He glanced at the layer of frost hugging the mug like snow on a branch and felt his stomach roll.

Things had been *off* since breakfast. John pressed the back of his hand against his forehead like his mom used to do when he was a kid. He couldn't tell if it was warmer than normal. He tapped his fingers on the counter. It was J.C. He'd infected him somehow.

"You gettin' married to that beer, Caban?" Al went to slap him on the shoulder and missed.

John waved a hand. "Shut up, Al. Not in the mood."

Al laughed loud enough to make John cringe and got a finger stuck in his beard. "You come n' find me when you've had a few. I'll whoop ya in that there pool game." He laughed again like he'd told the funniest joke ever and stumbled away.

"Blah-blah," John muttered. When he returned to the beer, two oval spots glared back at him from the frost. John gasped and pushed away from the bar nearly knocking over the stool. They were eyes drawn close together in a menacing sneer. He'd seen them before hovering above his bed on the darkest nights. He'd always been able to blame the alcohol.

Something snickered. John whipped his head around but there was no one near him. The place was surprisingly empty. His heart pounded against his chest.

You're disgusting, worthless…a failure.

The voice hissed and spat and John felt like a bag of bricks sat on his shoulders. He slowly turned back to the glass. The eyes were even closer and seemed to pull him in. He fought to get air into his lungs.

You're a murderer!

"No!" John reached for the counter as his knees buckled and knocked over the mug.

"Whoa!" Nellie was there with a rag, blabbing something about him not drinking. The dark voice was gone along with the eyes. He wiped the sweat from his forehead and looked around. Every face was downcast as if an artist without heart or passion had captured melancholy on canvases. Every eye was lifeless. Panic crawled over him like spiders on the heels of a question he'd never thought to ask: *do I look just like them?* He lifted his nose and bile churned in his gut. The odors of cigarette smoke and sweat mixed to form a foul stench he'd never noticed.

"Well?" Nellie persisted.

John looked her over. She wore a plain black top with shorts that would make Daisy Duke blush. On a normal night he would have been drooling. But this wasn't a normal night and he was looking into the same dead eyes he saw on everyone else.

"Well what?" John asked.

She rolled her eyes. "Why aren't you drinking?"

John yanked his stool back to the bar and plopped down. "Mind your own business."

Nellie stuck her hands on her hips. "This bar and everything in it *is* my business." She searched him with her eyes. "Are you sick?"

He glared at her.

Nellie tossed the rag on the counter. "What's wrong with you?"

John covered his face with his hands but couldn't shut out the world. "Can't a guy decide he doesn't want to drink *one* night of his life?"

"No," Nellie snapped. "Not when that *guy* has been in here every night pounding beers since I've been in this town. Like I said, it's natural, like breathing."

◄ finding home ►

John let his hands fall and shot her a look. "My drinking is like breathing?"

Nellie crossed her arms over her chest. "Yeah."

"That's stupid."

"You're stupid," she snarled and leaned closer. "And you'd better get yourself together if you wanna have any fun tonight."

John stared at her for a moment. "Yeah, I've got to get outta here."

Nellie leaned on her elbows letting gravity work on her loose top. "You sure you wanna do that?" The seduction weaved into her voice he normally found so irresistible now sounded like fingernails on a chalkboard.

"Not tonight, Nellie." He rose and strode to the door.

"John!" Nellie's angry voice rang through the bar and he turned just in time to duck a mug that exploded on the wall behind him.

Spit flew from his mouth, "What the hell's the matter with you?"

"Your loss," she sang and returned to the regulars down the line.

John punched through the door and stormed into the cold night. "Psycho woman," he muttered. The chill clutched his lungs and he shoved his hands in his pockets. Questions sped around his head like cars on a racetrack while he rounded the corner leading to his house.

"John!"

The desperate cry shattered the silence into a million tiny pieces. John searched the darkness through the dim glow of streetlights. He was alone, but the shadows falling across the street seemed to be moving. A shiver ran down his arms and legs. That voice, he would always know it. He walked faster.

"John, help us."

The words came from everywhere and slammed into John, knocking him to his knees. "Amy?" He whipped his head in all directions, but she wasn't there. The only sound was his erratic breathing.

Her urgent cry came again. "Hurry John."

The screech of tires trying to grab road echoed through the night. "*Amy,*" He screamed above the noise. He jumped up and turned in circles ignoring the ache in his knees. "Where are you?"

"*John, please.*"

"Arghhhhhh." John covered his ears as steel and aluminum screeched, popped, and broke as if he was standing next to a compactor. "Hold on." He guessed at a direction and started running. "I'm coming." *Oh God. Where is she?*

An explosion. John didn't see it, but the blast knocked him to the ground.

"John, it's so hot. It's burning!"

Her voice rose above the ringing in his ears. John shook his head and tasted blood in his mouth. "Amy no I…" He pushed to his knees and gasped for air. "Tell me where you are."

"John…"

She was everywhere, playing with him, tormenting him. He climbed to his feet and staggered forward. "Please," tears and sweat stung his eyes, "just tell me where you are."

"We're here John. Please help us."

All light vanished, the darkness was thick like mud. John stopped and put out his hands. He was dizzy and his head pounded. "Amy…"

"John…it's too late."

Sinister snickers echoed all around him. The same hissing from the bar. "NO!" He clawed at the dark. "I'm coming."

"I love you, John."

You're a murderer.

"Amy, hold on. Just…please wait." He ran. He couldn't think. He had to find her, save her. He wouldn't lose her again. "A few more minutes," he shouted. "I'm—"

Flames erupted in front of him. He barely stopped in time. The heat scorched his face and he turned only to find another wall of fire behind him. The flames spread rapidly. He was surrounded.

"Amy." He tried to shield his face with his arm. "Amy!" The roaring flames swallowed his words. It couldn't end like this. Not again.

"It's not real." He rocked on his knees. "They're gone. This isn't really happening."

John noticed the cool breeze first. Then the silence. He slowly raised his head and blinked his surroundings into focus. The streetlights lit small sections of the cracked street with a few flickering like they always had. Moonlight softly painted the sidewalk with its pale glow. No fire. No

‹finding home›

screams. "It wasn't real." His voice shook and failed to convince his brain. His heart hurt as much as it had ten years ago. "What's wrong with me?" He looked at his trembling hands. "I'm going—"

"John?"

John turned toward the voice and saw a car had pulled up next to the curb. He scrambled to his feet.

"John...is that you?"

"Yeah," John cleared his throat. "Yeah, it's me." He squinted at the light bar and police insignia. "Mike?"

Mike poked his head out of his window. "What are you doing?"

John brushed the dirt from his pants. "Nothing. I'm...nothing."

Mike looked him over. "Yeah, looks like nothing."

"Forget it Mike."

"*Forget it?*" Mike opened his door and climbed out. "I roll up on you laying on the ground and you tell me to forget it?"

"So what. Like you've never seen me on the ground."

Mike crossed his arms over his chest. "Not for a long time John. I know how much alcohol it would take to put you down."

John's eyes narrowed. "I'm fine."

"You're not fine." Mike stepped forward.

"I wasn't drinking." John took a step and felt his leg buckle.

"Whoa," Mike rushed over and caught him before he fell. "No drinking, huh?"

John shoved him away. "You can go pound salt."

Mike stared at him a moment and sighed. "I actually believe you."

"Don't care what you believe." John went to take another step but felt the same tremor work through his knees. "You gonna give me a ride home or what?"

"Oh, sure," Mike said and reached for his friend. "Aint' like I got a job to do or anything."

John pushed his hand away. "I got it."

Mike watched closely until John was in the passenger seat. "You sure you don't want me to take you to the hospital?" he asked and slid behind the wheel. "Something's wrong with you."

"I'm fine, Mike. Just take me home."

81

A few minutes later John stood in his room with the lights off listening to the hum of Mike's cruiser fade. He stared at the wall ready to admit he was scared. Images floated before him like ghosts. The stranger's face and a bar he didn't know anymore. Amy and flashbacks. Ashley and emotions he hadn't felt in years.

John kicked off his shoes and fell on the bed wanting nothing more than to escape. He instinctively reached for the bottle that was always on the floor but when his fingers found the cool glass disgust stabbed him like a dagger and John let it clatter back to the floor.

Defeated, he rolled onto his side and stared at the wall until it blurred into dreams of Amy and the kids. Of life before *that* night. A life that would never be his again.

⋖ finding home ⋗

⋖ chapter fifteen ⋗

"I'm going to kill you, Tabby!"

Alice peered out over the snowy edge of a thirty-foot drop. She stood next to Tabby on a small platform overlooking a double black diamond ski trail that wound through the rugged terrain of Whiteface Mountain. The Resort was one of the best in the world and just three hours from Redwood.

She shielded her eyes from the afternoon sun and surveyed the stunning landscape through the red tint of her goggles. Majestic fir and pine trees lined the trails, and snowy peaks highlighted the background. But none of that really mattered to her at the moment. How she'd ended up staring over the threshold of her imminent death was beyond her.

"I'm not even a good skier," she whined. "How about we finish up with a bunny trail and then head to the lodge."

Tabby laughed. "Come on, Alice. We didn't ditch work and school to hang out with the old people." She adjusted her goggles. "You wanna start eating supper at four and going to bed at eight?"

"You're crazy," Alice exclaimed. "I can't even see the ground."

"Yeah, but it levels out after the drop."

Alice gripped her ski poles. "I hate you."

Tabby laughed again and easily slid her skis across the powder. Jack and Melissa gave her a set for Christmas last year and she was a great skier. "No you don't. You love me. Plus, I didn't *make* you come up here."

Alice whipped her head around. "You told me there would be an easy trail back down!"

Tabby pointed across Alice's chest. "Well, there's another double black trail over there. I'm sure one is easier than the other." Tabby crouched and slid the tips of her skis over the precipice. "See you at the bottom," she chirped. "Oh, and watch out for the moguls."

"Watch out for what—" But Tabby was gone.

Alice leaned far enough to watch her best friend line her skis to the contour of the steep slope and glide over the snow in an "s" pattern. "She makes it look so easy," she grumbled and searched one last time for another way out. She finally inched her skis over the edge and glanced at the blue sky. "Lord, this would be a great time for a dose of supernatural skiing talent." A cold gust bit her nose in response. Alice took one last deep breath, closed her eyes, and leaned her body forward. "Though I walk through the valley of—"

Words turned to screams as Alice plummeted through the mountain air. Her eyes snapped open to find the snow-covered ground rushing up to meet her. Somehow her brain unearthed instructions: *Knees bent, weight back, and lift up your toes!* Her body obeyed like it was on autopilot and her skies aligned perfectly with the slope. Instead of crashing she began to level out.

But before she could exhale she was speeding down the steep incline of the trail itself. The trees lining the run were a blur as she raced by. She considered attempting the "s" pattern but the trail was too narrow. Another scream was lost in the wind whipping her cheeks.

Alice looked downhill and felt her heart flip flop. The trail. A sharp right turn was bearing down on her. She clenched her jaw and at the last second leaned hard and hit the curve dusting the trees with white powder, barely missing a big pine on the left edge. Her thighs were on fire and she tried to straighten, but yelped instead when the trail fell out from under her into another steep decline. The wind yanked at her goggles and her knees threatened to give up as she burst out of the canopy-covered trail.

And then she almost cried out for joy. The lodge. A two-story log structure with a trail of smoke coming from the chimney waited to comfort her. She fixed her eyes on the last stretch of trail separating her from glory and gasped. It was covered with moguls.

Alice leaned hard to the right in a desperate attempt to go around them but she was moving too fast. The first bump launched her into the mountain sky. She screamed and covered her eyes. She hit the ground and

‹ finding home ›

bit her tongue, but managed to stay up. The little cheer she gave herself was cut short by the *wobble* that swam through her legs.

She hit the next mogul and her world somersaulted. She hit the ground hard and flipped, kicking up a large white cloud. Her skis shot out in opposite directions along with her poles. Her cries were muffled inside a tumbling mess of hair, boots, sweatshirt, and ski pants.

"Alice!"

Tabby's voice sounded far away. Alice was afraid to move. She wiggled her fingers and toes. Nothing hurt as far as she could tell.

Tabby slid next to her throwing more snow across her face. "Alice," she cried out. "Are you okay?"

Alice moaned and pulled her goggles off. "I...I think so. Help me sit up." She held out her hands for Tabby who carefully pulled her up. "Yeah, I'm fine."

Tabby fell back in the snow. "I was on a curve up the trail when you came flying by. You were going *crazy* fast. I caught up just in time to see you hit the mogul. You know, the one that turned you into a snowball."

Alice scowled at Tabby who was doing her best not to laugh. "Hey," Tabby joked. "Do you think that sometime you can teach me how to run into those things? What was it, arms spread straight out and one ski off the ground?" Tabby jumped up and demonstrated the pose.

"Oh, that's just fine," Alice retorted. She stood and brushed herself off. "Go ahead and laugh it up. I'm so happy I could entertain you by almost *dying*. Owe," she groaned. "I think I bit my tongue."

"Were you praying?" Tabby was having trouble getting the words out between spurts of laughter. "I think I heard you shout, 'Oh Jesus help me!'"

Alice had her hands on her hips. "You about done?"

Tabby gave up and fell into the snow laughing.

Alice crossed her arms over her chest. "You're nothing but a—" something caught her eye. She looked up to see one of her skis dangling in the branches of a snowy fir. A giggle escaped despite her annoyance. Then she started to laugh.

Tabby wiped her eyes to see Alice pointing up at her ski. The sight brought another wave of laughter from Tabby. Alice fell next to her laughing so hard tears ran down her cheeks.

The girls lay like that for a while before getting themselves under control enough to fish the ski out of the tree and find the rest of Alice's equipment. The sun was setting when they finally huddled around a small table by the fireplace sipping hot chocolate with marshmallows. They watched it dip behind the peak casting a shadow over the trails but igniting the sky and delicate clouds with fierce reds and soft yellows. It was as if the sky itself was burning. "That's incredible," Alice cooed. "God's an amazing artist isn't he?"

"Definitely," Tabby echoed from behind her mug.

Alice felt her heart swell. Tabby was more than a friend. She was a sister. The closest she'd ever had to one anyway. She absently tapped her mug and thought about the conversation about to follow. It was going to be hard. She'd been ignoring the promptings she could only assume were from God, but after her encounter with Nita, and then the healed leg, she couldn't anymore.

Tabby felt Alice's eyes on her and swiveled. "What?"

Alice made a sound like a sad sigh. "I think I'm going to leave soon."

"Leave?" She cast a glance around the lodge. "What are you talking about?"

Alice dropped her eyes briefly before meeting Tabby's again. "I think I'm going to leave Redwood."

Tabby set her drink down. "Why in the world do you think that?"

"Well…" Alice grimaced. She'd known this was coming and was still making a mess of it. "Some strange things have been happening and I think God might be telling me it's time to go."

Tabby shook her head like a wet dog. "*Things?* What *things?*"

She told Tabby all about her crazy meeting with Nita and the miracle at the clinic. Tabby's eyes grew wide as she listened. "That's amazing," she sputtered when Alice finished. "But it doesn't explain why you think God is telling you to leave."

"Yeah, I know." Alice pursued her lips. "There's something else."

Tabby raised her eyebrows and waited for her to explain.

"I've been dreaming lately."

"So what? You dream all the time."

Alice wagged her head. "Not like this." She hesitated. "The dreams

‹finding home›

they're...really weird. I'm not even seeing full pictures of anything." She opened her hands imitating small explosions. "It's just me standing in the dark with random flickers ahead."

Tabby crossed her legs and leaned back. "Flickers?"

Alice nodded. "Flashes of light that feel familiar somehow. Like if I could see the whole picture I would know it. But for now they're just slivers of scenes I can't place."

"What do you think they are?"

Alice shrugged. "Memories maybe."

"Hmmm," Tabby raised her cocoa. "Did Dr. Felling ever figure out why you can't remember your childhood?"

"She thinks it's possible I could've had an accident that caused amnesia. But tests show that my brain's not damaged—"

"That depends on who you ask," Tabby joked.

"Ha-ha very funny." Alice circled the rim of her mug with her finger. "She thinks I'm the one in the way, that once I decide to remember I will." Alice let her eyes fall to the table. "I think she's right. I mean, I want to remember but I don't."

Tabby reached across the table and squeezed Alice's hand. "I get that. It's not like we've had the easiest life. I'm not sure I'd want to see the past in *my* dreams. New memories that is. I see enough of the old."

Alice took a look around the room and settled on a family near the fireplace. Laughter followed smiles as a young boy and girl climbed on their dad's lap while mom giggled. He gathered them both into a big hug while they squealed in delight. The scene stabbed her heart. It'd be nice to have memories like that. Maybe she did.

"How do these *flashes* make you feel?" Tabby asked.

Alice raised an eyebrow. "Now you sound like Dr. Felling."

Tabby grinned and stuck out her tongue.

Alice blew a stray hair out of her face. "Some make me feel happy and some are really scary."

"But you said you're not even seeing full pictures."

Alice raised her hands. "I know. It doesn't make sense. How could little flickers of light make me feel like this?" She'd been trying to come up with an answer to that question ever since the dreams started a few days ago.

Could tiny pieces of unknown memories really be strong enough to throw her emotions into chaos?

Tabby dabbed her mouth with a napkin. "Do you think you're seeing parts of all the junk you've been through in the last ten years?"

"No, I don't think so."

"Why not?"

Alice clutched her now lukewarm mug and thought carefully about her answer. "I guess because I don't remember feeling happy until I came to Redwood. And I remember *everything* about the last ten years. There's no blank spots. I don't know why anything from that time would only show in flashes."

"Weird," Tabby uttered.

Alice gazed out at the mountain whose trails were now highlighted by white lights. It was so beautiful, like everything in her life since she'd come to Redwood. She'd had nothing but despair, but somehow ended up with more than she even knew to hope for. But things were changing. Uncertainty raged inside of her trying to smother something else fighting to be heard, something inexplicable. It was a feeling, no, a *knowing* that the beauty of her new life wasn't fading, but transforming into something that would outshine anything she'd experienced so far.

A sigh rose from the depths of her heart. "I think all this has something to do with my childhood."

Tabby's eyes widened. "Really? I mean, I guess that makes sense." She paused. "Are you ready for that?"

Alice gave a sad laugh. "Probably not. I mean, I hope so. But I *need* to remember, Tabby." She felt tears sting her eyes. "I'm not whole. But I think I can be. I'm missing a pretty big chunk of my life and I need it whether it's good or bad." She sniffed. "I've been so scared to remember. But I think God is showing me that it's hurting me to leave it there. I think it's a door he wants me to open so I can finally heal."

Tabby handed her a napkin. "And you think that leaving can help you remember?"

"Yeah, I think so." Alice blotted her eyes. "There's a path in the dream. It leads away from Redwood and into the flashes. I know I'm supposed to follow it."

≺ finding home ≻

"You're serious about this," Tabby stuttered and for the first time Alice saw fear wind through her expression. "This is crazy Alice. You've got a great life here. For the first time you have a family who loves you, a good job, and you can go to school really close. Why would you want to give that up? You've never had it so good. None of us have." She motioned to the window. "Think about what we came from. You wanna to go back out there where all that...*stuff* is?"

"Of course not," Alice assured. "I know what I'd be leaving and what kind of world is out there. But I," she took a reassuring breath, "...trust God. And I want what *he* has for me more than anything."

Tabby rolled her eyes. "You don't even have a plan."

"But I trust *his*," Alice declared. "I trust in his plan because I know he loves me. He wouldn't hurt me. He's love, Tabby. He's on my side no matter what. So I *choose* to believe that if he's leading me away from Redwood it's because he wants to heal and transform me even more than he already has."

Tabby sank back into her chair but her eyes narrowed. "How can you do this to me?"

Alice flinched. "What?"

Tabby spread out her arms. "Dump all of this on me. What do you want me to say?"

Alice winced as the words attached her heart. But she could see Tabby's bottom lip quiver and hurt flash through her eyes. "I, I just want your support."

"Well, I can't give it," Tabby blurted.

Alice slid around the table until she was next to her best friend. "Yes, you can."

Tabby crossed her arms and stared straight ahead. "No, I can't."

Alice flung her arms around her. "*Yes, you can* because you love me and want what's best for me."

Tabby fought hard to hold onto the anger but couldn't. She dropped her head to Alice's shoulder. "But we need you here. I...need you here."

Alice took hold of Tabby's hands and smiled even though her grief was a knife to her heart. "You're gonna be ok. Know why?" Tabby shook her head and a tear slipped onto her cheek. "Because I know God loves *you* every bit as much as he loves me. He will never leave your side. He is the shoulder to cry on and the hand to lead you. I could never be there for you in the ways that he has been and will always be."

Tabby looked like she was going to say something to argue but swallowed it instead and sniffed loudly. "You're very brave you know."

Alice nudged her. "I'm only brave because I know that no matter what, God is going to be there with me." She paused and bit her bottom lip. "I love Redwood, but I don't think I can stay and become the woman God wants me to be."

"Arghhh," Tabby wiped away tears with both hands. "Fine brat, I support you."

Alice giggled. "Thanks. I love you too."

"I'm just worried about the boys of Redwood. I'm not sure they'll survive you leaving. They all think they've got you halfway down the aisle."

Alice laughed making her hazel eyes sparkle. "I'm sure they'll live."

"If you say so." Tabby slurped her hot chocolate. "Bleh, this is cold," she stated and pushed it away. "But seriously, I wonder if God has your man out there wherever he's sending you."

Alice scoffed. "Yeah, like we'd be good for that right now."

Tabby gave her a light shove. "I am!"

Alice laughed.

"What?"

"Nothing. I just, admire you."

Tabby cocked her head to one side. "For what?"

"For being able to put yourself out there like that."

"Me? You're the one talking about leaving town."

"I know but it's different. After all we've been through…" Alice shivered. "I'm not ready. How can you be?"

"I don't know. Maybe I'm just not willing to let my past control my future."

The words slammed against her heart. Is that what she was doing? "Tabby that was like, *really* deep."

Tabby lifted her mug, her eyes mixed with laughter and sadness. "How will you survive without me?" She sipped and made a face. "I forgot it was cold."

They both laughed and Alice glanced down at her watch. "Let's go. It's

≪ finding home ≫

late and we have a long drive home."

 Alice paid the check and they left talking and laughing with each other. They never saw the older woman staring at them. They didn't see her get up and follow them out of the lodge and they didn't notice the late model Buick following them back to Redwood.

chapter sixteen

God, why am I here? Ashley Cook forced her face from her hands. "Pfft," she huffed at the *Dino's Pizz* sign hanging on the opposite side of the window. It was supposed to say *Dino's Pizza* but the "a" was burned out. She replaced the two z's with s's and laughed to herself.

Ashley was early, as usual, waiting for the guy who almost killed her with a shopping cart. She ran her hand through her blonde layers and sighed. It had been a long time since she'd been on date. Not that she hadn't had opportunities. A Rolodex of masculine faces flipped before her. "What's wrong with that one?" her friends asked. "Keep turning them down and eventually the line's gonna disappear." At least her friends were nicer than her mom who never failed to ask, "What's wrong with you?"

She smirked at the window to her right that framed Main Street. Most of the time she couldn't even say why she declined. It was always a feeling. How do you explain *that* to someone without sounding neurotic? She fell against the cool glass and traced a heart with her finger. Maybe she was. But she'd had plenty of *good* reasons to decline this time. Anxiety wormed through her belly. So why hadn't she?

Ashley pictured John. A strong jaw and rugged features fell over a tall, muscular frame. He was attractive, striking even, but so were a lot of the men who had asked her out. What was it about him? His skin was sun-browned and tough, the way it got from working mostly outside. He was certainly different than the put-together men who'd approached her, the type she typically gravitated towards. Was that it?

The answer surfaced like gold in a miner's pan and she smiled in spite of herself. She was here because he'd shown her a part of himself he hadn't

⟨ finding home ⟩

meant to. For a brief moment in the middle of a grocery store there were no masks. There was no pretending and she saw the gentleness and vulnerability lying inside of him. She was here because his transparency, accidental or not, triggered a feeling she hadn't felt in a long time.

Ashley watched the streetlights flicker to life as the sun surrendered to the moon and stars. Did he feel the same way? Could a man like that fall for a woman like—

CRASH!

Ashley yelped and almost fell out of her chair. Every head wheeled around to the front of the restaurant where one of the waiters was frantically plucking jagged pieces of glass from the floor. A man hovered over him. The same man who had knocked *her* down just days before. She met his wide eyes and giggled into her hand.

John checked his watch. 7:03. He found odd relief in that he could still experience some sort of normalcy, even if it was being late. He stationed himself in front of the door. She was inside waiting for him. Ashley. Should be anyway, unless she got smart and decided not to come.

He kicked at a pebble on the ground and sent it skipping down the sidewalk. She'd had every reason to say 'no.' "So why didn't she?" He rolled his eyes. "Great, now I'm talking to myself. As if I don't feel crazy enough." He blew a stream of air into the door and remembered how she'd made him feel in the grocery store. Desperate. Out of control. His stomach flopped a few times. "Come on John. Stop being such a *girl*."

Ashley was alone by the window at a table for two wearing a white long sleeve shirt and jeans. Silky blonde hair flowed past her shoulders. Subtle jewelry sparkled in the light but her beauty wasn't subtle at all.

John hovered in the doorframe while his heart danced in his chest. His hands shook and he drew them into fists. She hadn't seen him yet. He could run. *Why is this happening to me,* he wondered. *Why am I*—The answer wrapped it's claws around his throat and cut off his air. Amy. He'd felt the same way the first time he saw her.

John stabbed for the doorknob and whirled right into a young waiter hauling a tray full of plates.

"Oof…" The kid staggered backward and went down while plates crashed around him. Fire burned in John's cheeks as every head turned. But he only cared about one. Ashley had one hand over her mouth, but he could see the laughter in her emerald eyes.

"Sorry," he mumbled and bent down.

"No." The kid raised his hand. "I got it."

"Suit yourself." John sighed and shifted back to Ashley who was waving him over. "So much for not being a jerk."

"Pfff, no kidding." The disheveled waiter shot a look at him from the floor.

John glared at him. "It was an accident, I wasn't talking to you, and shut up." His mouth worked a half smile at Ashley and he commanded his legs to move. He brushed the stubble on his face and wished he'd taken the time to look better. Wrinkled shirt and stiff jeans. He decided bums dress better than him.

"So," Ashley chirped when he arrived at the table, "You're kinda dangerous, John Caban. I mean," she held up two fingers, "That's two this week that I know of."

He crossed his arms over his chest. "You were laughing at me."

Her smile grew and tugged the strength from his knees. "I'm a sucker for irony."

John turned his eyes on the room, on anything but Ashley. She was doing it again. Drawing him in. Wrecking his wall. He wanted to run and be closer. A rock and a hard place. Morton's fork.

Ashley leaned over the table and lowered her voice. "Feel free to sit down." She motioned at a chair across from her. "I saved you a seat."

John snatched the chair only to have it get stuck on the table legs. It took a moment to yank it free and he slumped down with red-hot cheeks. He tried not to notice Ashley's amused expression. "I'm sorry, I'm not very good at this." He rubbed the back of his neck. "It's been a long time since I've actually gone on a date. I mean," he cleared his throat, "I've had women, but don't really date."

Ashley raised her eyebrows. "So, you've had hookers?"

‹ finding home ›

John stiffened and waved his hands. "What? No! Nothing like *that*." He felt sweat creep across his forehead. "I'm just saying..." his mind blinked off like a monitor.

Ashley giggled. "Relax, I'm just messing with you."

John studied her for a moment before exhaling. "You know, I'm not usually like this." He grabbed a napkin and pressed it against his forehead.

She dropped her head to one side. "Like what?"

He crumbled the napkin in one hand. "Pathetic."

To his surprise she reached across the table and took hold of his hand sending a jolt through his whole body. "What you call pathetic I call honest and sweet. I saw some of it the other day at the store. I don't think you *wanted* me to see it. But I did, and it's the main reason I agreed to see you tonight." She hesitated. "Look, I'm not interested in a guy that thinks he's got it all together and figured out. I've had my fill of those guys. But that other guy, the one who isn't afraid to stumble and fall and mess up, I wanna get to know *him*."

Ashley smiled and her whole body bloomed like a lily. John's heart skipped a beat. She was right. He'd been trying to be the guy that had it all together. Maybe it was working out that he couldn't. He lifted his eyes to hers. "You, look great tonight. I mean...really great."

Ashley tucked a strand of blonde hair behind her ear. "Thank you." She raised the menu. "What are we getting?"

John reclined in his chair and watched her eyes move over the menu while two slender fingers gently tapped the table. He'd made a complete idiot of himself more than once and she didn't seem to care. Anxiety pricked him like needles. If it didn't matter to her maybe it shouldn't matter so much to him. "Hey!" Ashley's voice brought him back to the table. "Not sure where you just were, but I'm hungry. Girl's gotta eat."

John smiled and signaled the waiter. "Supreme with a water, please," Ashley told him.

"Two slices of *the meats* and a beer," John added. "Did you grow up here?" he asked when the waiter was gone.

She shook her head. "No, I actually grew up in Glendale."

"Glendale?"

"Yeah. I moved down here a couple years ago."

"Wow," John teased as the waiter set their drinks on the table. "Big move. What's that, an hour from here?"

She laughed and threw her napkin at him. "Big enough. Far enough to live my own life but if my family needs me I'm close." She sipped her water. "Most of them are still up there. And it's an hour *and a half* thank you very much."

John chuckled and felt the tension finally fade from his muscles. Her laugh was nice. He wanted her to do it again. "What do you *do* Ashley Cook?"

"I, John Caban, am a nurse at Blackwater Memorial. Up in the ICU."

"Intensive Care Unit?"

"Yep."

John gulped his beer. "Do you like it?"

"Yeah, it's great most of the time. I mean, I get to meet lots of new people and help them on their worst days. Most are really nice and excited to have someone caring for them and about them." Her grin reached her eyes. "And I love seeing people get better, when they're well enough to move down to the lower floors." She hesitated. "But we also lose people in there. That's tough, you know?"

John's stomach knotted. "But you like it though?"

Ashley blew a stray piece of hair out of her face. "It's hard for me to see someone we can't help anymore. Those days can be long but yeah, I do love it overall."

John breathed relief that he dodged her question. Especially since he'd almost answered that he knew *exactly* how tough losing people was. Her passion was a riptide and he was getting swept away. Excitement about her job, happy about meeting people, joy when they get better, and sad when they don't. He had anger. And sarcasm. But he didn't think sarcasm was an emotion.

The waiter appeared and gently set Ashley's plate in front of her. He spun and dropped John's plate on the table and stomped away. John held up his hands at Ashley who was doing her best not to laugh. "I think they're a little mad at you."

"Ya think?" He inspected the table. "Did you get a napkin?"

She giggled and dangled hers in the air.

≪finding home≫

"And my beer's gone."

She laughed out loud at that and covered her mouth. "I'm sorry." Her green eyes sparkled at him. "You want me to go take care of this little uprising?"

"Naw," John replied. "I already knocked his buddy down and if you unleashed on them they'd never recover."

"How gracious of you," Ashley cooed and lifted her slice. "So, do you work?"

John swallowed his mouthful. "Yes." A few moments passed and he realized she was waiting. He cleared his throat. "I'm a contractor. I manage a construction crew."

"What kind of things do you work on?" She bit into her slice.

"We do all kinds of things."

Ashley swallowed. "Like?"

John felt his pulse quicken. Short, vague answers weren't working like they normally did. He wiped his mouth. "We do new homes and a lot of re-models."

"Like bathrooms and kitchens?"

"Yeah. We can do pretty much anything someone would want. Most of the new construction North of tenth is our work."

"Nice," she exclaimed. "Do you like it?"

"Bathrooms and kitchens? Yeah, they're useful." He filled his mouth with a large bite and wanted to kick himself. Maybe if he kept his mouth full he'd stop acting like a jerk. He stopped chewing when he realized that for once he actually wanted to be nice.

Ashley rolled her eyes at him. "Do you like what you do?"

John swallowed. "It's ok. I'm good at it and I like getting paid."

Ashley took a drink of her water. "How long have you been doing it?"

John worked his toes against the soles of his boots and his eyes darted around the room searching for something to save him from her questions. Desire to be nice or not, things were getting a little too personal. "About ten years I think."

"What'd you do before that?"

John gripped the edge of the table. His old job was gone, passed away along with so many other things that didn't matter anymore. Ashley nibbled on her straw and waited for an answer. Maybe he should tell her, let her in a little. Just to give her a reason to stay a bit longer.

"John?"

He cleared his throat. "Yeah, I'm fine." She smiled and the green in her eyes flashed. It wasn't fair what she was doing to him. He tapped a foot on the floor. "I was a, uh, Nuclear Engineer."

Ashley's straw fell back into her glass. "A Nuclear Engineer?" She gushed. "Really? Where? Here? No, there's nothing like that around here."

John waved at himself. "I'd be surprised too."

She shot him a look. "That's not what I meant. It's just not something you hear everyday. Where did you do that?"

John's options sprawled before him like doors. Lie, leave, refuse to answer, or…his stomach tied itself into a pretzel, tell her the truth. "I was the Chief Nuclear Officer at a plant in Ohio." His voice was so low he wasn't sure if she'd heard him. "A town called, Oak Harbor."

Neither of them spoke for a long moment. Then Ashley wrinkled her nose. "That seemed like it was pretty hard for you. You don't really like talking about yourself, huh?"

"You could say that."

"Is it harder for you than apologizing?" Ashley asked and gave him a teasing grin.

He leaned on his elbows. "Ooh, I don't know. That's a tough call." She laughed and tossed her crust on the plate. There were more questions. He could see them coming together in her head like a checklist. "Let's go for a walk," he spouted.

"A walk?" She threw him a sideways look. "You wanna go for a walk?"

John worked up some enthusiasm. "Sure, why not?" He tapped a knuckle on the window. "It's nice out and there are shops."

Ashley peered at him. "The shops. *You* like the shops?"

"Sure," John replied. "Who doesn't?"

She pointed at his remaining slice. "But you didn't finish."

John blew out his cheeks. "I'm stuffed."

Ashley studied him from across the table and he felt like a flower under the desert sun. He was sure she wasn't buying it but she suddenly pushed away from the table. "Okay fine, let's do it."

⊰ finding home ⊱

John paid the check and led her out into the crisp night air before she could change her mind. The sky was clear, showing off the brilliant glow of the moon and stars. Main Street was the oldest street in Blackwater. Family owned shops and little cafes lined both sides providing an attractive destination for locals and whatever tourists ventured south of Phoenix. A movie theater and ice cream shop kept the weekends busy with teens. But tonight the street was quiet, peaceful. Maybe he really did like the shops. He shook his head.

They strolled down the sidewalk side by side. Every now and then his hand grazed hers and sent waves of electricity through him. He wondered if she felt it too.

"I've always liked this place," Ashley remarked.

"Blackwater?"

She gave him a little bump. "This street, this area. I used to walk here a lot after work. It helped me settle down and unload the day…" Her smile faded.

"What's the matter?" John asked.

"Oh, it's nothing." She tried to recover the smile but it didn't reach her eyes. "Not really a first date story."

"Then you're on the hook for however many dates your story's worth." That earned him a laugh. "No really." He stepped in front of her. "What is it?"

She gazed at him for a long time. Long enough to make him think she wasn't going to answer. And then she sighed. "I was just remembering a day we lost a young kid in the ICU. He got a rare infection and died before we could get ahead of it." She pointed at a bench in front of an antique shop. "I came out here late that night and just sobbed on that bench." She cringed at him. "Told you it wasn't a first date kind of story."

The pale moonlight made her soft and alluring. Or maybe it was her honesty, her vulnerability. John almost reached to hold her but shoved his hands in his pockets instead. He commanded his brain to produce the *right thing* to say. "I'm uh," he rubbed the back of his neck, "sorry you went through that." He was pretty sure that wasn't it but she smiled at him anyway.

"Thanks." A light breeze moved over them sending a strand of golden hair across her face. She brushed it back before John could act and continued down the sidewalk. "So," her voice was thick, "tell me about your family back in Oak Harbor."

John slowed his pace. "My family?"

She winked at him. "Yeah. You were about to tell me that you grew up in Oak Harbor, right?"

John's tongue felt much to large for his mouth. The *walk* plan had failed. "Right…"

"Are your parents still there?"

John shook his head. "They moved away a long time ago, before I left."

"Where are they now?"

John kept his eyes forward. His heart quickened. "Not really sure."

"What do you mean?"

"I dunno I just," he rubbed his chin, "don't know where they are."

"Don't you talk to them?"

"Not for a long time."

"How long?"

"Long," John grunted.

"I can tell you *really* want to talk about this."

"Nothing I enjoy more," he answered trying to make his tone lighter than he felt. "We should probably head back."

She nodded and they circled back toward the restaurant. "Ever been married?" she asked.

"Nope," he lied.

"Kids?"

The question rammed him in the stomach and he winced. "No." Ashley squinted at him. She'd figure him out if he didn't do something. "What about you?" he asked. "Ever been married?"

Ashley pursued her lips. "Yeah, I was married once."

John couldn't keep the surprise from his voice. "Really?"

Ashley stopped and crossed her arms over her chest. "What's the problem?"

John faced her. "Nothing. I'm just surprised someone let you get away." It was out before he could close his mouth. He watched her through eyes half-open and saw her face blush under one of the streetlights. Maybe he

≺ finding home ≻

finally said something right.

"Well, thank you," she responded.

They ambled on towards *Dino's,* neither of them knowing what to say next. "So, what happened?" John finally asked.

"Oh, so you don't want to talk about any of your stuff, but you want me to talk about mine?"

John felt his face get hot and he looked away. Ashley giggled and squeezed his arm. "It's okay. We met in college and were married for eight years. He's a lawyer and wanted to be the best. He advanced quickly but it meant spending more time in the office than at home. We became strangers and one day he told me that it would be better if we went our separate ways."

"He's an idiot," John stated.

"He was just doing what he knew. To him work was life and there wasn't room for me. It's the way he grew up. His father was the same way."

John moved in front of her and found her eyes. Another blonde strand fell out of place but this time she didn't move. He swept it back, letting his fingers slide over her cheek. Her skin was soft, like velvet. Goose bumps raced up and down his arms. "Yeah." His voice was heavy. "He's an idiot." Her eyes were locked on his. He'd never seen anything so green and he was lost in them. Normally he'd already have the girl back at his place. But Ashley was different and he didn't know what to do. He tried to clear the moment from his throat. "We should get back—"

"Yeah," Ashley quickly added and fell back a step.

They drifted on, their arms bumping into each other much more often than when they started. *Dino's Pizz* flashed ahead of them. "Any kids?" John asked.

Ashley shook her head. "No, no kids." She opened her mouth like she was going to say more but then didn't. John made a mental note to ask about that sometime.

"When do I get to see you again?" John asked when they reached the restaurant.

Ashley gave him a gentle shove. "What makes you think I *want* to see you again?"

He kicked at a small rock. "I got the vibe."

She crossed her arms over her chest. "The *vibe,* huh?"

John nodded. "Mm-hmm, and it's telling me Saturday night would be good."

Ashley tapped her shoe against his. "Can't Saturday night."

"Why not," John asked. "Got another date?"

"Oh," she mocked. "Would that be a problem for you?"

He eyed her. "You're messing with me...right?"

She giggled and pressed her hand against his arm. "Of course. My church meets Saturday nights."

John flinched. The word was a nail on a chalkboard. "Church?"

"Yeah, but it's really more like a home group."

John took a step out of her reach. "So, you believe in Jesus and God and all that—" he stopped himself short of cursing.

"Yes." Ashley moved closer and alarm sounded in her voice. "What's wrong?"

The night pressed in on John from all sides like a vise. *God* was the ignition to the fire deep within him. Things like *Jesus* and *church* were fuel. And now it was raging. Ashley was in front of him, searching him. She knew. He saw her stiffen. Saw the laughter in her eyes vanish.

"John," she gripped his hand. "How big of a problem is this?"

John felt the old, familiar wall begin to surround his heart. It was being rebuilt by the hate that would always be a part of him. "Too big, Ashley." His voice was firm though his body shook. It was all gone. Everything he'd felt with her would fade into a memory he would never recall. She'd become just another face in a sea of forgotten faces. He lifted his head and her quivering lips intensified his rage against the one who continued to take everything from him.

"Wait!"

John clenched his jaw but slowly rotated to face her. Her eyes were brighter than they should've ever been with the available light. They were almost glowing. He steeled himself. "There's nothing to say."

"Stop," Ashley blurted. She closed her eyes and when she opened them they held resolve. "It's not his fault."

Her voice was soft, but the words slammed into him like bat. He stumbled back a few steps. "What?"

"You've been blaming God for so long," she told him. "Your hate has

‹ finding home ›

stolen so much. Don't let it take this too," she pleaded. "It's not his fault."
John felt the blood leave his face. "Who told you about me? How do you…" His eyes narrowed. "Who do you think you are?" he growled through clenched teeth. "You don't know anything about me or what I've been through." He pointed to the sky. "And you are not qualified to say what is and what isn't *his* fault!" He took off toward his truck.

"John, please stop," Ashley hurried after him. "If you would just—"

"NO!" He whirled around and stopped her with a look. "You think you know me, is that it? We take a walk, you ask me some questions and you think you know me?"

Ashley drew her hands to her chest. "No, I—"

"Stop it. Just *stop it!*" John stabbed the air above him and cursed out loud. "If *he's* what you want then take him. But I'm done." He didn't look back again. He couldn't see her hands cover her face or her body spasm under the force of a sob. He didn't see her knees buckle or her hand grasp a light post to keep from collapsing. He didn't notice the brilliant sparkle of life in her eyes fade under the shadow of pain. The only thing he saw was the familiar darkness of the life he knew, the only life he could ever have.

John jumped into his truck and hit the gas. Rubber squealed against asphalt as he sped off. Not toward the bar, and not toward home. Somewhere no one could find him.

chapter seventeen

John didn't mean to end up at the park. He hadn't even known it existed. He flipped off the moon and it seemed to shine brighter just to spite him.

He lumbered across a cracked sidewalk and plopped down onto a metal bench. Rust and peeling paint scratched against his jeans and he surveyed the scene. Weeds reached for knees in one place and crab grass for ankles in another. The ladder for a steep slide was missing a few rungs and leaned like an old woman on a cane. Pieces of trash blew in front of him, riding the random gusts of wind. It was an abandoned city left to its own demise.

John cradled his head and groaned. Every time his eyes closed Ashley's face appeared. He wanted to scream at the hurt that distorted her features. But scream what? Obscenities, or apologies? Both?

He wanted to sleep and wake up a week ago. His life had turned into a *Mad Libs* and he wanted to make some different choices. He exhaled the lingering rage into the night. Regret took advantage of the vacancy and pricked his heart. His fingers tingled at the memory of Ashley's cheek and he winced. She'd revived something in him dead and buried. Hope. Hope that he could still have good things, that he might not have to feel so heavy all the time, that he could peer into the mirror and look different than the people filling up his last ten years.

John noticed a star that was brighter than the rest. It pulsed clarity into him. He liked how hope made him feel. It was like a warm blanket on a cold night.

He picked up a small rock and tossed it at a tree. But Ashley ruined it. Or did he ruin it? John grit his teeth. Neither. It was *him*, God. His

⋖ finding home ⋗

stomach burned and he gripped the bench. God wrecked yet another thing that could have been good for him. "I hate you," he growled. "I *really* hate—"

"It's kind of chilly out here." The voice erupted from somewhere in front of him. "Didn't you bring a jacket?"

John jerked up and peered into the shadows. "Who's there?"

The moonlight caught a slender figure moving toward him. Tan pants, long-sleeved flannel shirt with a cap that used to be white, but was more yellow. Dark skin and piercing brown eyes.

John moaned. "Not *you*."

"You almost hit me with that rock," J.C. informed him. Weeds crunched as he closed the gap between them.

"I'm sorry my aim's not better." John held up his hands, "I'm really not in the mood for this."

He halted with one foot on the sidewalk. "Not in the mood for what?"

"What are you doing here?" John asked. "How did you…" He rose and narrowed his eyes on the man. "Did you follow me?"

J.C. wore an easy smile. "You're assuming you got here before I did. Maybe *you're* following *me*." He brushed a piece of crab grass off his pants. "Why are *you* here?"

John started for his truck. "I don't have time for this."

"Sounds like you've had a rough night."

"I don't care what anything sounds like to you," John retorted.

"Maybe I already know everything about it," J.C. said matter of fact.

John came to a stop as if hooks had seized his spine. J.C. was reclining on the bench taking in the sky. "Ashley Cook…" His warm breath rose like a cloud in the chilled air. "She's precious isn't she."

John blinked. It was statement, not a question. "What did you say?"

He glanced sideways at John. "I'll never forget the moment we met, Ashley and me. It was exactly eight years ago today, can you believe it?" He sucked in his bottom lip. "She was going through some pretty hard things. She shared just a small bit of that with you earlier."

John felt like he was in a car speeding down a hill without brakes. He took a few careful steps toward the man. "How do you know Ashley? How do you know what she told me?" And then he knew. "You followed us down Main Street didn't you? You're sick."

J.C. chuckled. "Again, you assume you're the first to arrive places. I was walking *beside* you on Main Street so let's just call it even."

Confusion wrung John's brain. He knew there was nobody around them earlier. The street had been empty. Anxiety fluttered through him. The man was crazy. Maybe even dangerous. Was he stalking Ashley too? "Who are you?" John meant to shout, but it came out in a short cry. He pointed his finger and willed it not to shake. "Tell me right now or I'll—"

"You'll what, John?" The man was still sitting, every muscle appeared relaxed.

"Tell me who you are!"

"I've told you."

"Yeah, you're J.C."

"Well, yeah."

John scoffed. "Tell me what you're doing here and how you know this stuff or we're gonna settled this right here, right now."

J.C. mulled that over for a few moments and then climbed to his feet. "I'm here to help you find what you've always wanted. To get back what you've lost."

Everything John planned to say vaporized. His voice lost the resolve he'd gathered. "What?"

J.C. took a few big steps toward John. "You've lost your life, John. I'm going to help you get a new one."

John reeled back. "You stay away from me. You're crazy." Sweat lined his forehead despite the chill. He needed to tell Mike. This guy needed to be thrown out of town or in jail.

"You asked me what J.C. stands for," J.C. mentioned, still coming at him. "I told you it stands for a lot. And it does."

"I told you to stay back," John warned.

J.C. ignored him. "Peace, Joy, and Kindness to name a few."

John sucked in a breath. Every word impacted him as if they were real, tangible.

"Freedom, acceptance, value, significance to name a few more." J.C. was in front of him now. "Reconciliation," he announced, "to name another. And the list goes on." He paused. "But above all else, I stand for *love*."

◄ finding home ►

John covered his ears. The last word resonated from everywhere and landed on his shoulders like a weight heavy enough to drive him to his knees. He threw out his hands desperate to find something that could help him back up. But all he felt was crab grass and weeds, and the weight on him that was increasing. "What's happening to me?" John cried and raised his eyes to the man who seemed to have captured the moonlight.

"I love you, John Rister."

The words felt like a caress and John dropped his head.

"I need to show you something."

Then, before he could react, the brilliant light was gone and total darkness engulfed him.

Chapter Eighteen

Claire sat straight up in bed as if fired from a cannon. She clutched her chest and scanned the unfamiliar walls, windows, and furniture. It was a hotel in a town called Redwood. She'd only laid down for a second. She rubbed her eyes and guessed she'd fallen asleep. But she wasn't certain. All she knew was that less than a minute ago she had been somewhere completely different.

The rustic bench had been in some kind of park. Trees surrounded her separated by patches of grass that were so green and uniform that they looked liquid rippling in the light breeze. Scattered sounds of birds chirping joined the song of leaves falling and wind gently caressing branches. She could even hear water moving through a stream or brook maybe.

Suddenly a man appeared in front of her. Her cry caught in her throat as she took in the figure towering over her. Kind features sat above broad shoulders. Life danced in his eyes along with a wary ferocity. A white garment draped his body to the ground and a large sword hung at his waist. He was glowing as if the light was buried somewhere within him. She crumbled to her knees.

"Stand up Claire." His voice was a quiet storm that shook her completely. "For there is *one* to whom your worship is due and I am not him."

She scrambled to her feet and her knees threatened to refused her weight.

"Don't be afraid," he said. "I've come with a message and you must listen carefully."

Claire could only nod.

"Go to the Redwood Clinic Monday morning. There you will find a young girl, a receptionist. Her name is Alice. Invite her to your home. She has been prepared. Do you understand?"

« finding home »

The trees spun around her. She was hearing, but having trouble comprehending. He was waiting for an answer and her voice was as quiet as the breeze. "I, I think so."

He nodded at her. "You will remember clearly when you wake up."

And then she was sitting straight up in bed. *Monday morning. Clinic. Alice. Invite her home.* The sudden ring of her cell phone made her yelp. She stabbed for it and read her husband's name off the caller ID.

"Mark?"

"Hey, hon. What's the matter? You sound out of breath."

"I called you earlier but you didn't…I mean you wouldn't—"

"Yeah I was stuck in a meeting with the elders. I'm on my way home now. Are you okay?"

She touched her chest. "I'm fine, Mark. I'm in Redwood."

"Redwood? What in the world are you doing there? Is the conference over?"

"Yes, I mean no. I spoke earlier today so my part is done but it's still going on."

"So what are you doing in Redwood?" he asked again. "I don't even know where that is. Are you in trouble? Do you need me to come get you? Stay right there I'm on my way. I'll just—"

"Mark just be quiet for a moment and let me explain."

"Alright," Mark agreed after a moment. "Please tell me what's going on."

"Well you know how Dave and Marjorie put up the conference speakers at White Face Mountain Resort."

"Yes, I remember."

"I was sitting in the lodge earlier tonight. Oh Mark, the sunset, it was so beautiful over the mountains. And then the stars, like diamonds lighting up—"

"Claire…"

"Sorry," she sputtered and waved a hand through the air. "Anyway, I was sitting there sipping hot chocolate when I noticed two young ladies at a table by the fireplace. Actually, it seemed like God shinned a spotlight on them. They got brighter while everything else dimmed. They were talking and giggling and carrying on. I thought they might be sisters. They were very precious Mark. When they stood up to leave I got that butterfly, fluttery feeling in my stomach. You know how that is."

"Uh-huh," Mark acknowledged.

"Well I got the impression that I was supposed to follow these girls. I sat still for a few minutes letting God know that it's not a good idea to follow strangers. You know how I do."

Mark chuckled.

"But goodness Mark, the girl with the long black hair. When she walked past me there was something so familiar about her. I couldn't explain it but it was enough to be sure this was a God thing. So I followed them back to Redwood. I'm pretty sure I'm still in New York, somewhere West of Lake Placid."

Mark took a few moments to process before responding, "Well Claire, our life together is certainly interesting."

"Mm-Hmm. Just a few years ago I wouldn't have even known that was God. Who says you can't teach an old dog new tricks?"

"Someone who doesn't know you," he offered. "So did you find a hotel or what?"

"Yes, the only one in town. I think the bed is really a cinder block...Oh Mark! Wait until you hear about the dream I just had!"

"That's incredible," he stammered when she was finished. "I don't even really know what to say."

"I know," Claire gushed. "It was far beyond anything I've ever experienced."

"You and me both. So, I guess you'll be there for the weekend. Is there anything you need, anything I can do at all?"

"I don't think so. Wait, pray for me. And let Ruth know I won't be at Bible study tomorrow night."

"Got it."

Claire heard the engine fade. "Are you home?"

"Yep, just pulled in."

"Okay, well I'll let you go. I love you, Mark Summers."

"Love you too Claire, and keep me updated."

Claire told him she would and hung up. She stared at the ceiling and tried to get comfortable on the stiff mattress. "You are my shepherd," she whispered and smiled. "Lead me and I'll follow." She fell asleep to the image of a girl with long black hair and sharp hazel eyes.

◄ finding home ►

◄ chapter nineteen ►

Heat spilled over John's back. He blinked in the sudden light and tasted dust. Ruts in the hard ground dug into his knees.

"Hello?" He lifted his arm to shield his eyes. There was no one around. His heart sputtered. Where was the park? Where was J.C.? He wiped away the sweat stinging his eyes. Wasn't it just the middle of the night?

"Hello?" He repeated. His voice cracked and strained against the dry air. He rubbed his throat and sensed something move behind him. He spun on his knees and gasped.

A thick, dark wooden beam reached high over John's head. It was gnarled in some places and chipped in others. Near the top it was married to another beam just like it. Together they formed a cross. It was cruel and it was ugly, and hanging on it was a man.

John thrust both hands at the ground to keep from falling over. The tan pants and long-sleeved shirt were gone. There was no old, yellowing cap, and there was a dark, coarse beard on his face. But John knew it was him. The piercing, brown eyes left no doubt.

John opened his mouth, but there was no sound, tried to reach out but his muscles wouldn't obey. J.C.'s feet twitched. They were dirty and caked with dried blood. The bottoms were rubbed raw. John's stomach lurched when he saw the thick, rusty nail that had impaled them.

His legs were colored purple and red from bruises, and too many lacerations to count, some of which still oozed. A red stained cloth covered his waist. John noticed his diaphragm sputter as he struggled to breathe. Bright red blood spilled from fresh wounds over his stomach and mixed with sweat and dirt. Black and blue arms extended straight out from his body. Nails speared each hand to the wood behind them. His head hung low and clumps of black hair had fallen over his face. He wore a crown made of thick, jagged thorns. They pierced his flesh and bright red blood dropped steadily from the wounds.

John leaned over and threw up everything in his stomach. He spit on the ground and looked up. Tears blurred his eyes but he could see a ragged piece of dark wood that was fastened to the vertical beam above the J.C.'s head. Words were scribbled across it, *Jesus of Nazareth, the King of the Jews.*

"My god," John stammered. J.C. is Jesus Christ. "No," he cried and rocked backwards as if he was shoved. "It's not possible."

He scrambled to his feet in a cloud of dust but his legs wouldn't hold him and he tumbled over. Jesus was taking deeper breaths now. He raised his head with a groan, agony etched into his expression. His eyes locked onto Johns. Tears streamed down his face and cracked lips parted. His eyes poured into John's and with his last of his strength proclaimed, "It is finished." Then his head dropped and his body became still and John was engulfed in darkness once again.

≺ finding home ≻

≺ chapter twenty ≻

Someone was screaming. It wasn't the sound of terror but of deep anguish, like a bleeding soul. John felt the cool earth under his knees before he realized the sound was coming from him. He cracked his eyes as the sounds of night invaded his ears. Crickets chirped and grasshoppers hummed as if nothing strange had happened. He was back in the park.

He wobbled on his knees and rubbed his eyes. The moonlight was still lighting up the dreary playground equipment. J.C,…Jesus, sat in front of him still emanating the glow, softer though, as if a dimmer switch had been pressed down.

John stood quickly, too quickly. A wave of dizziness attacked him and forced him back to the ground. His voice quaked. "You." He slung a finger at Jesus. "What did you do to me? I saw you, I saw you…die," he finished weakly.

Jesus stood without a sound and wiped his glistening tears. He raised his palms so John could see them. A round scar deformed the center of each hand. "I did die."

And I rose three days later, a voice spoke to John's mind. John was reeling. The headache and the tree stand. He closed his eyes against another wave of dizziness. "Why did you show me all that?" he asked.

"Because," Jesus answered and eased down beside him. "It's one thing to tell you how much I love you, but quite another to show you."

John pressed his fingers against his temples. "How could you be here with me? Am I dreaming?"

Jesus smiled. "No, John."

"But, I don't even believe in you."

"Well, you might want to make a theological adjustment." His smile faded a little. "Besides, you've always *believed* in me, you just haven't *wanted* me for a long time."

The statement rang John's heart like a bell. Somewhere in the trees the wings of a bat fluttered and he briefly imagined being able to soar high above the earth and all of its problems and heartache. He raised a shaky finger instead. "Amy, the kids…why?"

A few tears spilled onto Jesus's cheeks but his mouth stayed closed.

John felt the fire within him begin to burn. "I, I've hated you for so long."

"I love you, John."

"No," he spat. His shoulders sagged with ten years worth of weight. It was a life he was never supposed to have birthed from a night he never should have lived. Lifting his head to look at Jesus took all his effort and his voice cracked. "Why did you take them?"

Jesus's eyes begged him to understand. "I *love* you, John."

John erupted. "That's not an answer—"

Jesus was on his feet, "It's the *only* answer!"

"NO!" John shot to his feet and ripped at his chest like he could somehow soothe the pain in his heart. "You took everything from me. You took Amy," he paused and squeezed his eyes shut seeing their faces, "and the kids. Then you dropped me into this hell of a life. Ten years, it's been *ten years!*" John choked down a sob working up his throat and seethed at the source of his pain. "I need to know why you did this. How could this have been what you wanted?"

Jesus winced and fell back as if he'd been struck. "You think this is what I wanted? Do you think I was sitting above you with my arms crossed, smiling as I manipulated horrific pain and torment in your life?" A cold gust blew through the park agitating the dried leaves on the sidewalk.

John kicked the ground. "Weren't you?"

As soon as the words left John's mouth, Jesus doubled over at the waist and a sob mixed in a wail detonated into the air. At the same time a groan rose all around him as if the crab grass, weeds, trees, rocks, and nocturnal insects were lamenting in a cacophony of anguish. John grabbed his chest

◄ finding home ►

to keep his heart from ripping in two. He wobbled and nearly fell again. When Jesus straightened his face was streaked. His voice was thick and heavy. "You think I did this. You and so many others who have their lives ripped and shredded by the pain and suffering weaved into the fabric of this world. The truth of who I am is traded for the searing passion of hate and blame. But I was there John. I was there that night. Pieces of metal and debris were everywhere. Flames roared and reached and I held them." His voice cracked on the last word. "My tears splashed on their faces as I clutched them to my chest."

He took a step toward John. "I was there, watching you turn down plate after plate urging you to eat. I lay beside you when you couldn't get up and tried to hold you. My tears stained the bed sheets right next to yours. I stood beside you at the funeral. Your knees weren't the only ones to hit the wet ground. Your tears weren't the only ones to spill into the graves."

John slumped to the ground. Emotion hung on his shoulders. Every word Jesus spoke was like a pickaxe to his soul.

Jesus lowered himself and framed John's face with his hands. "I was there John, that night you used the bottle to numb your pain. I watched you hurl your anguish at the sky. I cried out for you but you couldn't hear me."

John tried to hide his face before the tears breeched his eyelids. A breeze flirted with Jesus's dark hair as it passed over them, cold on John's wet face. He could still feel the cool bottle in his hand before he threw it into the darkness. *I was there.* He rubbed his cheek with the back of his hand. "I, I didn't know."

Jesus gave him a sad smile. "You're beginning to see but far from understanding. I wasn't only with *you* during that horrific tragedy John. I was with your parents who'd lost their grandkids and daughter-in-law. I was with Amy's parents and extended family and friends. You suffered in your own pain and suffered greatly but I, I suffered beside every single person who had known and been impacted by your family. That's who I am, John. That's what you saw on the cross. I suffered so greatly *for* you so that you would know how much I'd suffer *with* you."

His pain was worse than mine. The revelation fluttered though John's mind. The grief in Jesus's churning eyes and wrought face silenced any objections. John could still feel the weight of his own pain so clearly. It was true he only carried his own and it had destroyed his life. He couldn't imagine carrying anyone else's. His voice was hardly louder than the wind, "Why?"

Jesus clutched John's shoulders. "Because I love you John. So often my love is difficult to understand. How you felt about Amy and the kids, how you wanted to be a part of their lives in every way possible…that's love and it's powerful but it's only a fraction of the love I have. I've invested my heart in you, John. I've given everything. And I'd have it no other way."

John could feel the bitter mortar securing bricks of hate groan. Could they really fall? After ten years? Something twisted in his gut and he slid out of Jesus's reach. "I can't do this. I survived. I—"

"There's a difference between surviving and living," Jesus declared. "In order to survive you tried to forget everything. You stuffed your pain deep inside and ignored it. You thought you were making it, that you were living." Jesus's eyes begged John to understand. "But you weren't John. You were rotting from the inside out." He lifted a finger. "But living, *truly* living is much harder. Pain is faced and hearts bleed openly. Living means making a choice to keep walls down and courageously face the reality of trials. At times it can make you feel like you're dying, but it's the only way to truly live again."

John cradled his head in his hands. He felt his heart leap at the possibility of living. *John, my precious son…*He jerked his head. The voice, it came from the ground. It was on the wind, in the leaves, and the trees. It was louder and yet softer than anything he'd ever heard.

I rose again but you haven't. You can John. You made the choice to survive. Now I'm asking you to live.

The words were a wrecking ball into John's heart. He trembled as a large section of the wall exploded. A hideous screech rose from the dust and stabbed his mind. "Arghhhh," John cried out and grabbed his head. He forced his eyes to Jesus. The invisible monster screeched again but stopped abruptly when he shouted, "I want to *live!*"

John had hardly blinked before strong arms hugged his neck. Jesus was laughing and John felt his tears on his shoulder. His next breath was smooth, as if it'd been oiled. He tested his shoulders and almost laughed

‹ finding home ›

out loud at the missing weight. He was a boat cut free from the dock. Love crashed over him like a wave, permeating his skin, tissue, bones, and organs. It flooded his soul.

Jesus scrambled to his feet and cupped his hands around his mouth. "Whoohoo! He's alive!" Jesus twirled and hopped in some kind of impromptu dance. "He was lost and now he's found," he sang out. "Come on," he urged and held out his hand.

"You want me to dance like that?" John climbed to his feet and laughed. *Laughter.* It felt foreign and right. Like riding a bike after many years. "That's okay. You go ahead."

Jesus shrugged and continued hoping around. John watched him, feeling joy pick at his heart. What now? He squinted at the moon. There was still pain. There were still questions.

"Hey," Jesus stood before him, his eyes glittering. "I know there's stuff that still needs to be healed. And I know that you still have questions." He put a hand on John's chest. "We can certainly wrestle with the questions you have, but there are things we need to talk about before we get there."

John scrunched his forehead. "What kind of things?"

"Losing your family was terrible, but there are other things that wounded you. Things that have been hurting *our* relationship for a very long time." Jesus took a few steps down the sidewalk before turning a gentle smile on John. "You've spent a lot of your adult life praying for me to be closer, to *draw near to you,* so to speak. And the results haven't exactly blown you away. Oh, there were times you were overcome by my love. You felt it, experienced it. But it never seemed to last more than a few days. The distance always returned. You did everything you could to fix it, but nothing seemed to work."

The hours spent in futile prayer blinked in John's mind like an arrow pointing to a run down motel. John picked at a fingernail. It was surreal to be told exactly what he'd experienced and felt. Especially since he'd always kept those things to himself. "Why were you always so far away?" he asked.

Jesus was silent a moment before he sighed. "John, I did everything I could to get close to you, to wrap you in my arms and never let go. But there was a problem. *You* had a problem John. One that you still have."

John straightened. "What kind of problem? I did everything I could."

Jesus nodded. "I know you did. That's not the problem. I know that you loved me as much as you could."

"Then what is it?"

Jesus stepped through the pale glow of the moon and leveled his face at John. "The problem was, and still is, you don't really believe I love you back."

John frowned. He recalled countless times he talked about God's love for him and others in church, small group meetings, and conversations with his family. Every Christian knows that God loves them. "Okay, I'll give you the last ten years, but before that I believed you loved me. I said it…" John did a count in his head, "I don't know how many times. You know though. How many times did I say it?"

"You said it a lot," Jesus agreed. "You even taught it to others. But just because you know something up here," he pointed at his head. "Doesn't mean you know it here," he touched the place over his heart.

John folded his arms. "What's the difference? Knowing it is knowing it."

Jesus smiled. "I know you don't understand. But you will. It's the place we must start. It's the foundation of everything. If you can't understand my love for you there's no hope for you to understand anything else. That's why my love is the only answer for those just beginning *and* beginning again." Jesus clapped his hands together. "It's late and we need to end this for tonight."

"Wait," John sputtered. "Just like that?"

Jesus chuckled. "Just like that."

John shoved his hands in his pockets and his keys fell to the ground. "When will I see you again?"

Jesus locked onto his eyes. "I'm always with you, John. I've never left you and I won't. Not ever. I love you. It's a love so deep you can't ever reach the bottom. It's a love nailed to that terrible cross."

John bent over to pick up his keys. When he stood up he was alone. He wheeled around to check the area and only the crickets answered him. But for the first time in a long time he didn't feel alone. He loped to his truck and eased behind the wheel. He wiped his mouth and chuckled. Who would he ever tell about all of this? Mike would lock him in the *crazy* cell, and then there'd be nowhere to run when he started in on all his *war* stories.

⊲ finding home ⊳

As his truck grunted to life and crunched over gravel and asphalt, the events of the night played on a loop. John didn't understand most it, and part of him still needed to be convinced it really happened. But things wouldn't be the same again. He thought about Ashley. Regret pierced him and he slapped the steering wheel. He would fix it.

He was absorbed into formulating a plan. It's the reason he didn't notice the vehicle swerve into his lane until it was too late. The crunch and scream of metal and aluminum silenced his cry. John's head jerked forward and slammed against the steering wheel. And then he was floating as glass shattered and plastic became shrapnel. He wondered why the moon was doing summersaults. It was the last thought he had before everything went black.

♡

Ashley squirmed on the couch and wiped her eyes for what felt like the millionth time. It was a small miracle she'd made it home in one piece.

She sniffed. "How did it go so wrong?" She'd been asking that question over and over, pleading with God for an answer. But he wouldn't answer. More likely she was too upset to hear him.

Her cat, Jeffrey, jumped on the couch and pushed his head against her hand. "Meeting him wasn't a mistake," Ashley told him. Jeffrey *meowed* at her until she scratched his head. "And he was letting me in," she muttered. "Well, sort of anyway."

Ashley sighed. "I didn't mean to like him that much, Jeff. It just happened." She rolled her eyes and gave a short laugh. "It's crazy but I feel like I've known him for a long time. I was just comfortable, you know?"

Jeffrey purred a response and curled on her stomach. Ashley felt her eyes fill again. She drew a finger across Jeffrey's back. "Maybe that's why it hurts so much. It's been a long time since I've felt like that. Somehow, it was much more than a first date." Maybe she should go find him. Maybe she should—Her cell phone rang. She snatched it off the table and glanced at the caller ID. It was the hospital.

"Hello?"

"Hey Ashley." It was her supervisor, Karen. Stress rang through her voice.

Ashley sat up and Jeffrey scampered off with a whine. "Hey, Karen. What's up?"

"I need you to come in."

"What? Why? I'm not on call today."

"I know but we're slammed up here and there's a bad trauma coming in. We need help."

Ashley sighed.

"Hello…Ashley?"

"I'll be there in 30 minutes."

"See you in 20."

Click.

Ashley tossed the phone onto the couch. "Yeah, can't wait."

Maybe this was good though. She would be busy and be able to forget about John. She threw on some scrubs, pulled her hair up, and walked out into the cool darkness into what had become a very long night.

« finding home »

chapter twenty one

The cold air found and invigorated everything within Alice. She cringed at the thought of year-round heat and humidity. Of course for all she knew that could be exactly where God was taking her.

She opened the glass door of the Redwood Café, a town icon, and stepped inside. The aroma of exotic roasted beans and fresh coffee filled her, held her, along with the soft voices of people starting their day, and the buzz of espresso machines promising to help them.

"Morning Alice," Sarah chirped from behind the counter. Sarah and her family bought the drowning business before Alice came to Redwood and turned it around. She wiped her hands on her apron. "What can I get started for you?"

"Hey, Sarah," Alice replied. "Can I get a regular with room, please?"

"Sure. You want me to put a shot of espresso in it?"

"Sure, why not."

"Be up in a sec."

Alice watched her bring the machines to life. A familiar thought ran through her head: *I could be happy as a barista for a long time.* She grinned. *Maybe forever.*

Sarah placed a steaming cup on the counter. "Here you go sweetie."

"Thanks." Alice raised the cup and felt the heat on her face.

Sarah grabbed a rag. "I heard about what happened at the clinic the other day."

Alice almost choked on her coffee. "You did?"

"Mmhmm," Sarah replied. "And I'm not the only one. Old Hank Tanner is telling anyone who will listen about how you prayed for his leg and it was healed."

"Really?" A tremor worked through Alice's hands. She was still trying to process what had happened herself let alone worry about how others would react.

Sarah must've noticed the anxiety in her voice because she dropped the rag. "Oh nobody's upset or anything like that," she assured. "Actually, it's the opposite. Seems that people out of church for years are starting to show up. Even some folk who've never been." She leaned toward Alice like she was about to share a secret. "Hank's been very convincing and people are interested."

Alice's eyes were round as plates. People were going to church because of what she'd done? It was hard to believe. But so was what happened to Hank. But she could probably let the lingering fear of getting fired go at this point.

Sarah folded her arms over her chest. "You look like someone poured pop in your cheerios." She lifted her eyebrows. "Maybe you should give people around here a little more credit."

"Sorry," Alice mumbled. In her experience, people didn't deserve any credit. She fingered the cross charm resting against her chest. "Its amazing, Sarah. Really. Maybe I should be telling people too."

Sarah rocked her head. "Maybe. It's about time things like that started happening in this town. I bet business picks up at the clinic." She laughed, but then gave Alice a serious look. "Thank you for having the guts to do something most wouldn't."

Alice felt her cheeks get hot. "Um, you're welcome." She waved goodbye and scooted out into the morning. She wrinkled her nose at the sky. The sun was shining brightly, chasing away some of the cold and making it very comfortable, unusually comfortable. Normally weather for this time of year was cold followed by more cold.

She shook it off and gazed at a fluffy cloud. Out of all the people God could have used, he picked her. She brushed her hair back and studied her slender fingers. She was the essence of ordinary. And she was broken. Being healed, but definitely broken.

Alice swatted a gnat out of her face and wondered how the lake looked. She had the day off and nothing important to do, but before she could take

◄ finding home ►

a step a voice startled her.

"Beautiful morning isn't it?" Alice spun around to see an elderly black woman standing behind her. A tight bun held her gray hair and her face was highlighted by smiling brown eyes.

Alice almost dropped her coffee. "NITA!"

Nita laughed like a grandmother seeing grandchildren and squeezed her hand. "It's good to see you again child. Hope I didn't give you a start."

"What are you doing here?" Alice asked. "I mean, I'm happy you're here, but why?"

"God tells me to go somewhere and I go." She extended a finger at Alice. "I suspect this trip has something to do with you. Oh my!" She cried out and rotated in a circle. "When he told me to come here I asked him to warm it up a little." She clapped. "And he did, didn't He."

Alice twirled a strand of hair around her finger. "Yeah...I guess."

Nita chuckled. "Oh child, half the things he does for us we never recognize and the other half we argue." She didn't wait for Alice to respond. "Would you like to walk a bit?"

"Yes," Alice sputtered. They drifted down the sidewalk side by side. She really was happy to see Nita, but the woman put her stomach in knots. Their fist meeting had changed her life. She sipped her coffee and wondered what it was going to be this time.

"Well, let's have it then."

Alice lowered her cup. "Let's have what?"

"You have some questions and I'm not getting any younger."

Alice hesitated. "How did you—"

"My-my-my," Nita clucked. "Listen for the shepherds voice and you'll hear him talk about all sorts of things, important things. And not just for yourself, you hear, but for others as well."

The knot in Alice's stomach went from a single to a double. Does God show you *everything* about someone's life? Like, even all of the bad things they've done?"

"You mean is he gonna go blabbin your secrets to everyone."

Alice waited for a man in a suit to shuffle past them before nodding her head. "I've never met anyone like you. Someone who knows what I'm thinking or what's in my heart. I want to know more but it makes me

123

nervous too." Alice noticed a couple, hand in hand, on the other side of the street. She heard their voices on the wind and imagined for a moment that they were talking about her and the darkest moments of her life. She wrapped her jacket around her body. "I just, I don't know, feel a little too open around you. *Exposed* I guess."

Nita pursed her lips. "Now you listen here. I only know the things God chooses to share with me. If someone's life opens like a book to me it's only because God opened it. But that's not normally how it is. Usually God only shows me a couple things." Nita stopped and faced Alice. "God has a certain reason for showing me the things he does. And that reason always seems to be about understanding his mighty love and growing into all he's created us to be." She motioned behind them. "You saw that man pass us in the fancy suit?"

Alice nodded.

"Mmhmm, well I saw the love of God pour over his head like liquid gold." She wagged her finger in the air. "I suppose he'll be my next stop so I can let him know." She paused. "There is darkness there to be sure. There is in everyone. But I didn't see that. Father's focus is on the things that are beautiful. God is not a gossip and he's not out to embarrass anyone. He loves us too much for that." Nita continued down the sidewalk with Alice beside her. "I hope that helps," she added, "but we should get to what you're *really* worried about."

Alice giggled and shook her head. "Last time we met you told me that it's safe to remember. Do you remember?"

"I sure do."

"Well, that night I told God I was ready and would trust him no matter what."

"I thought you might," Nita said matter of fact. "What happened?"

Alice pointed at a bench beside them. "Can we sit for a minute?"

"Of course, dear."

She'd had the dream again last night. Alice hugged herself as Nita eased on the bench beside her. "I, started to have dreams: dreams that I've never had before. I don't understand them. I mean, they're not even *full* dreams."

"I see," Nita uttered. "Go on, dear."

"I see pictures flash. They're there and gone. Most of them are blurry

‹ finding home ›

but some are getting clearer." She sighed. "It doesn't matter. I still don't understand any of them." She brushed a strand of black hair back as her eyes flooded. No matter how hard she tried she couldn't piece the puzzle together.

"What kind of pictures are you seeing?" Nita wanted to know.

"Different kinds. Sometimes I see smiling faces I don't recognize. Other times I see a backyard with a swing set and slide." Alice glanced at Nita. "But there are others."

"Go on," Nita encouraged.

Alice fixed her eyes on the ground. "They scare me. I hear screams all around me in the dark." Alice swallowed. She saw herself there, blinded by the black nothingness. The screams were terrible, worse than anything she'd ever heard. They cut straight to her heart, and the pain stayed even after she woke up. She clutched the bench to steady herself. "Then I see explosions of red and yellow with dark trees everywhere."

"Tell me about the faces you see."

Alice closed her eyes and images floated before her. "A boy and a girl," she admitted carefully. "They are young looking…kids. They seem happy. I mean, I guess they're happy because they're smiling."

"What else?" Nita asked.

"That's it. I see their faces but they disappear so fast." Alice dug her heel into a dry leaf that had floated under the bench. She couldn't make them stay no matter how hard she tried.

"How do they make you feel?"

Alice blinked. "Feel?"

"Yes," Nita answered. "How do you feel when you see them?"

Safe. The word floated through Alice's mind instantly as if it was hurled at her. She squeezed her hands together. The list of people she felt safe around expired after just a few names. She stared at her hands. "It's just a dream, and it's silly, but they make me feel…safe."

Nita clucked her tongue. "Oh child. None of this is *silly*. You wouldn't be here talking to me if you really believed that." She raised an eyebrow. "It's new for you isn't it? Feeling safe."

Alice fixed her eyes on the street in front of her. But instead of seeing cars and people meandering by, she saw dark streets and puddle filled alleys.

She saw cruel faces with slits for eyes. She felt hands like sandpaper twist her arms and felt bruises on her face. There were needles and syringes and a way out. "Nita?"

"Yes, dear?"

"Who are those kids?" Alice turned pleading eyes on the older woman. "Do you know?"

"No, I don't." She reached out and held Alice's face in her hands. "But I think *you* know them. I think you know them very well."

"But how is that possible?" Alice questioned.

Nita brushed a strand of hair from her face and smiled. "I think God's starting to heal your memories. I think he's healing your mind but being careful not to give you more than what you can handle."

Alice melted. It was exactly what she was hoping, and dreading. "Do you think those faces I see could be..." She hesitated and swallowed the lump in her throat. "Could they be my family?"

Nita fell silent for a moment. "If God chose them to be the first ones you'd see, well, they must be very important to you."

Alice spun a plain band on her finger. "I'm so afraid that my family, my parents, were horrible people." She saw the boy and girl again and a smile tugged on the corner of her mouth. "But I guess if the kids I'm dreaming about are my family I'd like to know more, a lot more."

Nita patted Alice's knee. "All in good time dear. You're on a journey now and he'll lead you down the road."

Alice's smile vanished. "But what about the *other* pictures?"

Nita clasped her hands together. "It would be wonderful if everything you've forgotten was good. But no matter how much we want it, that's just not the kind of world we live in. In order to fix your heart God is going to have to show you the things that weren't so good. A trauma that can't be remembered is still a trauma and, remembered or not, it keeps hurting." Nita pointed to the sky and grinned. "But don't you worry, child. *He* is with you and will hold you through it all. He'll rejoice with you in the beautiful memories and cry with you in the ugly. And if you follow him through it, your heart will heal through every experience, the good and the bad."

Alice dabbed a tear from her cheek as the woman's words anchored

≺ finding home ≻

courage, strength, and resolve to her spirit. "I'm ready to remember it all. And I'm going to trust that God will be with me no matter what happened back then."

Nita rose and held out her hand. "I know you will." They continued on together a minute or so before Nita spoke again. "I do have something else to tell you."

Alice cocked her head to one side. "You do?"

Nita laughed. "Of course I do. I didn't come all the way here just to talk about your dreams." She stopped and took both of Alice's hands in her own. "Now this is very important, dear. You're going to meet a lady about my age. She's going to invite you to go with her. You need to go. Do you understand?"

Alice felt the blood leave her face. "No, I'm not sure I understand."

"Mmhmm," Nita responded. "I think you do."

"B, but," Alice felt her knees shake. "Who is she? Where does she want me to go?"

"I'm sorry," Nita apologized. "The good Lord didn't tell me. He only told me that it's very important to go with her. You're going to be surprised and scared, but you must go. He will be with you and you're going to be just fine."

"But who is it?" Alice persisted. "Where's she gonna take me? Where will I meet her? Why does she want me to—"

"Alice!" Nita's firm hands grasped her shoulders. "Sweet lord, child. There's no need to get all worked up," she assured. "It's going to be alright."

Don't be afraid. I AM with you. The words came on a soft breeze, caressing Alice's face. But she also felt them hold her, wrap around her like strong arms, safe arms. Slowly the world stopped spinning. Questions spread before her like a buffet, but she was going to be fine.

"Well, it's time for me to get on," Nita announced. "I need to find that fancy fella." She drew Alice into a tight hug. "It's been a pleasure, child. He has so much for you. So much more than you think."

"So, I won't be seeing you again?"

"Hard to say, dear. Hard to say." She gave Alice a wink and started toward wherever she'd come from.

Alice watched her a moment and then remembered Hank. "Nita!"

"Yes?"

"I almost forgot to tell you about how I prayed for a man who broke his leg," she gushed. "God healed it! It was amazing."

Nita's face lit up and she clapped her hands together. "That's wonderful dear! Just wonderful!" Alice could hear her singing a song about the love of Jesus that grew quieter as the distance grew. An old hymn or gospel song maybe. She smiled to herself and began the trek home.

You're going to meet someone…go with her. A breeze came out of the North and chilled her. She raised her cup and made a face as the cold coffee shocked her lips. She thought about what Nita said about God changing the weather for her. There was so much she didn't understand.

Alice dumped the cold coffee on the ground and climbed the steps leading to her front door. She hoped that God's love was growing around her like a fortress. That it would be there in the times of doubt and when the ground seemed to shake underneath her feet. She wasn't quite there yet, but she would be.

‹finding home›

‹chapter twenty two›

John was a piece of debris drifting in a black sea. He tried to move but his arms and legs were gone, along with his voice. A sharp sound like a clap echoed all around him. He strained his eyes, but more darkness flooded in.

Clap! John jerked toward the sound and heard the inflections of a voice, but it was too muffled to understand.

Suddenly, a narrow beam of light breached the darkness and it cleared the cobwebs from his brain. He was awake. Awake and lying on something soft. Tingles spread down his arms and legs like tiny electrical impulses. He still couldn't move but now he could feel and someone squeezed his left hand.

"…squeeze back if you…"

A woman's voice. *Amy?* John thought. *No, she's dead?* John felt pressure on his left hand again.

"…squeeze my hand if…"

John poured all the energy he could summon down his arm. The pressure left his hand and the voice vanished. Maybe he'd done it. Maybe she just got tired and left. John sent all of his strength to his eyelids, which weighed a ton each. He strained and light overwhelmed everything turning the blackness into a blurry, bright haze. It was like looking at the sun. He blinked a few times and noticed a cloudy figure hovering near his feet.

"John," the ghost let out. "Can you hear me?"

John waited for the world to come into focus. The *ghost* gave way to a male caught somewhere between boy and man, examining a clipboard in his hands. White walls met the ceiling on both sides, but in front only a curtain separated him from people scurrying back and forth like mice looking for cheese. He licked his cracked lips. "Where am I?"

The guy flinched and almost dropped the clipboard. "You're uh, in the ICU at Blackwater Memorial. I'm Dr. Davis and I've been taking care of you for the past couple of days."

An ache spread through John's head and the right side of his face. A quick inspection found it swollen and tender. He traced a thin tube hanging from a bag of clear fluid until it disappeared into his left forearm. A thicker tube stuck out from the right side of his chest and hooked into some kind of canister. He took a breath and instantly regretted it.

Dr. Davis stepped lightly to John's left side. "Do you remember what happened?"

John winced. "No, I—" And then he did remember. It all came rushing back like a rouge wave. Ashley. Jesus. The cross. The truck. Rolling.

Dr. Davis tapped his pen against the clipboard. "Late last Thursday night you were driving your truck when another driver swerved into your lane and hit you head on. Your truck rolled. When the paramedics arrived you were unconscious and barely breathing. They rushed you here and we took you right to surgery." He paused and checked his clipboard. "You had a subarachnoid bleed. In other words your brain was bleeding. In addition, your right lung had collapsed with multiple rib fractures, your pelvis was shattered and your right tibia and fibula were broken. Those are the two bones in your lower leg." He placed the clipboard on the bedside table. "I'm happy to say that the bleeding in your brain has been controlled and is healing. All of your other injuries have been stabilized and are mending as well. You've got quite a bit of recovery ahead of you, but right now things look pretty good, considering. I've gotta say, I wasn't very confident you would ever wake up. It's Monday morning. You've been in a coma for four days. Part of that was the medicine we gave you and the other part was just wait and see."

Four days… The pounding in John's head was relentless and the overflow of information didn't help. *Accident, brain bleed, lung, and what else?* John licked his lips again. "So, get this stuff off of me so I can go home."

"I'll attribute that comment to the pain meds."

"The, uh," John swallowed. "The other car, did they…"

Dr. Davis sighed. "There was one guy in the car. He died at the scene.

‹ finding home ›

They think he fell asleep." He eased himself into a chair and leaned over his knees. "Listen John, we're going to take good care of you. We'll manage your pain and help you sleep. How well you do early on will help determine when we can get you out of the ICU and down to the floor. Once there we can start some rehab. But let's take it one step at a time alright?"

John nodded before he remembered the pain it would cause.

Dr. Davis rose and acknowledged someone John didn't notice had entered the room. His heart nearly stopped when he saw her. *I'm a nurse at Blackwater Memorial...in the ICU.* Ashley's blonde hair was pulled back in a simple ponytail. Her green eyes sparkled, but dark circles told a different story. Blue scrubs fell loosely over her tan skin. She cast a quick glance at him before focusing on Dr. Davis.

"Ashley's going to give you something for pain and sleep," Dr. Davis informed him and scribbled on his chart.

Ashley kept her eyes low as she approached with the pain medicine. He remembered it all, how he'd treated her, the things he'd said. The shame and guilt was worse than any of his physical injuries.

"I'll check in on you later, John," Dr. Davis called as he disappeared through the curtain.

Ashley reached for John's IV and her perfume washed over him. His heart raced and he gripped the sheet with his right hand. She was close enough to touch. He could call out, apologize, and tell her he was wrong. Let her know that he's different.

Heat raced up the back of his neck and he tasted metal. The medicine was in. It was in and Ashley was trailing away. Maybe that was best. The room began to fade and he felt much lighter, like he was floating on a cloud. Sleep yanked on his eyelids. But just before he drifted off he could have sworn he felt something. He wasn't certain. Maybe it was the medication but it felt like someone squeezed his hand.

❦

Ashley let John's hand slip from hers and hurried from the room. She managed to avoid all eyes and questions and closed the bathroom door just as four days worth of emotion finally breeched the surface. She slumped against the wall and buried her face in her hands.

Ashley cried until all her tears were gone and wiped her face on her sleeve. She closed her eyes and leaned her head against the wall. "God," she whispered. "Please tell me what to do." She swallowed and felt her eyes fill again.

"Ashley, darlin'? Are you okay?" It was Tina, a staple in the ICU like milk and eggs to a fridge. She was a southern bell in her 60's complete with a southern accent. She'd shared many teas, casseroles, and tears when Ashley's marriage fell apart.

Ashley dabbed her eyes and willed her voice to be steady. "Yeah Tina I'm fine." Her voice broke on the last word.

"You sound about as fine as a kicked puppy," Tina answered. "I'm comin' in, alright?"

Ashley hesitated, but then reached up and unlocked the door. Tina stepped through and sank to the floor beside her. "Oh, sweetie, what's got you in a fix?"

Ashley felt her bottom lip quiver. "I just…"

Tina draped her arm around Ashley's shoulder and pulled her close. "Does this have anything to do with that boy in 412, John Caban?"

Ashley felt her face flush and kept her eyes on the floor. She felt like a broken teenager. Sprawled on the bathroom floor because of a guy.

"I figured," Tina stated. "I took note of all the time you spent in there waiting for him to brighten up. It's easy to see just how much you care for him."

Ashley gave her a half smile and rubbed her eyes. "I really do, a lot."

"Well, that boy is sure blessed then," Tina declared and squeezed her hand.

Ashley sniffed. "But I've known him less than a *week*."

"*Ashley.*" Tina gushed. "When Fred n' I got engaged after two weeks people said we were actin' crazier than a couple of sprayed roaches. We've been married for 30 years." She gave Ashley a reassuring smile. "I reckon when you know, you know."

Ashley blinked. "I didn't know that about you."

"Well, you don't know everything about me, hon," Tina teased and

‹ finding home ›

motioned around the bathroom. "But you're not locked in here because of how long you've known him."

Ashley shook her head. "The night of his accident we were together and," Ashley swallowed the lump in her throat, "things didn't really end well."

Tina dropped her head to one side. "What do you mean?"

Ashley sighed. "Let's just say he pretty much told me it was over and he never wanted to see me again." Ashley winced at the memory. "Seeing him just a few hours later on the table, dying..." She straightened and faced Tina. "I was so scared. I prayed so hard that he would live. And God answered with two miracles. He lived and woke up." She snatched some paper towels and blew her nose. "It's amazing and I'm so happy but I don't know what to do now."

Tina drew her into another tight hug. "I'm so sorry, Ashley. Would you take some advice?"

Ashley wiped her cheeks. "Anytime."

"I've found that sometimes the best thing to do is nothin'."

Ashley made a face. "*Nothing.*"

"That's right. It's simple to panic and run around doing this and that. But that usually makes things worse. If you're patient you might be surprised at how things turn out." Tina covered Ashley's hands with her own. "Just give it some time, pretty girl. Give that boy a chance to come around."

Ashley closed her eyes. *God I need you now. I need your help.*

Ashley, I love you and I'm here for you. Find your rest in me. The words streamed peace through her. She opened her eyes and smiled. "Thanks, Tina. I think you're right."

"Of course I am, darlin'," Tina exclaimed and winked.

Ashley laughed and climbed to her feet. "I think I'm ready to get out of here."

"Thank the good lord for that," Tina spouted and stood. "Dear God in the mornin', you had to pick the smallest bathroom to cram yourself into."

Ashley giggled and smiled at her friend. "Thanks, Tina. Really."

"Oh, don't you worry about a thing," Tina replied. "Now go home and get some rest."

Ashley yawned. "Believe me, I'm on my way."

John woke up to a man in scrubs checking and fiddling with his IV and various tubes. He glanced at a clock on the wall, 1PM.

He picked the sleep from his eyes. He flexed his hands and noticed more strength than before. "Is it still Monday?"

The man didn't stop working. "Yeah, it's still Monday."

John surveyed the room. "Where's Ashley?"

"She went home," the nurse told him. "Had to happen sooner or later."

John lifted his head. "What are you talking about? What do you mean—ouch!"

"There you go," the nurse muttered and held up a needle in its sheath. "Had to replace your IV." He tossed the needle in a sharps container before turning on his heels to face John. "First of all stop being a baby and second, Ashley's been here pretty much every moment since Thursday night when you came in." He pointed to a chair next to John's bed. "She spent most of her time there waiting for something to happen."

"Did you say the whole time?"

The nurse rolled his eyes. "No, I said *pretty much* every moment. Couldn't make her leave. Believe me I tried." He scooped up a plastic container and set it on the table next to John. "Your lunch," he announced and left.

John briefly imagined wrapping his hands around the nurse's neck but there were more important things to consider.

Spent most of her time there…couldn't make her leave…

The words circled around John, making him dizzy. He pressed his fingers into his forehead as familiar voices sneered in his ear. *You don't deserve her. You're not worthy of anyone like that.* He blinked away tears.

John spent the next hour or so eating and watching re-runs of some sitcom he couldn't remember the name of. The food wasn't bad, turkey on wheat and Jell-O. The nurse who woke him up earlier was in and out to check on him and offer snide remarks.

The food felt good in his stomach, but he could still feel the ache in his head and body. He wondered how long it had been since his last dose of pain meds and when it would be time for more.

◄ **finding home** ►

"By god you've got a visitor," his nurse said from the curtain. "There's actually some besides Ashley that cares about you." He chuckled at his observation. "You up for it?"
Within arms reach, John thought. Just once. "They got pain meds with them?"
"That your way of telling me you're ready for the next round?"
"You cracked that code, huh?"
The nurse shook his head. "Visitor or not?"
John gave an exaggerated sigh. "Show them in I guess."
A couple seconds later his boss trudged around the corner and into his room. Stan was a large man. Tall and husky and rough around the edges.
John threw Stan a look. He wasn't known for making visits to anyone. Or for being personable at all. It's why they'd gotten along so well.
"You don't look happy to see me," Stan mocked hurt and shoved his hands in his pockets.
"I was just hoping it was someone much better looking," John replied.
Stan laughed a raspy, smokers sound and stepped to the foot of the bed. "Well, you just look terrible," he observed. "I mean really, really bad."
"I almost died," John retorted. "What's your excuse?"
Stan laughed again. "It's good to see you, John. When are you gonna stop being a girl and get your ass back to work?"
John gave him a smug smile. "Things fallin' apart without me, eh?"
Stan smirked. "Runnin' smoother than ever."
"I'll believe *that* when I see it."
Stan rubbed the back of his neck. "In all seriousness take all the time you need. I'll handle all the details. You just get better. There's plenty of incompetent idiots to put buildings together 'round here."
John gave him a slight nod. "Thanks Stan. I appreciate it."
They talked a bit longer about the things most men are comfortable discussing like sports and work and then Stan left. John was glad he didn't stay long. He was getting tired again and he could feel the pain in his head and body starting to intensify.
To his delight the nurse ambled in with another dose of dilaudid and it wasn't long till he was asleep.

chapter twenty three

John's eyes snapped open. He wasn't alone. Everything was still and quiet except for the soft sound of shoes shuffling across the floor on the other side of the curtain. He willed his eyes to adjust faster than they could.

"Who's there?" he asked. There was no answer, but peace surrounded him like a warm bath. John glanced at the clock. 2 AM. "Who's there?" he asked again.

A light flickered to life on John's left, bright enough to illuminate a man smiling at him from a cushy chair reserved for visitors. He wore tan pants, a long-sleeved flannel shirt, and an old dirty hat that used to be white. His voice was crisp like mountain air. "Morning, John."

John blinked. His throat was jammed with everything he wanted to say. "So, I got hit by a truck," he finally stammered.

Jesus's mouth formed a straight line. "I know."

"The other guy's dead."

Grief hung on his words like dew. "Yes, he is."

John toyed with his blanket. "I'm not very good at conversation."

A half smile pulled at Jesus's mouth. "I'm aware."

"Visiting hours are over." John pinched his forehead. "I'm sorry. I'm really trying not to be an idiot."

Jesus leaned over his knees. "It's okay, John."

John reached out and poked Jesus's leg. "You're *really* here, right? I'm not dreaming or hallucinating..." John fell back on his pillow. "Oh god, I'm hallucinating. I guess it's not surprising. I mean, they've been giving me some powerful drugs and—"

"Calm down, John," Jesus instructed and took hold of his arm. "You're not dreaming or hallucinating. I'll pinch you if you want."

John fixed his eyes on Jesus. *I don't know him,* he thought.

"I guess that's true, in part."

John stiffened. "Huh? What's true?"

"You *don't* know me very well. But there's nothing I want more than to change that."

John studied him and folded his fingers together. Jesus lifted his chin. "Something on your mind?"

"Wouldn't you know?"

Jesus blurted out a laugh. "That's very good John."

John rubbed the back of his neck and motioned to the entrance. "Can't they hear—"

"Nope."

"And they wouldn't be able to see—"

"Uh-uh."

"So, they're just gonna hear me talking to myself?"

Jesus grinned. "They won't hear that either."

John fell silent while he considered that. "Well then, I guess we've got some time."

"All the time we need." Jesus smiled while John pulled his sheet around in random patterns. "It's okay to ask," he assured.

John twisted the blanket a few more times before shooting a look at Jesus. "I almost died in a crash right after I left you."

Jesus's lips came together. *You think I did this.* John could still see his face gnarled like a tree trunk when Jesus stammered those words back in the park. He swallowed. "I'd...like to get to know you and believe you had nothing to do with all this." *And my family.* "But I don't know if I can."

Jesus' eyes danced like a colored flame as he leaned forward. "I most certainly want to explain. More than you could possibly imagine. And I *will* help you understand what you can."

John stared at the curtain and watched it change before his eyes. It blurred and became a dirt road lined by ditches that stretched away from his little room. Only the first foot or so was lighted. He couldn't see where it ended.

"There are answers scattered all along the road," Jesus explained. "We will find them together. With every step you'll understand more. We'll get where you want to be. But we can't start there."

John shook his head and the curtain reformed. The path faded like the end scene of a movie. "You're asking a lot."

Jesus's voice was so close, like a lover's whisper. "No, John, I ask for everything. Every part of you that stays in the world remains out of me. I love you. Because of that I can't ask for anything less than your *whole* heart. It's the only way you can truly know mine."

John lifted heavy eyes to Jesus. His voice strained. "I don't know if I can do it."

Jesus' face was steady. "I gave everything I possibly could for you, John. I'll help you every step of the way."

John stacked a scale in his mind. If he staggered forward there would be no turning back. He considered the old life that waited for him before fixing his resolve on Jesus. "Okay, where do we start?"

"The beginning."

"The beginning," John echoed. "What's that?"

Jesus slapped the chair. "LOVE!"

John yelped and jerked as if he'd been shocked. He scrambled for his now tangled blankets, flopping IV tubing and rattling the canister connected to his chest. He glared at Jesus who was bent at the waist laughing.

"I'm sorry," Jesus apologized and swiped a tear from his face.

"Yeah, real funny," John grumbled. "I guess WWJD means *scare the cripple.*"

"Whew," Jesus exclaimed and leaned back in the chair. "Really, I'm sorry. I wasn't trying to scare you. I just get excited about love."

"I noticed."

"There's nothing greater, John. Nothing more powerful. Laws are intended to modify behavior, but only love can change a heart. Only love can mend a broken relationship. That's where we start. You don't really trust me, but I want you to. In fact, I *need* you to trust me because it's the only way I can help you. The only way that's ever going to happen is for you to believe I love you fully and completely."

"But I do believe that. Or, I did anyway."

Jesus raised an eyebrow. "The mouth opens and anything can come out.

◄ **finding home** ►

But action is a statement of belief." He tapped the center of his chest. "Our true beliefs are tucked in our hearts and come out in the way we live."

John fell silent for a moment. "Do you know how strange it is for me to be talking to you like this?"

"I can appreciate that. Do you understand what I'm telling you?"

"I got it," John answered. "I can *say* I believe you love me, but my life or actions tell a different story. I'm not agreeing to that by the way," he quickly added.

Jesus folded his hands over his lap. "Is it okay if I ask you a question?"

"Can I even say, 'no'?"

"You can say whatever you want."

John drummed his fingers on the bed trying to decide if he believed that. "Okay, go ahead."

"Whose job is it to take care of you?"

John stiffened. "What?"

"Whose job is it to look out for you: to provide for you, to make sure that you have what you need to live. Who helps you in tough situations, holds and comforts you when you're sad, and rejoices with you when you're happy?"

Bits of Sunday school lessons and sermons John's brain had archived came rushing back. "Before Amy and the kids died I would've said that's your job."

"Right," Jesus confirmed. "But did you *really* believe that?"

"Yeah, I mean, I think so." He shifted. "Yeah, I definitely did."

"You had a supervisor at the power plant back in Oak Harbor. He made life very difficult for you."

John didn't answer. His boss had been a special kind of jerk. The kind that made him stay late and come in on weekends. Every time John messed up it was announced and circulated by the guy. Every now and then he would hear his tone in someone else and his blood would boil. "What about him?"

"It seemed like you could've used a hand dealing with him. Who'd you go to for help?"

John felt a knot twist in his stomach. "Nobody."

"What about when Kayla was born and you and Amy were struggling with money?"

John stared at the blanket. They could barely pay the bills. He still didn't know how they put food on the table. He cast a quick glance at Jesus as the edge of his point began to poke through.

"Did you come to me for help?" Jesus asked.

"No."

Jesus slid closer. His voice was soft. "Did you come to me and let me hold you when your family died? Did you come to me for comfort?"

John jerked away and clutched the bed rail. The scab being picked was different this time. "No, I didn't."

Jesus pressed on. "Can you remember one single time in which you asked me to help you through a difficult situation?"

No. The answer was there before he even thought about it. "I'm not the guy who asks for help," he muttered and faced Jesus. "Amy, she would ask. She would pray but I've always done everything myself."

"There's a reason," Jesus let him know.

John grimaced and suddenly wasn't in the hospital anymore. He was in the dank basement of his childhood home. The smell of stale rags drifted from dark corners. He was an eight-year-old kid standing on the concrete floor in front of his scowling father. In his hands was a broken model airplane. "Can you help me fix my plane?" His voice squeaked on the last word.

"Who's gonna help me fix *this?*" his dad spat and pointed at pieces of a carburetor that were spilled around a rusted lawn mower. "Nobody, and that's the way it'll always be. No one's gonna look out for you but you. Fix it yourself."

John sniffed. "But I don't know how."

"Then you'd best learn," he shot back. "And stop sniveling! Damn tears aren't gonna help anyone do anything." He pointed a wrench at John's face. "God helps men who help themselves. Don't you ever forget it."

And he never had. More memories poured in, each one carrying his fathers shaking head and stern voice telling him that the only one he could ever trust was himself. *People will always let you down,* his father pounded into him. John fixed his eyes on the wall. "I looked up to him, you know? My father. He always said nobody ever helped him do anything. I wanted to be like him. I wouldn't ask for help if he didn't." John bit the inside of his cheek. "I wanted to be a *man* just like him." He threw a look at Jesus. "You

◄ finding home ►

help people who help themselves, isn't that right?"

Jesus rose and paced to the window. John watched a look of admiration appear on his face as he studied the stars. When he circled back his lips were tight. "John, you need to understand something very important. Your father, I loved him so much. There were many things he did that made me smile."

John couldn't recall the man *ever* smiling let alone anyone smiling at him.

Jesus leaned over the back of the chair. "While there were parts of my heart he *did* reflect there were other things, things he learned from his own father and the world, that he passed on to you. Things that aren't a part of me at all."

John considered that. "What things?"

"Well for starters, he taught you that I only help those who help themselves. The truth is that the only ones I can help are those who understand they *can't* help themselves. Standing on the pillar of independence keeps me pinned to the sidelines where I have to watch sandy foundations crumble." Jesus moved around and fell into the chair. "It's the same ol' thing time after time. People forge ahead without me, experience a measure of success, and it all comes crashing down. Often times they begin to rebuild on that same weak foundation despite all my efforts to open their eyes."

John winced as he thought about the times he'd driven up the ladder only to have every rung fall out at the top. *That's life,* he'd say as bitterness and failure settled deeper into his heart. He was always on the lookout for the climb. "So what is it then, you get mad at not being involved so you destroy what we've worked so hard for?"

"A fair question," Jesus answered and his eyes sparked with fiery yellows and oranges. "But let me remind you that I AM light. There is no darkness in me at all. It's not about punishment. Every time you move forward on your own, you do so with a lack of wisdom and a lack of knowledge. *That's* what causes the inevitable fall. Independence is ignorance. I'm the only one who can see all of the curves, traps, pitfalls, and schemes, so I'm the only one who can lead you safely through it. When I'm invited to be a part of the journey there is *only* success. That's what it means to build your house on the rock."

The words were a battering ram against John's heart. *Negative consequences aren't divinely inspired but rather the natural result of choices.* He absently toyed with some of his IV tubing.

Jesus continued. "None of that matters if you don't believe that I want to be *everything* for you." His voice was softer now, closer. "John, I stood right beside you through every single difficult situation. I reached for you. You didn't see me but I was there. I was wisdom and insight. Provision and guidance. I was ready to give you rest, strength, courage, and the kind of peace that would've held you through it all." Jesus gave him a look that begged him to understand. "You didn't have to do it alone."

I'm not like your dad, John… John shut his eyes and saw the structure of what he'd known his whole life crash against the wave of what Jesus was now telling him. *Whose job is it to take care of you?* He started at the sensation of Jesus's hand on his own and examined his face. It was a calm sea.

"I've been trying to help and take care of you through every broken toy and every shed tear," Jesus lamented. "I wanted to hold you when your father had nothing to offer but anger. I could've helped you find a way to deal with your supervisor that wouldn't have led to your suspension. I had an answer for your finances that wouldn't have put your marriage at risk. There was a way to grieve that wouldn't have led you to the life you've been living for the past ten years. But you wouldn't let me in." His voice cracked on the last word. "You wouldn't let me because you didn't believe I loved you enough for all that. But you're wrong. I love you so much more than you could ever imagine."

John blinked the sting away from his eyes. "I didn't get it."

He felt Jesus's hand on his shoulder. "I know, John."

Grief and regret stabbed John in turn. "I'm sorry," he whispered. Tears dropped onto John's cheeks. "I'm sorry for all the pain, for the way I…" He couldn't make his mouth cooperate with his heart. "I just—"

Jesus caressed John's cheek and smiled in a way that lit the whole room. "I forgive you, John."

John wiped his face on the sheet and gave Jesus a sideways look. "Just like that?"

Jesus chuckled. "It's always just like that."

◄ finding home ►

Fingers of joy were flicking away John's guilt and shame. Jesus engulfed him in his arms and kissed him on the cheek. "I love you, John."

John rocked back. The words held substance this time. For the first time in his life he felt the power of them. "I, I think I know that now."

They sat together for a while longer as John let the events work through him. Truth displaced lies and began to take root. He was disappointed when Jesus leaned over and hugged him goodbye. "I'll be seeing you again soon," he assured and vanished behind the curtain.

John thought he might hear one of the nurses' yelp with surprise, but then remembered he wouldn't. It wasn't long before sleep took him and he drifted off, wrapped in peace he never wanted to let go of.

chapter twenty four

Alice stared at the fish gliding easily around the tank. "Do you guys hate Mondays as much as me?" She took a look around the waiting room. It was empty, save one elderly woman who was eyeing her. "Oh, not you Mrs. Jincy. I was talking to the fish."

"Okay, dear," the woman muttered before returning to her magazine. "I'm actually quite fond of Mondays."

"Of course you are you crazy old—"

"What's that, dear?"

Alice put on her best smile. "Nothing, Mrs. Jincy."

"Would you like a sweet?"

"No, Mrs. Jincy."

The woman rummaged through her purse. "I've got a caramel in here somewhere…"

Alice rolled her eyes and glanced at the appointment sheet. Mrs. Jincy was in for her check-up but nothing else was scheduled for another thirty minutes. She yawned and considered a quick nap. Sleep had been a stranger. Every time she closed her eyes the last meeting with Nita played on a loop. Fear and faith were locked in a fight to the death. God was preparing her to leave, but with a complete stranger?" Alice pressed her fingers into her temples. The whole thing was nuts. Nita must've gotten it wrong. God wouldn't—

"Excuse me."

Alice gasped and jerked her head to see a pleasant woman in her 60's stationed in front of the counter. "Good morning," the woman chirped. "I'm sorry, I didn't mean to startle you."

◀ finding home ▶

Alice blushed and cleared her throat. "It's okay. I didn't hear you come in."

Mrs. Jincy waved her hand through the air. "I found one, but it doesn't have a wrapper bless its heart."

"No thank you, Mrs. Jincy." Alice smiled. "What can I do for you, Ma'am?"

The woman studied her for a moment before answering. "Oh, yes well I'm here to see someone." She placed her purse on the counter.

"Okay," Alice said shaking off the awkward moment. She ran a finger down the schedule. "Do you have an appointment?"

The woman nodded. "I do, but not for a check-up or anything."

Alice eyed the stranger. Sometimes vendors stopped by to try and sell equipment or get patient referrals for Home Healthcare. But Alice thought she looked a little old to be a vendor. "Do you need to see Dr. Tishner?"

The woman shook her head and folded her hands on the counter. "No, I think I'm here to see you."

Alice straightened and scrutinized the older woman. She was shorter than Alice, but a lot of women were. Her shoulder length white hair was neatly styled. The lines in her face betrayed her years, but it was vibrant and fresh. She was dressed plainly, in slacks and an oversized sweatshirt. Her coat hung over her arm. Alice was pretty sure they'd never met. "Me?"

The woman smiled. "Yes, Alice. I'm here to see you."

Mrs. Jincy appeared and placed the caramel on the counter. "Here you go, dear."

"Thanks," Alice sputtered.

"A sweet for a sweet," she sang and chuckled her way back to the chair.

Alice swung her attention back to the stranger. "I'm sorry, do I know you?"

"No, I don't suppose you do," the woman said and extended her hand through the window. "Claire Summers."

Alice hesitated before taking her hand. "Alice Baker. But you already knew that. How did you know that?"

Claire fidgeted with a small diamond ring on her finger, "I don't really know how to say this so I'm just going to come out with it."

Alice pushed her chair back a few inches. "Okay."

Claire fixed her eyes on Alice. "Alice, I'm here to take you home with me."

You're going to meet a woman...you need to go with her. The words spun around her head making her dizzy. "What did you say?"

"I know how crazy that sounds but I, I think you were expecting this." She paused. "I hope you were anyway."

Nausea ripped through Alice. *Not now! Not this soon!* She tried to rise but her legs were jelly. The woman blurred like an undeveloped Polaroid and Alice grasped the edge of the counter.

"Alice? Are you okay?"

Alice felt the woman touch her hand and reeled back. "I..." she climbed to her feet fighting another wave of nausea. "Excuse me."

Mrs. Jincy raised her voice from her seat. "Would you like another sweet?"

Alice aimed for the break room using the walls for support. She made it to a chair just before her legs gave out. Feeling fled from her lips and needles stung her fingers. Panic attacks used to come all the time, but over the past few years they'd steadily decreased and then disappeared altogether. She was well on her way to one now.

Control your breathing! She clutched her tightening chest. Everything was moving, closing in around her and squeezing her like a python. She was losing. It was too late.

Oh, God! she prayed, *I need you. Please help me.*

Suddenly out of the pressing darkness of her mind a white dove emerged. She watched it glide to her and gently settle on her head. Heat began to spread through her, as if she was standing in the sun. It calmed and soothed as it worked through skin, muscle, organs, and everything else.

I'm here Alice. I'm always here. Don't be afraid because I am lighting your path and would never take you somewhere that's bad for you. Trust Me. It's okay, I'm safe.

Alice blinked and rubbed her eyes. The python, numbness, and needles were gone. "Thank you," she whispered. Another warm wave answered her. Her slender fingers flipped away a few tears as someone slid into the chair next to her. She flinched. "How did you get back here?"

Claire motioned over her shoulder. "The door was open. Look, I know

◄ finding home ►

this is a shock. It's just as weird for me as it is for you." She paused. "I'm just trying my best to follow the Lord."

Alice managed a weak smile. She felt Claire's hand on her own, but this time didn't pull away.

"I know you're scared," Claire affirmed. "So am I. I almost didn't come here. But I know God has something in store for both of us that's probably way beyond anything we can imagine. As unusual as this is, if we can just follow him I think we have a chance to experience something really great. Even when it doesn't make sense. *Especially* when it doesn't make sense."

Alice dropped her face into her hands. "I'm sorry. I should've been ready for this." She gave a frustrated laugh. "It's not like I wasn't warned."

"Oh, don't apologize. I can't say I didn't panic a little about this."

Alice dropped her head to one side. "How *did* you find out…er know…or whatever about this?"

"An angel told me in a dream. How about you?"

Alice grinned. "A woman on the street."

"Well, there you go."

Alice crossed her arms over her chest. "This is the most ridiculous conversation I've ever had."

Claire laughed. "You and me both. Oh," Claire pulled out a mint. "The woman out front wanted me to give this to you."

Alice giggled. "Good old Mrs. Jincy." She took the mint and plopped it in her mouth. "So, where are you taking me?"

"Oak Harbor," Claire answered with a twinkle in her eye. "Oak Harbor, Ohio."

chapter twenty five

Dr. Davis hovered at the foot of John's bed staring at the clipboard in his hands. Deep creases spread across his forehead. "I just don't get it."

John snorted and looked out the window. Sunlight was breaking through the scattered clouds. He tried and failed to remember ever feeling the kind of peace he felt now.

I love you John. I want to take care of you.

The words were freedom and even now they held him like strong arms. John stretched his hands above his head and almost laughed out loud. There was no pain in his chest. There hadn't been since Jesus visited him. Whatever they'd given him while he slept worked.

He rotated back to Dr. Davis, who was now peering at him as if he was a puzzle that needed to be put together. "Listen doc, I know I'm good-looking and all, but you're gonna have to keep the gawking to a minimum."

Dr. Davis sighed and spun his clipboard so John could see the black and white x-rays. "I was just saying that I don't understand this."

John made a face. "That's nice to hear from my *doctor*."

"Yes, well it's a miracle you're hearing anything." Dr. Davis flipped his clipboard back around. "But that's certainly not the *only* miracle."

John leaned forward. "You wanna share now or wait until you grow up and become a *real* doctor?"

He stepped to John's side. "I once attended a seminar devoted to managing the *difficult patient*. I'm thrilled to meet the inspiration."

"Pleasure's all mine."

Dr. Davis pressed his hands against the sides of John's chest. "How does this feel? Is there any discomfort at all?"

"No," John answered, "Whatever you gave me worked." He swiveled side to side. "It doesn't hurt to breathe or move. But it's kinda weird to know you can pump me full of whatever without waking me up."

"That's just it, John," Dr. Davis spouted and stood up straight. "I didn't give you anything."

"Right, the nurse did."

He shook his head and glanced at the chart. "The last time you had pain meds was 10 o'clock last night."

John studied the young doctor's face. "You're serious?"

"Yes."

"Then why doesn't my chest hurt?"

"I don't really know John." He hesitated. "Well, I guess I do know but I don't understand any of it." Dr. Davis lowered himself on the edge of the bed and help up an x-ray. "I don't see any injuries to your chest. In fact, I can't find any evidence that you even *had* an injury to begin with. He flicked the picture with the back of his hand. "The only thing there that shouldn't be is the tubing."

John gripped the bed rails. "I never even had an injury? Then what was all that pain from?" He leveled a finger at Dr. Davis. "If you think I was just making it all up—"

Dr. Davis waved his hands. "You misunderstand. Let me explain. The night you came to us we placed a simple chest tube to relieve the air trapped on the outside of your lung. Usually that works just fine and the lung inflates. But sometimes, in severe cases like yours, it doesn't work and we have to try something more invasive." He paused. "We used a chemical to scar your lung tissue. It's an effective procedure. It usually takes about five days for lungs to respond and then inflate. Then it's about a month before the patient can resume normal activities although it's unlikely the patient will ever be completely pain free again." He flipped through a couple of pages on the chart he was holding. "Yesterday morning your chest x-ray showed that your lung was only 40% inflated." He flipped back to the front page, another x-ray, and looked at John. "Today your lung is 100% inflated and I can't find any trace of injury *or* the scaring we put there Saturday night. Your lung, both of them in fact, look perfect. More than perfect. They look brand new." He ran a hand through his hair. "I have no explanation for you."

Trapped air. Scared lung tissue. Nothing wrong. Brand new lungs. John blinked at the doctor. "Are you sure about this?"

"I've been over the results a hundred times. I can't be any *more* sure."

"How?" John wanted to know.

"I don't know."

"Let me see those." John grabbed the x-rays. The black and white images were as good as ancient Arabic to him. He dropped them to his lap. "You've gotta help me out here, doc. Give me something."

Dr. Davis gathered the x-rays. "It's almost enough to make me believe God actually exists."

The words slapped John across the face. *No pain since Jesus. No pain meds. New lungs.* Dr. Davis was saying something about reduced pain meds and rehab and something else. John wasn't really listening and hardly noticed him leave the room. Instead, he was looking at the chair occupied by Jesus hours before. John could still see him sitting there smiling, loving him without even having to speak.

"Did you do this?" he whispered.

"Did I do what?" came a sharp voice near the curtain.

John sighed when he saw it was his nurse.

"Listen, John," he mocked. "You might not need pain meds for your chest but if you keep talking to yourself I'll have to get you a whole *new* set of meds."

"What do you want? And when do I get a different nurse?"

He grinned and held up a package. "Craft time, and never. Let's see your bird feeder skills."

"I'll tell you what you can do with that bird feeder."

"Why do you think I'm standing back here?" He tossed the package onto John's bed and scurried away.

Lunch came and went and eventually boredom beat against his head like a drum. He picked up the craft and got to work. An hour later he held up a diner any bird would be proud to eat at.

"That's a nice bird feeder," Mike commented from just inside the curtain. "Sorry ma'am, do you know where I can find my friend John Caban?"

"Look at you," John exclaimed. "You been hittin' the gym?"

‹ finding home ›

Mike stood a little taller and admired his arms. "I have been actually."

"Huh," John uttered. "Can't tell."

Mike rolled his eyes and found the chair next to John's bed. "Ha-ha very funny."

"I hope you didn't come all the way down here just to see me."

"Naw, I had some dry cleaning to pick up." He slapped John's shoulder. "Of course you're the reason I came you idiot. Who else?"

"I don't know. I just wasn't expecting to see you I guess."

Mike leaned back in the chair. "This may be hard for you to understand, but some people actually have hearts. I've been in and out since the accident."

John tossed him the birdfeeder. "Consider it a token of my thanks."

"Great," Mike murmured and turned the feeder over in his hands. "This'll be perfect for my new rifle."

"What's that you were saying about hearts?"

"Don't remember."

"Not surprised."

"So," Mike set the craft on the table. "How you holdin' up?"

John adjusted his blanket over his waist. "Pretty good, considering." He pressed a few fingers into his chest. "Really good actually."

"I came in a couple of times over the weekend. One of the nurses called yesterday to let me know you were up, but work was crazy and visiting hours were over once I got off."

"No worries man," John told him. "Who called you?"

Mike pinched his chin. "Um, Ashley I think. The same nurse that was here whenever I stopped by." A wry smile tugged at his mouth. "Real pretty. Much too pretty to be hanging 'round you. Something going on I should know about?"

John realized he was squeezing the sheet and relaxed his grip. "No, nothing."

"Didn't seem like nothing," Mike pressed. "Not with the way she was taking care of you."

"What are you talking about?"

"Like I said, she was here every time I stopped by. Anything you needed she'd already done it." He wiped his nose on a napkin. "At least when I was here."

Guilt grew fangs and tore at John's stomach. "She's just someone I met."

"Pfft, sure doesn't seem like *just someone*."

"She's just some *girl*, Mike," John blurted. "It's nothing." The edge of the curtain fluttered but when he looked no one was there.

Mike was holding up his hands. "Okay-okay." They were quiet for a few moments before Mike changed the subject. "Nellie's been asking about you."

Nellie. Her name held the appeal of snotty eggs. He tried to sound interested. "Oh yeah?"

Mike nodded. "Yeah, I told her to forget about you and that I'm available anytime she wants to trade up."

"Go ahead and take your shot, buddy."

Mike frowned. "You okay?"

John waved him off. "Yeah, I'm fine. What's new at Joes?"

Mike's voice joined the background noise of beeping machines and shuffling feet. *She was here every time I stopped in.* John studied the sunlight reaching towards him through the window. The forecast stated a 100% chance of rain, but not one drop had hit the glass. In fact, there wasn't a cloud in the sky. Was that the way of it then? Things that are certain becoming something unexpected? He flexed his toes. He was just being stupid. Weather changes but people don't. But hadn't he?

"You know what I'm sayin'?" Mike held an expectant look.

John blinked. "That's crazy," he offered a little too much like a question. It seemed to satisfy Mike who plowed ahead with whatever he'd been talking about. John chewed the inside of his cheek. Maybe there was hope for him and Ashley after all.

"Well, I'm gonna head out." Mike clamored to his feet and stretched. "I've got third shift tonight." He smacked John's leg. "Rest up."

"Mike," John called just as he reached the curtain.

Mike pivoted to face him. "Yeah?"

"Thanks for coming by. I really appreciate it."

Mike hesitated. "Sure, John." His eyes darted around the room. "Just uh," he cleared his throat. "Just don't make it awkward alright?"

John chuckled as his friend disappeared.

≺ finding home ≻

John woke as the last of the sun disappeared into the horizon dragging its orange and yellow display along. He lay still as his eyes adjusted to the blinking lights of the TV he'd left on and hoped he hadn't missed dinner.

John switched on the light in time to see a familiar figure leaving the room. "Ashley?" Her name was out before he could stop it. She stopped and stood still, as if trapped between two walls. John willed her to move. To speak. To do *anything*. The seconds stretched into an eternity and his hope buckled. The TV flickered. He'd already given up when she faced him.

Ashley's hair was a golden waterfall flowing around olive skin made darker by the soft lighting. Her mouth formed a straight line and the emeralds in her eyes were more intense than bright. Her voice was thick. "I heard you and your friend earlier today."

John stabbed for the TV remote and switched it off. "What?"

Ashley looked down at her hands. "You told him that I'm no one. Just *some* girl."

John pressed himself against the headboard. "Ashley wha…" Then he remembered the flutter of the curtain. No one had been there. A chill shot through John followed by hands of dread to choke him. "Ashley I—"

Ashley sighed. "I get it I guess. We'd just met and after the way you left…" She shot him a look. "Just some girl, John?"

She held her position beyond the end of his bed, but John could clearly see the hurt written on her face. This wasn't how it was supposed to go. Or maybe this was the only way it *could* go. "Have you been here…with me?" The words were quiet and weak.

Ashley made no answer. John summoned his voice and forced his eyes to meet hers. "Have you…stayed with me since the accident? Have you been taking care of me?"

He saw her stiffen at the question. She was quiet for a long time before finally admitting, "Yes."

"Why would you do that for me?"

Another long period of silence threatened to suffocate him and for a moment John thought she was going to leave. But then she fixed a look on him. Resignation weighed on her features. Her eyes were large and full. "Because I thought I was more than just some girl." She hid her face before he could see her wipe her eyes.

"Ashley wait!" Each step she took towards the curtain was a spike in John's heart. She was almost gone. "I'm sorry!" he cried out. She froze with one hand on the thick fabric. "I'm so sorry," he repeated. "I'm sorry for everything. I was wrong, okay? I was a jerk, a moron...you can call me whatever you want, just don't go. *Please.*"

Ashley didn't face him but she didn't leave either. "You're not just *some girl,*" he promised. "I've been...upside down since I met you, Ashley. Honestly, I'm not sure how to say what you are, but 'some girl' doesn't fit. Not by a long shot."

Ashley ran a few fingers under her eyes and stepped to the window. She gazed at the starry sky for a long time before finally turning. "That night," she hesitated and dropped her eyes to the floor. "I was home trying to figure out where it all went wrong." She gave a short, sad laugh and leaned against the glass. "Whew, this is hard."

John watched Ashley's eyes dart between him and the floor. She'd probably spun that ring on her finger a million times. There was probably something he could say. Something that would make this right. John gripped the mattress. He'd never been good with words.

Ashley crossed her arms over her chest. "My boss called. There'd been an accident. Two trucks. Head on. She needed me to come in. I got here about an hour before you." She brushed a strand of blonde hair behind her ear and looked at the ceiling. "I didn't know it was you until they brought you out of surgery. When I saw you..." Ashley swallowed a lump of emotion. "Arghhhh," she groaned. "I've only known you a week."

"Ashley—"

"A week, John! It shouldn't be this way. I shouldn't *feel* this way."

John was in a deep well without a rope and the water was rising. He searched the small room for an answer that wasn't there. *Jesus,* he pleaded. *Do something.*

The next minute stretched like an eternity and John decided that it was a stupid prayer. But then Ashley took a few steps toward him. "When I saw you it felt like part of me was on the table with you." She ignored the tears

‹ finding home ›

on her cheeks.

"Ash—"

"Shut up," She ordered. "I prayed so hard that God would save you. I told him that he couldn't bring you into my life and let you leave it so quickly." She carefully sat down on the bed. "And he saved you."

John took her in. So open. So vulnerable. And suddenly his heart bypassed his brain. "Thank you for staying with me," he whispered. "For caring so much about me, for praying." He reached out and brushed a hot tear from her face. And then he was drawing her toward him until only inches separated their lips.

John hovered there for a moment. He was a man leaning out over a cliff wanting to fall but chained to the ground. But then John found her eyes. Hope, courage, and desire flashed like green flame. And suddenly the chain was broken. He was falling. John closed the gap and for a few sweet moments he wasn't broken. He wasn't a man crippled by trials and loss. He was a teenager, a kid discovering love and life. The smell and taste of her drowned his senses. John pulled back and almost laughed before pressing against her lips again, harder, as if any more separation would mean the end of him.

Both of them were breathless when they finally parted. Ashley giggled and pressed her cheek against his chest. John could feel her heart beating against his lower ribs and whips of blonde hair tickled his nose. He couldn't keep the smile from his voice. "Does this mean you forgive me?"

"Getting there," she teased. "Just don't start talking and ruin it."

"But me talking is what got you over here in the first place."

She grinned up at him. The sparkle was back in her eyes. "Yeah, where'd you come up with that stuff?"

"Whatever gets you to make out with me." They both laughed and let a comfortable silence wash over them. Every so often he glanced down and noticed how bright she seemed. He stared through the wall thinking about the darkness of his own life and wondered how the two could mesh. It seemed almost unnatural. But wasn't Jesus making him brighter?

Ashley lifted her head. "Hey, are you okay?"

"Just thinking."

"About what?"

"My life compared to yours."

Ashley sat up and brushed her hair back. "What do you mean?"

John stared at his hands. "I've done a lot of things and I'm not sure you want to get mixed up with someone like me."

Ashley watched him. "Are you a fugitive?"

John reeled back. "What? No!"

Ashley grinned and raised her hands. "Just making sure."

John relaxed. "Fair question though."

Ashley took his hand. "Listen, life flows in one direction. Who you are today isn't who you're going to be tomorrow. We're always changing and growing. I'm not interested in the person you were yesterday." She gave him a shy smile. "I want to grow with the person you're becoming. The same should be true for you. You don't know who I was, the things I've done. But I'd like you to grow with the person I'm becoming."

John glanced at her hand resting on his. He might float down the river Styx if she asked him too. "Well, I'm in then."

"Me too," she whispered and touched her lips to his.

"You know," John stuttered when they parted, "if I knew you were dropping by I would have cleaned myself up a bit."

Ashley ran her hand through his hair. "This is the best you've looked since you got here."

"I've had great care."

"Oh yeah?"

"Well, Dr. Davis anyway." He lowered his voice. "Between you and me the nurses could be better."

Ashley laughed and rolled her eyes. "You're a brat." She stood and moved back to the window where moonlight framed her face. John's desire to kiss her again was almost enough to yank him from the bed. He could feel her silky hair on his fingers and—

"Why are you looking at me like that?" Ashley was studying him with her head tilted to one side.

John smirked. "I'll tell you, but it's probably rated *R*."

She raised an eyebrow. "I better check on my other patients. Make sure they're alive."

"Don't take too long," he told her. "I'm going to need *extra* attention

‹ finding home ›

from now on."

"Is that so?"

"My foot is starting to feel a little tingly so it might be good for you to check on me every ten minutes or so."

"You're a real pain in the butt." Ashley leaned over and kissed his forehead. Her perfume swam through his senses.

"Keep that up and my chest will start hurting again."

She gasped and covered her mouth. "I almost forgot! It's a miracle, John. A 100% miracle. I've never seen anything like it." She lowered her hands. "God gave you new lungs."

"Yeah, I guess he did," John agreed.

A smile formed on Ashley's lips and grew until her face shown with it. "You're different. Something in you has changed." She gave him a little wave and he watched her leave, his heart bouncing in time with her steps.

chapter twenty six

Two AM. The moon was a pale shard in the black sky. John peered around the dark room. "Hello?"

A light flickered to his left. "Hi, John."

John picked the sleep from his eyes. Jesus was smiling at him from the same chair he occupied the night before. "Should I expect this to be a nightly thing?"

"I don't get caught up in expectations," Jesus replied.

John pushed himself up against the headrest. "Well, I'm glad you're back."

"I appreciate that," Jesus answered and leaned over his knees. "But I never left."

"Don't do that," John complained. "It's too late for riddles."

Jesus chuckled. "It's not a riddle."

John yawned. "I get it. You'll never leave me or forsake me."

Jesus clucked his tongue. "Don't just repeat the words stamped on your brain. You're a person not a parrot and people are led by what they believe to be true in their *hearts*."

"Are you saying I don't really believe you're always around?"

"I'm saying that it's easy for the natural world to become the *only* world you see. Far too often I become the subject matter of reflections rather than a present help in times of need."

John pinched his forehead. "I'm not sure I understand that."

"That's okay," Jesus assured. "Just let it simmer."

"Well, it's making my head hurt."

Jesus laughed and tapped his head. "A little rust on those wheels?"

‹finding home›

John grabbed a cup of water from the bedside table. "Is that what you wanna talk about tonight?"

"That? No. That was just a fun little tangent."

John sipped from his cup. "Yeah, fun."

Jesus clapped his hands together. "So, you've had everything you've needed since last night?"

John spun the day through his mind. "You know, I did. And for the first time in my life I really trusted I would." He hesitated and fiddled with his IV tubing. "Trusted in you I guess."

Jesus pumped his fist in the air. "That's great John! Really, you have no idea how happy that makes me."

John rubbed the back of his neck. "Thank you for what you did last night. I feel better than I ever have and I'm not just blowing smoke."

Jesus leaned back. "I know you're not. And it's only the beginning for you."

John fell silent while that sunk in. Apprehension fired across his body. If this was just the beginning what in the world was next? "What do you—hey?" he almost shouted. "Did you give me new lungs?"

Jesus snapped his fingers. "That's where they went." He motioned at John. "Gonna need those back. Sorry."

John felt the blood leave his face. "You're kidding right?" Jesus held a straight face for another moment before breaking into laughter. Relief whooshed out of John like air from a balloon. "That's messed up, man."

Jesus wiped his eyes. "Sorry, John. Couldn't resist. Go ahead with your question."

"My question?"

The laughter was gone from his voice now. "You've been waiting to ask since Dr. Davis told you about your lungs."

Your lungs are brand new. There's no explanation. John could still see Dr. Davis shaking his head. *It's a 100% miracle,* Ashley's voice rang like a bell. *I've never see anything like it.* John swallowed more water. "Yeah, well I've been wondering why me." John raised his hands. "There's gotta be lots of people who deserve this more. The lungs I mean." *And your time,* he silently added. Jesus didn't reply. John clenched his jaw. It was true then. So why was Jesus wasting his time?

159

"Oh, John," Jesus lamented. His lips formed a line and the brown in his eyes seemed to weep. "There's so much more for you to understand." He lifted a bottle of apple juice from John's table. "Why, John. Why-why-why?" He rose and drifted to the window. The stars sparkled and pulsed as Jesus gazed at them. "You ask *why* hoping the answer will finally give you some peace." He rotated and leaned against the wall. "But you're wrong. The solution isn't in the answer but in discovering why you're asking the question at all."

John rubbed his jaw. "So why am I asking the question?"

Jesus tried the juice and wiped his mouth. "Because you don't believe you're really worth my time." Jesus stepped back to the chair and sat down. "You can't understand why I would heal you. Essentially, you think I see you the way you see yourself. But I don't. If you could see what I see you wouldn't question why I'd heal and provide for you. Why I'd want to spend time with you." Jesus paused. "What do you see when you look in the mirror, John?"

Unlovable, failure, worthless. John let his eyes blur. When they cleared he saw a meaty fist flying towards his face. The impact brought out the stars despite the noon sun.

"Look at him," someone was shouting. He moaned and rolled over. Above him Jimmy was grinning like a Cheshire cat. He was fourteen, four years older than John.

"He got you again, eh?" John's dad mocked when he'd stumbled through the door. "A man that don't know how to use the weapons God gave him ain't a man at all." He lifted his fists before tossing him an icepack. "Remember that," he scoffed before disappearing downstairs.

The scene glossed over and he was sixteen. The moon was bright and full. He stood stiff as a statue in front of a window watching his girlfriend Wendy and a guy named Pete. They were tangled in slow motion illuminated by pale light. There wasn't enough air to fill his lungs.

John pressed his fingers into his temples. "Please stop this."

Jesus' voice was quiet. "These are your memories, John."

"No more," John pleaded.

"Rister!" Jeff roared. John looked up to see his boss glaring at him. "Imagine my surprise when Allister asked me for the updated safety codes

‹ finding home ›

at the board meeting this morning."
John swallowed some bile creeping up his throat. "Oh, yeah," John stammered and glanced at the codes still sitting on his desk. "They're right here and I'm sorry—"
"Oh, you're *sorry*," Jeff sneered. "Hey everyone," he shouted. "John here is sorry. How 'bout that."
John could feel the stares as his stomach churned. "Listen Jeff—"
"No you listen you worthless piece of garbage. You're useless and now you're gone."
Jesus' voice lifted over the memory. "You've allowed people and experiences to define you. And you've numbed the pain with momentary distractions that let you down in the end."
Your family is gone, sir. I'm so sorry. The words floated into the darkest sky he'd ever seen. *You're a failure. You couldn't protect them.* John pulled at his hair and heard the clank of bottles. Amber liquid burned his throat. *Kill the voices. Kill the pain.*
"Pursuit, rejection, failure, and pursuit," Jesus continued. "That's the life cycle of a person who's had their identity formed by the world. They stand in wreckage amazed that the sand failed to provide an adequate foundation. And then they build on the same weak ground once again."
The tears were hot on John's face and he flicked them away. "I'm scum. Nothing's gonna change that."
"No!" Jesus grabbed his hand. "Let me help you understand who you've always been."
John gave him a skeptical look. "Okay."
Jesus stood and moved back to the window. "Those memories John, they're full of pain." Jesus shifted to face him. "But you missed something so crucial in each one."
"What?"
Jesus covered his heart. "*Me*, John." He stepped back to the chair. "You missed me. You didn't see my arms stretched wide and you didn't hear my words. In each of those situations, and so many others, I told you how much I love you. How much I care about you. How special you are to me."
Jesus kneeled beside the bed. "But you could only hear the other voice."
Failure, worthless, unlovable. John's eyes snapped wide. He'd been hearing

those words all his life, but never like that. Each word hissed and dripped venom onto his heart. "What was that?" he cried out.

"In every painful event you experienced, that was the voice taking advantage," Jesus replied. "It repeatedly told you how worthless, ugly, unlovable, and insignificant you are. It told you that you're a failure, that you'll never be good enough. Then it told you how to make yourself feel better."

John shuddered. *Failure, worthless, good for nothing.* Every word seared him. "What is it?"

Jesus seemed to grow taller. "It's a liar."

I'm the truth, the voice spat in John's head.

"No," Jesus bellowed in a voice that shook the room. "It's *not* the truth." His shoulders sagged. "But because you believed what it told you, you rejected yourself. Because you rejected yourself your heart was off limits to anyone and everyone, including me. You weren't willing to risk others rejecting what you already had."

"Sometimes I don't think I know you at all," Amy told him one night. She slumped on the edge of their bed with her arms crossed. "Tell me what you *feel* John."

"About what?" he'd snapped from the doorway.

"About anything," she cried and stood. "What do you hope for? What are your dreams, your goals?" She stepped to him and framed his face with her soft hands. "What makes you afraid? What makes you happy?" She dropped a hand over his heart. "I want to know what's in *here.*"

The memory faded but the shame was piercing. John's voice quivered. "What's the truth then?"

The tenderness never left Jesus's face but his brown eyes were suddenly ablaze. He opened His mouth and the words reverberated throughout John's body, shaking him to the core of his being. "You are loved because I love you. You are valuable because I value you. When I shaped you I sang of your beauty. There was a shout from Heaven when you were born. There is no one quite like you. You are unique and I adore you. I've rejoiced with you in your successes and cried with you in the failures. You are the smile on my face and the sparkle in my eye. You're the one I died for. You're an overcomer not a failure. A son not a slave and a co-heir with me in everything our father has."

Jesus's words swirled and beat against John's heart like a drum in a relentless beat. "All I've done—"

"Has only changed *your* perception of who you are. Step away from your mirror and look into mine."

A shriek pierced John's mind like a hundred needles. He grabbed his head and moaned. When he opened his eyes a mirror floated in front of him. John stared at the image in the glass. He knew the reflection was his own but it was a stranger nonetheless. The lines etched in his face and eyes by worry, stress, and trials were gone leaving smooth, shimmering skin in their place. Round hazel eyes were filled with hope and joy. A sincere smile shaped his lips. On his head rested a crown set with various jewels and a white robe fell over his body like a sparkling waterfall.

"What is this?"

"This is you," Jesus answered.

John lifted a trembling hand to his face and the reflected image did the same. His skin was silk on his fingers. "This can't be me."

"Why not?"

"The, the things I've done—"

"Don't define who you are."

The tears rolling down John's cheeks were drops of sunlight on the image in the mirror. He touched the glass. It sent a shockwave through him before disappearing.

He wiped his face on the sheet and looked at Jesus who was kneeling again beside him. "I want that."

Jesus smiled. "You *are* that."

"How do I...what do I do."

"Speak out the truth."

"The truth." John hesitated. "Is it supposed to be this hard?"

Jesus shook his head. "No John, it was never supposed to be this way."

John gripped the bed. *Speak the truth.* "I am loved—" Another shriek hit his brain but was cut off as if choked.

"Go on," Jesus encouraged.

"I am worthy and valuable. Whoa!" He felt light enough to float. "That's weird."

Jesus laughed and John cleared his throat. "I'm not a failure, I'm an overcomer. I'm loved." He inhaled as joy pulsated through him. "Am I supposed to be feeling like this?"

Jesus clapped his hands and gave a shout. "This is freedom, John!"

John couldn't stop the laughter rising in him. "You love me. No matter what."

"No matter what," Jesus echoed.

And then, despite his swirling emotions, John stopped laughing and fixed his eyes on Jesus. "I just want to, uh, say how sorry I am for not listening to you. For—"

Jesus' arms were around him, squeezing him tightly. "I forgive you," he exclaimed. "I love you."

And then John uttered words he thought he would never say again, especially to Jesus. "I love you too."

They stayed like that for some time. Exactly how long John didn't know, or care.

They finally separated, but not really. John could feel the imprint of Jesus on his heart.

Jesus climbed to his feet and wiped His eyes. "Well, you better get some sleep."

John chuckled. "Yeah, I guess. If I can."

Jesus grinned. "Oh, you're gonna sleep like a baby tonight."

Jesus swiveled toward the door, but then stopped. "Hey, one more thing." He put his hands in his pockets. "You can trust Ashley. Trust is a gift that we must *choose* to give others. Without it relationships die. It's risky to trust, but the risk is acceptable because I love you. Even if the risk becomes a reality my love will hold you together." He smiled warmly and disappeared behind the curtain.

« finding home »

chapter twenty seven

"Do you need to stop at this Rest Area?" Claire asked. "It's the last one for a while."

"I'm okay, thanks," Alice replied and peered at the windshield. "Claire, do you know the last thing to go through a bug's mind after it hits the windshield?"

"No, what?"

Alice grinned. "It's butt."

"Oh!" Claire covered her mouth and laughed. "I don't think I can argue with that." She fell silent for a moment. "Poor bugs though."

Alice laughed as they zoomed West on I-90 at eighty-five miles per hour. "Do you always drive this fast?" Alice had asked when they were still in New York. It was faster than she would've expected from the older woman. They were on schedule to make the eight-hour trip in seven.

"Oh, heaven's no," Claire cried out and winked. "I usually drive faster."

Alice laughed and faced the window. The last two days were a haze, like a part of her brain short-circuited. She picked at a nail and recalled Dr. Tishner taking the news fairly well.

"You're leaving?" she'd asked, wide-eyed.

Alice nodded slowly. "Yes."

Dr. Tishner shot up from her chair and came around her desk. "When?"

"A couple days probably."

"Where are you going? Who are you going with?"

Alice bit her lip. "I'm going to Oak Harbor with a woman named Claire."

Dr. Tishner gave her a queer look and leaned against the desk. "Claire? Alice, you're gonna have to explain what's going on."

So she did in the least shocking way possible. When she was finished Dr. Tishner was still before shaking her head. "A week ago I would have referred you for a psych consult but I," she pointed towards the waiting room, "I just saw a man with a broken femur get up and walk." She wrapped Alice in a hug. "You're very brave Alice. I'm going to miss you. We all are."

Alice let her forehead rest against the cool glass. Explaining what was going on to Jack and Melissa had been much harder. Saying good-bye was worse. In the end, after they'd spent hours with Claire and had a chance to process as best they could, they were supportive.

Melissa had outlined Alice's face with her hands. Her voice was thick. "We love you. It's been such an honor to see you grow and become the young woman God has always planned for you to be." She paused to swallow a sob. "We thank God for every day we've had with you. You're a princess," she declared. "Never forget that."

Alice blinked back tears and remembered how Jack came and took her hands. "You're our daughter," he'd expressed. "I can't even remember a time you weren't." He touched the side of her head. "I bless you, Alice. I bless you and release you into God's care, into his love. I bless you with the courage to follow him wherever he leads." He paused. "You're our daughter, but you're *his* first and he loves you more than we ever could." Jack drew her into a tight hug. "We're sure gonna miss you, but you'll be just fine. You're ready."

Alice kept her eyes on the sweeping landscape and ignored her wet cheeks. She'd spent the last night with Jessie, Anna, and Tabby. They went to dinner and strolled around town. There were sad moments, but they laughed a lot and Alice was grateful. She wanted to remember their smiles rather than tears.

They ended up at a small community park near the restaurant. Her and Tabby fell back a few steps. "Are you sure about this?" Tabby had asked and kicked at a pebble. "I mean, it's *crazy*, right?"

Alice shoved her hands in her coat pockets. "Yes."

"Yes you're sure or yes it's crazy?"

"Both, I guess." It was quiet enough to hear the wind blowing softly through the trees. Alice shivered, but not from the fall chill. Uncertainty bit at her heart making her feel like a little girl. "I'm not sure." A sad

≪finding home≫

laugh escaped into the air and Alice shook her head. "I'm not sure about anything."

A breeze fell from the trees and tossed the hair around her ears. *I am the good shepherd.* The voice was brick and mortar to her heart. "No, wait," she said half-aloud. "I'm sure about him, about Jesus. I'm sure that Jesus will be with me. He's not gonna take me to a bad place." She took Tabby's hand. "I'm still sure that he loves me enough to be my everything."

Tabby nodded and hugged herself. "I'm gonna miss you so much." Her voice broke on the last word. And then her arms were around Alice. "Call me every day," Tabby whispered into her ear.

"I promise."

A few blinks later Tabby was gone. The Bakers were gone. Redwood was gone. The only light in her life vanished as simply as someone flipping off a switch. But maybe another light had been switched on. Excitement flickered like a flame despite the damp sorrow of change. What did God have in store for her? It had to be amazing if it meant leaving the only home she'd ever known.

"There's that smile," Claire cooed and held out a Kleenex.

Alice wiped her face and dropped the tissue into a trash bag. "Thanks."

"Mother Teresa said, 'Peace begins with a smile,'" Claire stated and changed lanes to pass a truck. "She was a very wise woman. Now my mother was also a very wise woman and she told me that peace begins with a good pot-roast."

Alice grinned. "So, who was right?"

Claire flicked her hand. "Oh, they both were sweetie. Although, my pot-roasts have been known to bring peace AND smiles."

Alice laughed at the woman who had turned her world upside down. "So how long have you lived in Oak Harbor?"

"Goodness," Claire remarked and tapped the steering wheel like a calculator. "Must be close to fifty years now."

"Wow," Alice exclaimed.

"Mm-hmm, most of our lives. Mark was looking for a lead pastor position and a small Baptist church in Oak Harbor offered him the job. We were so young…" Claire glanced at Alice. "Many pastors don't even make it five years. Mark's been going ever since." Claire laughed. "He's like that silly bunny with the battery on its back. Energizer I think. What's that called?"

Alice stifled a laugh, "An energizer bunny."

Claire clapped her hands. "Yes! That's it. My Mark, the energizer bunny of pastors." They both laughed at that. "It hasn't always been easy," Claire continued. "Working to meet the needs of the church and the needs of our family. Keeping them from bleeding into each other can be a real trick. Some days *bleeding* was all we felt like we were doing."

Alice thought about her old pastor. He always seemed so put together preaching from his podium. A model of Jesus for the rest of them. She never considered him being anything other than that Sunday morning reflection. She looked at Claire. "I'm sorry."

"Bah," Claire waved her hand. "Keep your 'sorries' for someone with regrets, sweetheart. The beautiful things that have happened in that church and on the streets of Oak Harbor shine brighter than any darkness could hope to swallow."

Alice smiled. Maybe Oak Harbor would be the same for her. They chatted on as the Buick bore down for the final leg of the trip. "So, do you have any kids?" she asked Claire.

Claire hesitated before giving Alice a weak smile. "No, not of our own anyway. There was a family Mark and I were very close with. They had children." Claire made a sound like a laugh and sigh twisted together. "Cookouts and parks. Camping and school activities. My-my, we had some times."

Alice glanced at Claire's hands, which had tightened around the steering wheel. A shadow crept across her face. "That must've been nice," Alice offered.

"Whew," Claire let out quickly and forced a smile. "That's certainly enough about me. It's your turn, Alice. Tell me about yourself."

Alice tugged on the sleeve of her sweatshirt. Talking about herself was like trying to dig up cement with a shovel.

"It's okay Alice," Claire assured and gave her hand a squeeze. "You can tell me as much or as little as you want. I just want you to know that it's safe to do so."

Alice looked out the window to trees and grass passing them in a

«finding home»

whoosh. My first ten years passed way faster than that, she thought. *The next eight slower than tree sap in the middle of winter.*

It's okay, Alice. The voice startled her. *You can trust her.* Alice glanced at Claire. *Is that you Lord?* She only heard the hum of tires on highway but peace began to drown the anxiety. She gave Claire another quick glance, and shared about her lost childhood. Alice mentioned the years before Redwood without details, but kept none out regarding life *after.*

Claire was chuckling softly when she finished. "You are very blessed Alice." Claire looked at her and smiled. "And very, *very* special."

The words dug into her heart. Alice could've hugged the woman but folded her hands instead. "Thank you."

Oak Harbor was small. In that way it reminded her of Redwood. Claire squinted through the afternoon sun and pointed to thick trees lining the two lane road. "Got its name from all of the Oak Trees. The Portage River also runs through here on its way to Lake Erie." She leaned towards Alice. "That's where the *Harbor* came from."

The car weaved its way through the worn streets like it knew its own way home. They passed Main Street. Then Ottawa. A young looking couple waved to Claire as she turned into a residential neighborhood.

Claire waved back. "Such a nice family."

Alice smiled and then touched her stomach as the familiar feeling rumbled through her again. She smothered a groan. It was maddening, like waking up in the morning knowing that you dreamed, but can't remember any of it.

"Are you okay?" Claire was eying her. Alice straightened. "Yeah, I mean no…" She ran a hand through her hair. "I just keep feeling like I've…"

Claire threw her a sideways look. "Like you what, dear?"

"Arghhh." Alice grabbed her head. "Like I've been here before. It's driving me crazy."

"Hmmm." Claire studied the road ahead of them. "Lots of people come here for the festivals and activities at the harbor. Maybe you *have* been here."

Alice sighed and let her hands drop. "Maybe…" Another family waved as they passed. *10 lost years.*

"Here we are." Claire pulled the old Buick into a driveway and killed

169

the engine. They both got out and stretched.

Alice took in the single story home. The exterior was brick, a shade of nutmeg that seemed to soak in the sun and glow. A large bay window looked out over a front yard carefully filled with varieties of bushes and flowers. A stone path weaved through the colors and ended at an Oak front door.

"Claire," Alice exclaimed. "It's *beautiful*."

Claire gave a satisfied sigh. "Thank you, Alice."

Alice stepped towards a flowerbed. "Did you do all of this?"

"Oh, yes," she answered. "My husband goes on his visitations and I go on mine." She motioned to the path that weaved through the landscape and gave a short laugh. "The backyard is my *ministry* as well."

Alice was bent over a group of flowers that were a deep shade of pink. "What are *these?*" she asked and carefully touched a soft petal. "They almost look like butterflies."

Claire held her coat to her chest as she leaned over Alice. "Ooh, those are my Cyclamen. Yes, they *are* beautiful aren't they? It's about time for me to bring some inside before winter really gets going. It's been mild enough for them so far but it won't last."

Alice nodded and noticed a flash of purple to her left. "What are those?"

"Mark!"

Alice scrunched her nose. "Mark? What's a Mark?"

"A particularly stubborn old weed," a voice boomed.

Alice noticed a man walking towards them down the stone path. "Hard to kill," he added. "Can't do a thing with it." A breeze tossed his thin, gray hair and an easy grin sent deep creases through his skin.

Before Alice could stand Claire was in his arms. She kept her eyes somewhere between them and the ground as they laughed and hugged and kissed. The way they carried on reminded her a little bit of Jack and Melissa. Alice blew warm breath into her bare hands. That was a good thing she decided.

"Alice," Claire called. "Come on over here. I want you to meet my husband, Mark." Alice commanded herself to relax. Meeting men had never been easy for her.

"Well, it's an absolute pleasure to meet you, Alice," he gushed. Mark

≪finding home≫

stood a few inches taller than her and broad shoulders made him look strong. A warm smile reached his eyes and eased her stomach. "It's very nice to meet you too, Mr. Summers."

"Ugh," he expressed and waved his hands. "Please, call me Mark." Alice gave him a tight-lipped smile and hid her hands in her pockets.

"Alice...," Mark murmured and pinched his chin. "Ah!" he snapped his fingers. "Noble."

Alice shot a look at Claire who shrugged. "Mark is a bit of a name... nerd, if you will." Claire swallowed a laugh at Mark's frown. "I keep telling him not everyone cares what their name means," she half whispered and winked.

"Now, just hold on a sec," Mark interjected and poked Claire in the ribs making her squeal. "Alice, your name means *noble* which is another way of saying full of honor, virtue, goodness, and integrity."

A cold gust licked at Alice's nose. *Alice.* She'd called herself that after finding an advertisement for *Alice In Wonderland* on Broadway. It was soaked and half ruined in a gutter but she'd picked it up and taken the name hoping it might transport her to her own wonderland. If she'd known what it meant back then she would've chosen a different one.

She thought about her first night in Redwood. Melissa's voice floated through her heart. *We just want you to remember that you're a princess.* Alice lifted her eyes and smiled sweetly. "Thank you Mr...Mark."

"Ack," Claire grunted and rubbed her arms. "It's cold out here and if I know you there's a fire going."

Mark nodded. "You two go on and get warm. Alice, I'll set your bags in the guest room."

A short time later Alice was warm and sitting on a surprisingly comfortable double bed in the room they'd prepared for her. It wasn't extravagant but she didn't need extravagant. She stood and ran a hand along a wooden dresser set against the wall and stopped in front of a full-length mirror. "Bleh," she spat. A nest of black tangles sat on her head and she looked pale and worn from the drive. She tried to smooth out a few wrinkles in her sweater but gave up. Her bags sat in the corner like children in trouble and she rummaged around for a change of clothes. The moving van would arrive tomorrow with the rest of her stuff.

Alice blew a strand of hair out of her face and felt her heart leap at the idea of a shower. She'd almost danced when Claire told her that the room came with her own bathroom. Noble indeed.

A few hours later she was clean, unpacked, and comfortable in jeans and an oversized sweatshirt. Alice grabbed her phone to call Tabby but the clang of pots and pans drew her to the kitchen. Mark raised a raw chicken breast when he noticed her. "Dinner will be ready around six."

"Don't worry," Claire teased. "He's going to cook it."

Mark inspected a bottle of paprika. "Just not sure how."

"Hmmm. Why don't you try making a rub with these." Alice picked out three of the spice bottles and positioned them in front of Mark. "They're great with some brown sugar, salt, and pepper mixed in."

Mark lifted his eyebrows. "Sounds like you know your way around the kitchen?"

"I helped out at home every now and then."

"Well you're welcome to help out in the kitchen any time you'd like," Claire let her know and put a hand on Marks shoulder. "Hun, can you manage while I show Alice the rest of the house?"

Mark grabbed a measuring spoon. "Yeah, I'm going to mix up this rub and throw them on the grill. Medium rare right?"

"Ha-ha," Claire retorted and nudged him. "Come on Alice, let me give you the grand tour."

Claire showed her the other rooms on the ground level and then the finished basement. "We've repaired and remodeled through the years," Claire explained and patted a plush blanket lying on the couch. "Our goal has always been comfort. We want people to feel at home here."

Alice followed Claire back up the stairs. The fireplace in the living room, soft blankets on couches, warm colors on the walls…she couldn't deny the house felt comfortable. But could it be *home?* Did God want it to be? Did she?

Claire led her out to the back porch where there was a propane heater and a wooden swing. "Whoa," Alice blurted. The setting sun washed the vast backyard in deep oranges and rich yellows. Flowers and bushes pushed out from the porch and stretched into an elegant network bordered by decorative stone. Thick trees shimmered where the yard ended. "Claire, this is amazing."

"Thank you, Alice. Why don't you have a seat on the swing and I'll turn this heater on."

A few moments later they were sitting together enjoying the gentle sway of the swing and warmth of the heater. "You and Mark must come out here all the time."

Claire nodded. "It's gorgeous in the spring when all of the flowers bloom. I can almost smell them now."

"There's a lot here that reminds me of Redwood," Alice admitted. "The smell of the air and the trees…" She looked down at her hands. "But it's so different."

Are you sure about this? Tabby had asked her. *You can't just leave with some old woman you just met. Redwood is your home.* Maybe Tabby was right. *You're the bravest girl I know,* she'd said. More like craziest.

"Sweetie, are you okay?"

No. Alice forced a smile, "I'm fine."

Claire squeezed her shoulder. "Alice…"

Tears were on her cheeks before she could blink them away. "Arghhhh," she cried and hid her face in her hands. "All I wanna do right now is go back home. I know God led me here but I have no idea why and I feel so… lost." Alice wiped her eyes on her sleeve.

Claire sighed and watched the last sliver of the sun disappear behind the trees. "It can be so hard. Life, I mean. Following God and doing what we think is right." She gave Alice a sad smile. "A few years ago I was ready to leave."

Alice sniffed. "Leave?"

Claire folded her hands. "Oh, yes. I was done with church and this town and even Mark if he wouldn't come with me. I told you earlier that the things God has done here shine brighter than the darkness." She wagged her head. "That hasn't always been true for me. *Fifty years* of ministry. The way I'd come to see it, fifty years dealing with the death of loved ones, anger of those offended by what was preached or sung or whatever else, endless meetings and hospital visits and so many other issues that kept Mark away. Add that to the typical struggles of *any* marriage and I was just done. I was lost Alice. I really was."

A swirl of air combed through Alice's hair like fingers and then through Claire's like it was tying them together. Despite the cold Alice felt warmer. "What changed?"

Claire smiled. "I was sitting right where you are, telling God that I was done and leaving and…" she paused. When she continued her voice was thick. "And he said, 'Claire…I love you.'" She wiped a tear from her cheek and giggled. "It was as clear as we're talking now. I'd never heard him like that before. I always knew in my head that he loved me but the next thing I knew I was on my knees sobbing." Claire pointed at a flowerbed just beyond the porch. "I felt like a dry and withered flower finally getting a drink. Over time he showed me things to forgive and burdens to let go but it always came back to those three words, *I love you.* They're the answer for everything. I realized I could never be lost." She fixed her eyes on Alice. "And neither can you."

Alice hugged herself and looked up at the stars just beginning to wake. Discouragement was fading and hope was shining. *I'm not lost. I can never be because you love me.* She smiled and faced Claire. "Have you done anything like this before, bring a stranger home I mean?"

"Oh, goodness no," Claire exclaimed. "This is a first." She reached for Alice's hands. "But I want you to know that Mark and I will be here for you and help you however we can. No matter what. We'll walk this road together. This is your home for as long as you're with us."

Home. Alice swallowed a lump. God had brought her two homes when she never thought she'd even have one.

"Oh, my," Claire beamed and placed her soft hand on Alice's cheek. "Your sweet face shines with the light of Jesus. I can't wait to see what God has in store for you."

Alice beheld Claire though blurry eyes. "Thank you so much."

"Dinner's on the table," Mark called from the kitchen.

"Okay," Claire hollered back and stood. "Alice?"

"Yeah?"

"If you ever want to talk, about anything, I'm here."

Alice nodded and hugged her. "Thanks."

Roasted broccoli and baked sweet potato complimented the grilled chicken that earned Alice rave reviews. Mark wanted to know about her life

‹finding home›

in Redwood and she told him all she could. She expertly dodged a question about her childhood and they seemed to take the hint. Mark shared some of his favorite stories from a life spent in ministry.

Conversation with him is easy, she mused as he talked about a drug addict he'd been able to help get sober and eventually lead to Christ. She almost dropped her fork as the revelation struck her. Conversation with men was never easy for her.

She considered that the rest of the night and was still thinking about it when she climbed into bed. She clicked off the light and stared at the ceiling. *Mark Summers.* There was no anxiety or jittery feeling around him. There was no oppressive need to hide or stand back. Jack was the only other man who made her feel comfortable and relaxed, but that took a year. Why Mark?

♥

Later that same night on the other end of the house in the master bedroom, Mark was lying on his side listening to the soft rhythmic sound of his beloved wife's breathing. He'd fallen asleep to it for so long that it was part of him. He even heard it when she wasn't there next to him.

Mark was usually asleep in minutes, but tonight he was wide-awake. Something was grabbing his spirit, nagging him and refusing to let go. Something was strangely familiar about their guest. He had no idea how or why but something wasn't right. It wasn't upsetting or unpleasant at all. Quite the opposite in fact. The fleeting feeling of familiarity brought a sense of peace and even a flicker of joy.

He rolled over to face his lovely wife. He was so thankful for her and how faithful God had been to them. Trials and tragedies. Joys and triumphs. Losing people they loved and new people rising up around them. Mark grazed her hand and she stirred just a bit. He smiled and closed his eyes.

chapter twenty eight

Thirteen hours earlier and almost two thousand miles Southwest, John's Wednesday began in a familiar way. Dr. Davis occupied the exact place he'd been almost 24 hours before and wore the same perplexed expression on his face.

John rotated his pelvis again. Not even an ache. He knew something was different as soon as he woke up. He'd moved all around, manipulating his hips however he could and it all felt fine. No, more than fine. It felt great, even better than before the accident. He'd told his nurse and x-rays had been ordered.

Dr. Davis slapped his clipboard. "This is really something." He eyed John. "By the look on your face I'm assuming you already know what I found here."

"I think it's what you didn't find."

Dr. Davis fell silent.

"This is a strange place," John crowed. "The less *you* do the better I get."

The young doctor threw John a glare. He started to say something, but stopped, shook his head, and hurried from the room.

John lifted his chin at the nurse. "I guess we're down to just the broken leg, eh?"

"And then we can finally remove the pain from my ass."

Once he was gone John exhaled and let his face fall into his hands. *Twice! Two miracles!* He'd done his best to keep it together for the kid doctor and that obnoxious nurse, but now his eyes misted over.

He seized his head as if his memories might fall out and be lost forever. The chair was empty but he could see the one who'd breathed life into his

«finding home»

cold, dead heart as if he was really there. *I love you John.* Emotion stung John's throat. This time he wouldn't ask questions like *Why?* and *Is this really happening?* "Thank you," he whispered into the air. "Thank you for everything."

The sudden rustle at the curtain startled him. Dr. Davis peered around the room. "Who were you…I can come back."

"No," John almost shouted and cleared his throat. "It's okay."

The doctor hesitated as if unable to make up his mind.

"You gettin' married to that doorway? Get over here."

Dr. Davis approached the bed and fidgeted with a stethoscope looped around his neck. He threw a nervous glance back at the curtain and for a moment John thought he might leave without saying anything. But then he eased himself into the chair. "I've, uh, seen a lot of things in my relatively short career. Some crazier than others. But I've never seen *anything* like what I've seen happen to you." He rubbed his mouth like he wasn't sure if he would continue. "I've tried hard to find a medical explanation and…I want you to tell me how these things are happening."

John nearly choked on his tongue. The young doctor leaned closer. "What's going on with you? How are these things possible?"

John felt the bottom drop out of his stomach. *Help him understand?* He drummed his fingers on the bed. *Jesus healed me. Go on, say it.* But John could hardly envision those words coming from his mouth. "I could maybe help you find a pastor who might, I don't know, explain it to you better than I ever could."

Dr. Davis scratched his nose. "A Pastor? So, it has to do with Jesus or God or something in that arena?"

John rushed a prayer. *Oh God, what am I supposed to tell this guy? I'm not qualified for this.*

Dr. Davis shifted in the chair. "You know, I'm sorry, if you don't want to, or can't, it's fine."

For a second John thought he was off the hook. But then a familiar voice echoed through him. *Just share your heart. Share what I've done for you.* John forced his eyes on the doctor. He'd never looked as young as he did now. Anticipation lit his face like a kid on Christmas morning. The voice spoke again, urgent this time. *He wants to know me.*

177

And then memories of all John had been through over the last week, everything God had done for him invaded his mind. He could see them play through, like clips from a movie. Every feeling and emotion was fresh. He turned full eyes on Dr. Davis. "I'll tell you all about it."

The doctor's features didn't change as John laid out his experiences. When John was finished he stayed quiet before finally declaring, "You've given me a lot to think about." He rose to leave but halted at the curtain and informed John he would be moving out of the ICU later that afternoon.

John thought he caught a small smile on Dr. Davis' face before he left. *It's only the beginning, son.* He inhaled the peace and joy circling him. "I'm ready."

She's safe John. It's okay to risk your heart. I love you.

Jesus's words rang in John's ears. He twirled his thumbs and rotated on the bed in his third floor private room. He'd left the ICU a couple of hours earlier just as Dr. Davis had promised. "There are some things I need to tell you."

Ashley was beside him with her legs stretched out. She gazed at him with eyes reflecting anticipation and a hint of anxiety. "Okay, bring it on."

"Gotta love that attitude."

"I'm kinda feisty."

"I'm aware. Okay, so the first thing is that I've given my heart back to Jesus and I—"

"What?" Ashley gasped and covered her mouth. "John that's amazing I…" she stood with a hand on her chest, turned and took a few steps away from him.

"Ash?"

She giggled and blinked in a way that made her green eyes sparkle. "God keeps answering my prayers. I knew something was different and I thought that maybe you had." She bounced a couple of times on the mattress and wrapped her arms around his neck. "Tell me all about it."

John laughed at her eagerness. "I will but promise to listen cause some of

‹ finding home ›

it might sound a little strange."
Ashley held up her right hand. "I promise."
She's safe John. "So Jesus was sitting next to me last night and—"
"Hold on a second," Ashley interjected and pulled a leg underneath her.
"He was...what?"
"A lotta good your promises are."
"Sorry. Now answer my question."
John swallowed. "He was sitting next to me. In the chair next to my bed."
Ashley paused and then gave a nervous laugh. "You mean like because he's always with us?"
"Well yeah but he was *physically* sitting next to me just like you're sitting next to me now."
"Like, you could *see* him?"
"See him, touch him, hear him, yes. All of the above."
Ashley's lips were slightly parted and John could see her brain working to process the information. He reached over and poked her in the ribs.
She squealed and slapped his hand. "What'd you do that for?"
"I wasn't sure if you were still with me."
Ashley rubbed her side. "Cut me some slack. You're telling me Jesus, in the flesh, was sitting next to you. That's a lot to take in."
"Are you good for me to keep going?" John asked. "Cause there's a lot more."
She tucked a strand of hair behind her ear. "Just don't poke me again."
John swallowed some water from a paper cup and noticed Ashley's eyebrows lift when he talked about Jesus in the diner and the bar. He watched her eyes grow wide when he recounted the park and vision and last few nights at the hospital. "Do you think I'm crazy?" he asked when he'd gotten through it all.
Ashley cocked her head to one side. "No, John. Not at all. What you've been through is amazing." She giggled. "I'm actually a little jealous. I want to see Jesus like you have."
John reclined on the bed. "You've been seeing him much longer than I have." The room blurred with the years of his life. "I've wasted so much time."
Ashley patted his knee. "So let's not waste anymore. But I'm not sure

God views our lives like that. He probably wanted parts of those years to be different, but I don't think he'd consider them wasted."

"I love it when you get all *deep* like that."

Ashley went to shove him, but he caught her hand and tugged her into him. John caught the fresh, clean smell of her hair as it tickled his chin. He sighed and lightly traced her bare arm with his fingers not wanting the moment to end. But there was more to say. He felt his heart beat faster and muscles tense.

"What's wrong?" Ashley asked. He didn't answer. She pushed herself up to face him. "John?"

John grunted. The bed suddenly felt hard and lumpy. "Ashley, I was done living. I had been for ten years. I only cared about beer, women, and the grave that would one day end my misery. There weren't any other options for me. I'd accepted my lot." He hesitated. "The moment I saw you I knew you were gonna wreck everything. That scared me. But not nearly as bad as realizing I *wanted* you to wreck it." John lowered his eyes to the bed. "I'm sorry, I'm terrible at this."

Ashley's hands were the smoothest silk covering his own. John's heart lifted and he found her eyes. "I care about you, Ashley. I *really* do. It doesn't even make sense how much. I want you to know me. I want to tell you about my family."

John closed his eyes and let his mind breech the place holding memories he'd done his best to bury and forget. But neither time nor depth could erase them. Their faces floated before him, frozen in time ten years ago. Four lives began to flood the room. John winced as raw pain stabbed the deepest parts of his heart. The grief was still thick enough to choke him.

"Kayla was my youngest," he began and stared through the wall that became a portal to the past. "She was a surprise. Amy and I thought we were done having kids and then one day we weren't." John wasn't in the hospital anymore. He was home, ten years younger watching his brown haired, green-eyed little girl hold a handstand. *How long was that daddy? Had to be at least a minute.*

"She was our little gymnast. Her dream was to be an Olympian and, you know," John raised a fist, "bring home the gold." He paused. "She loved animals and was always trying to turn our house into a zoo." John closed

⟨ finding home ⟩

his eyes and saw her running to him arms open, grinning and laughing wildly. He felt her thin but strong arms around his neck. Somehow she always smelled of strawberries. His precious baby girl. He would always remember her that way. Sweet, innocent, carefree, and full of love. Tears streaked his cheeks. The warmth of memories battled against the pain of loss. "That girl loved better than I knew how. And when she hugged you… she was eight."

Ashley's voice was strained, "John, if you need to stop—"

"No," John asserted. He brushed his face with the back of his hand. "Jill was my middle child. She was beautiful. Long black hair like her mothers', and hazel eyes that absolutely lit up when she was doing what she loved, usually cooking." A proud smile pulled on his mouth. "She was an amazing chef. Won all kinds of awards and always talked about opening her own restaurant someday." John paused and remembered…remembered her eyes, how they always seemed to say, *I'm going to surprise you.*

"Jill was a tough kid, determined. She wanted an explanation for *everything*. She really challenged us. But she was so sweet. She would, uh, get all dressed up and want me to dance with her to practice for her wedding someday." He blinked and Jill was there, standing in front of him wearing her favorite blue dress. Tears spilled onto his face. He heard her voice. *Dance with me daddy.* He held his little girl as they swayed to the songs she loved. He lifted his hand and saw her twirl in a smooth motion like she'd done more times than he could count. His little Jilly Bean. "There was so much love in her heart. She was ten."

He glanced at Ashley. Though tears streaked her face she nodded at him to keep going.

"Andy was my oldest," John trudged on. "He was tall," John pointed to his head, "and somehow ended up with curly hair. We gave up trying to figure it out. He was *so* smart. He could just look at something and know how it fit together. Sometimes he'd get a little carried away." John remembered the morning he found the coffee maker in what had to be at least twenty pieces. He smiled and shook his head. He'd been so angry. Now the memory stung his heart with grief, with loss.

"He was a natural leader. People were drawn to him. When he saw something that needed to be done he just went after it. And that kid could play a guitar." The sound of acoustic strumming sang through his mind. It was seamless. Worship music. "He'd been on the worship team at church." He opened his eyes as the music faded. "He was twelve."

John gathered his remaining strength. "Then there was Amy. We met in college and after a few dates I knew. One year later we were married."

The hospital room faded. Amy relaxed against him on a balcony looking out at the Gulf of Mexico. "Mmmm," she sighed as the last sliver of the setting sun cast a soft glow across the water. A gentle breeze stirred her long, black hair. Her shampoo and perfume mingled in a way that was all hers. "It's so beautiful." Amy lifted her ice blue eyes to his. "Let's just start *here*. Forget that job at the plant and…snow, bleh." She grinned and touched his face. "It could be just us and the beach…and babies of course."

John smiled and squeezed her tighter. They'd been married for a day. The Sanibel Honeymoon was a gift from her parents. "I can't give you the beach." He lowered his mouth her hers. The taste of her spread through him like fire. "But I can help you with the babies."

The scene changed and John saw her giving birth to their children. He saw her loving them, teaching them, nurturing them. He watched the memories of dates, private vacations, and anniversaries play like a slideshow. There would be no slides of them retiring together. There were no slides of them growing old together.

John blinked. "She had so much passion for life. I saw it every time I looked in her eyes. She lived for God and us. She never stopped believing in me, even when I thought there was nothing to believe in."

John steadied himself. He knew what he had to do next and how hard it would be. He wasn't sure how much more strain his heart could take. He breathed a desperate prayer for help.

◄ finding home ►

chapter twenty nine

"Did you talk to Deb today?" Claire asked from the kitchen. She switched on the stove and made sure the teakettle was centered.

"About what?"

Claire shot a scowl toward the dining room. Mark was staring at notes spread across the table with a pen in one hand and a cup of steaming tea in the other. "Mark!"

Mark took note of her tone and tried to remember. "Oh, about the job. No, I didn't." He motioned to the table. "But I'm supposed to preach in a few days and I still don't have a topic. You think anyone would notice if I just preached all of my old sermons again?"

"Pfft, after fifty years I wouldn't even notice," Claire teased and sat down next to her husband. "Something wrong?"

Mark sighed and leaned back. "I guess I'm a little distracted."

"By what?"

"Alice I think. I've just had this feeling..." he leaned in close to Claire like he had a secret. "Do we know her from somewhere?" Before she could answer he flipped his hand and leaned back again. "Oh, never mind. That's impossible."

"Impossible?"

"Well, unlikely anyway." Mark lifted his tea, but stopped it short of his lips. "But do you ever get that feeling about her?"

"Shhh..." Claire pressed a finger against her lips and peered towards the guest room.

"Oh, don't worry," Mark remarked and puttered to the singing teapot for a refill. "She wanted to walk around the neighborhood." He poured the steaming liquid into his cup. "Do you want some of this?"

"Please. Half a packet of equal and—"

"A little bit of honey, I know."

Mark fixed the drinks and carefully returned to the table. "Lord help me if I don't know how you take your tea after fifty years."

Claire smiled and dunked the tea bag a few more times before laying it on a napkin. "You still haven't figured out laundry."

Mark raised his tea. "That's been a willful ignorance my dear."

Claire laughed and sipped the hot liquid. Tangy lemons and oranges spread over her tongue and down her throat warming her whole body. She glanced at the fogged windows. It'd been cold and was only getting colder. Summer was relegated to memories at this point.

"So do you?"

Claire blew at some steam. "Do I what?"

"Do you ever get the feeling that we know her?"

Claire set her tea down. "Sometimes I guess. There were moments in the car and then a few since we got home. It never lasts more than a second or two." She titled her head to one side. "But it doesn't mean that we know her."

Mark picked up a page of notes. "Maybe. But it's strange that both of us feel it." He raised an eyebrow. "Maybe she reminds us of someone. Let me know if you figure it out."

"Likewise," Claire replied. "Now, what are you going to talk about on Sunday?"

Mark dropped the notes on the table and leaned back. "Oh, probably Jesus."

"Ah," Claire gasped. "You never lost that smart mouth."

They were both laughing when the front door opened. A cold gust whipped down the hallway and around the table. "Wow," Mark exclaimed and rubbed his arms. "It's winter out there isn't it."

Alice trudged into the room and yanked off her stocking cap. Her cheeks were pink roses and she shook out her raven hair. "It's not too bad out there," she claimed and wiped at her nose.

"Oh, dear," Claire gushed and moved toward her. "Let me get your coat."

‹ finding home ›

"Hang on a sec," Mark ordered and climbed to his feet. "If it's not too bad then maybe it's a good night for a fire."

Alice glanced at Claire. "A fire?"

"Bah," Claire dismissed. "There's a pit in the back yard but it's too cold."

Mark's hand covered his heart while mock offense colored his face. "Too cold for a fire? As Lucy Larcom once said, *If the world seems cold to you, kindle fires to warm it.*"

"Lucy Lar—who?"

Alice giggled. "A fire *does* sound nice."

Mark clapped his hands together. "It's settled then."

Claire took a stance of resistance, but Mark pointed at her as a silly grin spread across his face. "Baby, it's cold outside."

Claire tried to hide a smile. "Don't mind him, Alice." She tapped her head. "A few too many birthdays I think."

Mark swayed toward her. "Come on, you know the words."

Claire flirted with her options for a moment before dropping her arms. "I really can't stay."

Mark grabbed his chest. "But, baby, it's cold outside."

Claire's smile spread as she sang out. "I've got to go away."

"But, baby, it's cold outside."

"This evening has been…"

Mark linked his arms around her waist. "Been hoping that you'd drop in."

Claire giggled as they moved together. "So very nice."

"I'll hold your hands, they're just like ice."

"My mother will start to worry."

Mark held up Claire's hand so she could twirl away from him. "Beautiful, what's your hurry?"

"My father will be pacing the floor."

Mark pulled her back to him and kissed her. "Listen to that fire *pit* roar." They all laughed together.

"Okay-okay," Claire gave in and pushed him back. "Go make it roar, honey."

Mark disappeared down the hallway and returned with his coat. "I'll shout when it's ready."

"Phew," Claire uttered and straightened her hair. "Alice, would you like some tea?"

Alice followed Claire outside holding her warm mug with both hands.

"All set," Mark declared. Behind him flames climbed over each other stretching as high as they could. A stone ring set their boundary and three chairs were positioned around it. Alice could already feel the heat cut through the chill.

Claire tossed a bag of marshmallows to Mark and waved a bar of chocolate. "I had to dig a little but I found them. Here's the graham crackers."

Mark held his hands to the warmth. "What's a fire without s'mores, right, Alice?"

Alice felt her cheeks flush as she sat down next to Claire. "What's a s'more?"

"You've *never* had a s'more?"

"What's that?" Mark gawked at her with three sticks in hand. "Never a s'more?"

Alice stared at her feet and tried to dig a hole in the hard ground with her shoe. Maybe she could fall in and climb out as a little girl. Alice let her shoulders sag. The pain of a forgotten decade stung her heart. S'mores were probably just one more thing that had been stolen from her.

"Well, I think we found the reason," Mark offered.

Alice raised her head and noticed his smile reach his eyes. "Reason?"

Mark nodded. "That God brought you to us. Claire and I are a couple of s'mores experts."

Alice couldn't help but laugh at that and soon she was burning marshmallows with the best of them. "Take it easy," Mark teased. "We're not making torches."

Claire pointed at his own flaming marshmallow. "Worry about yourself, mister."

"Ugh," he grunted and jerked his stick away from the fire. He lifted the

«finding home»

charred blob. "This one's yours, Claire."

The night continued with laughter, squeals, scorched marshmallows and melted chocolate. "These are *amazing*," Alice sputtered through a mouthful of her third.

Mark produced the bag of marshmallows. "Ready for another?"

Alice held her stomach and groaned. "I can't. Any more and I might explode."

Claire laughed. "I can't do more than one these days. Oh, I almost forgot. A member of our church, Deb Swoon, owns a coffee shop here in town and just had a position open up. Mark was going to check with her to see if it was still available—"

"*Is* going to check with her," Mark spoke up.

Claire shot him a teasing smile. "We'll see. Anyway, if it's available would you be interested?"

Alice licked her sticky fingers. "A coffee shop? That sounds perfect."

"Yay!" Claire squealed. "I've known Deb for ages. You'll love her, she's…"

Don't come near me with that thing. EEK! Alice straightened and scanned the yard. "Claire, did you hear that?"

"Hear what?"

Alice searched beyond the reach of the firelight. "Someone's out there. A little girl I think. She was—"

Mom, make him stop! He's got a bug and won't leave me alone. Another yelp and then a woman's voice. *Leave your sister alone.* Alice jumped to her feet. The voices were all around them. She gave Claire a desperate look. "Please tell me you heard that."

Claire's blank stare was her only answer.

Mark stepped up and blew into his hands. "What's this now?"

Claire pointed towards the dark trees. "Alice thinks she hears someone out there. A little girl."

"Sometimes the wind can play strange tricks I suppose. It might sound like voices when it gets to swirling around the tree tops."

Alice felt her stomach drop. "You didn't hear anything?"

Mark shook his head. Alice looked around the yard again. Maybe it was the wind. Yes, that's all it was. Alice felt her heart returning to its normal pattern. "Y, yeah," she stuttered. "You're probably—"

I'll take a hot dog, a young girl made known. *I wanna burger. A fat one, with cheese.* A boys voice that time. *There's plenty for everyone.* Adults. Men and women. *Now-now, don't shove.* Squeals and laughter.

"Alice?" Claire touched her shoulder. "Are you okay? You look like you've seen a ghost."

Or heard one, Alice reasoned. She brushed her hair back and forced a nervous laugh. "Yeah. I'm just…maybe I ate one too many s'mores." She motioned to the house. "I think I'll go to bed if that's alright."

Claire nodded, the concern sinking deeper into her expression. "Of course. Get me right away if you need anything."

Alice smiled politely and thanked them. She took one more look at the yard before disappearing inside.

‹finding home›

‹chapter thirty›

You need to do this. I'm right here.

It was his voice, Jesus. And then Ashley had squeezed his hand. He didn't have to do this alone. Resolve filled the air and John sucked it in until his heart steadied. "It was the week before Christmas, almost ten years ago. I'd just been promoted to Chief Nuclear Officer when the plant came up for inspection. They are completely random. We never knew until the day before and all personal plans were cancelled. Everyone came in. Everyone *needed* to come in. A failed inspection wasn't going to happen. I wouldn't allow it."

John could still hear the staff grumble. He'd been hard on them. A freshly promoted big-shot bent on proving he'd do it better than anyone else. A bitter taste filled his mouth. It all seemed so stupid now. It had for a long time.

"The inspection ended on Christmas Eve. It was getting late and the state officials were finishing up some paperwork. Just some formalities. I didn't need to be there. My crew could've handled it. They told me to go home but I, it was my first inspection." John tried to shift on the bed, but his blanket had turned to cement around him. He took in a ragged breath and willed himself to keep talking. If he stopped he'd never start again.

"Amy and the kids were with her parents, about two hours south. Before they left, she asked me to take the night off so that I could be with them. I told her I, I couldn't. She called me on it. She knew my part in the process was over. Before she stormed out the door she let me know a bad storm was supposed to hit and the roads would be terrible. She gave me one more chance to change my mind but I let her leave without me."

John squeezed his fists until they turned white. More than once he'd pulled Amy and their van out of a snowdrift. Everything was a blur. He turned his eyes on Ashley and begged her to understand. "I couldn't leave." *Guilty.* The word thundered through him. *Guilty-Guilty-Guilty!* John sank into the bed as the gavel crashed around him.

"The storm hit like she'd said," he whispered. "Black ice." John swallowed a sob. "They were almost home. There was a semi in the oncoming lane. A gas tanker. The driver started to slide, hit the brakes, and jackknifed."

Ashley and the room were gone. The hospital was gone. John was pacing in his office at the plant listening to OnStar tell him they'd registered an impact to his minivan and were unable to reach the occupants. "We called 911," the operator reported. "Emergency crews are on their way. The address we're showing is…"

John was stone on the black highway in the freezing night. Heat from roaring flames licked his face. Jagged pieces of aluminum and crumpled metal marked a nightmarish trail leading into the inferno. One piece in particular reflected the firelight more than the rest; the Toyota emblem of their Sienna.

Emergency vehicles covered the scene. Bright flashes of blue, red, and yellow reflected off mixed fluids pooling on the highway. John caught the sound of more sirens in the distance. He detected the inflections of urgent voices. None of them were Amy or his kids. Time crawled forward in slow motion.

Paramedics hung around their ambulances with arms crossed and heads down. John tried to scream for them to do something, but the cry never made it past his lips. One of them lifted his eyes and John knew why they were still. There wasn't anyone to save.

The road was quickly becoming a sea of white foam trying to smother the flames. Bits of it caught random gusts and escaped the nightmare. A sob racked John's body. It was the first sound he'd made since the call from OnStar. Wobbly knees gave up and he crumbled to the ground. There were shouts he couldn't discern. The paramedics were running his way.

One of them bent down. He stunk of fire and sweat. His face was streaked with grime. Or was it tears? John tried to sink into the ground, but strong arms tugged him up and hurried him toward a stretcher. He

‹ finding home ›

curled into a ball when they placed him on the hard cushion. He couldn't move, couldn't think. He could only gape at the firestorm raging from the cylindrical trailer. He closed his eyes and embraced the darkness. When he opened them he was back in the hospital room.

Ashley had wilted like a daisy in the desert. Grief had spread over her face, mirroring his own. She twitched as if to move, but then hesitated for a moment before her arms were around him, holding him, squeezing him. He melted into her and gave himself to the sobs. His voice was barley a whisper. "It's my fault."

Ashley wiped her eyes and searched his face. "What did you say?"

His head felt as if it had an anchor hanging from it. "I should've gone with them. I should have been driving. I told her that my job was more important." Guilt and self-hate tightened around his lungs. His last moments with Amy had been sealed in a fight. He never got to tell her so many things. The victories of the last several days seemed so far away. In the end he was the same. He groaned and hid his face. He was guilty. He was—

"John!" Ashley's tone was firm and her eyes uncompromising. "I'm so, so sorry for what you've been through and what you've lost. My heart hurts for you, my heart hurts *with* you. I can't begin to imagine..." She let the words hang in the air for a long time before lifting his head so she could look into his eyes. "There are things that we should take responsibility for and things we shouldn't. We own the things we can, forgive ourselves, and ask God to heal our hearts." She paused and pressed her hands against his cheeks. "We release the things we aren't responsible for. John, you aren't responsible for the weather. You aren't responsible for the patch of ice. You aren't responsible for the decisions of the semi driver and you certainly aren't responsible for the explosion."

John felt his heart harden. He'd heard the judgment, felt the sentence. "It doesn't matter. If I would've—"

"You've got to let this go. Please, let it go. Forgive yourself for not being with them and release the blame and guilt for what you had no control over."

Guilty! "It's because of me." John's voice cracked on the last word. "They're dead because of me."

I forgive you John.

John gulped air and cast a glance around the room. He ignored the confused look from Ashley and strained to hear that familiar voice.

I forgive you for not being with your family. I forgive you for choosing work over them that night.

John felt his heart spasm and grabbed his chest. How can you forgive me after what I've done? They'd still be here.

Son, you listen to me now. Hear the truth. What happened was not your fault. It wasn't because of you. I need you to forgive yourself before I can take you where I want you to be. Self-hatred, guilt, and shame want to keep you in prison but I have come to set you free. I have wiped away your stains. Now, forgive yourself and let me love you.

But I'm guilty.

Does your judgment rise above mine? Is your court higher than mine? I have pronounced you forgiven. You are not guilty. Forgive yourself and you will be free.

He fixed his eyes on Ashley. "Was it my fault?"

"No," Ashley assured him. "It wasn't."

Fresh tears spilled onto John's cheeks. If Jesus said that he was forgiven, maybe he could believe it. "I can't live like this anymore. I want to be free. I forgive myself for the way I treated my family that day." He gasped and clutched his chest. Each word spoken was ripping him to shreds. He threw a desperate look at Ashley.

"Go on," she encouraged.

"The accident wasn't my fault." As soon as the words left his mouth something stirred deep inside of him, like a heavy weight being dislodged. It moved, slow at first, but then faster, rising with emotion so strong it hurt.

The wail was loud enough to shake the walls. Ten years worth of blame and self hate poured from him like a geyser. The sound ended and he collapsed back on the bed. He stayed like that for a few minutes before turning wide eyes on Ashley. "It's gone." He moved his hands over his body as if checking for injury. "All that weight is just…gone. I feel so light."

A slow grin took Ashley's features and she began to giggle. John held out his arms. "I think I could just float away."

Ashley sniffed. "You're free."

‹finding home›

John reached for Ashley and traced her face with a shaky hand. "I'm free." It didn't sound real, but it was. "Jesus set me free." He clapped once and gave a shout. "I'm free!" Then he pulled Ashley's lips to his own. "Thanks, Ash. For everything."

She grinned and buried her face in his chest. "You're welcome. Thank you for sharing your heart with me."

"One more thing," he added. "My last name's Rister. I'm John Rister."

chapter thirty one

Seven AM had never smelled better. Alice let the aroma of freshly ground exotic coffee beans overtake her senses. Espresso machines hummed and the roar of steaming milk filled her ears. Tired voices played in the background as the team, her team, worked seamlessly to get the sleepy customers their energy fix. The morning rush was on and the Morning Shot was busy as usual.

Alice held up the latte she'd just made and admired the foam. *My best yet,* she decided and handed it to a sagging woman who glared at her while mumbling something like, "It's about time." Alice watched her take a sip and waited. The woman's eyes brightened and a smile pushed the weariness from her face. She lifted her cup at Alice before disappearing into whatever the day had for her.

Alice smoothed her apron and giggled at the guy in line with a shirt that said, *Caffeine isn't a drug, it's a vitamin.* A satisfied sigh rose from her heart as she took in the room. Warm reds and yellows colored walls that held pictures of steaming cups and piles of whole beans. Soft lighting finished off an ambience that beckoned patrons to stay and get comfortable. Some did. Alice glanced at a couple shuffling papers and pecking at laptops. Joey with plates in his stretched ear lobes and Crissy with her frizzy red hair. Regulars. After two weeks Alice knew most of them.

"Hey, Alice."

She turned as her manager tossed a white rag on the counter. Judy was a hard woman who'd fled New York City with the accent and famed *charm.* "Wipe down these counters for me will ya."

"Yeah sure," Alice responded.

Judy rubbed her hands on her apron. "Good, I don't want none of them

≪finding home≫

smudges here. Hey you!" She pointed at a thin barista named Matt. "I need a minute. No, stay there." She leaned toward Alice. "He's like a eunuch in a whorehouse that one. No, I said stay there ya schlep."

Alice sprayed cleaner on the counter and wiped while Judy's voice blended into the background. *Poor guy.* Matt's eyes darted back and forth while Judy's finger cut through the air like a conductor. *She could huff and puff and blow him right outta here.*

"Don't worry about her. She's really not that bad." Alice rotated to see Nikki smirking at her. "Underneath all that other…stuff."

Alice covered her mouth so Judy wouldn't hear her laughing. Nikki had been working at the cafe for a couple of years and had been tasked with making sure Alice could do the job. She was a skinny girl with milk chocolate skin and curly black hair that bounced when she laughed. Something she did a lot of.

"For real though," Nikki went on. "She's fine once you get to know her."

Alice balled the rag and tossed it into a bin marked 'dirty.' "You keep telling me that."

Nikki flicked at a crumb. "Say somethin' enough and it'll happen."

"I'm pretty sure that's not true."

"I've got one year left to find out. Then I'm outta here. College, fame n' all that." She dropped her rag in the bin. "So how you doin' with everything?"

Alice leaned against the counter. She'd shared general details about her recent move from Redwood. "Pretty good I think." It was the truth. She'd been in Oak Harbor for a month and was settling in well. Maybe even better than well.

"You get to talk to your family at all?"

"Yeah, I actually talked to them last night. They miss me like crazy, but everyone's doing great. And they've been nothing but supportive." She paused. "Maybe that's why I feel so good about being here."

Nikki carried an empty creamer container from the counter to a sink holding a few other dishes. "What about the people you're staying with? How are they?"

Alice tucked a strand of hair behind her ear. "Honestly, I think they're the biggest reason I haven't freaked out."

"I can see that," Nikki expressed. "I went to his church once. Long time ago." She snapped her fingers. "Mark right? Mark..."

"Summers."

"Yeah, that's it. Anyway, he seemed like a really nice guy."

"They're both great. They include me in everything but I never feel like they're intruding, you know?"

Nikki made a face. "No. Sounds like intruding to me."

Alice waved her off. "It's not like that. They're not pushy. I get room to breathe but I," she smiled shyly, "they make me feel like part of the family."

"What do y'all do together? Checkers? Pigeon feeding?" She hopped up and sat on the counter. "You ever get tired of eatin' dinner at 3:30?"

Alice laughed and smacked Nikki's arm. "Stop it. They're good people. A couple of times I've even felt like they know me or something." She shook her head. "I mean like, before I even moved here."

"*Have* you met them before?"

"Not that I can remember."

"Well, lots of people come for the festivals. You probably came one year."

"That's what Claire said. Maybe..." The feeling was always so brief, like a twig in a current that snagged momentarily before floating away. Alice straightened some flavored syrups. "There's something else." Alice lowered her voice. "I don't usually do well with men." Nikki raised an eyebrow. "I had some bad...it's complicated. But with Mark its easy. I don't get it."

"What do you mean?"

Alice sighed. "I don't know like, okay, the other night we were all playing a game and I didn't even notice Claire leave. I just looked up and she was gone. I had no idea it'd just been Mark and I. That's not *normal*. For me anyway."

"Girl..." Nikki twirled a finger around Alice's head. "You're just all kinds of crazy up in there aren't you?"

Alice laughed and shoved her. Something else had been distracting her. There'd been more dreams and the pictures were becoming clearer. She saw pictures of a boy and girl she didn't know. Kids. They smiled and held out their arms out inviting her to go with them. She wanted to, but couldn't make herself move.

≺ finding home ≻

They would run and disappear inside of a house that took her breath away. It was a brilliantly white, two-story home. Large windows faced her on both levels and the wrap-a-round porch highlighted the front. The door was all wood, the color of maple with glass arranged in rectangles lining the top section. The house was big but not gaudy. Not a mansion. Not an estate. But bigger than anything *she'd* ever lived in.

Thick trees lined the winding driveway. Green grass colored a backyard that stretched into hills before meeting dense woods.

"Hey!"

Alice blinked at Nikki. "Sorry I—"

"Ladies!" Judy was glaring at them from the register, her mouth a taunt line. "Not fuh nuttin' but if you're done exercisin' your mouths and, oh I don't know, feel like *working...*" she gestured to the line. "And you'd better get off that counter."

Alice hurried to the espresso machine aware of Judy's scowl, but unable to keep her mind from wandering back to her dreams.

They hadn't all been fluffy and nice. One night Alice dreamed that she was flying, at least she thought she was. She couldn't be sure because it was so dark, but she felt air rushing past her. At the very least she was moving very quickly. It made her feel disoriented and dizzy, like she'd just been on the teacup ride at the Redwood county fair.

And then things would change. The darkness was the same, but loneliness, confusion, and fear were new. She'd still be moving through the dark, but walking instead of flying. Alice could feel the hard, uneven ground beneath her feet. She kept bumping into objects that felt rough and tall like trees, like she was in the woods somewhere. When the fear became so intense she thought it might kill her, she would wake up. Instantly peace would fill her and she could almost feel God's arms wrap around her saying, *It's alright. I'm here. That's enough for now.*

Alice filled a cup and wished with all her heart that Nita would walk through the door. She could untangle it all.

Just then the door chime sounded. Alice whipped around expecting to see the old woman. But it wasn't her. It was something else, *someone* else.

chapter thirty two

Caleb Parker stepped into the café and rubbed his burning eyes. He sighed and took a look around the room. A line of crossed arms, tapping feet, and sleepy scowls greeted him. The only smile came from a guy wearing a shirt that read, *caffeine is not a drug, it's a vitamin.* Caleb rolled his eyes. Caffeine is a drug and the withdrawals turn people into jerks. He glanced at the cheery shirt guy again. Except for that guy. It made him weird.

"Excuse me…" A stump of a woman thrust her finger over Caleb's shoulder. "The line's back *there.*"

Caleb feigned surprise. "What? I can't just step into line wherever I want?" He threw his hands up. "I guess I'll just go to the end then. I thought this was *America.*" Caleb felt her glare on his back and heard a few snickers as he took his place at the end of the line. A streak of regret stung him. He didn't mean to snap, but his patience was a strand of angel hair pasta against a table saw.

The crowd shuffled in front of him, but instead of moving forward a few people just seemed to trade places. Actually just one. Caleb stifled a groan. The *shirt guy* was now facing him wearing a toothy grin. He was thick and heavy and stood a head taller than Caleb. "Hi, I'm Ralph," he chirped and held out a Cheetos stained hand.

Caleb tried to see past him to the front of the line. "Weren't you just up there?"

Ralph shrugged and a strand of oily brown hair slid across his forehead. "Eh, it's okay. I wanted to come talk to you."

"Lucky me," Caleb muttered.

"What?"

⯇ finding home ⯈

"Nothing." Caleb shook they guys hand and instantly yearned for a sink. "Caleb."

"Nice place, huh?" Ralph covered his mouth and hacked. "Haven't seen you here before."

Caleb watched him wipe his hand on his corduroy pants. "Yeah...I haven't been here."

Ralph pointed at Caleb's chest. "You're a firefighter, right?"

Caleb glanced down at the department patch peaking out from beneath his jacket. "Firefighter/Paramedic," he corrected. School was long and hard and he was proud of it. He slid his thumb over the rough patch. He'd forgotten he was wearing his work shirt. *Should've been nicer to that woman.*

They moved forward with the line. "I thought you all loved coffee," Ralph blathered and picked at something in his teeth.

"Sorry to disappoint you."

"But you're here now." Ralph raised both eyebrows. "Long night?"

"You could say that."

Ralph shot him a queer look. "Yeah, I just did. Anyway, I was up all night too."

"That's nice."

"Finally," the stump woman grunted somewhere ahead of him. She stomped to the door with her coffee but stopped long enough to spin and flip Caleb off.

"Have a nice day, ma'am," he hollered after her.

"...Warcraft."

Caleb turned his attention back to Ralph. "Huh?"

"Are you a *gamer*, Caleb?"

The line moved again. "A gamer?"

"Yeah, you know." Ralph jerked a pretend controller through the air. "Computer games, RPG...a *gamer.*"

"No Ray—"

"Ralph."

Caleb pressed his fingers into his temples.

"Gotta headache, huh?" Ralph tugged at the bottom of his shirt making the letters yawn. "Must be from your job. Do you like it?"

Caleb loved it. Though the warm fuzzies were hard to feel after being awake for 24 hours straight. It wasn't always like that. Some nights the emergency tones didn't go off at all. He forced a smile at Ralph and pointed at the register. "You're up."

Ralph turned and for a moment Caleb could see past his thick body. That single moment was all it took to have every coherent thought chased away by a set of piercing, hazel eyes.

❦

Alice watched him linger for a moment before heading to the line. Curly blonde hair bounced over round ears with each step. Alice measured him. He was tall and lean, but not lanky. Maybe her age. The chill outside had left a pinkish tint to his cream colored skin.

She forced him from her mind and pressed a button on the espresso machine. It roared and spit a shot into an empty cup marked: Margo. Alice carefully poured in steamed milk and watched black and white create swirly caramel. Who was the last boy she'd actually paid attention too? She held up the latte and blinked. There'd *never* been anyone like that for her.

"...*America!*"

Alice almost spilled the drink. The boy with the curly blonde hair was almost at the end of the line while a short, thick woman glared a hole in his back. "Crazy coffee drinkers," she said half aloud and put on a smile. "Latte for Margo." A pleasant looking woman accepted the cup and disappeared through the door.

Alice tucked a strand of hair behind her ear and searched for the blonde curls. For some reason the guy with the funny shirt had moved right in front of him. She leaned to the side to try and get a better look.

"Girl, *what* are you doing?"

Alice felt her cheeks get hot. "Nothing," she blurted and slid behind the espresso machine. "Just seeing how many are waiting."

"There's eight," Nikki reported. "Somethin' about that number make you blush?" She leaned in. "Or maybe it's that fine piece of man I saw you starin' at?"

Alice's hands flew to cool her face. "What are you talking about?"

‹‹finding home››

Nikki gave her a 'do I look stupid' look and muttered something about white girl drama. Alice studied the pending orders, but all the letters mashed together. A flame rolled through her belly. Boys are just men. And eight years before Redwood had taught her about men. Some of their voices still haunted her. *You think you're better than this? This is all anyone will ever want from you!*

Alice centered all of her focus on the next few drinks. Maybe if—

"Alice," Judy called. "Come take the register for a sec."

Alice gave the Americano she'd just finished to a grateful man and hurried to relieve Judy who pointed at the big guy with the shirt. "He's all set and you've got it from here."

Alice settled behind the register as the mountain moved. "I can help whose next." His ice blue eyes were wide and slightly parted lips were pulled into a half smile. *Men. Eight years.* Her cheeks flushed again. Neither of them seemed able to produce words and the guest behind him was starting to notice. "How can I help you?" she finally managed.

"Wow," he let slip.

It was the loudest, quiet word she'd ever heard. "Did you just say, 'wow?'"

His face turned cartoon red. "No, I mean...who are you? I mean..."

The line behind him rustled. Alice leaned over the register and lowered her voice. "We serve coffee here. Would you like some?"

He seemed to remember where he was and forced a crooked smile. "I'm sorry, I haven't really slept..." He threw a pleading look at Alice for mercy. She wasn't dealing. "Uh, just a medium, regular, please."

Alice rung him up and took his money. "We'll get that right out for you." She turned her focus to the line. "Can I help—"

"I'll take it from here." Judy bumped her back toward the prep area. Alice swallowed her annoyance. "Yeah, sure."

Nikki took a pitcher of half n' half from the fridge. "I'm all caught up here. Just have the *medium regular* left."

"Very funny," Alice returned. "Should be a quick one for Matt."

"Uh-uh, I don't think so. That boy's cryin' in the back somewhere."

"Can you take this one?"

"And get in the way of true love?" Nikki teased. "No way."

Alice sighed. "Fine." She found the red-blonde boy waiting at the end of the counter. "Sir, what was your name?"

"Caleb with a C," he answered and turned red all over again. Nikki snickered and Alice wrote his name on a cup. *Caleb with a C.* She threw one more glare at Nikki, who she thought might be the worst person in the world, before heading to the dispenser.

Black coffee filled the cup while excitement and dread churned in Alice's stomach. When she lifted her eyes Caleb was staring at her, but quickly averted to the counter. Alice left some room for cream and lingered at the machine. She wasn't stupid. She saw the attraction in his eyes. She'd seen it before in many others. But there was something different in the way *he* looked at her. She snapped a lid on the cup. What was it?

Lust, Alice suddenly knew. Her heart fluttered. Raw, perverse, and unbridled desire was missing. She snuck another peek at him. His arms crossed loosely over his chest and the bright red skin was returning to normal. She traced the hot cup absently with her finger and Nikki nudged her. "You gonna give that poor boy his coffee or stand here and drink it yourself?"

"Shut up," Alice shot back. Caleb was sitting now, on a stool with one arm on the counter. He smiled as she approached. She set the cup in front of him. "Here you go Caleb with a *C*. One medium, regular coffee with enough room for you to make it taste like something else."

He glanced at the cup and then back at her. "How'd you know?"

"You just kinda seem like a guy who doesn't drink a lot of coffee."

"Two weeks and the girls a pro," Nikki called from somewhere behind her.

Alice raised her hands. "It's a vibe I guess."

"You got me," Caleb admitted. "I don't really like coffee but occasionally I need it." He leaned on his elbows. "Any other vibes you're picking up?"

Alice felt heat on her cheeks and started her retreat.

"Hold on a sec," he blurted.

She held a moment before rotating back. "Yes?"

Caleb drummed the counter with a finger. "I, uh, just wanted to, you know, apologize for what happened over there. I'm just gonna blame it on sleep deprivation."

Alice studied him and tried to keep her expression neutral. She was a

‹ finding home ›

wall, impenetrable to cute boys and slick words. But the way he stumbled over himself kept knocking her sideways. "Well, I'm sure it's been worse somewhere...somehow."

He grinned. "I appreciate the lie." She spun away before he could see her smile.

"So how many sugar packets should I—"

Alice whirled around and brought her hands together. "Look, I've got alotta work to do so if there's nothing else..." The outburst surprised her. She peered at him expecting to see the damage she'd done reflected in his face, but he didn't look hurt. He appeared steady and determined like some old statue of a town founder.

"Okay forget the sugar. But if I left without knowing your name I'd hate myself." He worked up a sad look. "Don't let me hate myself."

She eyed him. "You'll hate yourself."

"Yes."

"Like before at the register?"

He scoffed. "Yeah, I definitely hated myself over *there*."

Alice banished another smile back into the reserves.

Caleb motioned to where Nikki stood trying not to laugh. "I mean, I'd hate to have to ask your friend."

Alice gaped at Nikki. "Have you been there this *whole time?*"

"Come on, girl," she exclaimed and laughed. "If you don't tell the poor guy your name I'm gonna tell him mine."

Alice glanced between the both of them a few times before finally surrendering. "Alice, alright. My name is Alice."

"Alice." Caleb said it like hearing it from his own mouth would make it real. "Well, okay then."

Anxiety pricked her skin. "That's it then? You're going to leave now?"

Caleb adjusted his jacket and Alice noticed the Fire department patch for the first time. "That's the deal I made." He caught her eyes and she let him hold on longer than she'd meant too.

"It was very nice to meet you, Alice." He gave her one last smile before vanishing through the door.

Alice bit her tongue to keep it from forming words. Part of her wanted to stop him, tell him to wait.

"Back to it, girl," Nikki hollered. "We've got like a *zillion* drinks to make."

Alice pointed at her friend. "I'm gonna kill you."

Nikki laughed and handed her an order.

«finding home»

chapter thirty three

Ashley's ponytail swayed back and forth on her back as she hurried into the Pink Tea Room, a cozy little shop nestled at the corner of Main and Peach Tree. "Good morning," she chirped to a pretty girl standing at the podium with a sign that read, *please wait to be seated,* in an elegant font.

"Good morning," the girl echoed. "How many?"

"Oh, I'm meeting someone and I think she's already here."

The hostess ran a finger down a page. "Name please?"

"Tina."

The girl smiled sweetly and showed her a closet. "Please hang your coat there and follow me." She led Ashley through pastel flowerbeds and rustic décor accented by soft music. They stopped at a table for two where Ashley's longtime ICU friend was crunching on a weird looking pastry. Ashley smiled at the hostess who sang an, "*Enjoy,*" before floating away to the next guest.

Tina brushed a few crumbs from her mouth and gave Ashley a guilty look. "I couldn't let these poor things just sit on the plate."

Ashley waved her off and sat down. "Sorry I'm late. What are those anyway?"

Tina plucked up one of the round snacks and studied it. "*Anarse Ki Goli.* Don't ask me what it means. Tasty though." She plopped it in her mouth.

Ashley sized up the room. "It looks like we're in a courtyard or something."

Tina swallowed. "Nice, isn't it?"

Ashley sipped water from her glass. "I can't believe there's a place like this here. The hostess looks like she was transplanted from a fairy tale book."

Tina laughed. "Wait till you see our waiter."

"What's with our—"

"Good *afternooooon ladiessss.*" A spectacled Mr. Belvedere clone complete with the accent hovered over them. Ashley covered her mouth to hide a smirk.

Tina winked at Ashley and gasped. "Ah, good afternoon, sir." Her English accent was terrible. "Could we trouble you for a spot of tea? Maybe a crumpet or two?" She pointed at Ashley. "Maybe something with an English name for my friend here?"

The waiter studied Tina down the bridge of his nose for a long moment before letting out a long sigh. "Always lovely to see you." He swiveled and started for the kitchen. "Heaven forbid you start drinking *coffee.*"

Tina turned a wide grin on Ashley. "We go back, him and I."

Ashley laughed. "Sometimes I forget how much of a *brat* you can be."

"It's how I stay so young, deary. We need that sass, working where we do." She flipped her hand through the air. "But enough about me. How's that man of yours?"

Ashley smiled. John had been out of the hospital for a few weeks. They'd spent nearly every day of it together. Picnics and walks under starry skies. It was like something out of a Nicholas Sparks novel. "I don't want to be a total *cheese ball* but I've never felt this way about someone before. I mean, yeah I was in love with my ex but this is different. I'm," Ashley balanced her hands, "more complete I think. No, I *know*. I always thought people only had one level. What you see is what you get. But then Jesus changed everything. The more I pursued him the more my superficial layer disappeared. I discovered I have so much *more* to give than I ever thought. And it's like that with John. That day in the store he tried to be so, concrete maybe? But I saw the layers underneath and I've watched him become someone I can know and connect with in a way I haven't before." Ashley nibbled on a pastry. "I don't think I'm making any sense."

Their server set down a chic teapot and assorted pastries. "Cream? Sugar?"

"*Pleasssssse,*" Tina drawled. He set down two smaller jars and muttered something about the homeland.

"Oh my dear sweet Ashley," Tina cried out and filled their dainty cups

≪ finding home ≫

with tea. "My husband and I spent the first ten years of our marriage getting to know that *superficial layer*. Sugar?" Ashley held out her cup and Tina dropped a spoonful in. "We had divorce paperwork signed in that tenth year. Never filed. Jesus got to us in a tiny church in some Podunk Kansas town just in time. Ran out of gas right in front of the sucker and wandered in. Spent the next five years getting to know each other for *real*." Tina sipped carefully. "So, I know what you're saying. I get it. I just wish Fred and I could've had that right from the beginning. You're in a good place, sweetie."

Ashley turned the pastry over in her hand and listened to parakeets chirp from a cage to her right. *A good place*. It was nice to hear. Tina had a way of making her feel grounded, stable. Like her world wasn't as topsy-turvy as it sometimes seemed. "Thanks, Tina. Thanks for not telling me I'm crazy."

"Bah," Tina uttered and poured a bit more cream into her cup. "The kettle doesn't call the pot black, sweetheart."

Ashley smirked. "Stones and glass houses?"

Tina's eyes sparkled. "Let's not get carried away." They both laughed before Tina asked in a serious tone, "How's John doing? It's still hard to believe all he's been through. And then you just found out his real last name."

Ashley placed her teacup on the table. She'd already told Tina all about the night John explained about his family. How he'd lost them. "Uh, pretty good I guess considering this is the first time he's ever really grieved the loss." There'd been more smiles than tears since that night, but when the anguish hit him it was rough. "It breaks my heart when I see the pain in his eyes. And I can't say I wasn't surprised about his last name but in a way it fits. He's not that person anymore. I get to be with the man God is making him instead of the one pain made him."

Tina gave Ashley's hand a squeeze. "I can't imagine having to deal with the things he has." Tina sipped her tea. "Remind me where they were from."

"Oak Harbor, Ohio." *Oak Harbor*. "Tina?"

"Yes?"

Ashley twisted a cloth napkin around her finger. "John's mentioned Oak

Harbor a few times over the last couple days. He's talked about people he used to know and different parts of the town he grew up in."

"Okay."

Ashley dropped the napkin that was now a ball onto the table. "I think he's going back. Or wants to. He hasn't said anything like that to me but I can tell." She gave Tina a defeated look. "Do you think he'd leave without me? I mean, I think about how long we've been together and how nuts it would be for me to leave Blackwater. And then I wonder if he would even ask me…" Ashley held her head to keep it from spinning off. "Sorry, I just—"

"Don't you dare apologize," Tina ordered. "Following you on this roller coaster put's life in these old bones."

"Everything okay here?" their stuffy waiter asked.

Tina slapped the table. "Smashing my good man. Simply *smashing*."

Ashley giggled as the man left. "You're so bad."

Tina dipped her head. "It's the highlight of his day I'm sure." She chewed a bite of pastry. "But I'm not sure what to tell you, Ashley. If he's really planning to leave you might wake up one day and find him gone." She flicked her hand. "*Vanishmo.*"

Ashley feigned relief. "Whew, thanks so much for putting me at ease. And that's not even a word."

Tina raised both eyebrows. "First of all, yes it is a word, and second, you didn't let me finish."

Ashley gestured for her to continue.

"I was *going* to say how unlikely it would be for him to leave without you. It seems like he's come a long way in a short time and he's done it with you by his side. It's hard to just up and leave someone who's shared in the deepest parts of your life."

Ashley brushed a pastry flake off of her lap and sucked in her bottom lip.

"What is it, Ashley?" Ashley shifted in her chair and Tina leaned back. "Oh. You're not even sure you'd go if he asked."

Ashley let her shoulders sag. "Do I have it written on my forehead?"

Tina smiled. "More or less."

Ashley picked up a spoon and stirred her tea into a whirlpool. The

‹ finding home ›

thought of leaving with John was exciting, but she had a life here. Tina leaned over the table. "Do you love him?"

Ashley felt some of the tension melt as the question weaved in and out of her heart. There was no doubt. "Yes."

"And does he love you."

Ashley stopped stirring. John's voice echoed in her ears. *I care about you Ashley. More than I thought was possible.* The things he'd told her in the hospital. The time they'd spent together. But did he *love* her? She lifted heavy eyes to Tina. "I don't know."

Tina reached over and squeezed her hand. "Well, I'd *figure that* out before making plans to go anywhere."

Tina sipped her tea and changed the subject to crazy ICU stories. They left the Pink Tea Room laughing but Ashley also had an ache in the pit of her stomach. An ache that could only be relieved by knowing that the man she loved, loved her back.

chapter thirty four

It was one o'clock and Alice's shift was over. She gave a short wave over her shoulder. "See you tomorrow, Nikki."

"Alright, girl," she called back. "Make sure you do something fun today."

Alice blew a strand of hair away from her face and wondered what she meant. "Something fun," she muttered and rummaged through her purse. Mark and Claire had an extra car they'd given her permission to use, but she couldn't find the keys. There was more junk in her purse than Marry Poppins.

"Need some help?"

Alice snapped her head up, startled. *Caleb!* Her face flamed and she nearly dropped her purse. "What are you doing here?" She finally spotted her keys and fumbled them out.

Caleb shoved his hands in the pockets of his jeans. "I just thought you might need a tour of the town since you're, you know, new to the area and all."

Alice raised an accusatory finger. "Okay, how did you know that? And how did you know when to show up here?"

"Your friends are pretty helpful."

"My friends?" Alice almost ordered him to explain but then she knew. *NIKKI!* She whirled around to the counter, but couldn't see the traitor. Probably hiding.

She pivoted back to Caleb and glowered at him. "You asked Nikki about me?"

"I thought that might be easier based on the whole *name thing* this morning."

‹ finding home ›

"Stalking is against the law."

"Then it's a good thing I'm just a concerned tour guide."

Alice crossed her arms over her chest and took a step back. "You had no right. Nikki had no right to—"

"Whoa," Caleb stammered and raised his hands. "I'm sorry if I upset you. That wasn't my intention…*really*." He rubbed the back of his neck. "When I left this morning I just needed an excuse to see you again. Any excuse. And this is what I came up with."

Alice studied him and fought to keep her righteous indignation. She wished the small part of her that was glad to see him was a bug so she could squash it. "It's fine," she finally murmured keeping her eyes away from his. "Don't worry about it."

They hung there for a long time each daring the other to speak first. Alice won. "So are you gonna let me show you around?"

"It's a small town and I've been here awhile."

Caleb winked. "Maybe there's something you haven't seen yet."

"Did you just *wink* at me?"

"What? No, sometimes my eye twitches." He tried to convince her by rubbing it.

"Uh-huh."

"So, what do you say?"

"I can't. I'm still unpacking and, you know, really busy." She felt a stab of remorse for the lie but she couldn't go with him. The thought of saying *yes* was equally thrilling and terrifying.

"Come on," he pleaded. "How about you let me show you around now and I'll help you with your stuff after."

"I don't need your help with my stuff."

"You say that now but after our walk you might be pretty tired."

Alice almost cracked a smile. "Fine."

Caleb smiled with victory as he held the door. Alice closed her eyes briefly as she passed him. "Just a quick look around," she told him without turning her head.

"I'll take it."

The sun was out and shining brightly in the clear, blue sky. The air was cold and fresh and carried the faint scent of burnt leaves. She tightened her coat around her body.

Caleb stepped beside her and blew into his hands. "Are you okay with walking? Everything's pretty close."

"I guess so." She watched him blow into his hands again. "That is, if you can make it."

"I'm good," he assured and motioned down the sidewalk. "Shall we?"

Alice answered by moving forward, and was careful to keep space between them when he fell into step beside her.

"Just about everything is here on Main Street," he announced and pointed to her left. "The library and post office. And then you've got a bunch of little shops like hardware, grocery, and some stuff for tourists."

"Tourists, huh?"

He grinned. "Well, we're a little *slow* right now. Head left here."

They rounded the corner on Church Street and Alice stopped. Snow banks, naked trees, and a blue sky gave it a classic winter look. Beautiful, but empty. They were the only ones in sight. Panic raced through her colder than the air.

"You okay?" Caleb asked.

"Yeah, I'm fine. This way?" She started moving before he had a chance to ask any more questions.

"Hey are you sure you're—"

"I said I'm *fine*, Caleb." He fell silent and she stole a glance at him. His eyes were fixed ahead and his mouth was a straight line. Remorse hammered her again. "Caleb, look I'm—"

Thud! Whoosh! A cloud of white powder struck her arm. Alice squealed and saw Caleb bouncing another snowball in his hands. The laughter in his eyes matched the smile on his face. "You can't just yell at me and not expect to get hit by a snowball."

Alice raised a finger. "Don't you dare."

He laughed, reached back, and let it go.

"Caleb!" The snow was in the air and exploded on her chest before she could get out of the way. She was too stunned to be mad.

He raised his hands at her. "Let's see whatcha got."

Alice hesitated but felt a coy smile form on her lips. "You sure about that?"

≪ finding home ≫

Caleb lifted his chin. "Bring it!" He fired again but Alice slid to the left and it sailed past.

"Okay," she sassed. "But just remember *you* asked for this." Alice raced behind a snow bank and had an arsenal in minutes.

"Hey," Caleb called. "Where do snowmen keep their money?"

Alice carefully peaked around her barrier. Caleb was about 15 feet from her.

"In a snow—"

His last word disappeared in a cloud of white as Alice's snowball exploded on his chest. "Keep telling jokes funny man."

Caleb spit snow out of his mouth. "So, that's how it is." He launched a wobbly snowball that Alice dodged easily. She fired two more that hit him center chest.

"Okay-okay," Caleb cried waving his hands and laughing. "I surrender." He jogged to her. "What are you some kinda professional snowball thrower?"

Alice was breathless. "Yeah, something like that. I didn't hurt you did I?"

"Just my pride. But it was worth it."

She caught his eyes. The look he gave her sent a quiver through her knees. Alice broke the spell. "What are you talking about?"

He paused long enough for her to notice he'd stepped closer. "I finally got to see you smile."

Alice reached for her face and forced air in and out of her lungs. Time seemed to take a break from its relentless push forward to give her a chance to stay in the moment. He was so close. She could touch him if she wanted. Alice wondered what that would be like, to touch his face. Her fingers tingled but she fell back and squeezed her eyes shut.

Caleb's voice was thick. "Shall we go on?"

She brushed her hair back and nodded. They shuffled down Church Street in silence until they reached an open, grassy area with scattered trees. A large fountain stood near the center.

"This," Caleb pointed out with a dramatic inflection, "is where we have our annual Frosty Fest."

Alice raised an eyebrow. "Excuse me?"

"Yeah, it's a few days before Christmas. It's pretty neat. The whole town comes out and has a good time. There's games and music." He paused. "Even a dance at the end."

Alice pressed her lips together. Redwood had thrown some festivals and she'd always had fun.

Caleb kicked at a small pebble. "There was actually a Frosty Run a few weeks ago. People take off through the town in shorts and tank tops." He flashed a teasing grin at her. "Too bad you missed it."

"Yeah, too bad." Alice took a step onto the frozen grass. "Lots of Frosty stuff here."

Caleb slid beside her, close enough for his arm to graze hers sending a tingle across her skin. "Are you going?"

She put some space between them. "Will you dress up like a snowman?"

He laughed. "I will if you will."

"Sorry, white's really not my color."

"Right," he scoffed. "Like there's any color that *doesn't* work for you."

Alice raised her eyebrows at him. "Ooh, he's got *lines*."

"No, not lines. Just trying to be honest. If I tried a *line* I'd probably choke on it."

Alice kept her head down as they moved back to the sidewalk, but let herself smile at the way he continued to surprise her. "I'm guessing you've lived here your whole life to be able to give me this fabulous tour."

He grinned. "Yeah, I was born here. Never left." Caleb spread his arms wide. "Twenty-four glorious years right here. Well, mostly glorious anyway."

A sudden wave of homesickness washed over Alice. She wanted her *own* small town. "You ever want to? Leave I mean?" Alice reached up and flicked a blonde curl. "You know, maybe find a beach and surf board?"

"Hardy-har-har," Caleb returned. "You joke, but try growing up somewhere everyone is convinced you're some coastal vacation love child."

Alice laughed out loud at that before she could get a glove over her mouth. Caleb feigned offense. "Oh, she laughs. At my *suffering*." That only made Alice laugh harder. A second later Caleb was laughing just as hard.

Alice could feel anxiety and reservations melt as she held her sides and wiped tears. Mark had just quoted something about laughter a few days ago. Something like, 'There is nothing in the world so irresistibly contagious as

≪finding home≫

laughter and good humor.' Charles Dickens, he'd informed her.

"Anyway," Caleb continued after they'd composed themselves, "no, I never seriously considered leaving. Oak Harbor isn't the kind of town people wanna get away from. I know that small towns can get kinda *weird,* but this town is different." He faced her and walked backward. "People really care about each other here, you know? For the most part anyway."

Alice did know. She rifled through a Rolodex of friendly Redwood faces. "I moved here from Redwood, New York. It's a small town like this one. I could've lived there my whole life."

Caleb bumped her. "It's home right? Not perfect, but home."

Alice tried to ignore the sensations shooting through her from his touch. She watched him blow a smoky breath cloud into the sky and then smile as it rose and disappeared. *I'm a real boy!* It was an odd time to remember the line from *Pinocchio,* but it fit. There might be a real boy walking next to her. No mask. No angles. Just Caleb.

"So, what do you *do* Caleb? There was some sort of patch on your shirt this morning."

"I'm a Firemedic for the county." He gave her a serious look. "That's a Firefighter *and* a Paramedic."

She exaggerated a gasp and covered her chest with her hands. "You're a *hero!*"

He rolled his eyes. "Oh, stop it."

Alice didn't try to hide her smile. "How long have you been doing that?"

"Um…About four years."

"Do you like it?"

"I love it," he gushed. "There's nothing else I'd rather do."

His passion touched her. "What do you like about it so much?"

Caleb considered that for a moment. "There's definitely an adrenaline rush," he admitted. "And I'm kind of a junkie. A few months ago we got dispatched to a house fire in the middle of the night. It was a smaller home, single story. Smoke was pouring out of the front and flames had burned through the back. I took the nozzle through the door and searched for that orange glow. The one that says, *spray water here.*

"It took us a couple minutes to find it because the smoke was so thick. I crawled to the end of the hallway where a room broke off to the right.

And there it was. The four walls and floor of that room were solid flame. Every few seconds a wave would work through the room and make it look almost liquid. I grabbed my partner and made him look at it before we hit it with water."

The way Caleb talked about it, Alice could almost smell the smoke and feel the heat. She shivered as they started walking again and not from the cold. "Well I'm glad *you* love it. Campfires are good enough for me."

Caleb laughed. "More than that though, I think I love it because I see people on their worst day and get to help them. It's what Jesus did and I feel honored to be able to take his love to those who desperately need it." Caleb coughed. "How's that for broaching the subject of religion?"

"Slick," Alice replied.

Caleb fixed his gaze on her. "You love him too, don't you."

Alice stopped and crossed her arms. "Why do you say that?"

"I saw something this morning in your eyes and I've been seeing it in every smile you thought I didn't notice. You're tough, Alice. But I see Jesus in you. This is Mill Street." Caleb scratched his chin. "Let's go left."

Alice followed the sidewalk down Mill trying to hold herself together. Trying to remain a mystery. *It's a good thing he sees Jesus in you,* she told herself. *But what else can he see?* She felt like a half opened present that needed to be rewrapped. But in a moment it all unraveled as the blood left her face and the world turned silent around her. She made a wild stab for Caleb's shoulder as her surroundings swayed around an image straight from her dreams. It loomed at the end of a stone driveway winding through scattered Oak trees.

‹finding home›

‹chapter thirty five›

"Are we really doing this?" John asked Mike who was busy adjusting the side mirror. "And aren't you supposed to fix those *before* you start driving?"

Mike returned both hands to the wheel. "There, ten and two, you happy? It's like driving with my wife." John gave him a queer look. "You know, if I had one I'm sure she'd nag me like you. And this is our new slot for a few weeks. The guys have been taking special detail overtime in the evenings."

John sighed. "Poker night during the day. It's unnatural."

"What's *unnatural* is you being out of the hospital for two weeks and this is the first time you've joined us. I almost strapped your legs to the car."

Two weeks. The details of his hospital stay were etched into the permanent part of his brain. The part that would never surrender to time or illness. Jesus had come after midnight the day he was discharged. John explained how he'd forgiven himself and Jesus' smile lit the room like a sunrise. His laughter and shouts lingered in John's ears.

"The Holy Spirit dwells inside of you, John," Jesus had explained when John asked if he would continue to see him like this. "He's just like me. Listen to him because he'll tell you everything you need to know. He will guide you in all truth. You'll never be alone."

John could still feel the warmth of Jesus' arms, and the love wash over him.

"You're going home later today," Jesus let him know. "You've been made whole and you are *being* made whole." He'd turned to leave but stopped short of the door. "I love you John and I'm going to show you how much all day, every day, forever and ever!"

John glanced at his right leg and stretched it out. His leg, the last of his injuries, had been completely healed when he woke up a few hours after his meeting with Jesus. He chuckled inside as he remembered sneaking up behind his nurse and doing jumping jacks. She'd almost fallen over from shock. He was discharged a few hours later.

"You okay?" Concern flashed through Mike's face.

"Yeah, it's fine." John raised an eyebrow. "Although a massage wouldn't hurt."

"You can't afford me. Ah, here we are." Mike steered his Honda into a parking spot and killed the engine. "They've probably already started. Let's go."

John beheld the building and grimaced. Maybe it was a building at some point. It looked more like a lean-to of rubble ready to collapse at the next sneeze. The sign swung from the front like a lazy pendulum held by a few weak nails. It had those big old-fashioned bubble lights and none of them worked. *Blak water og trac* is what it read as if it drank all day like most of the people inside. *Feed me your soul,* is what it should've spelled out. Ladies Night and strip club ads blew across the parking lot.

"Wow," John muttered and started after Mike. "How have we been coming to this place all these years?"

"Everything looks better in the dark."

"And after a large number of shots," John added.

Mike chuckled and held the door. John ducked under the sign and stepped into his old life. There were no races anymore. Not for years. Poker and blackjack was the game 24 hours a day, seven days a week, blah-blah-blah. John let his eyes adjust and took a long look around the room. He recognized many of the regulars. Smokes in one hand and bottles in the other. Greedy eyes focused on cards and chips that would both be gone by the end. John almost gagged on the crescendo of despair. He felt an ache in his heart. Maybe he could help them. If he could get free they could too.

"Come on, John." Mike led him to a very familiar room with three very familiar guys. All cops.

"John!" Bo jumped up and almost spilled his scotch. "It's good to see you, buddy."

"You too, man," John spouted with half the enthusiasm. "Good to see

≺ finding home ≻

you're not letting the fact that it's noon keep you from drinking the hard stuff." He glanced at the man next to Bo. "Hey, Sam. What's up?"

Sam smiled and pumped Johns arm a few times. "Workin' hard for that money n' all."

The last guy to stand was Bond. That was his *real* name. Poor guy couldn't be anything but a cop. Maybe an assassin. John thought he caught a beat of guilt in his expression. "Hey the hospital...you know how cops... we were gonna..."

John slapped Bond's shoulder and chuckled which seemed to ease their collective conscience. "Don't worry about it. No words needed."

Sam took a drag from his cigar. "Just so you know we're not gonna take it easy on you."

John plopped down ignoring how the smell made his stomach roll. "Then I guess I'll finally stop taking it easy on all of you. I've got an hour, guys. Then I've gotta be at a job site. Make it count."

"Mike," Bond hollered at however many decibels *tipsy* is. "Get the man a drink and a cigar."

"At ease, Mike," John asserted before he could move. "Soda and nothing but flushes and straights."

John felt every eye bore into him. Eight. Eight eyes making it awkward. "You can all stare at me for an hour or we can play some cards."

"Deal em up, Bo," Sam ordered.

Thirty minutes was all John could take. Thirty minutes of smoke, booze, *ef this,* and *ef that.* That, combined with stories of what girl Sam had and what girl Bo wanted to have, and how, formed a lethal claw squeezing the air out of his lungs.

John pushed away from the table. "I'm gonna get some air. Put me in for the blinds." He quickstepped through the dark room and almost lunged for the door. The sunlight hurt his eyes but the clean air felt great. It was chilly enough to cool the fire in his chest.

"What's the matter with you?" John felt a hand on his shoulder. He turned to see a worried Mike. "You look sick."

"Pfft," John uttered and rubbed his eyes. "I *feel* sick."

"Well, take a minute and come back in. Clock's ticking," Mike tapped his watch to illustrate.

John stiffened and followed a piece of wadded paper smut as it tumbled across the parking lot. He couldn't remember why he'd agreed to come. Something about preserving a friendship. "I can't go back in there, Mike."

"What'd you say?"

John studied him and saw a friendship that he couldn't commit to anymore. He couldn't hold up his end of the old agreement. "I can't, Mike. Not now and not ever again."

Mike straightened. "What's gotten in to you?"

"Lot's of things. But mainly Jesus. And I know how that sounds, but it's true. And I'm not some phony TV guy trying to sell you miracle water. You know I'm not."

Mike's eyes narrowed and his eyebrows squished together. "Jesus, John? *Jesus?*"

John wouldn't relent. "In the hospital things…happened. I'm different, Mike." He pointed at the chipped door. "I can't be *that* guy ever again."

"And who is that exactly? The one who's *balls to the wall* and can out drink and out play anyone? The guy who has the respect of everyone that matters. You can't be *that* guy anymore?"

John noticed the confusion in Mike's face but there was hurt in his eyes. He sensed years of history about to be undone. "You're wrong, Mike. I had the respect of some but not from the only one who truly matters."

Mike drew back like he'd been stung. "Ashley," he snarled. "She did this to you didn't she?"

"No."

"You're gonna let *her* wreck who you are?"

"Careful…"

Mike's alcohol induced volume increased and he stabbed a finger into John's chest. "You're gonna let some bit—"

The whole wall shuddered as John slammed his friend with a forearm across the throat. John felt the rapid pulse in Mike's neck against his skin and caught the scent of his hot, stale breath. A small whimper escaped Mike's parted lips when he noticed the club of a fist aimed at his face.

John was burning like an accelerated fire. He held his fist for a long time before finally relaxing. "Don't do this, Mike. It doesn't have to be like this."

Mike's relief morphed into fight, but only briefly. "I'm sorry, John." He

‹finding home›

glanced up at the sky and massaged his neck. "I knew it that day at the hospital. You were different, better than me in every way that matters."

John beheld his friend. The torment hung on him like lead. Everything he'd begun to come out of still had a tight grip on Mike. "It's not just for me."

Mike gave a sad laugh. "That stuff's not for me." He held out his arms and made a small circle. "*This* is my life. Catch the bad guys while being one myself." He nodded toward the building. "I've still got my crew. Don't you feel sorry for me you big, stupid oaf."

John didn't smile. The sign creaked at them offering its own useless input. *The sign. The dream.* It's been a recurring one, a first for him. He always started on a road, a two-lane highway to be specific. The sun was high and the sky a deep shade of blue.

A hazy sign appeared in the distance. He knew it was a sign because of the shape and the way it fell off the road a bit. It was too far away to read, but then it floated closer to him...or him to it, he wasn't quite sure, but eventually the words cleared, "Welcome to Oak Harbor."

John would shield his eyes and see a figure just beyond the sign. Flannel shirt and tan pants. Jesus would smile and motion for him to cross over the town line.

He would shake his head, defiant, refusing to take one step. Jesus would smile and assure him it's okay. Relief and disappointment were John's companions each time he woke up.

"Mike, I think I'm leaving."

Mike showed no emotion. "I'm trying not to overreact any more today. But you're making it very hard on me."

John laughed. It was still strange to hear the sound come from him.

Mike managed a small smile. "Where you goin'?"

"Oak Harbor, Ohio. My home town."

Mike scoffed. "Ten years is all it took for me to find out where you're from."

John pressed his lips together and considered how much Mike didn't know. There was only so much the poor guy could take.

"When?" Mike wanted to know.

"Soon."

"With Ashley or without?"

John stared out across the parking lot. It was weird, hearing the question out loud for the first time. The back and forth had hardly stopped since he first had the dream a week ago. He could only shrug.

Mike scratched his nose. "What? It's not working out?"

"It's not that. She's great." He'd given more of himself into his relationship with Ashley than any that'd come before her. Even Amy. The mere thought of losing that, leaving it behind scorched his throat. But uncertainty stabbed him. She had a life here, family, friends…a career. Would she give it all up to follow him to Ohio? Could he even ask her to do that? He forced a smile at Mike. "Take me outta here will ya?"

Mike hesitated and bounced his keys a few times, but surrendered, and soon they were nearing the job site where John would spend the rest of the afternoon. The days after, he wasn't sure.

‹ chapter thirty six ›

The two-story white house stood tall, making a joke of Alice's sanity. *Are you sleeping or awake?* It sang to her like something out of a horror movie.

Alice felt her knees wobble and tightened her grip on Caleb's shoulder. She pinched her eyes together hoping the action would eliminate the apparition. But the house remained. And it looked even bigger.

"Alice!" She snapped her head toward the worried sound. Caleb's eyes were big as plates. "Are you okay?"

Alice relaxed her death grip on his shoulder and fought for composure. "Yeah," she answered. "I'm fine."

"Don't tell me you're *fine*," Caleb squawked. "You were about a second away from being carried outta here."

Alice ignored him and peered through the trees. "Do you see that house?" Either answer held its share of problems.

"The white one? Sure. It's been there most of my life." He took hold of her arm. "Now can we go so you can sit and rest? I'll get you some coffee or something."

A few strands of black hair fell over Alice's face and she blew them back. It was just a house. But it wasn't *just* a house. It was a house that was an exact copy of the one in her dream, complete with matching driveway and front yard.

The only thing holding you back is you. You can't remember because you've decided that you don't want to.

Dr. Felling's words raced across her heart and she cast a quick glance at Caleb, before setting her jaw and marching toward the driveway.

Caleb took off after her. "Where are you going?"

Alice didn't answer and picked up her pace.

"Tell me what's going on," Caleb demanded when he caught up.

"Nothing," she replied and squinted through the naked branches stretching over the driveway.

"It's not nothing," Caleb countered. "*Something's* going on."

Alice's wrapped her coat tighter around herself. "Caleb I—" They'd reached the end of the driveway and the house loomed before her. A small patch of grass separated them from a staircase that led to a wrap-a-round porch. A maple door was fixed at the center with glass rectangles lining the top section. With every second she was more certain. This was the house.

"It's just an old house," Caleb jabbered. "I'm pretty sure it's empty."

Alice took a few careful steps and pressed her hand against the rail. The wood was smooth. Not chipped. Not warped. She tested one of the steps. Well maintained. It all spread before her like a hidden treasure, a pearl waiting to be found. And then a rush of warmth struck her face. It spread through her whole body and suddenly she wasn't outside of the house, she was in it.

Her feet echoed off the hardwood floor as she sped through a hall. *That's not fair. I found her so she's it. No, you have to catch her.* They sounded like kids and the laughter and squeals confirmed it. Alice smothered her own excited giggles as a staircase flew by on the left. She aimed for a room off to the right and gripped the knob. But when she burst into the room she found herself back at the bottom of the porch steps. Caleb gaped at her through frantic eyes.

"Okay, we're leaving," he announced and placed a firm hand on her back.

Alice whirled away from him. The happy shrieks of children still floated around her ears. She tried not to shake. "I'm not going."

Caleb lifted his hands. "Alice, I was calling you and you wouldn't answer. We've got to go."

"I've been here," Alice told him. "Inside."

"What? In the house? When?"

Alice wasn't altogether sure what was real and what wasn't. "I, I'm not sure exactly when." She crossed her arms and shivered. "Who lives here?"

"No one," Caleb replied. "The last owner took off years ago. Why do you want to know?"

⋖ finding home ⋗

She studied Caleb for a long time. She wanted to explain everything and nothing. Neither seemed like a good option. She finally slumped on a step halfway to the porch. "This might sound a little...strange."

Caleb eased himself next to her. "I think I've been prepared for crazy." He gave her a smile to let her know he was teasing.

Alice's heart pounded in her ears. This had been one giant mistake. She should've never agreed to go with Caleb and now she was stuck in the middle of nowhere with him and a house yanking on the last thread of her sanity.

"It's okay Alice," Caleb said and slid a bit closer. "You can tell me."

She gazed into his blue eyes and desperately wanted to believe the sincerity she found there. Her stomach flip-flopped. Maybe she could. God please help me, she prayed.

The answer was quick. *I'm right here.* After a long time she blew the air out of her lungs. "I've, uh, been having this dream." Alice tapped her foot on the step. "There's a house in it. *This* house."

Caleb gave her a skeptical frown. "You dreamt about this house?"

"Yes."

His eyes alternated between the house and her. "This *exact* house?"

She nodded.

"You're saying you've been here, inside it even, but only in your dreams?" His tone held a note of disbelief.

"Arghhhh!" Alice scrambled to her feet and put some distance between them before whirling around. "I'm *not* crazy Caleb! I'm just..." She threw her hands up. Her brain didn't have any words to offer.

Caleb jumped up. "I didn't say that you're crazy. I'm just trying to understand."

"So am I," she cried and started to pace. "They're more than just dreams." She stopped suddenly and shot him a pleading look. "I think they're memories."

"Memories?"

Alice could almost see the hole she was digging. She could hardly see over the edge. "Never mind."

Caleb took a long look at the house before fixing his eyes on Alice. "Earlier you told me you've been inside. Maybe you have. I don't think you're making it up. Doesn't mean I understand it. But I know God can speak to us through dreams like what you're describing. He could be trying to show you something."

"That's what I thought," Alice replied. "But when would I have been here?"

Caleb put his hands on his hips. "You sure it's the same house?"

"Yes."

He shook his head. "It's not a happy story."

"What do you mean?"

"Long time ago a family lived here. They were all killed except for the dad. Car crash I think. The whole town was a wreck. The dad skipped town not too long after. Can't say I blame him." He lifted his eyes. "Maybe you knew one of the kids."

Alice shook her head. "I just moved here."

Caleb was about to say something but changed his mind. "Why can't you remember anyway?"

Alice pretended not to hear him. "Who owns it now?" She admired the rail again. "Someone's been taking care of it."

Caleb blew heat into his hands and closed the space between them. "I think a church bought it."

A *church*. His arm grazed hers. She briefly wondered what it would feel like to have them wrapped around her. Her heart thumped. "What church?"

"I can't think of the name but the Pastor is a guy named Mark Summers."

Alice gasped and fell back a step. "Mark Summers?"

"You know him?"

"Yeah, I mean, I'm living with him, with them."

"You're living with the Summers?"

"It's a long story."

"Ah." A grin formed on his mouth. "For another time?"

Another time? *They'll only ever want you for one thing.* The words were a knife in her gut. Frustration began to boil inside of her. Her dreams, the house, but mostly the way Caleb had smashed barriers she'd sworn would protect her heart. She narrowed her eyes at him. "What do you *want*, Caleb?"

He stiffened. "Huh?"

"This morning you harassed me till I gave you my name. Then you

≺ finding home ≻

talked to my friend and wouldn't leave me alone until I agreed to let you show me around." She threw her hands at him. "Is this some kind of *game* to you?"

The color had left Caleb's face. "It's not a game."

"Then what is it?" she cried. "What do you want from me?"

"I just wanted to get to know you," Caleb fired back. He took a few steps back and stared at the ground. "When I saw you this morning I was done. I couldn't take my eyes off of you and when I left I couldn't stop thinking about you." He raised his head. "I just want to get to know you, Alice."

Alice's heart beat like a drum. It would never work. Her voice was shaky, "There's things you don't know that would change your mind."

Caleb's tone was gentle. "Let me be the judge of that."

He reached forward and Alice flinched. "What are you doing?" He hesitated just for a second and lightly swept a strand of black hair out of her face. The touch of his fingers sent a wave of electricity through her body, forcing the air from her lungs. They stood like that for a long time. Fear battled desire inside of her, neither gaining definitive victory. She almost reached for his face, but finally fell back, breaking the spell.

Caleb's voice was thick. "We'd better get back."

They walked back together mostly silent, but less concerned with keeping space between their swinging arms. When they reached the café Caleb faced her. "Ask Mark about the house. He can tell you much more than I can."

"I will," Alice promised.

Caleb rubbed the back of his neck and gave her a shy look. "There's a place down the street that makes the best burger you'll ever eat. I'd love to take you there…tomorrow night maybe?"

Alice hugged herself. "I don't know."

"If you don't do it for me, then at least do it for the burgers." His eyes sparkled. "They're *that* good."

She grinned and felt her resolve weaken. "Well, if they're *that* good."

"Pick you up at 6 then. At the Summers?"

Alice watched him slide into his car and twirled a ring around her finger. When did something like this become possible for her? She shook her head and got into her car.

chapter thirty seven

John stared at the doorknob while he spun the ice in his glass. Any minute now it would spin and Ashley would walk through the door. She would cross the room and sink into his arms. He sipped his water and smelled her shampoo like she was already there. Her perfume infiltrated his senses and he felt her soft lips on his.

A drop of condensation fell from John's glass and hit his hand with a cold splat. It snapped him to reality. He was going to tell her about Oak Harbor and then she was going to leave. Probably angry. He touched an ache in his stomach that had already formed.

Knock-Knock-Knock

John hesitated and set his glass down on the coffee table. Maybe he should ask her to go with him. But he didn't want to be the crazy guy who asks the girl to give up her whole life. *I'm doing the right thing aren't I Lord?* Silence. Maybe he was more afraid that she wouldn't go if he asked.

Bang-Bang-Bang

John rose and furrowed his brow. Why was she knocking? He crossed the room and paused next to a picture they'd taken together at the park. Next to it was another one of them at a café. Then at the Grand Canyon. Three weeks together and he already felt like they had a long history.

He picked up a piece of paper resting next to the pictures. It crinkled a little in his hand as he held it up.

Hey John,

You rock! Have a great day and I can't wait to see you tonight. You're the best part of my day. -Ash

John smiled. He lowered the note and glanced at the pictures again. Maybe she'd say yes.

‹ finding home ›

Bang-Bang
"Okay-okay," he hollered and opened the door. "Why are you kno—"
It wasn't Ashley. That was the first thing John became aware of. The second was Nellie's face warped by rage, and the third was her fist flying at his face.

"John." He blinked. The sound of his name was bouncing all around like an echo.
"John."
It was a little clearer. He blinked again. A blurry mass hovered over him. Something slapped his face. "Arghhhh…" Another slap. "Stop it!"
The blurry figure materialized into Mike. "Ah, there you are."
John groaned. His head was pounding and things were still blurry in his left eye. He touched it and winced. He worked his jaw back and forth. Intact. "I've got a busted eye and you're gonna slap me in the face?" he growled.
"You were out man. Don't question my life saving methods."
I've got a *method* to show you." He got to his feet and balanced himself on the edge of the couch. The drum in his head grew louder. "What happened?" *Nellie.* He held up his hand to Mike. "Never mind. I remember."
Mike crossed his arms. "Neighbor saw the whole thing and called it in. She went old school on you, bro. Brass knuckles. Tossed them into the bush outside. Not a very smart girl is she?"
John reflected on the incident. "Why would she…?" Then he knew. "Ashley!" He stumbled for the door.
Mike took hold of John's arm before he could fall. "Whoa, take it easy. You need to get checked out. Let one of my guys take you to the hospital."
"No thanks. I've been slapped enough for one night."
"Let me help you," Mike pleaded. "What's the deal with Ashley?"
John had to admit Mike was right. He was in no shape to go running off like a hero. "I think Nellie will go after Ashley."

"You think this is some kind of jealous rage? You really think Nellie is that type?"

John recalled a few times he'd talked to some other women at Joe's. Each time they'd left early because Nellie wouldn't serve them anything. He'd laughed it off at the time. "I don't know, man. There were a few times she had that…look."

Mike rolled his eyes. "Because all women are under your spell?"

John pointed at his face. "She did this to *me*." He started for the door. "If you're not going to do anything then I will."

Mike blocked his path. "We're looking for Nellie now and I'll send someone for Ashley."

Bond poked his head in the door. "We just picked up Nellie a couple streets North of here."

"Thank God," John spurted.

"See," Mike bragged. "We've got it taken care of." He nodded at Bond. "I need you to pick up a woman named Ashley. John will give you her address."

Bond glanced between them. "There's a woman out here saying *her* name is Ashley."

John's head snapped up. "How long has she been here?"

Bond shrugged. "Just got here."

"Let her in," Mike ordered.

John massaged his temples as the tension left his body like a deflating balloon. He lowered himself onto the couch and felt Mike plop next to him.

"Knocked out by a girl, huh?" Mike teased and chuckled.

John sized him up. "She would've killed you."

"John?"

They both turned their attention to the front door where Ashley stood wringing her hands. Her hair was pulled into a sloppy ponytail and fear colored her expression.

John waved her over. "Hey, Ash."

She gasped and hurried over to him.

"It's not that bad," he told her. "Don't get all worked up."

"Have you looked in the mirror?"

⋖ finding home ⋗

"No, and I don't really want to."

"What happened?" She asked and kneeled in front of him.

"Just my old life catching up with me." Ashley narrowed her eyes and John relented. "An old girlfriend with a little more *crazy* than I thought."

Ashley sighed and examined his face. "It's actually not that bad. I'm surprised. I mean, I knew you had a thick skull and all but..." She lightly touched his eye and he winced. "Sorry. Doesn't look like anything's broken, but only an x-ray can tell for sure."

John shook his head. "It's fine, Ash."

"It's not *fine*," she scolded and scurried to the kitchen.

Mike produced a note pad. "You wanna press charges?"

John thought about court and paperwork. It wasn't going to fit into his timeline. "Just let her go." If this was the worst he got from his old life then he was getting off easy.

Mike shoved the notepad back into his pocket. "We'll hold her tonight. It'll scare her a little. She'll stay away from both of you." He glanced at Ashley who'd returned with an ice pack. "Take care of this guy."

She smiled at the man on the couch who was so used to taking care of himself. "I will."

Mike cast one more look at them both before closing the door behind him, blocking out all the noise and chaos the night had become.

Ashley sat down carefully next to John who nudged her. "I knew I could get you to spend the night."

Ashley handed him the ice. "Put that on your face. And who said I'm staying the night?"

John reclined and set the ice pack on his head. "You will. I can tell." He adjusted the ice pack and felt her eyes on him. "What?"

"Why won't you press charges against her? She nearly took your head off."

"Pfft, it's just a scratch." The ice pack slipped. "Ouch."

"Did you want that mirror now?"

"No, thanks." John paused. "Nellie was mad and got me. Kudos. Mike has her now. We won't be seeing her again."

Ashley clucked her tongue. "If you say so." She sighed and squeezed John's leg. "Are you sure you're gonna be okay?"

John sat up a little straighter securing the ice with one hand. "Not the first time someone took a shot at me. When I was a kid I—" John suddenly recalled an incident from their first date. The walk down Main Street after pizza. He'd asked her about kids and it seemed like she was going to say something, but stopped herself. She'd been open that night, much more than he had. But she'd held back. "Hey, I've been wanting to ask you something."

She threw him a wary look. "Okay."

"On our first date we walked down Main Street."

Ashley raised her eyebrows. "I'm with you so far."

"Be serious."

"Sorry." Ashley reset her face. "Okay, walking down Main."

John cleared his throat. "I asked you about kids and you got weird."

Ashley's eyes went wide and she sat up straight. "Weird?" She tugged on her ponytail and tried to laugh her words. "I didn't get weird."

John eyed her. "Yes, you did. And you're getting weird now." He lifted his chin. "Maybe a bit deranged."

"You'd be the expert on deranged women wouldn't you." She sprang to her feet and retreated to the kitchen.

John tossed the ice pack on the table. "Very funny. What's with the kid thing? Why are you acting like this?"

Ashley gulped water she'd poured in a glass and kept her back to him. When she finally faced him a shadow had fallen over her eyes. She leaned against the counter and was silent long enough for John's stomach to twist itself into a knot. "Ashley," he offered and winced as his head throbbed. "You've got to start talking."

His voice seemed to break whatever trance she'd fallen into. Ashley gave a quick nod and tucked a strand of hair behind her ear. "My ex husband and I…we'd talked about having kids. Tried for a year or so. Never happened. We had tests done, but they all came back normal. The doctor told us to just keep trying and if nothing happened in a few months come back."

Ashley gripped the edge of the counter she was leaning against. "My marriage was over. We both knew it. He was a stranger. But we kept trying to get pregnant anyway." She sighed. "I don't know. Maybe I thought a baby could save the marriage. At least give me something to be happy about."

‹ finding home ›

John held his place on the couch trying to digest what was happening like a tough piece of steak. He was the one who was supposed to have past issues. *He* noticed her face had lightened a shade. He saw himself wrapping his arms around her. Running his fingers down her soft check and telling her everything would be okay. But the tension in her eyes was a seatbelt around his waist.

"The morning sickness started a few weeks after he gave me the divorce papers." Ashley gave him a desperate look. "I hated him, John. With everything I had in me. When the test came back positive, all I thought about was the daily reminder of the man who'd stolen years of my life." Ashley's eyes watered faster than she could blink it away. "I wanted a baby so bad. I really did. But I couldn't…"

Ashley ripped a paper towel from the roll. John stepped to the woman he cared more for now than he did even a few minutes ago. The tears on her cheek were needles into his heart. He halted with a few feet between them and found her eyes. "You had an abortion."

Ashley nodded, losing a fresh flow of tears onto her cheeks. "A few months later I met Jesus while holding a handful of pain pills." She sniffed and John wiped a few tears with his thumb. "I didn't plan on waking up but he saved me that night. It was a long journey of healing but eventually I was able to tell my ex." She blinked at him. "You're the only other one I've told."

John brushed her damp hair back and let his hands linger, framing her face, before tenderly touching his lips to hers. He drew back only a second before kissing her again, pressing harder this time, letting his passion touch her heart. Words weren't his specialty but they didn't feel necessary.

When they parted again Ashley searched his eyes. "I was afraid to tell you."

John leaned in and touched his forehead to hers. "Why?"

Ashley hesitated. "Because you lost your family and I…" A sob swallowed the next few words.

"Ah, Ash." John held her shaking body. "Don't you ever think…" He lifted her chin so he could see her eyes. "Don't you ever think I'd hold that against you." He grabbed another paper towel and dabbed her face.

She gave him an uncertain look. "But I—"

"What you did has nothing to do with what happened to me. *Nothing.*" He could see the pause in her eyes. "I'm in a lot of trouble if we're going to start taking things we've done in the past personally."

Ashley made a sound that was part sob and part laugh and pressed her face into his chest. "Sometimes I think I'm completely past it and then… this." She lifted her eyes. "You know what?"

John traced a line on her face. "What?"

"I still want a baby. I really do."

John pulled her into him. "Well, maybe we can find one you can visit."

Ashley gasped and jabbed his chest before the giggles came. Then they were both laughing. "Is this messed up?" Ashley asked between laughs.

John raised his hands. "Who knows." He leaned down and kissed her. Her lips were salty and when they parted he saw desire in her eyes.

Ashley ran her hand through his hair and hung an inch from his lips. "I love you, John," she whispered. "You don't have to say it back. I just can't keep it in anymore." She smiled shyly. "I love you."

Time froze capturing John at a crossroads. He hadn't been ready for that. Her words struck his heart and played a song to his core. *I love you too.* It's what he wanted to say but his tongue and mouth wouldn't cooperate. Or maybe it was fear. Or maybe Oak Harbor. He staggered back a step. "Ash, you know…you know the way I feel." He saw her eyes lower a notch. "I'm sorry. I, I didn't get the way I am overnight so please give God more time to work on me."

Ashley smiled at him. "I can do that."

They made their way to the couch and in no time Ashley was asleep on his chest to the low hum of the TV. John lightly ran his hand over her hair, now convinced of one thing. There was room for two on the trip to Oak Harbor.

chapter thirty eight

"Phew." Mark stuck the shovel into the snow and wiped a bead of sweat from his brow. The remaining half of the sidewalk mocked him. "I think there's more snow on that half than the one I just did," he muttered into the air.

Mark cast a glance at the bay window. Edith Jones peered out at him through sunken eyes, a skin-tight face, and hair that'd turned white instead of gray. She raised a frail hand in a short wave while lifting a coffee mug with the other that wobbled all the way to her lips.

Yeah, hello, Mark conveyed by waving back. He grabbed the shovel and buried it into a layer of snow. "So happy to be out here shoveling this extra long sidewalk you couldn't possibly walk down even without snow." He grunted and tossed a load to the side. "Thank goodness I'm a pastor and get to help people."

"Hey, hon."

Mark whirled around to see Claire carefully making her way up the driveway. "Hey, Claire." He stuck the shovel in the snow and grinned. "You're just what I needed—careful, don't slip."

"It is a little slick isn't it." Claire made her way to Mark and seized his arm for balance.

Mark kissed her cold lips. "What are you doing here?"

Claire sniffed the air a few times as a corner of her mouth curled up in a smirk. "It smells a little bitter over here."

"Ha-ha-ha," Mark let out. "In my defense, nobody was supposed to hear my disgruntled ramblings."

Claire chuckled. "Well, you mumble louder than you think."

Mark wiped his nose. "Whatcha got there?"

"I brought cocoa." Claire lifted a thermos. "Want some?"

"You, my dear, are amazing." Mark drew her close and kissed her again. "I'd love some."

Claire laughed and poured the steaming liquid into the thermos cap. "Knock it off or Edith might have a heart attack."

"Well, at least I wouldn't have to finish the sidewalk," Mark whispered into her ear.

Claire exaggerated a gasp and handed him the cap. "Mark Summers, you're *terrible*."

Mark slurped his hot chocolate. "Don't tell anyone."

Claire shook her head. "What am I going to do with you?"

Mark gave her a toothy grin. "Love me forever, like you promised."

Claire's eyes sparkled. "I did, didn't I."

"Mm-hmmm." Mark drained his drink and looped his arms around Claire's waist. A small smile played across his mouth. He still felt them in times like this, the butterflies. Just like the day they met. He was sure she wouldn't look at him twice. And then she did and he thought he'd need to nail his feet to the ground. They began to sway back and forth as if a song was playing just for them. "You're the marshmallows in my hot chocolate."

Claire giggled and rested her head on his chest. "Ever the romantic." They stayed like that for a long time before Claire suddenly touched her nose and looked up. Mark followed her gaze. Tiny snowflakes were falling all around them like a silent audience. Claire grinned. "Time for me to go."

Mark scowled at the sidewalk. "I'd better double time it to get this done before it piles higher." He kissed his wife one more time before she started timid steps to the car.

"Dinner's a little early tonight," she called. "Alice has something with Caleb later."

"Okay," Mark acknowledged and went to grab the shovel, but stopped. "Claire?"

"What?"

"Alice asked me about the old Rister house the other day. She'd gone by there and seemed a little out of sorts about it. Has she said anything to you?"

≺ finding home ≻

Claire scrunched her forehead. "No. What did she want to know?"

"About the family that lived there. The Risters." Mark touched his stomach. Despite the years and the way God had healed his heart, the emotions had a way of lingering. Of popping up at unexpected times. Sometimes the pain was still sharp. "Caleb had filled her in on some of the details."

Claire nodded. "So what did you tell her?"

"Just that we were close with the family. Some general details. I told her we bought the house and sometimes use it for ministry purposes." Mark fixed a look at the gathering snow. It wasn't the whole truth. They made use of it to help people and store supplies, but they didn't need a house for that. The real reason they'd bought it was hope that refused to disappear into the night.

"Do you think he'll ever come back?" Claire's voice was soft like the falling snow.

Mark sighed and wished he had a different answer. "I don't know."

Claire held his eyes for a few moments. "You know who she looks like, right? Alice, I mean."

Mark pinched his eyebrows. For the first few years after the accident every little girl with long black hair made his heart skip a beat. "Jill is dead."

"They never found her body."

Mark stared at his wife. "They didn't have to. The fire—"

"But what if it didn't?"

Mark raised his hands. "So what are you saying? You *really* think she's alive? We looked Claire...we searched for years." He saw her lips tremble and felt his own shoulders sag. It was a replay of an exhausting argument they'd had many times before. He went to Claire and hugged her tight. "I agree. She really does look like Jill." He leaned back so he could see her face. "But she's not."

Claire brushed a tear from her face and forced a smile. "I know. See you at home, okay?"

Mark kept watch to make sure she reached the car safely. But before she got in she turned to face him. "I know it's not her. But...but if she was wouldn't that be just like God?" She gave him a curious look before sliding behind the wheel.

Mark didn't grab the shovel until Claire vanished around the corner. *Wouldn't that be just like God?* He raised his eyebrows and buried the head under a pile of snow. *It certainly would.*

♥

"How can you stand to be out here?" Caleb rubbed his arms like a boy scout trying to get fire from two sticks. "It's freezing!"

Alice giggled as she skipped across the frozen ground. "Because it's so beautiful," she answered and spun in a slow circle. The light of the setting sun reflected off the snowy ground turning it into a sea of red and orange diamonds. The festival was just a week away. Caleb had volunteered to be part of the committee and she'd agreed to help him set up. They were the only ones still there. The rest of the volunteers had retreated to the warmth of heaters and fireplaces.

"Beautiful or not it'd better warm up for the festival," Caleb remarked. "It's gonna be hard to dance through 15 layers of clothes."

"Isn't that what the heaters are for?" Alice gazed at the red and green lights twinkling from the large tent like a little girl on Christmas Eve. It would soon be filled with Oak Harborites dancing and celebrating Christmas just around the corner. They'd hung wreaths and other holiday decorations on the fabric walls, and positioned large propane heaters at each opening, and a few inside to keep the cold out. "I am wondering where all the snowmen are." She fixed her eyes on Caleb who was actively blowing into his hands. "It's supposed to be a *Frosty* fest right?"

"You're hilarious," Caleb sputtered through chattering teeth. "There's actually gonna be a snowman contest. Although right now I'm a little too frozen to care."

Alice threw him a look of offense. "Where is your Christmas spirit? A little chill turn you into the Grinch?"

"My Christmas spirit?" He pointed up. "It's disappearing with the sun."

Alice watched him stumble over a patch of frozen grass and covered her mouth so he wouldn't hear her laugh. *Laughter.* She pulled her cap further over her ears. There was a lot of that with him. She twirled and took a

◄ finding home ►

couple steps on the hard ground. She almost didn't show up for burgers the day after their *tour*. She'd called him twice to cancel, but he was very persistent. Since then they'd spent almost every one of his days off together. She traced a little circle pattern in the thin snow with her boot. Day after day Caleb continued to surprise her, refusing to be squeezed into the general mold she held for men. She glanced at him; he'd found a bulb that wasn't shinning and was trying to work out the issue. Maybe it was time to make a new mold.

Alice noticed the moon just starting its nightly shift. The pale light outlined a single cloud crawling across the sky. That's how she needed it to be with Caleb…slow. Just being close to him pushed her to the limit. Desire and fear. A cocktail better left on the table. But it burned through her stomach when they were together.

She buried her hands in her coat pockets and mulled over a phone conversation she'd had with Tabby a few days ago.

"It sounds like you really like this guy," Tabby had offered with a smile in her voice. "I just knew you would go off and find someone. Miracles *do* happen."

"I wasn't looking for it. He just showed up and wouldn't leave me alone."

"So what do you think?"

"About what?"

"Alice!"

There was a pause and Alice could almost hear Tabby roll her eyes. "What are you gonna do?"

Alice sighed. "I don't know, Tabby." She rose from her small desk chair and shuffled to the bed. "Probably nothing. I mean, how could it ever work?"

"By telling him how you feel."

Alice made a frustrated sound. "How can you even say that? You've been through a lot of the same stuff I have. Who would stick around for that kind of baggage?"

"So, you're saying people like us are destined to be alone? There's no chance for us, is that it?"

"No, I'm just—"

"Worried you're not good enough."

Alice fell on the bed as her stomach tied in a familiar knot of fear. Fear of rejection, of not being accepted...not being loved. It was like cancer that yields in remission, but refuses to die completely. She'd felt it with Melissa and Jack during that first year in Redwood and then again the night she gave her heart to Jesus. She sighed into the phone. "He won't stay, Tabby." She blinked back tears. "He won't."

"There's only one way you'll know that for sure." Tabby paused for a moment. "You're not *that* girl anymore, Alice. But that's how you still see yourself sometimes. Still dirty and broken...but you're not. Aren't you the one who kept telling me that Jesus made you clean and put you back together?"

Alice could only nod at her voice and wipe at tears freely rolling down her face.

"You told me Jesus showed you that you're worth something. That you're worth *everything*. If that's true, you're worthy of this too, of a guy like Caleb."

Alice pressed her fingers into her temples. "I don't know."

"Alice, you think you're standing in front of this guy wearing...I don't know, rags you found in the dumpster or something. Like, dripping with old food slime and—"

"Got it, Tabby," Alice let her know unable to keep a small smile from her voice.

"Right. But remember that dress we saw at the mall. The white formal one I made you try on?"

The dress caught their attention from the window of a boutique. It was a full length strapless gown that fanned out slightly below the waist. And it was pure white, a white was so brilliant it seemed to radiate off the fabric. After a few minutes of Tabby's insistence, she discovered it was softer than silk as it hugged her form. Her heart had skipped when she faced the mirror. "I remember."

"That's you, Alice. Sparkling, pure, and beautiful. That's what you're wearing. That's who you are...all the time."

"Tabby..." Alice hesitated, but then sniffed and laughed at the same time. "You're ruining my makeup."

Tabby giggled. "I don't know if this guy will stay or not. But I *do* know that you'll never find out unless you give him a chance. And *you're* the one who kept telling me it would be okay because God'll always be with you." She paused. "He still is right?"

Alice sat up and tucked a strand of hair behind her ear. Every now and then she felt the rush of peace against her heart as God reminded her that he was still there, still walking beside her. She was learning to hear his voice in the quiet hours before the sun came up and saw him in the lives of Mark and Claire. "Yeah," she admitted. "He still is."

"Then don't throw away something you really want just cause you're afraid."

"And what are you?" Alice stood and paced in front of the bed. "You've told me how scared *you* are. Why does it get to be different for you?"

Tabby was silent for a long time. "I've got a ways to go on my journey. That's between me and God, but you were always so much further than me. And you still are, I know it. If there's anyone that could be ready for something like this after what we've been through, it's you."

Alice ran a hand through her raven hair and smiled at the window. "Have I told you how much I love and miss you?"

"Not nearly enough," Tabby teased. "So what's God got to say about this *Caleb thing* anyway?"

Alice pressed her boot into the snow making it crunch like a handful of chips. She sighed and rubbed her arms against a chill that didn't come from the cold air. She didn't know what God had to say about Caleb because she hadn't asked him. She hadn't included some boy from a coffee shop into her idea of what it meant to trust God.

"Hey." Caleb was jogging towards her.

"Get that light fixed?"

He threw a hand at the tent. "Bah, I got that one to work and two more went out."

"Hope you're better at taking care of sick people," she joked and winked at him.

He grinned and bumped her. "Haven't heard any complaints." He repositioned one of the heaters so that it was facing them and switched it on. "Are you allowed to mess with that?"

"Perks of being on the committee," he claimed and faced her.

Something about the way he looked at her made Alice start to fidget with a ring on her finger. And then he said the words that unleashed the rest of her anxiety.

"Can I talk you to about something?"

Alice felt her legs go stiff beneath her. "Everything okay?" She noticed his eyes were a little rounder than normal. He bathed his hands in the heat and motioned her over. She slowly moved into the warmth. "What's going on?"

Caleb tried to smile at her, but his lips twitched like they did when he was nervous. He glanced up at the stars and blinked a few times before gently taking her gloved hand. "I like you, Alice. I mean, I *really* like you." The way he shrugged made him look like a little boy with a crush. "When I'm not with you I'm counting the minutes until I can be."

Alice willed her hands not to shake and leaned on her back foot. "Okay…"

"I've tried hard not to push you into something you're not ready for." She started to object and he raised a hand. "And that's not what this is. I just want you to know how I feel." He paused and searched her eyes. "What are we, Alice? Just friends? Is that all you want out of this? Cause if it is, I'll deal with it, but I don't think you…" He raked his hand through his blonde hair and took a few steps away. "I know this is hard for you. I just don't know why."

Why? It was a question with a myriad of answers. Air hovered beyond Alice's lips refusing to enter her lungs. Her heart galloped in a rebellious beat. *Why?* She finally squeezed her hands together. Coming to Oak Harbor was supposed to be about finding her memories. It was supposed to be about a journey with God into her past. Not this. Not about having feelings for a boy who would stand in the moonlight and ask her why she couldn't open her heart. Alice fixed her eyes on the ground. "Caleb I—"

"Alice." Caleb's voice was soft and he moved close enough for her to hear the quiet pattern of his breathing. "That morning in the café changed my life and I'm not sure I can go back. This," he motioned to the space between them, "is great but I…" He let his hands fall to his side. "I just wanted you to know. And if you feel the same way, even a little bit, I need you to do something for me."

A gust of cold air weaved through them and tossed Alice's hair. She felt unsteady, like the ground beneath her feet was cracking and would and fall away any second. Her voice was barely above a whisper. "What do you want?"

He gently brushed the hair from her eyes. His lips were no longer twitching and his eyes were steady. "Let me know you."

Alice crossed her arms over her chest and tried to laugh but it sounded more like a choked cough. "You know me, Caleb."

He shook his head. "I don't. Not really. I know how to make you laugh and where you like to eat. I know you hate bowling and that you're a great cook. I know you love the Summers and God. You lived in Redwood and Tabby is like a sister to you." He paused and his features fell. "But I don't know what makes you sad or what makes you cry. I don't know what trials you've faced or they pain you've walked through. I've seen the same fear in your eyes I see now, but I don't know what causes it. What do you dream about, Alice? What do you hope for? What about your family? What about—"

"That's enough, Caleb!" Silence hung between them like an awkward marionette. *It's okay Alice.* The familiar voice scrolled across her heart and she closed her eyes. *Don't run. Listen to him.*

"Alice…" Caleb hadn't moved. "What do *you* want?"

She didn't trust her voice enough to answer. As if she even *had* an answer. Before Alice could figure out what to do she felt his gentle hand on her shoulder. "What do you want, Alice?"

Alice kept her back to him as the truth tumbled around her heart. Being with Caleb had become the best part of her day and it was getting harder to imagine a life he wasn't a part of. But Tabby was wrong. He wouldn't stay. So she would lie to him, because it would hurt less to see him go now. She turned to tell him, but when she saw his face the words caught in her throat. A tremor ran through her bringing new words that fell out on a breath, "You, Caleb. I want you."

He smiled and took her hands. "Then share your life with me."

She felt her eyes pool. "I, I can't. You don't understand."

He brushed a strand of hair from her face. "I want to. Please just tell—"

"No!" Alice reeled back and searched the darkness for her car. Her eyes stung and blurred and she couldn't see where to run.

"Why are you so afraid?"

She whirled around and a tear spilled onto her cheek. "Because you won't stay." She swiped at the tear. "You'll leave."

"Try me."

"You don't know what you're saying."

He clutched her shoulders and found her eyes. "Try me."

It's okay Alice. Don't run.

Alice almost screamed at the sky like it was God's face. She felt she had a good argument for it not being okay. Wasn't running the only option? If she could see straight she would be already. Tabby's voice pulsated through her head, *You'll never know unless you give him a chance.*

Alice bit her bottom lip hard enough to taste blood and felt a little resolve leak out. Maybe she should give him that chance. She felt sick, like she was on a raft in the perfect storm. After a few more minutes of rocking she gave in. "Okay Caleb," she whispered. "I'll tell you."

« finding home »

« chapter thirty nine »

Alice dropped onto a bench near the propane heater and worked a ring around her finger. "I told you that Jack and Melissa Baker are my parents. They're not. I met them three years ago when I moved to Redwood. I was 17."

Caleb eased down next to her. "Okay…"

"I don't know my real family." She threw him a quick glance. Questions swam through his eyes, but his expression remained neutral. "I can't remember being a kid. I don't know why," she quickly added. "I just can't. The first thing I remember is riding with some guy, a truck driver. I was around ten I think."

"Ten is still a kid," Caleb interjected.

Alice's mouth formed a straight line. Ten's a kid for many, but not for her. She saw past the ground and into her memories. A road stretched far ahead with tall buildings rising in the distance. They were all lit up like Christmas trees. "He drove me into the City. New York City."

Alice climbed to her feet and scooped up some snow with her toe. "The buildings were getting smaller and darker, but we didn't stop. He wouldn't tell me where we were going." She could still hear the man's snarling threats when she'd started crying. Confusion warped her mind like it was yesterday. *Why is he so mean? Who am I? How did I get here?* "I was just a scared little girl with a stranger and a huge truck." She shuddered and prayed for God's strength. "When we finally stopped there were only a few street lights."

She eyed Caleb. He already knew more than anyone. Dr. Felling had only gotten the minimum…in very general terms. Same with Jack and Melissa. Her and Tabby shared a mutual understanding without the need for words. Alice rubbed her throat.

"The truck driver made me get out and motioned to another man who called himself, *Boss*. He'd come out of some shack that looked like it was half caved in." Boss was bald with the face of a bulldog and a stomach that hung over dirty jeans. Body odor, stale cigarettes, and beer transcended the line between memory and reality and filled her senses. Bile crept up her throat and she swallowed it down. "He gave the truck driver some money. I didn't know what was happening. I thought maybe someone inside knew me and could help."

Caleb tried to remain neutral. But the creases in his forehead betrayed him. Alice guessed he'd seen a lot as a paramedic, but not this. *If you stop now there's a chance this could go back to normal.* Her brain was in full panic mode. But panic makes a myth out of reality. She set her jaw.

"He pulled me into a dark room where there were other girls. I was happy at first because I wasn't alone. But then I *really* saw them." Alice hung her head and hated the way her eyes still flooded when she saw their expressions. "Their hearts were beating, but there was no life. They were like…zombies. That was the only time I screamed." She touched the left side of her face. "Boss hit me hard enough to make the room spin. A few minutes later one of the older girls made me swallow a pill and tugged on my arm. I heard voices of men. One of them mentioned something about getting back before his wife woke up."

Alice flicked a tear from her cheek and blinked at the moon. She hadn't believed in God back then, but it didn't stop her from praying that the pills would erase her memories, to have them join the others she'd lost. But the reel played day after day, growing thicker night after night.

She sent a cloud of warm breath into the sky and gave Caleb a quick look. Tears rolled down his face like sullen raindrops. Alice considered leaving without another word. But he'd asked for it. He wanted to know her. She couldn't stop now. "Girls stayed in the house until they looked old enough for a different *clientele*." She rubbed her arms. It'd rained her first night on the street, but she didn't feel the drops. By then she didn't feel anything at all. "I took a lot of pills. All different kinds. And not just pills." She gave a sad shrug. "Drugs made things easier."

Caleb ran a hand through his hair, but didn't make a sound. The darkness hid most of his face. But the strain of emotion told its story. She

❰ finding home ❱

didn't miss the quiet way he swallowed sobs.

"It took two years in the Red Light District for me to understand things were never going to change, and only a couple days after that to know I couldn't go on." She turned her back to Caleb and spotted the tent. It was impossible to imagine that very soon this place would be filled with laughter and dancing instead of tears and heartache.

"So…" Her voice cracked. She willed her emotions down and started again. "So, one night I filled a syringe with enough heroin to kill me and hid in an alley." She could still feel the frigid concrete on her back. Her arm had gone limp and splashed in a puddle. Darkness closed in like thick, black clouds. Death had come for her. She pivoted back to Caleb. "I woke up in a hospital room. The nurse told me I'd stopped breathing, that it was a miracle an ambulance found me and gave me medicine in time."

Alice's sigh sounded like a groan. "I was furious. All I could think about was the hell I'd have to go back to once they made me leave." She paused and felt a little lighter for the first time since she started talking. "But there was a woman…Sheri. She was a nurse. She told jokes and brought me food and, I don't know, just took care of me.

Alice took a few light steps towards the bench. "I didn't know what to say to her. No one had ever been nice to me." Alice would never forget Sheri's tender face and bright eyes. "She came in the day I was discharged and told me about a group home for girls. She let me know I was in if I wanted to be. I didn't believe her, but she said there was a cab waiting outside and that everything had been arranged. I didn't know what to do. So, I told her to give it to someone else and ran.

"The cab was there just like she said. I saw it as soon as I was outside. I meant to leave but something wouldn't let me walk away. I remember looking down the street knowing I'd be dead in a few days if I went back." She settled on the far end of the bench. "Then I looked at the cab and felt the faintest spark of hope. I know now it was God drawing me in even though I wanted nothing to do with him. That night I was in Redwood."

Alice pressed her lips together. It was over. But instead of relief the air grew heavier. She cast a glance at the boy on the other end of the bench. Her voice was small, "Caleb?" His head was down and his fingers twitched in a variety of erratic patterns. He was smaller somehow, a mere shadow of whom he'd been.

A sad sense of finality squeezed Alice's heart. She'd done what he'd wanted. She'd given him a chance. This is what she'd expected. But his silence lit a fire in her stomach that burned out the sorrow. Her eyes narrowed. "You're not going to say anything?"

His head dropped even lower than it already was. "This is what you wanted, Caleb. *You* asked for this." He didn't respond. "This is why I told you we couldn't—" She stopped before he could detect the sob climbing her throat. The only thing she wanted to do was leave as fast as possible.

Her knees wobbled and threatened to collapse as he started for her car that was parked along the road. Every step she took away from Caleb jarred her heart. In the movies he would shout and run to her. He'd wrap his arms around her and say he didn't care about her past. He'd tell her how much he loved her and that's all that matters.

The seat was cold as she slipped behind the wheel. When the door was shut she finally allowed a few tears to fall. This wasn't the movies. There would be no fairy-tale ending. She started the engine and turned up the heat.

The tears came faster and gave way to sobs that didn't ease until she was in bed with the covers draped around her body. She wiped her eyes on the sheet and knew two things for sure: God's love had healed her from more than should ever be possible, and that he would be the only man able to love her as she was. She stared at the ceiling as a few more tears landed on her pillow. That would have to be enough for her.

«finding home»

«chapter forty»

Ashley dropped her paintball gun on a worn picnic table. A pink and purple mask muffled her voice. "Do you hate me, John?"

John glanced at Ashley who tapped her foot on the ground like an obstinate teenager. "Why would you think that?"

She moved her mask so it held on her forehead. "Call it a hunch."

John shielded his eyes as the bright pink on her mask caught the midmorning sun. "Last chance to pick some different head gear. Maybe something not so reflective…and bright. You might as well wear a sign that says, 'please shoot me in the face.'"

"Worry about yourself, *commando*," Ashley exclaimed and stuck out her bottom lip. "I can be cute *and* deadly."

John grinned and removed a camouflage mask from his bag. Ashley had refused the paintball plan at first, but surrendered when he reminded her of the medical seminar she'd dragged him to. He lifted his chin. "That gun okay for you?"

"No. It's heavy and my arm's already tired. Isn't there one that doesn't weigh a million pounds?"

John cringed. Her voice had risen an octave, rapidly approaching a whine. He wiped some grime off his gun and motioned at the table of rental guns. "I think you've got the lightest one. It's that or nothing."

"Is *nothing* an option?"

"Sure, if you wanna be the bait."

"The *bait?*"

"Yeah, you know, wave your arms and draw enemy fire." John pointed at the side of her head. "Just make sure to cover your ears. A paintball there is enough to make a grown man cry."

Ashley shoved him away. "You're a jerk."

John laughed and returned to his bag. He pulled out his Planet Eclipse GEO 3.5, a paintball gun that'd seen a lot of victories. He tested the electronic button that let him switch modes and stared down the extended barrel.

Ashley eyed his weapon. "What are you, some kind of Terminator?"

John gave her a wink. "Something like that." He secured the hopper and carefully began pouring paintballs into it. "Mike and I used to come out here a lot. Great way to blow off some steam, you know?"

Ashley followed a renegade paintball that slipped from John's hand and fallen to the ground. "By shooting a bunch of kids with paint?" She plucked the ball off the ground and offered it to John.

He shook his head. "Can't put any in after they hit the ground. It'll clog the gun." He motioned across the field. Hay bales, partial fences, plywood, and other objects were spread around ready to be used as tactical barriers. "Plenty of adults over there too."

Ashley peered at the other team. "If you say so. Most of them are what…15, 16?" She aimed her gun in their direction. "Shouldn't be too hard, right?"

John beheld her with amusement as she tried to steady her gun at eye level. "Yeah, sure. Just stay behind me."

Ashley followed him to a plywood wall where the rest of their team were gathering. A piece of blue fabric hung over a rusty nail. "It's capture the flag, Ash. We get theirs and bring it back here. We're blue and they're red. Get shot and you're out, so don't get shot."

Ashley put a defiant hand on her hip. "I was a kid once too, John. I know what capture the flag is."

John rolled his eyes. Maybe her getting shot wouldn't be the worst thing. He lifted his gun and stared down the sight one last time. "Okay, you ready?"

"Yeah I'm—"

The blast of a horn drowned out her words and John dashed for a hay bale. He slid in just as a flurry of paintballs sailed over his head. He wanted to shout as the thrill of war washed over him. "Okay, now we try

‹ finding home ›

to advance while our team draws fire on the other side of the field. Got it? Ash?" He glanced over his shoulder. "Ashley?" The only thing behind him was a cloud of dust.

John jerked his head around and finally saw her scurrying from one side of the starting wall to the other. "Ashley!" He punched the hard ground. "Get over here!"

Ashley hurled some choice words in his direction and carefully leaned out from behind the wall. Nobody seemed to notice her and John only heard the occasional paintball hit his hay bale. Maybe she could make it.

Ashley shot a wild look in his direction and braced for a sprint. John looked her over and suddenly noticed her hands were empty. He frantically waved his hands and pointed behind her. "Your gun!"

Ashley whipped around and snatched up her weapon that was leaning against the wall.

John rubbed his forehead. "Oh, Lord, help her."

Ashley cast one more look at John, and made a break for the hay bale. She made it halfway before the first paintball screamed by her head. She yelped and dipped as another one barely missed.

For a moment, time seemed to slow long enough for John to see that all reason had fled the poor girl. John sensed what was coming a fraction of a second before the air around her exploded with enemy fire. Her squeal was strangled by the sound of paint hitting wood and hay. She covered both ears and crouched in a ball.

"Ashley, run!" John fired blind shots trying to draw some attention, but it had minimal success. He started to wonder how long it would be before she spoke to him again, but then heard her shout.

"John!"

He turned just as she dove on top of him. They both grunted as they crashed to the ground. "Ashley..." He pushed her off and scrambled to check her clothes for paint. "You were *supposed* to stay right behind me."

Ashley's voice quivered like popcorn about to pop. "Those...those aren't kids, John. Those are little monsters. Little demon-monsters from some sort of evil...monster...place."

John quickly checked her back. "I don't think you got hit." He stared into her mask. "How did you not get hit?"

She glared at him. "I'm a walking frickin' miracle."

"Wait a minute." He climbed over her careful to keep his head below the barrier. "Where's your gun?"

Ashley leaned against the bale. "I don't know. I, I threw it I think."

"You what?"

"I threw it, John." She jumped up and directed a shaky finger between his eyes. "You left me alone in paintball *hell* and I threw my gun."

"Ashley!" He yanked her on top of him just as a payload of paintballs erupted where her head had just been.

"Oh, god." She clutched his mask. "Don't make me be bait."

John stifled a laugh. "I won't, Ashley."

Her eyes darted back and forth like she'd swallowed an upper. "Take them out, John. Take them all out."

John raised an eyebrow. "I kind of like it when you get all nutty."

"I'll remember you said that."

Someone shouted from the field, "Blue team *forward...*"

John popped up from behind the wall and eliminated someone from the red team trying to advance up the field. "Ok, Ashley, remember, this is capture the flag."

She pressed up against his back. "Yeah, get their stupid flag, bring it back to our stupid side, and we win the stupid game. It's not rocket science."

John leveled his weapon. "Stay low and right behind me. Here we go."

John moved in a low crouch, quickly removing a few red players who poked their heads above barriers. The blue team moved up the field in a strategic line. Most of them were on the far side of the field.

"Alright," John almost whispered. "Most of our team is over there drawing attention. There's probably just a few between us and the flag. You ready?"

Ashley nodded like a bobble-head doll having a panic attack.

They crept around a piece of fence and surprised two red players guarding the flag. A few seconds later John was tying the red fabric around Ashley's arm. "All we have to do is get past the center line."

Ashley rubbed the thin cloth between her fingers. "All this for something probably pulled out of a dumpster."

John ignored her and pointed ahead. "Do you see that big wooden spool?"

Ashley shielded her eyes from the sun. "Yeah."

‹ finding home ›

"When I tell you, make a run for it."

"They've got our flag!" someone shouted.

John fired a flurry toward the voice. "*Now*, Ashley."

Ashley sprinted for the spool. "It's the girl," someone hollered from behind a bale. "Get the girl!"

John unloaded on those daring to show skin, connecting with a few, and hurried after Ashley. He was just about there when something small and hard slammed into his left ear and sent him rolling. He groaned and pressed his ear. When he drew back his fingers they were covered in blue paint. He was out. A figure in a red jersey was approaching.

"Well-well-well," taunted the masked gunman. "It's John, isn't it?"

John steadied himself on his knees and lifted his mask. "Do I know you?"

"You don't remember me?"

John fingered his weapon. The voice *did* sound familiar. It was young... and very upbeat at the moment. His brain raced to try and match it. "You're wearing a mask. Pretty hard to tell."

"This should help." He raised his mask.

John's stomach rolled. "Oh, no."

A smirk formed on Sid's face. "Your team's almost dead. My guys are taking care of the few that are left." He motioned to someone who'd stepped up beside him. "Josh and I would like a word with you."

John eyed the barrel of Sid's gun. "Hey, listen. The other day...you caught me on a bad morning." John examined his face. "Your nose looks great."

Josh scoffed. "Better than your ear right now."

"What's going on?" Ashley wanted to know. "How do you all know each other?"

John caught her eyes and willed her to understand the plan coming together in his brain. "Josh and Sid here were about to invite us to their church to have coffee and doughnuts."

The boys leveled their guns at John. "No," Sid argued. "That ship has sailed. But you're about to eat *something*."

"Ashley," John cried and thrust his gun toward her.

The boys flinched at the outburst, but Ashley seized John's gun out of the air, twisted around in a tight circle, and aimed at the shocked duo. Before they could react she squeezed the trigger and a stream of paintballs screamed 300 feet-per-second straight into their chests.

For half a second John was frozen on what had just happened. But then he remembered there was a game to win. "Ashley..." She whirled stunned eyes at him and he stabbed his finger at the centerline. "RUN!"

Paintballs whizzed by her ears and exploded on the ground, but she raced ahead. Then suddenly the line was behind her and she was clean.

John was on his feet when she crossed the line. He sprinted to the blue team's hero, scooped her up, twirled and kissed her on the lips. "That was unbelievable," he blurted between laughs.

Ashley grabbed his face. "Did you see me shoot those guys? Wasn't that awesome?"

John grinned. "I can't figure out how you didn't get hit. You're like Wyatt Earp in *Tombstone*."

"I don't know what came over me. I just turned and shot and ran."

John could only laugh as he set her down and stepped back to let the rest of the blue team gathered around to congratulate her.

When the last person wandered off, Ashley hurried to John. "So..." she clapped and hopped up and down like a crazed bunny. "What do we get?"

John cleaned dirt from his eyes. "What do you mean?"

"*Hello*, we won," she jabbered. "What do we get for winning?"

"Satisfaction. And usually a beer."

"Satisfaction?" She spat the word like it was rancid in her mouth. "Are you kidding me?" She pointed at a few of the losing team members. "Someone better give me a friggin' trophy."

John took her in. Her hair looked like she'd been in a wind tunnel and her face was streaked with sweat and dirt. Her oversized sweatshirt was ripped up one side and the knees of her dark jeans were caked with mud. Dirty hands were firmly planted on her hips. "Would you, uh," he coughed to cover a laugh, "settle for lunch?"

Ashley lifted her chin. "Depends on where?"

He plucked a leaf out of her hair. "Wherever you want."

Her green eyes sparkled. "I guess that'll have to do."

John wrapped his big arms around her as they strolled to the car. "You

‹ finding home ›

had fun out there, didn't you?"

She tried to curb her enthusiasm. "It was alright."

Forty-five minutes later, John was staring at pieces of raw fish arranged on top of rice. He'd never eaten sushi and didn't want to start today. Chopsticks remained neatly concealed in their wrapper, discarded for a fork. Ashley observed him with amusement pulling at her delicate features.

"You might as well go ahead and laugh," he let her know. "It can't be good to hold it in like that."

Ashley giggled. "No-no. You're doing great." She threw him a cheesy grin and a thumbs up.

John rolled his eyes and prodded a piece of opaque fish with his fork. "Is this stuff even safe to eat?"

She waved him off. "Don't worry. I'm a nurse."

"Not sure I like that answer," John replied and shot her a playful smile. "If I fall over after eating this stuff just give me some good mouth-to-mouth and I'll come right back."

Ashley laughed. "Any more trouble from what's-her-face, who punched you?" She expertly used her chopsticks to move a piece of sushi to her mouth.

"Naw," John answered and sniffed at a piece of fish. "Mike said there's nothing to worry about. *Somehow* she's moved on."

"Oh, brother," Ashley uttered and lifted her chin. "Does that mean I get to be the only girl who punches you from now on?"

John scooped up some rice with his fork. "After watching you today I'd be lying if I said I wasn't worried." Ashley laughed and John finally tasted his food. "Hey, that's not bad."

Ashley leaned on her elbows, "I've been trying to tell you. Try a piece of that." She pushed a piece of tuna at him. "Put a little soy sauce on it."

John stabbed the thin slice with his fork and dipped it in the sauce. He swallowed and licked his lips. "Okay, I'll admit that was pretty good."

Ashley smiled and told him about her week between bites. *This* guy and *that* girl and medication shortages and doctors' egos. It was like a soap opera. John chewed and wondered if he was the one who'd had it easy all this time.

The waiter collected their plates and returned with hot tea. "So, have you seen Jesus lately?"

"No," John answered. "Not like I did anyway." He took a sip of tea and pictured the face of Jesus embedded in his brain for eternity. "He told me it wasn't going to be like that anymore. But he did say that he'd never leave me. I've heard pastors and churchers say that more times than I can remember, but I never really got it. I think I'm finally starting to." He paused. "I kinda feel him right now. It's weird…but good."

Ashley was grinning at him. "*Churchers?*"

John set down his cup. "Yeah. Someone who goes to church enough to think everyone's business is their business." John shook his head. "Old Betty at the church I grew up in. She was a giant *churcher*."

Ashley laughed loud enough to draw a couple of looks. "It's okay," John assured and waved at them. "I'm hilarious."

Ashley threw her napkin at him. "*Stop it.*"

John chuckled. "Is the Jesus thing still weird for you?"

"No. A little, maybe. I mean, it's easy to believe everything you've told me, but at the same time it's hard. God loving us enough to interact with us on the level you've experienced is amazing but," she let her hands fall to her lap, "at the same time it's hard for me to wrap my mind around."

"Yeah, I get that," John conceded. "There's still times it all seems like a dream." *Dream. Oak Harbor.* John rubbed his stubbly chin. The decision he'd made pounded against his heart.

"Hey!"

He jerked his eyes up to the deep scowl etched in Ashley's face. He straightened. "How do you look so beautiful even when you're so mad?"

That softened her some and she sighed. "Did you hear anything I said?"

"No but listen, I've got something to tell you."

She threw her hands up. "Oh, *you've* got something to say? Please," she motioned to him, "Let's hear it while I fade to God knows where."

"Ok, great." Ashley stared at him like he'd grown an extra head while he swallowed a mouthful of tea. "I'm just gonna say it, okay?"

"Say what?"

"I think it's time for me to go home, to Oak Harbor."

She flinched and cleared her throat. "Time for what now?"

John launched into his dream explaining every detail. She fidgeted with

‹ finding home ›

her hands on her lap as he went on about the sign and Jesus. When he was done she sat silent for a long time and some of the color had left her face.

"So, you're leaving?"

John reached across the table and took her hand. "Yeah, but I want you to come with me."

Ashley stiffened. "For how long?"

"I don't know."

"Why now?"

"I don't know that either." He ran a hand through his hair. "I hurt some people there. People I really cared about. I need to make that right, but I don't know why it has to be now."

Ashley drew her hand back. "I have a life here, John. Family, friends…a career. You're asking me to leave all that and move to Ohio?"

John rocked back in his chair and felt a spark of frustration. "You can have all that in Oak Harbor. And it's not *moving* for sure." He glanced around the room to make sure no one was listening in and leaned forward. "I wasn't even going to ask you because—"

"You weren't going to ask me?" Ashley's voice rose a bit and she clutched her napkin. "You were what…just gonna leave?"

John sighed and gulped some water. "No, I was going to tell you…it's because of everything you just said. I wasn't sure you'd leave all that for me but I, I just couldn't imagine leaving without you."

"John." Ashley's voice was soft and there were tears in her eyes. She stroked his hand. "I would go with you in a second but…" She glanced at the ceiling and wiped her face. "Do you love me?"

John's shirt was a noose tightening around his neck, and a bead of sweat crept across his forehead. "You know how I feel about you."

"I know you care about me…a lot." She hesitated. "But that's not what I asked you. I'm not going to pick up my life and move across the country with someone who just *cares* about me. If you want me to go with you I need to hear you say it. I *need* to know."

I love you. It'd been more than ten years since he confessed those words to a woman. He gazed at Ashley and felt his heart move and rip at the thought of leaving her. She was the centerpiece of every way he pictured his future. He'd do anything for her. But the words wouldn't come. "Ashley

I…" his words died and he had the terrible feeling what he had with Ashley was following suit.

Ashley sniffed and rubbed a few more tears from her face. "When do you leave."

His voice was a whisper. "Soon. Couple days."

She got to her feet and gathered herself. "I'm gonna call a friend to pick me up."

"Ash—"

She stopped him. "No, it's okay." She held his eyes for a long moment before forcing a sad smile. "I hope you find what you're looking for."

John lowered his eyes to the table. When he looked up she was gone, and a wrinkled old man was glaring at him. "What?"

The guy shook his head. "You're an *idiot.*"

He hobbled away and John covered his face with his hands. The old corpse was right. He just allowed the woman he loved to walk out of his life. *The woman he loved.* He grunted in frustration. He could admit it to himself but…no. He slapped the table making the silverware jump. It couldn't end like this. He didn't have to live like *this* anymore. He jumped to his feet. It wasn't too late.

He found her in the parking lot. "Ashley!" When she turned he saw the streaks on her face. "Ashley, wait."

"No, John. I understand."

"No you don't." He hesitated, searching for the right words. "I was scared, Ash." He threw his hands in the air. "All I know of love is *pain*. My whole life, nothing good followed those words. I thought it might change with Amy, but it didn't. I told myself I'd never say it again to anyone."

Some of the tension faded from Ashley's expression. "What about now?"

John sighed. "I met you and Jesus and…it's still hard, no matter how I feel. But I need you to know something."

Ashley trembled as he moved close enough to touch her. Her voice was brittle, "What do I need to know?"

John fixed his eyes on hers. "You need to know how much I love you."

Ashley sucked in her bottom lip as the remaining tension disappeared. John gave her a small smile and ran a hand through her hair. She was silent until a few tears ran down her face. Her voice was a whisper, "I thought

‹finding home›

you were gone."

John brushed away her tears with his thumb. "I know. I'm so sorry." And then he drew her lips to his. "I love you, Ash," he professed into her ear. "More than anything."

He kissed her again. When they parted Ashley's face was wet but she was smiling. "So, is there still an open seat on that trip you're planning?"

chapter forty one

Caleb laid his forehead on the steering wheel of his Honda as it churned heat into the space around him. But the cold was stronger. It had been for the last few days. Heavy weights pushed down on his shoulders and hung off his legs. He'd been unstable, snapping at co-workers and patients.

He lifted his head and smeared some condensation on the windshield. Naked trees were positioned ahead and on either side. The service road was rarely used and perfect for someone who wanted to be alone. Away from people and injustice. *Men* and injustice.

Rage sparked in his belly and sent a flame through his chest. In his dreams they surrounded Alice and he killed them, crushing the cartilage of their tracheas with his bare hands. "Arghhhhh," he hollered and beat on the steering wheel with his fists.

"Hey-hey-hey."

Caleb snapped his head to the window and rubbed his eyes. A man shivered in the snow. Caleb made a quick scan for the man's car, but his was still the only one there. He peered at the figure but didn't recognize the stubbled face. He motioned for him to go away.

"Come'on man," the guy pleaded. "Give me a chance to warm up. It's freezing out here." He tugged his flannel shirt tighter around his body and gave Caleb a desperate look.

Caleb was about to tell him to get lost, but then changed his mind. Maybe it was the gleam in the guy's eyes or the strange rush of compassion or even the fact that, at the moment, he didn't particularly care if the dude killed him. Whatever it was, Caleb unlocked the passenger door.

The man hurried around the car and slid into the seat next to Caleb.

‹ finding home ›

"Thanks," he gushed and rubbed his legs through tan pants. "It's a cold one out there today."

Caleb turned up the heat. "Who are you?"

The man held his hands in front of the vent. "Just a guy passing through."

Caleb made a face. "That's a little vague."

"Well, sometimes it's better to keep things to yourself. I didn't ask you why you were going a round with your steering wheel." He moved his face in front of the heat. "Ahhh, that's better. Little heat in these bones and I'll be right as rain."

Caleb shook his head. "Whatever man. You need a ride?"

He adjusted the cap covering his dark hair. "Naw, I'll be fine in a few minutes."

Caleb lifted his chin. "Looks like that hat's seen better days."

"Well, it's pretty old." He cleared his throat. "So, why were you beating up on your car here? Must be somethin' about a girl, eh?"

"How did you…some things are better kept to ourselves right?"

"Sometimes. Not in your case I don't think."

Caleb's eyes narrowed on the man. It was time for him to be moving on. "You warm yet?"

"Almost. So what'd she do? Break your heart?"

Caleb grimaced. The guy was a boot stepping on the shards of a life he'd dreamed Alice into. A dream that had turned into a nightmare. "*She* didn't do anything. You know," Caleb leaned toward the man, "people are *sick*. The world is full of monsters. They just walk up and down the street every day and nobody does anything about it." He swiped at his wet eyes and noticed the man's features had fallen a bit.

"Someone hurt her."

Dark faces swirled in Caleb's mind, blank except for an evil sneer on each one. He kept his eyes on the trees ahead. "Not just one."

For the next few minutes neither of them spoke. "I'm sorry…"

"Caleb."

"Yes…I'm sorry, Caleb." He drew a line in the window fog. "I've been around…experienced this world for a long time. I know what it's like to have someone you love hurt terribly by someone else."

Love. He'd stopped short of telling her that night because he was afraid it'd be too much. But he loved her. There was no question in his head. Caleb wiped his nose. "How'd you deal with it?"

"Got mad. Punched a few holes in the wall." He removed his hat and turned it over in his hands. "Went to her with open arms and cried enough to flood a river."

Caleb stared out his window and blinked back tears. That was the other thing crushing his soul. He'd just sat there. Alice had practically begged him for something…anything. Something had happened to her, that much he guessed. But nothing could've prepared him for that night. He just hadn't known what to do. "How did you do it…go to her?"

"That's what love is, Caleb. It always holds and comforts. It bears up under anything and everything that comes. It cries with, shares with, shouts with, and is just *with*. It never fails no matter how deep the valley or sharp the sword…or how ugly the monster."

Love never fails. But Caleb had. He'd run when love would've stayed. He leaned against the headrest and wished he could go back. Back to that night and be the kind of love the guy next to him was talking about. "What about the people who hurt her?" He faced the man. "What about them?"

"Ah, yes. The antagonists. I forgave them."

"Just like that?"

The man sighed. "Forgiveness…yes. But it's never as simple as *just like that* when emotions are involved. And I'm not a robot."

Caleb leaned forward as anger poured through him like lava. "Why forgive them? The things they did to her…no one should have to experience things like that."

He clucked his tongue. "You're right, but try living without forgiving the people who hurt you and the ones you love and see where you end up. Not in the abundance you learned about in Sunday school, I'm sure."

"How did you—"

"I see it in your eyes." He rubbed his hands in the heat. "Bitterness will give you a rotten heart and the same past. But more importantly, forgiveness is what it means to love others…even those you call monsters." He raised an eyebrow. "Or are those kinds of people excluded from the command to *love one another?*"

≪finding home≫

Caleb tried to swallow the man's words. At the moment, forgiving the men who'd hurt Alice seemed impossible, but the other thing, loving her... "Do you, uh, think it's too late for me to make it right with her. I really screwed up and I just..." The last word broke in a sob.

The man reached over and squeezed his shoulder. "Son, you'll never know unless you go to her. Fear runs, but love goes."

A sliver of hope flickered through Caleb. Maybe there was still a chance. Maybe she could forgive him. He wiped his eyes and gave the man half a smile. "You sure you don't want me to take you somewhere?"

The man popped the door and shoved it open with his hand on the window glass. "I'll be fine." He climbed out and bent over before shutting the door. "Thanks for the heat, Caleb."

Caleb nodded and watched the man vanish into the trees. He was about to turn the car around when the handprint on the passenger side window caught his attention. He leaned closer and felt his heart jump to his throat. In the middle of the handprint was a jagged circle.

chapter forty two

Alice blinked at the blurry ceiling and groped wildly for her notebook. She had to draw before the images faded from her memory.

She hadn't meant to fall asleep, but with Mark and Claire out shopping it'd been quiet enough to lure her into a dream she was trying to capture on paper. Much of the dream was familiar, the kids and house. The laughter, the desire to know them...the oppressive feeling that she already did.

But there was something else this time. Two new faces...a man and woman. They were with the children, laughing and pushing them on swings. The man was tall with dark hair that blew in the wind revealing specks of gray, even though his face was young.

The woman stood next to him with her arm draped loosely around his waist. Her jet-black hair fell around her shoulders and spilled down her back. Her expression wrote life and love into the scene like a Thomas Kinkade painting.

Draw them Alice. It was the last thing she'd caught before waking up. She lifted four pieces of paper and eyed them like she was judging fine art. Not bad. She cocked her head. It was a little creepy that faces from her dreams had crossed into the *real* world. She placed the portraits on the nightstand next to her bed and lifted her cross charm from under her shirt. *Love never fails...* The man and woman had to be the kid's parents. She smiled as the scene played again through her mind. If love and hope was anywhere it was there.

Alice rolled on her side toward her bedroom window and watched the late afternoon sun shimmer across a blanket of fresh of snow. It was so white, so pure, like she might've been before being thrust into the underbelly of

‹ finding home ›

the world. Then again, as far as she knew, she'd always been there.

A sigh rose from her heart as she fell onto her back. *The dreams, the house...Caleb.* She blinked back tears inspired by the last few days. Claire and Mark knew something had happened. Even Nikki wanted to know what was wrong with her. In times like this she remembered what it was like to be *numb* and part of her longed for it. She knew she was deeply loved by God. She'd come a long way in believing what that meant for her worth and value, but she had exposed the filth of her life to someone she really cared about, and been rejected.

Alice slowly climbed to her feet and paused in front of the mirror. Her paler-than-normal skin hid behind an oversized sweatshirt and sweatpants. Her eyes looked more red than hazel, and drooped.

She swept her frazzled hair into a loose ponytail and felt the burn of betrayal in her stomach. She'd made the impossible choice to open up and was discarded like garbage. She touched the cool mirror where her face looked back at her. The cross charm was suddenly ice-cold on her chest. She pulled the necklace over her head and dropped it on the dresser. The cross lay face down so she could see the inscription, *1 Cor. 13:8.* Her eyes narrowed.

"Why did you even bring me here?" The pain was acid on her heart and she jabbed the air with her finger. "Answer me! You wanted me to leave everything in Redwood and come out for what...this?" She spread out her hands and a few tears tumbled down her cheek. "Was it for this? To see that I'm gonna be alone my whole life because I'm so *damaged?*"

A knock startled her. She ignored it, but a minute later it came again. Alice sniffed, wiped her eyes, and gave the mirror a dissatisfied glance before heading to the front door. She carefully peered through the peephole and instantly fell back a step as if she'd been pushed.

Caleb! She covered her chest with her hands and reminded herself to breathe. She rotated toward the back yard and imagined the thick woods lying just beyond. She could hide there for the rest of the day.

Alice returned to the door and felt heat burn through her chest. She should just leave him out there. But she couldn't deny the way hope jolted her heart. Maybe she should just see what he wants. She hesitated a long moment before she gripped the knob and opened the door just enough to see him.

Caleb stood with his hands shoved in his pockets, one foot slightly in front of the other and shoulders slumped. He quickly lowered his eyes and shifted, like he was standing on nails instead of concrete. "Hey," he managed weakly.

Alice's mouth was a straight line as she watched the boy who'd broken her heart search for words. After a moment that stretched for an eternity, Caleb cleared his throat. "Alice, I, uh," he glanced at the ground and then back at her, "That night…what you told me—"

"You just sat there." Alice's voice was venom. "I told you things I've never told anyone and you couldn't even look at me."

Caleb sunk even further into the ground. "I know and I—"

"You said you wanted more." Alice opened the door a little more and clutched the frame. "You asked me to share my life with you and I *did*." She looked away so he wouldn't see her eyes pool.

"Alice—"

"I saw your face, Caleb." She wiped angrily at a tear. "The look of disgust—"

"Alice!"

His tone silenced her and he ran both hands through his hair. "I'm trying to say that I'm *sorry*…and that *wasn't* disgust. At least not for you." The words broke through the cold air and flooded her. She didn't back away when he took a step closer.

"That night it was…I didn't know what to do. I never expected…" He sighed. "It's not okay what I did and all I want to do is go back and hold you on that bench. I'd tell you that it's gonna be okay. That I'm not going anywhere." He exhaled and Alice felt her knees wobble. "I'd thank you for sharing your life with me."

He pressed a hand against the door and Alice let it fall open. She could feel her anger melting away like snow in spring, but she scrambled to hang on to a portion of it. Her voice was strained, "You hurt me."

Caleb winced and looked away. "I know. And I'm so sorry." He found her eyes. "All those things I wish I'd said, I'm saying them now, Alice. I couldn't that night because I…" The last word caught in this throat. "I want to run backwards in time and rescue you before you ever got in the truck with that scumbag. I want to kill them, Alice. Every single one. I

◄ finding home ►

want to choke the life out of them before they ever laid a finger on you. But every time I try I run into a wall." He dropped onto the porch step with his back to her and head in his hands.

Alice hung in the doorway like a child weighing the safety of the house against the dangerous world. Compassion coated her eyes and she felt herself moving forward and sitting down next to him. She saw the pain in his face and it stabbed her heart. She drew her knees to her chest and angled her body towards him as he lifted his head.

"I'm so sorry, Alice," he repeated. "For letting you walk away. I've seen myself running after you a thousand times." He paused. "Please forgive me."

Alice chewed her lip. This was all more than she had hoped for, but there was just too much. "Caleb I, I forgive you." She forced a sad smile. "But *please* understand that I'm not asking you to save or rescue me. What's done is done." She paused. "God's been healing me for the last three years and the change is bigger than I have words for."

She sighed and kicked a piece of hard snow off the step. He was saying all the right things, but she didn't know if she could ever forget how her story had broken him. And she didn't want to be the reason for that ever again. Her voice was thick, "Caleb I—"

"Alice, don't do this."

Alice stared at her hands. "I think it would be better if we just went our separate ways. It's not fair to ask you to be with someone like me." She clenched her jaw and gripped the step like a vise. "Someone who's been through the things I have."

Alice glanced up at him as her heart broke. He focused straight ahead, his jaw and mouth a tight line. She didn't want him to go. She wanted him to stay. She wanted to order him to forget everything she'd just said and melt into him.

Caleb's legs twitched as if he was going to get up and leave, but suddenly faced her with rekindled fire in his eyes. "Maybe you're right. Maybe we move on, live our lives, and eventually find other people to share it with. Who knows how things could turn out. We both love Jesus so I'm sure we'll be fine." He hesitated and peered into her heart. "But I don't want *fine*, Alice. I don't want *pretty good*. The day I walked into the café you ruined both of those options for me."

He took her hand. "I want *you*, Alice. I want the adventure and passion living in your heart. I want the pure and precious woman that you are." She blinked and he slid closer. "Alice, I even want the mess because I know I can help you clean it up. If you don't want to be with me then that's your choice. But don't hide behind your idea of what's fair for *me*." He paused. "I want to be with you. What do *you* want?"

Alice had to remind herself this was real. He was willing to sacrifice so much to be with her. There was no doubt in the way he gazed at her. Maybe she was wrong. His fingers traced down her cheek and instead of pulling away she felt herself lean into him. "Caleb, I," her words were a whisper, "I didn't expect…" Fresh tears dropped onto her face. "I want to be with you."

And then his lips were softly pressing against hers. Alice was swept into a world she couldn't have imagined as passion for Caleb flooded her. It was a world where every sensation was new and fresh. One where she was experiencing it all for the first time. She couldn't keep the smile from her face as Caleb drew back. God had erased all of the dirt and perversion and made her new. Made *this* new.

"Wow," he exclaimed as he weaved his fingers in and out of her own.

She giggled and sniffed. "…Yeah."

"Does this mean you'll still be my date to the dance?"

She grinned and pulled his mouth to hers.

"I guess that's a 'yes'," he said half-aloud when they parted.

Alice giggled and leaned into his chest as he draped an arm over her shoulders and pulled her close. Snowflakes had begun to fall all around them covering footprints and disturbed snow as if God was telling her, See, *I make all things new.*

They stayed like that for a long time until Alice suddenly sat up straight and gasped. "I need a dress."

"Better hurry." Caleb climbed to his feet and held out his hand. "Do I get to go?"

Alice took his hand and let him help her up. "No way. I'll see if Nikki's busy." She gave Caleb a shy smile still feeing dizzy from everything. "So, what do we do now?"

‹finding home›

He slid his arms around her waist. "Tonight would be a great night for our first date."

"My first date *ever*."

Caleb kissed her again. "Then it better be special." He held her close while they moved toward the warm house. "Oh, wait till you hear about this guy I met earlier."

chapter forty three

John squinted at the sign through the afternoon glare. *Welcome to Oak Harbor.*

"Oh, thank goodness," Ashley exclaimed and ran a hand through her tangled blonde hair. "I was starting to wonder if we'd *ever* get here."

John focused straight ahead and tried to shrug the weight off his shoulders. Thirty-four hours on the road had taken its toll on both of them.

He noticed an old gas station as they passed through the outskirts of town. A few cars lined the pumps, and the store window held a familiar bright orange *OPEN* sign with black letters. His stomach turned into a twisting rope of nerves.

Ashley squeezed his thigh. "You okay?"

"I'm fine," John lied. His eyes darted up to the rearview mirror. Just a quick U-turn and he could jet out of town as if he'd never been here.

"Don't even *think* about it," Ashley warned.

John shot her an innocent look. "What?"

"If you're gonna bail it'll be alone." She tested her breath and wrinkled her nose. "I need a shower and everything else a bathroom has to offer."

John surrendered. "How do you know me so well?"

"You're not that hard to read, John. Now tell me how you're *really* doing?"

John let the question hover like fog. His feelings were a jumbled mess. Every building they passed brought familiar comfort, but also stabbed him with memories of why and how he left. "It's strange," he finally expressed. "After ten years it still feels like home. But I hurt people here. After the accident I made a pretty big mess of things." He winced. "I, I think I threw

‹ finding home ›

a bottle at one of my neighbors who tried to talk to me about God."

Ashley grimaced. "Did you hit them?"

John scratched his head. "No, I missed and broke my mailbox."

Ashley covered her mouth to stifle a laugh.

"I left people here I'd known my whole life. People who loved and cared about me. I was just," John chopped his hand through the air, "gone. I didn't say goodbye or anything."

He fell silent as they passed a brick elementary school. Ashley gave a short wave to a few teenagers on bikes who examined them through curious eyes. "Isn't that why you're here?" she asked. "To fix the things you broke?"

John felt a wave of nausea as Mark and Claire's image hovered before him, his desire to follow God warred against the pain he'd left in his wake. He gripped the wheel tight enough to chase the blood from his hands. "*If* they can be fixed."

Ashley brushed some cracker crumbs from her shirt. "I don't think God would've told you to come if it wasn't possible." She raised an eyebrow. "Did you see *him* at the welcome sign?"

John shook his head. He'd almost expected to see Jesus standing at the town line motioning for him to hurry up.

Ashley shrugged. "Well, I know he's here."

"Doesn't make it easy to keep going." John hauled his truck into the hotel parking lot and killed the engine. "Okay, first thing's first." He tugged on a strand of Ashley's disheveled hair. "Let's find you a bathroom."

♥

Mark Summers shivered at the chill permeating the walls of his office. He held his hand up to a silent vent and huffed at the work order on his desk. "Someone will be out to fix the heater between one and five," the receptionist had informed him. He glanced at his watch and rolled his eyes. The deadline had come and gone.

"Betty?" he called to his longtime secretary. She was an anxious woman, the kind that takes everything as it's said. But the *no nonsense* complexion made her very good at her job. "Can you call the heat company again?"

"I've called them three times," came her shaky voice from the foyer. "They said they'd be here as soon as they can."

Mark fell into his cushy desk chair and looked over his sermon outline. Just a couple spots left to be filled in. If he could finish up early he might be able to help put the finishing touches on the festival. There wasn't too much left to be done thanks to volunteers like Caleb and Alice.

Alice. He stroked the stubble on his chin and smiled at how nice it was to have her around. Her love for Jesus was infectious, and she seemed to make things brighter.

But something had happened to her. Something traumatic involving men and maybe more. Mark frowned and drummed his fingers on the polished oak desktop. In the beginning, it stood like a brick wall between them. But he credited the love and grace of God for how quickly it crumbled.

His knees crackled as he rose and moved to the window. Small clumps of snow scattered across the landscape as if the sky had specifically decided where to dump its icy contents. Alice informed him with glittery eyes that it was supposed to warm up a little in time for the festival.

"Betty, you're in for a treat."

Betty appeared in the doorway, the wrinkles in her face creased with concern. "What's that?"

"Alice is going to bake for the festival. Don't be surprised if it causes a riot."

"Oh, dear," Betty muttered and scurried back to her desk.

Mark pivoted back to the window and rocked on his heels. To say the girl can cook was a colossal understatement. Claire was a great cook from a long line of great cooks, but even she was astonished at what Alice could create.

He sighed and saw his breath on the window. But why did God bring her to Oak Harbor? He rubbed his stomach. It had to be for more than helping him gain weight. The harder he tried to figure it out the further away he felt from the answer.

"Some people here to see you," Betty let him know from her desk.

Mark motioned with his hands. "Yes-yes, well send them—" He stopped suddenly like he'd choked on his tongue. A broad shouldered man

≺ finding home ≻

hung in the doorway. Unkempt dark hair with specs of gray shimmered like sunlight bouncing off minnows in murky water. The skin of his face was covered with a day or two's worth of growth and tight hands fidgeted like they were foreign objects he didn't know how to handle.

Mark staggered and groped for the edge of his desk. His next word was thick and no louder than a breeze. "John." The man in the doorway lifted hazel eyes as past and present clashed into one. Mark gasped and covered his mouth.

John's eyes darted between the floor and Mark. "Hey...Mark."

Mark couldn't recall the steps that took him to John, but suddenly his arms were wrapped around his friend as laughter and sobs melded into an overdue symphony.

John tensed, but only for a moment as every muscle relaxed and his own tears joined his friend's.

Mark held him at arm's length. "I can't believe it. Where have you been?"

John wiped his face on his sleeve. "Arizona."

"Arizona? Why in the world...you know what?" he waved his hands, "it doesn't matter." He gave a shout that was mostly a laugh and gripped John's shoulders. "You're home. That's all that matters."

John fell back a step as the heat of shame burned his cheeks. "Mark I..." he let his hands fall to his sides. "I'm so sorry for...well, I don't even know where to start. Everything I guess."

Mark fixed a steady gaze on John. "I forgive you. I forgive you for it all."

John lifted his chin. "Just like that?"

Mark chuckled. "Just seeing you here has healed more than you can imagine. There's just nothing left for you to do, my friend." He laughed again and slapped John's shoulder. "I just can't believe you're here! And you've changed haven't you?"

A small smile tugged at John's mouth. "You could say that."

Mark pursed his lips. "Well, it was Robert Short who said, *The church is the great lost and found department.*"

John tapped his head. "Still a steel trap for quotes, I see."

"Well, I've got another one for you. *Long lost friends are like old wine, they get better with age.*" He grinned and caught sight of someone behind John. "And who's this?"

John rotated to see Ashley cautiously approaching with hands folded behind her back. She wore a look like she'd been caught taking cookies from the jar. "Sorry I'm…I'll just wait outside."

"Nonsense!" Mark strode to her and scooped up her hand, patting it like he was forming a hamburger. "Did you come with this guy?"

She giggled and nodded.

John stepped beside her. "Mark, this is Ashley."

"It's so nice to finally meet you," Ashley gushed. "I've heard so much."

"It's my pleasure…really." Mark stepped back and studied them both like an artist putting the final touches on a masterpiece. Suddenly he clapped his hands together. "Well, I'm assuming you don't have dinner plans?"

John cast a quick glance at Ashley. "Well, we were just gonna find a restaurant and—"

"John." Mark shook his head. "You didn't think I'd let that fly, did you?" He grinned at Ashley. "Dinner's at my house."

"Oh, you don't have to do that," John objected.

Mark shot him a look like he'd just snored during one of his sermons… again. "John Rister, I will pick up this phone and call every food-serving establishment in this town with strict instructions not to let you in." He dropped his chin. "And you remember how they treat Pastors in this town."

"We'd love to have dinner with you," Ashley assured him through laughs. "Thank you."

Mark paused and fixed a satisfied look on John. "I'm just so glad you're home." He gathered up his unfinished sermon outline and motioned to the door. "Alright then, let's go."

«finding home»

chapter forty four

John swayed on Mark and Claire's porch swing overlooking a backyard that was as beautiful as he remembered. He still knew the landscape, knew how thick the woods were beyond the border. It was deeply comforting, the familiarity. Like a child reunited with its blanket or favorite toy after a lonely night.

He pushed his feet against the ground giving the swing more momentum. Claire had just about tackled him to the ground when they walked in.

He'd forgotten just how good of a cook Claire was. She gave all the credit to their absent houseguest for the recipe. He smirked when he considered whether or not Ashley would take notes.

Mark and Claire had lots of questions, but listened intently as John recounted his experiences with Jesus, the crash, Ashley, and how he'd been reconnected with the heart of God. He'd hesitated before sharing about meeting Jesus, unsure how they would react, but his concerns were misplaced. He'd found out why when they shared some of their own journey into the deeper waters God has to offer, including inviting a stranger to live with them.

"Room for one more?" Mark asked.

John slid over and Mark settled next to him. "House looks great."

"Thank you." Mark sipped steaming coffee and studied his friend. "You doing okay?"

John lifted his chin. "Better than I expected."

Mark adjusted the propane heater to funnel more heat at them. "Just checking. The last time you were in this house was pretty rough."

The funeral. John rubbed his legs. "I'm aware. I'm not gonna tell you it's been easy." He glanced at Mark. "Earlier I looked down the hallway where the guest room is and felt some of the same things I did that day. Not as strong but still, it was a tough moment."

Mark blew the steam from his mug. "It did take you a long time to use the bathroom."

"Yeah, well it made me realize you and Claire aren't the only reason I'm here. I didn't see it until now. There are parts of the trauma I couldn't heal in Blackwater."

"Ah, but God knew all along." Mark set his mug on the coffee table in front of them. "You drive by the cemetery on the way in or did you manage to avoid it?"

John shot a wary look at Mark. He could still navigate every road in town. Knew exactly which roads to take to miss things that should be missed. "The yard still looks great. Claire hasn't lost her touch with the flowers."

"I see you haven't lost your ability to change the subject. But I appreciate the compliment."

John sighed. "I'm not leaving without going there. I just couldn't today. It's—"

"I know, John. Take your time. There's no rush."

"How's my old place doing? Still over there anchoring Church and Mill?"

Mark nodded and picked up his mug. "Sure is. And I'd say it's held up quite well."

John pictured the house he'd deserted. It had become a dark shadow holding demons of despair and broken dreams, but now he could see there were far more happy memories than bad. Seeing it was another item on his *to do* list.

"We bought the house after you left," Mark continued. "The church did anyway. We've been using it for ministry, people in need." He stood and stepped to the rail, looking over the snow-covered ground before turning back. "We couldn't let it go, John. It was our way of holding on to you. Not just you, but Amy and the kids as well. It made me smile every time we showed it to someone."

John swallowed the emotion climbing his throat. There was a well of love in the man he'd never appreciated. It was another reminder that what he'd missed stretched further than ten years. "I don't know what to say."

Mark chuckled. "You don't have to say anything."

The ambient melody of winter wind blowing through bare trees joined the sounds of dessert being prepared inside. John thought he could've been inside some kind of holiday special, but a question pressing on his heart was wrecking the serenity. He peered at Mark. "I need to ask you something."

Mark returned to the swing. "Go ahead."

"It shouldn't surprise you that I blamed God for what happened to Amy and the kids. But when I saw Jesus in the park he seemed really upset, sad I mean, that I thought he was responsible. He said I didn't understand, but that I would." He lifted his hands. "I'm not sure I do. What do you think he meant?"

"Hmph," Mark grunted before crossing his arms. "The issue is so distressing most people ignore it completely." He paused and drew in a deliberate breath like John remembered him doing before launching into a Sunday morning sermon. His tone was heavy, almost labored. "Son, you don't serve as a Pastor without quickly realizing the issue of God and tragedy can't be ignored." He paused to pinch the space between his eyes. "We can try, but tragedy in this world is an inevitable eventuality. When we find ourselves on the wrong side we've *got* to do something with the loving God we've always tried to believe in.

"Amy and the kids made me face the issue with greater strain and travail than ever. My office went from a place of inspiration to the bane of my existence." He gestured to the sliding glass doors leading into the house. "My room became my own personal fortress of solitude. I didn't preach for months. Wasn't sure I ever would again."

Mark paused and tasted his coffee. John watched his friend but saw his own life, how he'd handled things when his nightmares became reality. But comfort worked through his heart knowing he hadn't been alone, that Mark had cared *that* much. "So, what happened?"

"Oh, I screamed and cursed and did everything a man filled with the rage of injustice could do. I even threw things." He lifted his chin toward the kitchen. "Scared her a couple of times." Mark tapped the swing with his fingers. "Eventually, I ran out of things to holler and decided to try listening."

John leaned forward. "And…"

"Uh-uh, we're going to talk about you and what you've come to understand about the mess of it all." He agitated the swing enough to keep it moving. "What do you think?"

John got to his feet and waved his hand through the air like a conductor. "*The Lord gives and takes away, who can understand the mind of God, Don't worry because God's in control, there must be a reason, God wanted them in heaven more than here…*" A bitter laugh escaped into the air. "I heard them all before, during, and after the funeral. So many reasons why God is responsible and, much to their chagrin I'm sure, so many reasons for me to blame and hate him."

He blew out frustration with a grunt. "But I just can't see it. It doesn't make any sense. The Jesus I met wouldn't do it. He just *wouldn't*." He pivoted to face Mark. "When I accused him in the park it looked like I'd punched him in the stomach." John took a couple steps towards the back yard. The moonlight bounced off the snow and ran into the trees until it disappeared.

"God is light and there is no darkness in him at all. I read that the other day in 1st John." John paused. "The funeral was the darkest day of my life." He wiped his nose and shook his head. "No, the Jesus I met wasn't responsible. He healed me from the pain. He didn't cause it." He eyed his friend. "Feel free to jump in at any time. You're the pastor."

Mark chuckled. "You're doing just fine on your own." He raised his mug. "A theologian is born."

John rolled his eyes and lowered himself on the swing. "Why can't God be responsible for the good and Satan for the bad? I mean, isn't Satan the ruler of this world? I thought that was in the Bible somewhere."

Mark nodded. "John 14 verse 30 and 2 Corinthians 4 verse 4."

John leveled a look at his friend as if to say, "And…"

Mark held his stomach and laughed. "I wrestled with these questions for years. It's your turn. Seriously though, you'll need to come to your own conclusions about God and suffering."

John cleared his throat. "You know, for years the *why* question has driven me crazy. I just needed to know. But over the last few months I feel like my need to know why has decreased. And I think it has something to do with

❮ finding home ❯

the love of God growing in me." He glanced at Mark. "Does that make sense?"

"That, my good man, is incredibly profound. And it *does* make sense." John reclined. "Maybe you can talk about all this on Sunday."

"I expect you to be there you know."

"Yeah, yeah. Just like old times."

Mark winked at him. "Maybe not *just* like old times. I expect you to stay awake." John laughed and Mark studied him. "You *are* different, John." He waved his hands. "I know you've been through a lot and experienced things with God I can only imagine, but the John I knew he…we wouldn't have a conversation like this. I'm proud of you."

"Well," John cleared the emotion from his throat, "who knew there was hope for this old mule." He paused as fresh snowflakes began to dance their way to the ground. "Thank you, Mark."

They sat in comfortable silence for a while. "Hey, I wanted to ask…did you and Claire keep looking for Jill after I left?"

Mark's mouth was a straight line. "For awhile, yeah." He made a sound heavy with regret. "But we had to stop. Like I said, I was in a terrible place and our health was being affected. We just had to accept it…eventually."

John sighed. "Yeah, well, I know. I guess I've just always hoped—"

He felt Mark's hand on his shoulder. "I know John."

John tried to lighten the mood. "You know she's up there serving Jesus and whoever the best food they've ever had." He laughed, but Mark stiffened and his eyes glazed. "Mark?"

He jerked. "Yeah?"

"What's the matter?"

"Huh? Uh, nothing."

Before John could ask again Ashley appeared. "You deep thinkers ready for some cobbler? Come get it while it's hot."

John threw another look at Mark before smiling at Ashley. "I could get used to this you know." He stood and poked her side. "You cooking dinner and desert for us hard working men."

She slapped his hand. "Watch yourself." She turned, but not before he caught the glitter in her eyes. Yes, he could definitely get used to this.

chapter forty five

"Mark!" Claire's voice rang through the drywall. "Almost done?"

Mark dried himself off as fast as he could, puffing in the steamed bathroom. "Just about," he hollered back. "Did you get in touch with John?"

"They're going to meet us there," Claire answered from the doorway. She glanced at her watch. "I knew we should've gone to dinner with Alice and Caleb."

"Yeah, I'm sure they would've *loved* having us along."

"I wanted to take pictures of them arriving at the festival." She stuck out her bottom lip. "Probably too late now."

Mark took a long look at his wife. She wore a pale blue dress that sparkled on top and fell smoothly to her feet. She still took his breath away. Even more so now than on their wedding day. "You still light a room like no other."

That earned him a smile. "Thank you."

"Ready for another Frosty Fest?"

Claire lowered her chin. "After all these years I can't imagine not going. What about you?"

He spread his arms. "Save me a dance. That's all I ask."

She tapped her watch. "Then you better get dressed or we'll have to dance here."

"Fine with me." He raised an invisible microphone to his mouth and did his best Sam Cooke impression.

"Lights tuuurned way down low…" He spun and shuffled towards Claire who had covered her mouth trying to hide laughter.

‹finding home›

Mark closed his eyes. "And muuuusic soft and slow, oh…" He slipped his hand to Claire's back and took her hand in his, swaying side to side.

"With someone you love soooo…" She yelped as he caught her in a dip.

"That's where it's at, yeah."

"Mark Summers we are too old for this kind of thing," Claire teased.

He gazed into her eyes seeing the ups and downs of the years, convinced yet again that there's no one he'd rather travel that twisted road with. "I've still got gas left in the tank," he claimed and helped her up.

"Good," she exclaimed and gave him a meaningful look. "I'm just not interested in being here without you."

He leaned in and kissed her. "I'm not going anywhere."

"Hmmm." Claire gave him a pat on the butt. "Now hurry up so we can at least see a little of the Festival."

A short time later Mark was fully dressed and giving his thinning gray hair one last look in the mirror. "I'll meet you in the car," he called.

"Make sure the front door is locked."

Mark snatched the keys from the kitchen and checked the front door. He noticed the guest room door hung open a few feet on the way by. He grabbed the knob to pull it shut when something in the room flashed like a spark.

Mark flipped on the light and scrutinized the room. Nothing seemed out of place. He watched a few more seconds and rubbed eyes he figured were playing tricks on him. But as he went to close the door a mix of colors caught his eye on Alice's dresser. He hesitated, not wanting to invade her privacy, but curiosity won out.

Four pictures lay on the dresser. "Now what is this…" His eyes widened. The first image was rough, but the man looking back at him bore a strong resemblance to John. "Claire," he hollered and shuffled the papers to a picture of a woman. A tremor worked through his fingers. Jet-black hair and ocean blue eyes yanked Amy's face out of his memories. He let the page fall and held up the final two. "*Claire!*" A boy and a girl, smiles etched into their faces.

"No." He refused to believe it. "It's just art." He swiped a bead of sweat from his forehead. "Maybe she saw a picture of them somewhere." Relief flooded him. That was it. Had to be.

Mark returned the images to the dresser but flinched when his fingers brushed against something cool. He looked closer. It was a small charm, a cross. The silver was worn and faded like it'd been through a million washings. His fingers shook but he managed to turn it over. *1 Cor. 13:8.*

He'd been there, that day John brought out a small package. She was turning ten and they'd just sung an awful rendition of, *Happy Birthday.* Her eyes sparkled with excitement as she ripped into the paper.

She slowly lifted a thin silver chain that glittered in the light. A charm hung from the bottom. A cross. The princess adjusted her birthday tiara and gently turned the charm over: "*1 Corinthians 13:8*," she read and glanced up at her dad.

"Love never fails," John answered and kissed her head. "I love you, Jill."

Mark squeezed his eyes shut in an attempt to right the world but when he opened them the cross was still there. He clenched his jaw against a wave of nausea. Pieces of a puzzle that'd haunted him for months were slowing moving together forming a picture that was perfect no matter how implausible. *The festival!* He had to get there as quickly as possible. He staggered out of the room using the frame and wall as supports.

Behind him the faces of John, Amy, Kayla and Andy Rister fluttered silently to the floor like butterflies landing in a field flowers.

‹finding home›

‹chapter forty six›

The cobblestone path to the tent was lined with soft, pale light as if parts of the moon had been captured and recast in elegance. Laughter ebbed and flowed on the heels of conversations just beyond the entrance.

Alice took slow steps trying to stretch every second as long as possible. So far the night was a dream that started at the Summers'. Caleb had been talking to Mark, but stopped abruptly when she stepped into the room.

The dress she'd chosen was deep purple and sleeveless, falling just above her knees. The chiffon fabric was light and silky against her skin. Two sequin straps anchored the V-neck and spilled over her back in an intricate design. A band of sparkling beads lined the front in an empire style.

Caleb stuttered, but finally managed to tell her how beautiful she looked. After the flurry of pictures he took her to Georggios, an upscale Italian restaurant worthy of her dress. The soft lighting and music was a thrill even though she felt a little out of place. She'd reached for the cross charm only to be reminded she'd temporarily traded it for a silvery necklace that fit the dress better. But Caleb's warm smile and the feel of his hand on hers calmed her nerves.

Alice marveled at the steps that took her from the streets of New York to a festival in Ohio on the arm of a boy she was falling in love with. She hugged Caleb's suit jacket around her body. Maybe she could stop time and exist here forever.

"Alice, come on." Caleb motioned to the entrance. "It's freezing out here."

Alice giggled and let him lead her into the party where he helped her out of his coat. Shimmering dresses and dark suits danced to soft music from a live band. Red, green, and white lights twinkled and bounced off of expertly constructed faux icicles and snowflakes suspended from the ceiling. A chandelier made of crystal floated in the center.

"Wow," Caleb said after he hung his jacket on a rack. "This place looks great!" He leaned close to her ear, "Have I told you how *gorgeous* you are?"

Alice grinned and rubbed her bare arms, thankful that the heaters were doing their job. "Maybe once or twice."

He fixed his blue eyes on her. "Not nearly enough."

Alice felt heat in her cheeks and took him in. He'd never looked better in his pale blue oxford shirt and black dress pants. "You look great, Caleb." She glanced up at him and felt her heart flip-flop. "Really great."

Caleb lightly brushed his lips against her hand sending chills through her body. "May I have this dance?"

Her stomach fluttered as he led her to a spot directly underneath the chandelier. She'd never danced with a boy and the ground felt uneven. She observed the happy couples moving in tune around them. Maybe she should apologize in advance.

But when Caleb's blue eyes locked onto hers, everyone else began to fade. They were the only two there, dancing on a stage built just for them. His hand on the small of her back was a gentle guide moving her through steps in smooth motions. He was leading her, but she was doing it as if she'd done it a million times.

"*Take my hand, Take my whole life too…*"

The words from Elvis' hit were slow and long, churning the air around her into an array of thrilling impulses that swayed with her slender frame. The expression on Caleb's face told her that he was feeling the same way. It wasn't until his fingers gently brushed a strand of hair from her eyes that she realized that they'd stopped dancing. She felt his fingers move through her hair and watched him mouth the next words of the song.

"…*Cause I can't help falling in love with you.*"

Caleb's lips were silk on hers and his arms held her like she might disappear if he let go. Alice titled her head to rest on his shoulder and a few tears vanished into the fabric of his suit. It was all more than she could've hoped for.

The people around them were blurry figures in a haze of lights and decorative frost. She blinked a couple of times and they cleared, like an old Polaroid.

She scanned the faces and settled on a man positioned next to the drink table. At first she didn't recognize him and almost moved on. But then she caught his eyes and the blood left her face.

"Hey, Alice." Caleb's voice held a measure of urgency. She hadn't noticed he'd pulled away and lifted a phone from his pocket. "I've gotta take this."

The tent titled and began to spin. "Yeah...okay," she managed.

Caleb muttered something that sounded like, "sorry" but his voice was muffled as if cotton had replaced his tongue.

Alice blinked, but the impossible picture remained. The man had abandoned the pretty woman with black hair and kids on the swing in the land of dreams and stepped into *her* reality as if only a thin curtain separated them. And he was staring straight at her.

♥

John fidgeted with the cuffs on his suit coat.

"You gonna be okay?" Ashley stroked his arm and calmed some of the nerves panicking like soldiers without a commanding officer.

"Yeah, I think so." He almost laughed at the lie. His stomach was way too small for the number of butterflies in it. He was home and a stranger at the same time. The faces moving around him were familiar, but time had formed an inevitable rift.

John quietly cursed when he couldn't find Mark and Claire. Ashley had convinced him to come after Claire's invitation. She reminded him of Mark's reaction and that others might want the same opportunity to welcome him home. It all sounded great and noble last night, but now... everywhere he turned there were eyes that darted away when he met them.

John wrung his hands. Maybe he was just being paranoid. He cast a look at Ashley. "You *are* beautiful."

She made a display of covering her mouth. "Well, I'm glad you remembered I'm here."

He shoved down all his fear and lightly touched his lips to hers.

"Everyone in this tent is gonna remember you."

They floated in the moment before she cleared her throat. "You keep that up we'll have to find a place to get married tonight."

John chuckled and took in her lean form wrapped in a green strapless dress that fell to her feet and accented what he considered some of her best features. Blonde hair lay smoothly over her tan shoulders beckoning for his hands. His voice was low and guttural. "Yeah, you're right about that."

Ashley grinned. "If your eyes were any further out of your head I'd be holding them." She stood on her tiptoes and kissed him with a passion that made him dizzy.

"You're not helping," he let her know when she leaned back.

"Not trying to."

John laughed and shook his head. "Can I get you something? A cold shower maybe?"

"A drink would be nice. I'll go find Mark and Claire. They should be here by now."

John lugged his concrete feet toward the drink table. He kept his head down but could feel eyes working him over as if he was a pauper at a king's feast. He didn't blame them for not coming over and was glad they didn't. What would they say? *Don't make it awkward people.*

He raised a cup of red liquid to his lips hoping it was at least half alcohol and turned to the dance floor. A band belted out the melody of, *Can't Help Falling In Love.* The lead singer was young, but did a pretty good Elvis.

John tasted the punch and was disappointed that it didn't burn his throat. He slowly rocked to the band and remembered the festivals he'd shared with Amy and the kids. He could still see Andy trying to breakdance like it was yesterday. An upside down turtle had more grace.

He watched couples move to steady music until a pair of eyes stole the air from his lungs. They were big and intensely hazel and produced something within him from a deep and forgotten place. *I've seen eyes like those before,* he realized.

They belonged to a young girl caught up in the arms of a tall boy with curly blonde hair. Her face had a smile that seemed to draw the light in the room and John slid a few steps to the side to try and get a better look.

All of a sudden the blonde boy stopped and tugged a phone out of his

‹finding home›

pocket. After a few apologetic gestures, he hurried off and was lost in the crowd. For the first time John had an unobstructed view of the young woman. He didn't feel his glass slip from his hand or notice the heads that whirled toward him. He wasn't aware of conversations ending in midsentence as if their words were being hurled back down their throats. A groan, sob, and whimper joined into a single sound and forced its way out of his throat.

John gripped the table as his knees buckled. *We only found the remains of three...It's not unusual with a fire that hot...Jill's dead, John. They all are. Don't do this to yourself...*

He squeezed his eyes shut and when he opened them he expected her to be gone like a wisp of smoke. But she remained, highlighted like a priceless painting and she was staring at him through wide eyes.

Go to her!

John took a heavy step forward, his body following like a faithful dog. *Ten years older.* His eyes blurred but he saw her tremble and suck in her bottom lip. The questions shredded him like swords leaving his heart a tattered heap. *She looks so much like Amy.* There was a mile of dance floor between them. The voice of reason started in. *It's not her. Turn around before you make a fool of yourself.* But his feet trudged forward. He swallowed a lump in his throat. He *had* to know.

John reached her just as the band started the intro to Bruce Springsteen's, *When You Need Me*. Those around them slowly backed away and John wondered what they thought. *A pretty girl in a purple dress and crazy John Caban who bailed ten years ago with a truck full of bottles.*

But then all he could see was *her*. Nothing else mattered. All other voices were gone. It was just him, her, and the music. His heart thumped like a drum and she stared back, neither of them sure of what to do next.

But then an ache began to tear into John. An ache so strong it nearly split him in two. He had to hold her, to sway with her in the soft notes resonating from the stage. He slowly offered his hand to her. His hand hung suspended in the air, quivering. He'd let go of every need for control or composure. She hesitated, her eyes bouncing between his face and his hand. She appeared to wrestle silently with her options. Finally, slowly, she placed her hand in his.

If you miss me, I'll be there…to brush the sunlight from your hair…

They moved together in a cocoon of slow music and words sharing what neither understood. Ten years older. Impossible. But as John peered into her eyes he was transported backwards in time to a beautiful little girl who loved to dance.

When you need me…call my name…'cause life without you just isn't the same…

John silently forbade the music to ever stop. With each step he became more certain and when he lifted her hand every remaining doubt died. She slowly twirled in a circle. That same graceful movement, the same sparkle in her hazel eyes. It was ten years ago and he was holding up the hand of his precious little girl so she could practice spinning for her wedding day.

He dropped her hand and fell back a step. His sobbing heart wouldn't be restrained any longer and a wail exploded from his lips. She still didn't get it. He could see confusion and apprehension cloud her eyes.

John's knees finally gave up and he crumbled to the floor hardly noticing the impact. He kept his eyes locked on hers, parted his dry lips, and forced two words over the sound of his pounding heart, "Jilly-Bean."

♥

He looked older than the man in her dreams. The hard lines on his face mapped the trials and struggles of life. But it was him. She was certain in the same way she was about the house.

The closer he'd gotten the less she'd breathed and when he'd held out his hand she'd stopped altogether. She'd considered it as if it was a white rabbit waiting to lead her through a hole in the ground. Now she danced with him following his gentle lead as the band played something soft and slow.

The lights around Alice were a shimmering haze. She felt his hand tremble and tried to keep hers still. Her heart raced and her stomach rumbled just like it had the day she came to Oak Harbor. Moving with him was so familiar and yet beyond her grasp like a road disappearing into the horizon. Maybe she really had fallen into Wonderland.

She noticed the pale glow of the chandelier bounce off moisture filling

≺ finding home ≻

his eyes and saw his bottom lip quiver. Did he know something she didn't?
If you miss me...I'll be there...
His eyes were a striking shade of hazel. Just like hers.
When you need me...call my name...'cause life without you, just isn't the same...
The words drifted and swirled around them. Her hand lifted suddenly as if caught in the updraft. Alice was almost through the spin before she realized she'd moved.

When she faced him again he stopped and dropped her hand like it'd scorched him. His face lightened a shade and his eyes were planets arranged in a space way too small. He blinked and tears spilled onto features streaked with a complex mix of joy, awe, and surrender.

Alice almost reached for him as he sank to his knees, but uncertainly held her like glue. She glanced nervously at the faces around them until a deep wail jerked her attention back to the stranger. His shoulders heaved as if the remaining strength in his soul had been expelled through the sound. She watched as he raised his head and parted his lips enough to utter the words, "Jilly-Bean."

Alice gasped and stumbled backward. She wasn't at a dance anymore. She was gazing up into the eyes of a man smiling down at her, the same man but younger. She was younger. They were dancing and he was spinning her. Squeals of delight echoed all around her.

The scene blurred into a kitchen where the woman from her dreams measured out flour before dumping it into a mixing bowl. Alice handed her the salt and ripped open a bag of chocolate chips. They were baking cookies. It was a recipe Alice created.

She flinched when the woman tossed flour at her with a laugh. A battle ensued leaving both of them caked with white paste. They collapsed into giggles and found each other's arms. She felt the soft touch of her hand, the tenderness in her light voice.

The interactive slideshow continued with a square, maple colored table surrounded by chairs, five of them. Alice sat beside the man and woman but now the others, the two children, joined them. The picture erupted with life as excited, young voices described adventures in school and the woods. Laughter and squeaks followed food being handed around.

"Jill, pass the chicken!" She fixed her eyes on a boy…her brother smiling at her through a mouth full of potatoes.

The memories started to unleash like a flood sweeping in faster and faster. Birthdays and Holidays and vacations. School and church and bedtimes. Ten years of forgotten childhood restoring what was lost.

Jill opened her eyes and blinked at the man. At some point she'd fallen to her knees and he'd buried her hands in his own. His eyes frantically searched hers and her throat wasn't big enough for the sobs trying to barge through at once. She covered her mouth as tears tumbled down her cheeks. She fixed her eyes on his and cried the words she'd longed to say her whole life, "Daddy!"

"Jill!" It was a shout wrapped in a sob and instantly his strong arms were around her neck holding her like he'd never let go. "My Jill!" He laughed and cried and kissed her face over and over again.

"Daddy!" Jill never wanted to stop saying the word but her voice was swallowed by wave after wave of emotion. She buried her face in his chest soaking his shirt and letting the beat of his heart chase away the years they'd lost. It didn't matter now. She was a little girl in her daddy's arms.

John allowed as little space between them as possible and sniffed. "I just can't believe…" He stroked her hair and framed her face. "It's really you isn't it? This isn't some messed up dream?" She shook her head sending more tears to the floor. His eyes drooped slightly. "I looked everywhere…I did everything I could to find you. Where did you—"

Jill pressed her cheek into his shoulder. "I'm here now."

His hands clutched her firmly. He was saying her name, her real name, over and over and it was honey coating her heart. Her daddy was here. She was where she'd always wanted to be.

John began to laugh as he looked around at the gathering astonished faces, "My Jilly-Bean is home!"

Jill sat up and he wiped her tears. A moment later she was giggling. Then wholehearted laughter merged with his creating a melody rivaled only by angels.

She suddenly became aware of their surroundings for what felt like the first time in hours. They huddled together in the middle of a large circle formed by people wiping their eyes and sniffing. She noticed Mark and

Claire on their knees, their faces and clothes drenched with tears, and joy carved into their faces.

"So, it's Jill, huh?" Caleb appeared and lowered himself next to her.

Jill wiped her eyes again. "You heard?"

Caleb brushed a strand of hair from her face. "I saw the whole thing."

"We've got a lot to talk about."

"And I thought we were finished with all our serious conversations," Caleb teased. But his grin never reached his eyes, which held notes of grief and apprehension.

Jill leaned back and studied his face. "What's the matter?"

"Huh? Oh...nothing." He cleared his throat and thumbed the phone in his pocket. "Introduce me to your dad."

Jill's excitement canceled her suspicions and she swiveled back to John who was glowing like he'd swallowed a sunbeam. "Dad, this is Caleb."

They laughed and shook hands and Jill was so caught up in the surreal moment that she didn't notice the beautiful blonde woman until she was kneeled beside her dad. Streaks of mascara colored her cheeks and a careful hand touched John's shoulder.

John glanced back and cleared his throat. "Wow, okay." He grasped the woman's hand. "Ashley, I'd like you to meet my daughter, Jill."

Ashley opened her mouth, but nothing came out.

A thousand questions hit Jill at once. Why was she kneeling beside her dad like that? Why was she touching him? Why did he seem to know her so well? She felt her face tighten. "Dad?"

"Yeah, sweetheart?"

She squeezed his hand to match the sink in her stomach. "Where's mom...and Kayla and Andy?"

John's features fell and he kissed her forehead. "Let's get out of here so we can talk."

♥

The man in the tan pants and long-sleeved flannel shirt adjusted his yellowing hat and swiped a tear from his stubble as he took in the reunion from a distance. His full heart sighed as a smile worked through his mouth. Reconciliation…it's what he came for, his bride to him and to each other. He glanced at his scared hands. It's what he died for. He'd have it no other way.

He strolled in the glow of the stars. Branches of trees he passed bent in acknowledgement. The plants rotated to behold their creator. A book had closed on John and Jill. But that only meant it was time for them to write a new one.

Jesus slowed as Caleb's phone conversation played through his mind. They would all need each other in the days ahead and he would be right beside them every step of the way.

The End

≪ More from Jesse Birkey ≫

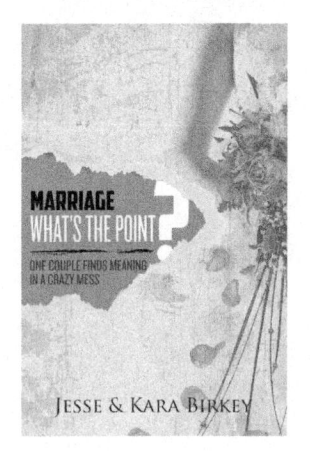

Life Resurrected, Extraordinary Miracles through Ordinary People
The dead come to life as ordinary people discover we all have the ability to live the extraordinary life of Jesus.

....

Marriage What's the Point? One Couple Finds Meaning in a Crazy Mess
Jesse and Kara share the testimony of their marriage with bold transparency. Draw encouragement and hope from their story as God brought them from the depths of despair into the joy of restoration.

....

Connect with Jesse and Kara
Visit and interact with them on their blog at www.jessebirkey.com

....

Email, Facebook and Twitter:
jbirkey@jessebirky.com
https://www.facebook.com/jbirk
https://www.twitter.com/jessebirkey

Available at www.jessebirkey.com and www.amazon.com

Made in United States
North Haven, CT
03 February 2024